The Dreamwatcher Diaries

A St. Louis Love Story

Lawrence Gabriel

STRATTON
—PRESS—
Publishing Life

THE DREAMWATCHER DIARIES
Copyright © 2020 **Lawrence Gabriel**

All rights reserved. No part of this book may be used or reproduced by any means, graphic, electronic, or mechanical, including photocopying, recording, taping or by information storage and retrieval system without the written permission of the author except in the case of brief quotations embodied in critical articles and reviews.

Stratton Press Publishing
831 N Tatnall Street Suite M #188,
Wilmington, DE 19801
www.stratton-press.com
1-888-323-7009

Because of the dynamic nature of the Internet, any web addresses or links contained in this book may have changed since publication and may no longer be valid. The views expressed in the work are solely those of the author and do not necessarily reflect the views of the publisher, and the publisher hereby disclaims any responsibility for them.

ISBN (Paperback): 978-1-64345-664-5
ISBN (Ebook): 978-1-64345-920-2

Printed in the United States of America

Part One

Discovery

CHAPTER ONE

Soul Mate Blues

"What am I going to do with you, Lindsay Louise Parker," Lindsay chided herself out loud as she turned south down Market Street. She glanced at her rueful smile in the rearview mirror and saw the smile give way to a tremor in her lips. The tremor belied a crack in her resolve to hold back the sob that had been building over the past several miles. Lindsay pulled her focus back to the road ahead of her, blinking back the tears, thinking to herself, *It's been four months since the divorce, why does it still hurt so much?*

Because you still believe that true love is forever, she thought, answering her own question. You still believe in the soul mate fairy tale.

"So believe then, if you have to," she scolded herself aloud, "but take a break from the crying already, will ya?"

She really had no reason to be feeling as gray and cloudy as the St. Louis skyline on this rain-swept afternoon. It was early March, and while the damp weather was expected, the sadness was an unwelcome visitor that threatened to taint what should be one of the brightest days of her life. At twenty-eight, Lindsay was rapidly earning a reputation as the most innovative data analyst in her field. Her most recent project on random data analysis had produced a program that targeted the detection and identification of individuals who avoided or withdrew from typical computer and paper trails. Dubbed the GDP (Ghost Detection Program), Lindsay's project was drawing attention from high levels in both government and private sectors. She had just signed on with Data International, a booming data resource company based in St Louis. She had managed to negotiate a six-figure salary and a signing bonus. Just three days earlier, she had closed on a loft in a rehabbed section of Downtown St. Louis.

Today was moving day, and she at this moment was only a few miles from her new home. Career wise, life couldn't get much better. Professionally she felt confident, secure, and even blessed. It was regarding her love life, where she courted grave suspicion, that she may very well be cursed.

After completing graduate school, Lindsay had found herself longing for a relationship with a future. The postcollege work-a-day world had awakened a dream that she had been able to avoid with help from the lures and distractions of college life. This recurring dream, once sweet but now soured at the fresh memory of her recent divorce, was responsible for the ache that even the heady balm of her recent success could not dissolve. It was the dream that there was one man out there who was her equal, one man whom really believed in her. The man who could see the worst in her without feeling a reluctance in his longing to hold her in his arms, one who wanted to stay with her forever just because he saw the real Lindsay the same way that she saw the real "him." If only she could meet the one man who could take her beyond the roots of her parents' love, to a new place, a place that she never dreamed existed. "It's your fault, Mom and Dad," Lindsay whispered to herself, blotting a single bittersweet tear. "It's your fault for living the fairy tale."

As far back as she could remember, her parent's romance had made Hallmark cards look like plastic flowers on Valentine's Day. Sometimes she found herself wondering if maybe their passion would dim, but each time that she visited her childhood home in Silverton, Colorado, she found their affection unwavering. Soul mate is what they called each other, mysteriously matching step for step their rhythmic appreciation of their togetherness. Demonstrative to a fault, whether engaged in a warm embrace, or each catching the other's eyes from across a crowded room, they expressed their love every day like there was no tomorrow. Lindsay's mind flashed back to that memory, the one that always popped up when she heard the words *soul mate*.

* * *

Lawrence Gabriel

It was a June day in Colorado, and she had just celebrated her twelfth birthday a few days earlier. Disco was dead (much to her parents' chagrin), hair bands were in, and *Dirty Dancing* was her favorite movie in the whole world. The Parkers were on one of their famous adventure hikes. Lindsay and her brother Evan, then seven, and sister Erin, then nine, were hiding behind some trees along the mountain trail plotting to scare the living daylights out of their parents. Lindsay, who was just beginning to see this game, that made her brother and sister so giddy with excitement, as child's play, looked back down the trail to get a fix on her parent's approach. What she saw was a picture postcard that would make a deep and lasting impression on her romantic soul.

Her parents, in their own wonderful world as they so often were, were holding hands, walking with secret smiles and shining eyes. In that moment, her parents seemed to radiate a togetherness that pulled at her heart. She felt a yearning that she could not quite explain, nor seem to think how to satisfy. They stepped into a light where the sun broke through the trees casting its warm smile on the shaded path. As the light turned their blonde hair to gold, she watched her father slowly turn and tilting her mother's face toward his, he pressed his lips to hers. Parting slowly, they gave each other that look, the one that came with the words, sometimes spoken and sometimes not, "You are my dream come true."

Walking again hand in hand, they continued toward her, when her father suddenly whirled and

The Dreamwatcher Diaries

swept her mother off her feet. He spun her in a circle, until his balance gave way, spilling them to the foothill floor. They fell together laughing with the passion of love's resolve and the freedom of an innocence that does not fade after the first kiss but grows stronger in both its wonder and exuberance.

Lindsay came back to the here and now, finding her hand on her mouth, with a tear tracing its salty path down her cheek just as one had when she had come out of her entranced state, fourteen years ago, behind that tree, some seven hundred miles to the west.

It was magic, she thought to herself. "My God," she teased her self aloud, "you sound like Meg Ryan in *Sleepless in Seattle*."

"Only with Mom and Dad it wasn't a movie, it was real," said the twelve-year-old girl from deep inside her. "Why couldn't you make it real Lindsay, why?"

"It just doesn't work that way honey," she answered, trying to cajole her younger self. "Besides, you remember what Mom said about making my own path and not trying to match up to theirs."

She was referring to the talk that took place several years ago. The time was just after her engagement to her ex-husband, Bruce. It was early morning in Silverton, and Lindsay could remember feeling warm and snug in her old bed, in the room where so many childhood dreams had been cast. She was properly engaged in another dream, this one of the adult variety, when she heard a tap on her bedroom window. She pulled the curtain back, and there was her mother sitting astride Sisco, smiling and beckoning for her daughter to join her. Knowing that she would never get back to sleep anyway, Lindsay gave her mother the pinkies up sign. (In the Parker home, agreement was thumbs up for the Parker boys and pinkies up for the Parker girls.) She pulled on jeans, a college sweatshirt, and old riding boots. Fastening her hair back in a ponytail, she tiptoed through the sunlit kitchen careful not to wake the sleeping members of the Parker clan. She paused to grab a buttermilk biscuit before slipping silently out of the house.

She was greeted by an early September sunrise so beautiful that it hurt inside, in that place where she sometimes missed home. The air was Colorado crisp, energizing but far from the paralyzing cold that was waiting in the weeks ahead. Anticipating Lindsay's assent to an early morning ride, Shelley Parker had saddled her daughter's favorite horse, a spirited Appaloosa mare named Sundance.

Lindsay's mouth broke out into a wide grin at the memory of her mother's teasing smile as she commented, "Well if it isn't that pretty little thing from the city, and up before 9:00 a.m. Well howdy, miss, and how are we feeling this fine country morning."

"Fine enough to beat that country smile of yours to Silver Creek." Lindsay had returned with a smile of her own.

"Oooh and an uppity city girl at that. Well I guess will just have to see about that," her mother came back in her best country twang.

The smiles on their lips gave way to determined lines as they urged their mounts into a quick gallop. Identical blonde ponytails bounced in rhythm as they made their way across the pastures of the Parker ranch toward Silver Creek.

The "Creek Talks" as Lindsay and her mother had come to know them were those conversations unique to the bond of mother and daughter. The talks were special, not only in terms of content but even more so, in the experience of leaving, for a moment, the tradition of familial roles to sense an endearing feminine equality, as women who had come to share the secrets of their souls.

Lindsay had labeled this particular Creek Talk, "Soul Mate Blues." Her unusual abilities at memory recollection and reconstruction had developed to the level where she had command over a Dewey decimal three-dimensional, DVD, lifetime so far, memory library. This particular memory DVD that was now playing was well worn and was in the top 3 for memory DVDs that soothe and nurture.

Having decided the race to the creek was a draw, mother and daughter tethered their horses to a familiar fallen tree and, after pulling some bottled juice from their saddle packs, made themselves comfortable on their "creek lounges" consisting of horse blankets and flat-surfaced, creek bed stone. Had there been onlookers, each would swear they were seeing double Sharon Stones, whose features required close inspection in order to identify mother from daughter.

"So what's the topic?" Lindsay asked her mother with a mischievous grin.

"Oh, I think you know exactly what the topic is, Lindz," Shelley replied with a smile of her own. Her mother always shortened her name when talk became sensitive or serious.

"So what do you think? Do you think he is the one?" Lindsay asked, looking hopefully at her mother.

"No, it's what you think, honey," Shelley replied gently.

"I know that, Mom, but I really want to know what you think."

"I think it's important to know what you want. Is Bruce what you want?"

"I think so. I mean I'm happy when we are together. It's just I couldn't think of any reason to say no when he asked me. I mean everything seems so right with us. But sometimes I feel like something is missing, and then when I think about you and Dad, I'm sure something is missing. I just don't know what that something is, or even if whatever *it* is, is that important. I mean, you know what I mean?"

"I know exactly what you mean, sweetheart, and believe it or not, you actually said it quite well."

"So what's missing, and why can't I find it?" Lindsay queried anxiously.

"I'm not sure I have all the answers, Lindz, but I can tell you what I see."

"I'll take it," Lindsay said, sitting up with rapt attention.

"Well, sweetheart," Shelley began, "I see that you have a vision, a picture, in the mind of your heart. It is a picture about what you believe a marriage should be. It's a beautiful picture, Lindz, and such a picture comes with many deep and important feelings. It comes with feelings that live in the picture and feelings about those feelings in the picture. The picture is your father and me on a path in the foothills. The feelings in the picture are your parents feeling lucky in love. You were watching winners of the "soul mate lottery," enjoying their good fortune. The feelings about the picture are coming from an extraordinary twelve-year-old girl just beginning to sense the potential of true love."

Lindsay felt a tremble play across her lips. "You remember that day, Mom?" she asked, the tremor traveling to her voice.

"Of course I do, honey. The way that you looked at your father and me that day was so precious to me. Why it's just about page 1 in my treasure book of mother-daughter memories. You didn't even say anything as you stepped out from behind that tree. It was your eyes that told us how you could really see the love your father and I have and how you gave us that wonderful hug before telling your father and me to act surprised when Evan and Erin jumped out to give us a scare. I'll always remember your words to me later that night. We were in your room just before you went to bed, remember? You said, please don't ever stop looking at Daddy that way, OK, Mom."

"I remember," Lindsay said, her eyes taking on a shine, "I made you pinky swear. You said, this will be the easiest pinky swear I've ever made, and then you gave me the longest hug."

"One of our best I think," Shelley said, blinking as a tear well overflowed. "Of course," she continued, "the dead giveaway about the importance of that day was the way you took most of your boyfriends on that same hike, down that same path."

Lindsay smiled in spite of her confusion. Shelley smiled back adding, "And I'll bet you the bill on your wedding cake that your first kiss took place on that very same path."

"No deal," Lindsay said, her smile taking over her face. "You're a psychic and you cheat."

Shelley broke into laughter, reaching toward her daughter who was doing the same.

"OK, alright, you got me," Lindsay conceded, her smile giving way to a pensive frown. "So what you're saying is," Lindsay started, attempting to understand, "I've got like, the soul mate blues or something."

"Wow talk about getting down to it," Shelley said admirably.

"But what does that mean?" Lindsay said more to herself than to her mother.

Shelley took her daughter's hands into her own. "It means that maybe it's time to let go of the picture, Lindz, set it free. Set it free so that you can find your own picture. How can you find your own dream if you keep trying to match ours? Your father and I believe that we are the most blessed parents in the world to have a daughter that can see and feel so clearly with her heart. Your ability to sense what another soul is feeling, and then make a personal connection with that soul's experience is extraordinary. But, Lindsay, you must see your own heart's desire, even more clearly than you so capably see the hearts of those around you. I must confess, Lindz, I'm not the best at this, at being able to show you exactly how to find your own dream when I've lived within a dream as real and wonderful as your father's and mine. All I know for sure is that only you can find the way to the dreams that are just yours and yours alone. The only direction I can think to give you is this—for all things, there is a season. I'm saying that there was a season for that path on the foothill. There was a season for the dream to have the love you see between your father and me, but today, Lindz, is the season to dream your dream, to find your path and your way to that place you never knew."

"I believe, Lindz," Shelley said, wiping a tear from her daughter's eye, "that you will find that path, that dream, and that place. Somehow I sense that help will come from a 'wisdom' much greater than mine. Until then, consider this, don't worry so much about shoulds and should nots. Instead follow your heart, and remember that you already have that love that you saw on the path that day because, you daughter, are that love and that dream came true."

* * *

The memory DVD faded to black with mother and daughter embracing while tears of growth stained a creek bed stone in Colorado.

Moving slowly back into her driver's seat, Lindsay sighed a little sigh, as the tension in her ache subsided. "Are you feeling better, little Lindz?" Lindsay asked her twelve-year-old self.

"Yeah, lots, and it was a great idea to remember the talk with Mom, thanks," came the grateful reply.

"Anytime, girl, all you have to do is call."

CHAPTER TWO

Moving In

Stan took a break from his work, leaning for a moment against the open gate of his moving truck.

"Take five, Mitch," Stan directed up to his partner.

Coming out of the truck, Mitch jumped lightly from the truck gate, landing easily on his feet. Leaning against the gate next to his boss, Mitch pulled out a pack of Marlboro Reds and lit up.

Stan wiped his brow with the blue and gold of the St. Louis Rams. Putting the cap back on, he looked down Castleway. His eyes caught the silver of an SUV pulling into a space ten, maybe twelve, cars back toward Fourteenth Street. As the driver stepped out, he let out an involuntary whistle.

"Blonde fox alert," Stan said, pulling Mitch's attention with a distracted slap on his back. "Would you look at the gams on that minx, I mean that actually hurts, kid," Stan commented, his eyes fixed on the woman who seemed to be heading toward them.

"The term, Stan, is *hottie*," Mitch replied with a teasing smile. "I hate to be the one to break it to you, but *fox* and *minx* has been out of circulation for about thirty-years now. As for *gams*, I have to travel so far back to find when it was last used, it makes my head hurt just thinking about it," Mitch said, massaging his forehead for effect. "However, your general point is well taken, and your powers of observation in the area of female anatomical assessment are both accurate and astute. That hottie does have some pair of gams," Mitch finished, flashing a wide grin at his boss.

Stan, with effort, pulled his attention from the blonde woman. "Alright, college boy," he jibed back, rapping his young partner smartly on the chest with the back of his hand, "why don't you take your wise ass up front and grab the paperwork. My bet is that's our girl."

"You got it, boss," Mitch replied, tossing his cigarette into the gutter and running around to the front of the truck."

* * *

Turning right on Castleway, Lindsay smiled as she caught sight of the sign that marked the entrance to her new home. The Castle Lofts were housed in a seven-story structure that occupied a square block bordered by Castleway and Colfax to the east and west and Sixth and Fifth Streets to the north and south. The building, at one time a shoe factory and warehouse, was the most recent addition to several renovation projects aimed at rejuvenating Downtown St. Louis. Washington Street just one block west of Eight Colfax, and several blocks north of Fourth Street was the primary region targeted for the downtown facelift. The area along North Washington once considered a "no man's land," and owned more by the local street gangs than by the residents, was gradually overcoming the forces of age and neglect. Several nightclubs had popped up as well as renovated restaurants and small businesses. Crime in the area was down, and commerce was up. The city planning committee was pleased to find people overcoming the region's "bad neighborhood" identity. A recent quote from a *Post-Dispatch* editorial stated, "This renovation project lends credence to the notion that it's the whole town working together that makes a city a great place to live. It gives plausibility to the concept that a city is only as rich as its poorest soul. This group effort over there is a living testament to the word rehabilitation, which essentially means to put back, and to restore to its original potential. I believe that is exactly what's happening downtown."

Lindsay pulled into a space along Castleway almost a full block down from the entrance. She grabbed her briefcase and climbed out of her silver SUV. She secured the door, bleeped the car alarm, and headed toward the entrance where she could see the two movers leaning against the tailgate of the big yellow truck. As she passed alongside an old loading dock that ran down the west side of the rehabbed structure, Lindsay wondered how long it had been since the gray warehouse door had been open for business. She slowed her walk and breathed in the ambience of the building's historic presence.

This is your moment, she thought, *enjoy what you have earned*. Lindsay mentally hit record on her memory player and gave full concentration to her five senses, linking with them one by one. The smell of the rain, which had all but stopped, mixed with the sharper taste of rusting metal. Feeling the touch of the moist air and a soft breeze that seemed to plant misty kisses on her cheeks. The noise of traffic blending with the song of streaming water, creating the singular sound of many travelers impatient to reach some important destination. The sight of the ethereal sculpture across the way, which seemed to pull at her with some mysterious invitation.

Lindsay recalled the day that she had first seen the sculpture and how its mystical presence had somehow conveyed to her that this was home. The sculpture was of a young woman opening her arms to release a bird that seemed to take wing from out of her heart. As the arms extended back, they melded into what appeared to be wings, giving the young woman the appearance of an angel. Utilizing subtle combinations of light, angles, and shades, the sculptor had created the altering perception that the angel was human or the human, angelic. The observer's eyes were initially drawn to the bird and the arms of the young woman giving the subject a human form. As the observer's gaze continued its study, there was the sudden appearance of wings altering the form of the sculpture into an angelic being. More astonishing was the woman's face, which appeared youthful and innocent at first glance, but with additional focus gradually including the perception of wings, the woman's features seemed to take on an ethereal wisdom. The sculpture, which stood approximately ten feet high, rested on a pedestal in the courtyard across from the entrance. The benches surrounding the sculpture were occupied by small gatherings of homeless men and women. Lindsay made a mental note to visit the sculpture again someday soon when she was settled.

The sound of laughter from the direction of the moving truck pulled her out of her personal trance. She sensed the gaze of the movers monitoring her approach and began to wish that she had taken the time to change out of her corporate attire. Lindsay wore a navy-blue Calvin Klein suit, with white blouse and low navy-blue heels. Her hair was pulled back with a professional air, accenting her prominent cheekbones and clear blue eyes. At five feet, eleven inches and long legs toned and shaped by daily five-mile runs, Lindsay walked with the grace and poise of a model on the runway. As she got closer to the movers, the younger of the two flicked his cigarette into the streaming gutter and ran around toward the cab of the truck.

"Miss Parker, I presume," Stan inquired, extending his hand.

"You presume correct," Lindsay replied with a smile, giving his hand a firm shake.

"Well, I think we've got you all set, Ms. Parker. Everything is moved in, and all the big furniture is set up along the taped lines per your instructions. We took the liberty of pulling up the tape you laid to mark the furniture setups, and all the boxes are labeled and in their designated areas."

"Sounds perfect," Lindsay replied.

Mitch arrived with the paperwork and handed the clipboard over to Stan.

"Just sign here," Stan pointed, holding the clipboard while Lindsay penned her signature.

"How long did it take the two of you?" Lindsay asked as she watched Mitch pull down the truck's back door and secure the gate.

"Round about six hours, Ms. Parker," Stan replied as he handed her the paperwork. "Now there's a card inside that packet there. Should any problems come up, you call that number and we'll take care of you. There's also a service satisfaction survey with a self-addressed envelope. I'd be much obliged if you would slip it in the mail for me when you get some time."

"No problem, and thanks for all of your work," Lindsay said.

"Good luck to you. Ms. Parker," Stan tipped his cap, walked around to the front cab, and climbed in next to Mitch, who was smoking and staring transfixed at the alabaster angel in the courtyard.

* * *

Lindsay moved around her new home multitasking like a butterfly, moving from flower to flower, lighting and lingering with some strange internal rhythm. First to the kitchen with its multipurpose island, hanging pots, pans, and utensils on the overhead rack. Now to the living area arranging pillows cushions and shelves, now the bathroom unpacking towels and toiletries, then suddenly back to the kitchen to locate her spice rack and pasta jars, leading to a left field impulse to begin a clothes closet project in her bedroom. Catching a look at herself in the vanity mirror on the way to her closet, she smiled at the look of studied concentration on her face. Her smile grew as she recalled past comments from others who had seen her when she was in the "zone," as she called it. While friends and coworkers expressed puzzlement at Lindsay's seemingly random work methodology, she secretly knew that there was logic to her apparent lunacy. What Lindsay knew about herself was the way that her energy flowed. Spend too much time on one project and her energy evaporated. Not enough time and her energy expanded and evolved into a frenzied anxiety. The timing of her lighting and lingering had everything to do with the maintenance of a creative energy stream. She also knew that staying in the shelter of the zone was a good way to avoid the "ghost of marriage past," who was already beginning to knock on the door of 707 Castleway.

Back in the kitchen again, she sipped on a chilled glass of Chardonnay enjoying a quick break, as Steve Perry sang about a road-weary musician who really just wanted to be home with the woman he loved. Lindsay smiled to herself as the song conjured up the picture of her father bailing hay in their barn back home. He was singing along with the legendary (as her father called them) tunes of Journey as he worked. She remembered giggling at his off-key efforts as he tried to match the extraordinary voice of the band's lead singer while using the pitchfork as a microphone. The moment had occurred some months after her sixteenth birthday. She had been bringing apples out to the horses for an afternoon treat when she had caught her father in this rare performance. Lindsay's smile faded into a look of serious reflection as she recalled smothering her giggle somehow sensing that the moment was sacred. Settling into the memory, she inhaled deeply almost able to smell the familiar scent of horse and hay. Quietly stepping to a better vantage point, she had watched her father as he moved back and forth between work and play. His hair was askew, its color almost blending with the straw pieces that had taken up temporary residence there. Sweat glistened on his chiseled features, and small streams ran down his shirtless form. The muscles of his sculpted body bunched and flexed as he moved seeming to radiate a scent of strength and vitality. She remembered holding her breath as she watched the most important man in her life transform from superhero to endearing human and back again. As Lindsay watched herself watch her father, she again felt the bittersweet tug of war between the young girl who wanted the hero worship to last forever and the young woman who was ready to allow the notion of a father who was human. Then he saw her. Their eyes locked, and for just a heartbeat, his smiling eyes seemed to see what she was thinking.

He winked and his mouth broke out into a wide grin. "How long have you been standing there?" he'd asked.

"Long enough to know you better not quit your day job," Lindsay had come back, her giggling escalating quickly into full-blown belly laughs.

The air was suddenly filled with hay, and she was soon buried in the straws' sweet fragrance as her father made mock threats of severe consequences should she reveal the moment to another living soul. Lindsay's smile returned as she felt the laughter echoing from the Parker barn some twelve years back down memory lane.

* * *

It was raining again. Lindsay sat on the window seat watching the gray world outside dissolve into the wet dusk of early March. She had completed all of her initial move in projects and was feeling the beginnings of a weariness that was pulling her toward the soft bed in the next room. Toni Braxton was singing now urging her to "let it flow, let it go now baby." So she did.

"It was that picture, that damn picture," Lindsay consoled herself as the tears began to fall. "How did that get in there?" she wondered out loud referring to a picture of her ex-husband, Bruce, that she had found a short time earlier.

After the divorce, she had packed away every memory of Bruce that she could find, even telling her friends and family not to mention his name in an effort to purge herself from any and all marriage recollections. The marriage memories had gone into boxes, which went home with her parents who were in town for support during the final days of her divorce. While unpacking the last box in the bedroom, she had come across a picture of her and Bruce taken on the last day of their honeymoon.

They were sitting in a little bar in Maui. The space just above the bar was papered in one dollar bills left by "couples only" as the handwritten sign had read. The owner, a Harley-Davidson lover as well as a hopeless romantic, required only a "how we met story" to become an addition to his wall of romance. The bartender, who also happened to be the owner's wife, had taken the photo after they had signed and placed the bill in a vacant space on the wall. For Lindsay, that moment had seemed like an encouraging wind that filled the sails of their marriage ship on its way out of honeymoon harbor.

The Dreamwatcher Diaries

"What more do I need to move on?" she wondered aloud. "Can anyone tell me what more do I need to do?"

A flash of white suddenly appeared along the window ledge outside. At first she thought it was some paper caught up in the wind, but after wiping her eyes with the back of her hand, she found to her surprise that it was a bird. Too small to be a pigeon was as close as she could come to identifying the specific species of the winged visitor. The bird just stood there on the ledge, moving its head from left to right as if it were scanning the room for a familiar face. Lindsay pulled the cushion off the window seat hoping to work the window up a little. She thought she might put some crumbs out for her unexpected guest. As she looked down to locate the slots to lift the window, she discovered three brass hinges. The window seat was actually a window box. Curious, she lifted the lid and looked inside the dusty compartment. It was empty except for a dark-blue pillbox with gold lettering across the lid. Lindsay took the box from the compartment and studied it as she put the window cushion back in place. She gave the box's lid a quick birthday candle wind to blow off the dusty coating. The box was round like a hat box but only about half as deep. Staring at the lettering on the box with questioning eyes, Lindsay read aloud, "The Dreamwatcher Diaries."

Sudden activity at the window startled her and the box flew from her hands. Looking up at the window, she caught the fluttering of the white bird, which disappeared into the damp night. As Lindsay reached down to retrieve the box, she discovered a thick white envelope along with a diary colored in the same dark blue as the box, which she had fumbled. She collected the box, envelope, and diary and sat down on the sofa, subtly aware that all signs of grief and weariness had fled from her body. She placed the box and the diary on the marbled surface of the coffee table and sat on the edge of the sofa cushion ready to give the envelope a thorough inspection. It was a plain white envelope, in fair condition, aged and worn as if the unsealed lip had been open and tucked closed many times. The front of the envelope had no distinguishing markings save an abbreviated address that read "To My Little Fay-Fay, From Grandma Gracie." She pulled the thick fold of pages from the envelope and carefully unfolded what appeared to be a letter twenty-some pages long. Laying the letter facedown, she gently but firmly pressed on the folds of the letter to smooth out the pages. Satisfied with the result of her efforts, she settled back into the sofa's cushion and began to read.

CHAPTER THREE

The Letter

Dearest Faith (my little Fay-Fay),
    I've much to tell you precious, so you may as well make yourself a nice cup of coffee and settle in for one of our spirited chats. I know that your mother is probably in bed, and I am off to see your grandpa at the hospital. As you're out of school today, I thought this would be a good time to say some things that I've been wondering how to tell you for quite some time now. Why don't you get that coffee and grab a cinnamon roll (your favorite made fresh this morning), and I'll meet you at the second paragraph.
    I'm writing you, Faith, because I'm afraid that my tears would get the best of me if I tried to say these words out loud.
    My cancer is back, dearest, and as it turns out, the sand in my "life-here glass" is much less than I had originally thought. I hope that you can forgive me for waiting and for telling you like this. It's just that I really needed to have my last days with the Faith that was free from the anticipation of sad

goodbyes. I know it's a bit selfish for me to ask for a gift that I designed, but the last few weeks with you have been my gift to myself. Your grandfather is the hope in my heart, my sweet dream, and your father was my heart's pride, but you, my little Fay-Fay, are my joy, the joy in my heart.

I must go to Grandpa now as his time is said to be even shorter than mine. I have found a hospice where we can stay together. The location is very close to the beach where we first met. We are still so in love, Faith. I miss him so when I'm away. Actually it was only the thought of giving myself a gift that really gave me the courage to come out here to be with you. For once I'm glad that I did the selfish thing and had you all to myself.

I need to ask you not to worry and to please wait for my call for dates and directions on the hospice plan. I know that you are probably the only person on the planet who understands just why your Grandpa and I really want these final days all to ourselves, and for your understanding, precious granddaughter, I thank you.

Maybe you need some time to pause and let some feelings go before you read on, and if you do, it's a great idea. If you don't, you are amazing cause it took me about three days to write a little, cry a little, just to get this far. Take your time, honey, and call me if you want as I will always have time to hear your sweet voice. When you're ready, I'll meet you at the next paragraph.

I wanted to say a word about you and your mother. I know you think that your mother does not see you, and I can only imagine how lonely you might feel without someone close who really does see the real Faith inside. I don't think she misses who you are on purpose. I think that she is so busy defending herself from the fear that she is not good enough that she just has so little left for anyone else. I know that it has been hard having her depend on you and that she tends to put her needs first. I know that we have talked about this before and that you've come up with good ideas on how to handle being the caretaker of the house. I just want to say that I know that your mother loves you and that she is very proud of you. Maybe you don't know this, but one night at the last drama performance of your freshman year, she cried. Yes, that's right, she actually shed a tear. Yet even more surprising was hearing her whisper to herself, "That's my girl, that's my Faith." There was adoration in her eye at that moment, heartfelt, almost in spite of herself, springing from a place inside her that she has somehow not yet discovered. I just wanted to let you know that in hopes that it might help you see something significant. That something is that maybe she would help you with that deep down empty spot in you (the one that only a mother's warmth can seem to soothe), if she only knew how to find that warmth inside of herself. Maybe she will find that strength one day. Who knows, sweetheart, stranger things have happened. In the meantime, I believe your strength and wisdom are faring well, but should you need the hope that comes from an old soul who believes in you, I wish to give you a gift. This is a gift that will last forever. It is a gift for your soul and one that was also given to me.

Before I give you this gift, let's talk about our favorite subjects: friends and romance. I know that you are having trouble finding friends who are real and not "gamers" as you call them but just the fact that you can recognize the gamers has you one step ahead in the quality of life category. One real friend is better than the adoration of one thousand gamers. I know we both agree on that.

I know that you are only fifteen years old, and yet as I've told you many times, I can see that you have a wisdom well beyond your years. This wisdom is both beautiful and uncommon. It will set you apart from many, but you will find a chosen few who will see you for who you are and fall in love with you. They will be forever friends and very special souls just like you. They will see a woman who has a passion for life, second to none, and a woman who enriches every life that she touches. You will have to learn on your own this truth, a friendship with you is something with a lifetime value because you truly do bring out the best in the lives I've watched you touch. It's OK if you don't realize your true beauty and worth yet, though in my sweet daydream, I can see that you will wake up one day soon and embrace this wonderful truth about yourself as your own. So love, no worries in the friend department.

Now let's take a walk along the beach and have some serious "girl talk." Meet you at the beach of your choice in the next paragraph. I'll bet I know which beach you chose... Fifty bucks says it's New Smyrna... A check will do fine, dear, but cash has always been my favorite.

I remember well our last beach walk and how you asked me, "Tell me again, Grandma, tell me the 'sweet dream' story." It is a story that I will never tire of telling. I must have told you that story a thousand times, and to tell you a secret, I've always been delighted to find that like me, for you, the magic has never faded. For the first part of my gift to you, Faith, I would like to write the introduction to your sweet dream story. The introduction to my sweet dream story, the one that you know so well was actually written by my grandmother Angel Andrews in 1941 when I was fifteen. Grandma Angel's introduction was written in 1916 by my great-great grandmother Hope Asher. I included the first part of my introduction (the one written for me by Grandma Angel) in what I've written for you. I knew that you would appreciate that, and I know that Hope and Angel (Grandma Angel included some of grandma Hope's words in my introduction) will most definitely approve. Most important, I included the first part because I sense it to be true about your sweet dream. So now I give to you, granddaughter Faith, these words of introduction to your sweet dream.

To each and every soul, there is designated one sweet dream. Your sweet dream will be the man who while seeing the "real you" will also see "jewels of you" that you have not yet discovered. He will take great delight in showing them to you one by one. He will be passionate about freedom, the freedom of the soul. He will be on a journey to free his self. He will touch, with just one look, that place inside you that longs to be held. He will know when to embrace and how to give space. He will make you feel secure in who you are, and in his arms, you will find that you can fly or you can cry. He is intense with the ability to feel every last drop of a single emotion. When he focuses his energy on you, he will sense your energy to a place where he can almost feel your feeling as if it were his own. He will resonate with a deep and uncommon wisdom that has long been seeking an equal. You, Faith, are that equal. He will see that truth almost at once but may hesitate to believe in what he sees. He will be a romantic with a rich sense for the rhythm of intimacy and her mysterious ways. He often feels like a traveler from a strange land and has yet to see a face that is more than yet another stranger. It seems that you will meet him at a time when he is troubled by an ancient wound that has come up for healing. He is hurting at this time, although he stands on the threshold of a discovery that will alter the course of his life. Strangely, Faith, you will not see his troubled countenance until later as it appears you are also healing from a recent wound. You will sense first the strength of his hope before meeting the severe beauty of his vulnerability. It is the bonding of some deeper wisdom that will see you both through the early days of the most intense romance I have ever sensed. It is almost as if there is some "angel" that is so certain of your divinely intended union that it magnifies your true inner selves when you are together. This magnification makes your original designs so clear that you are both quickly able to shed the inessentials to reveal the original shape of your "us." I get a strong sense of the embryo of your us, but I am not clear on the date of its birth. What seems most clear is that he is a healer, a teacher, or a writer. It seems that you will meet him sometime just before your thirtieth year.

I know, Faith, that you might be wondering if your life can hold a sweet dream of such promise. You may wonder how you will ever appreciate all that your sweet dream is without feeling small or overwhelmed. Well I've just the remedy for that wonder, honey, which brings me to the second part of this four-course gift. Before I bring some illumination to one of the most beautiful miracles within your soul, I just want to say that you already have everything you need to have and to hold your sweet dream. However, it will be up to you to not only discover the treasures of your being, but it will also be yours to own those treasures. This process of discovering and owning your own soul is your primary journey. This is the path that will determine the outcome of each and every relationship you have. It is this soul journey that will also forge a quality and a meaning to your life that will be forever yours. Here is a gift that will help you find "your" way. As it happens, Faith, you not only clearly possess this gift, but even at the age of fifteen, you are wakening to the presence of a divine prudence. Now let me introduce you to your wisdom angel.

It is said that there exists deep within the unconscious mind an angel of wisdom. This sage spirit acts as guide and gatekeeper for the treasures of the soul. The angel knows when and what treasure to release in accordance with the soul's progress on the inward journey of self-discovery.

The soul by design cannot appreciate its own treasures without the completion of "soul journey" milestones. The wisdom angel may never release soul treasures that cannot be fully appreciated and cared for by that individual soul. The capacity for the care and appreciation of a soul treasure is learned and earned on the soul journey path. Upon the completion of each milestone, the wisdom angel will be there to embrace you, to thank you for believing in "you" and to leave with your soul another "jewel of you." Deep within the soul's internal universe, each and every soul contains more treasures than could be discovered in several lifetimes, which is to say there is more than a lifetime of you to discover, nurture, and appreciate. Incredibly a vast majority of souls will live out their entire life without discovering even a fraction of their own soul treasure. You, Faith, have already made a conscious connection with your wisdom angel. You will never be alone because your angel will always be there for you. Your angel wants very much for you to have all that she holds for you. Trust this spirit sage, find her residence in your heart, and call her by name (a name that only you will discover) should you lose your way. She will help you find the path and light the way to your next destination of "you."

I want to tell you a story, Faith, about the first time you revealed this mystical presence. I remember the day your father died and thinking to myself that hope and joy would never visit me again. But it was only a few days later, the day after your father's funereal. It was what I called a chinook (an unseasonably warm day). Your grandfather and I were sitting in the swing on your front porch. We were watching you play with your books and colors. As I remember, we could not take our eyes off of you. You were only four, and we could see so much of our William in your eyes and most especially in your smile. You kept looking up at us, giving us that smile each time. It was after the third or fourth smile that I lost it, bursting into tears and asking your grandpa to please bring my Will back to me.

All of a sudden, I felt your little hand patting my head. I looked up, and with this intense look in those deep green-gold eyes, you said, "Don't cry, Mamaw Casey (your four-year-old way of saying Grandma Gracie), Daddy's still here."

I was so shocked to hear your words that my tears shut off like a faucet. I asked you, "What do you mean, Faith, sweetheart?"

You said, "Daddy told me that he would always be with me, and that if I wanted to feel him here, all I have to do is smile. I really do feel him when I smile, Mamaw, and I know it's him cause I can smell Daddy, you know, like the smell after he puts the whip crème on his face."

"She's talking about his aftershave," Grandpa Micheal guessed.

Then your eyes turned sad, and you said, "But I miss his arms, Mamaw. I miss his arms." That's when I pulled you close, and we three had a good cry. It was that moment that told me that your wisdom was uncommon and that your wisdom angel lived very close to your heart.

Lawrence Gabriel

* * *

Lindsay's swelling emotions forced her to stop as tears of wonder, amazement, and sympathy rolled in succession out from the well of her deep blue eyes. Taking a moment, Lindsay sat with her disoriented thoughts and emotions, hoping in vain for some semblance of equilibrium. "OK, girl," she comforted herself, wiping her eyes for what seemed to be the umpteenth time that day. "It's time to call for reinforcements." Tucking the letter carefully back into the worn envelope, she pushed herself up from the comfort of the white suede sofa and made her way to the kitchen. Pulling her cell phone from the charger, she dialed a number and silently wished, *Pick up, Gaby, please pick up.*

"Lindsay? Is that you, Lindz?"

"Of course, it's me," Lindsay said, smiling in relief at the sound of her best friend's voice. "Who else would be rude enough to call you an hour before midnight on a Friday night."

"Rude, there is no such thing as rude with you and me. We're family, girl."

"In that case, can I convince you to meet me at KK's in about forty-five minutes?"

"Sure, Lindz, but I want you to stop right now and tell me what's wrong. I can hear it in your voice. Is it Bruce, honey? Did he call?"

"No, Gaby, he didn't call. It's just I thought I could make it through my first night downtown, by myself, without thinking about him. I almost did too, but then I'm unpacking this box in the bedroom and I find this picture of me and Bruce. You remember the one from our honeymoon in Maui?"

"I remember, Lindz, the one at that place with the dollar bills on the wall."

"That's the one. So I'm sitting there on the window seat watching it rain and trying to work out the blue you know and…"

Lindsay recounted the events of the past hour, bringing Gaby up to the moment of her tearful response to Grandma Gracie's letter to her granddaughter Faith.

With enthusiasm now added to concern, Gaby eagerly confirmed the plan to meet at KK's. Placing the box and the diary back where she'd found them, Lindsay scooped up the mysterious letter, placed it her purse, and with renewed energy headed out to her car.

* * *

Breathing a prayer of appreciation for her friend, Lindsay reminisced as she made the short drive to KK's by way of an all-night Kinko's. It was early fall in the year 1995 when she first met Gabriella Carmelita Menendez.

It was her first day flying solo, as she had called it, freshman year, Washington University—no parents, no familiar faces, new school, new city, sky's the limit. She had just survived registration, and after dropping her books off at her little apartment on Kingsbury, she had set out to canvas the neighborhood. While biking along the business district on Delmar known as the Loop, she had been seduced by the Cajun fragrance of a bar and grill called Blueberry Hill.

She had gone in and ordered a burger as she pored over book lists and class schedules. Seated at the bar, she was just finishing her late lunch when she heard the noisy approach of what appeared to be a group of fraternity guys. The group of five all had the same conservative style haircut. Their dress and demeanor fit snug and firm into the preppy groove of the campus social strata. She could still recall how their boisterous tone and unrestrained banter had seemed to convey convictions of an entitlement that was brewing its way to a border town recklessness. She remembered quietly slipping her papers into her pack, hoping to make a discreet getaway as she sensed an unexpected urgency to evade this sudden intrusion of cologne and testosterone. No such luck, she was spotted, marked, and moments later surrounded by the intentions of five unsolicited suitors. As one who had enjoyed the security of a close knit, small town shelter, she had been unaccustomed to the experience of unbridled anxiety. She was genuinely surprised in those moments, at her tremulous responses to their probing queries. She remembered trying to "buck up" (as they said on the Parker ranch) and not appear so fragile, but she could not seem to help herself. Her mouth had become desert dry, her tongue uncooperative, and she recalled the growing panic as she began to feel that her legs were too weak to trust.

That's when she saw her. The face was striking, resonating with a Latin American beauty that stunned the beholder. Her cheekbones were high and sharp, in contrast to her nose that featured a softer line. Her full mouth was framed by generous lips, with corners that dimpled when she smiled. Her deep brown eyes belied both a fire and an intelligence that saw far more than the average beholder might expect. Her long dark hair complimented a light cocoa–colored complexion that dared you to find a flaw. The face had given Lindsay a shutter speed, conspiratorial wink, and then she had watched the young woman's perfectly proportioned body move effortlessly into action.

"There you are, girl," she'd said as five pairs of eyes whipped around at the sound of her voice. Before anyone could respond, she was standing next to her, stuffing her papers into her pack and grabbing her arm. "What did you think, we had all day to shop and eat?" she'd said as she rolled her eyes at the frat boys as if to say some people just have no concept of time. "Let's amscray or we're going to be late." She'd pulled her out of her chair while placing her pack over her shoulder.

Her legs had somehow transformed from rubber back to flesh, and she had half walked, half stumbled with her rescuer toward the door. The frat boys, still in shock (a couple with their mouths actually hanging open), followed their exit with unabashed stares that, as Lindsay recalled, seemed to crawl up and down her body long after leaving the restaurant behind. They had been just a few steps short of the door when one of the frat pack found his voice, "So what's the big rush? What are you going to be so late for?"

"Lingerie party," Gaby threw back easily as she pushed Lindsay out the door. "Why so much fuss over something as mundane as underwear, I'll never know." She shrugged innocently as she backed out the door, smiling demurely at their scope-locked concentration on her long brown legs. Once outside, she had casually linked arms with Lindsay, and together they strolled on down the sidewalk.

Recalling vividly Gaby's first words to her, Lindsay smiled to herself as she pulled into a parking space at Kinko's.

"You did good, kid. You could use a little work on improvisation, but overall not too bad I'd say, not bad at all.

"Me? Not bad?" Lindsay had responded incredulously. "You were amazing in there. I mean that was the scariest, coolest, most exciting thing I've ever seen. How did you do that?"

"Oh just a little trick that I learned from my mother when I was in junior high school, which those toads back there maybe graduating to any year now. So what's your name, kid?"

The Dreamwatcher Diaries

Lindsay paused in her selection of a copier as she watched the response of her eighteen-year-old self standing in front of a sidewalk café called the Red Sea.

"Stop calling me kid," she'd said, beginning to feel some anger. "I'm not some helpless child. I-I just got ambushed and I wasn't prepared."

"There you go, now I see the claws. I knew you had nails, girl, yea you got 'em alright. By the way, where did you get yours done cause they definitely rock."

Realizing that she had just helped her regain her dignity and equilibrium in what seemed like nanoseconds, Lindsay's anger dissolved in a blink and she burst out laughing, "What are you, a psych major or something?"

"That's me, the campus shrink. Wait a minute, who told you? Is this written somewhere or something? I thought I washed that Freud tattoo off my forehead? And here I went to all the trouble of leaving my cigars at home." By the time she was able to stop giggling, they had arrived at the sidewalk rack where she had parked her bike.

"My name is Lindsay Parker, and I wanted to say thank you. That was a really nice thing that you did back there. I want you to know that I will never forget the gorgeous Latin girl with no name who rescued me from the 'Blueberry Hill' gang."

Gaby held out her hand. "Gabriella Carmelita Menendez at your service. I know, it's a mouthful.

My friends just call me Gaby," she'd said with a smile so sincere that Lindsay could actually see the heart of the girl within the mind of the young woman that stood before her. "So where to now, off to teach more of the local males about the ins and outs of sexual frustration? Oh my god, I did not just say ins and outs what a perfectly horrid thing to say to a young impressionable mind."

Lindsay had caught herself giggling again. "I think I'm going to take my bike, my trusty backpack, and the serendipitous fortune of meeting you back to my apartment while the going is good."

"You've got an apartment? Where is it?"

"Just down the street on Kingsbury."

"Jump back! For real?" Gaby had exclaimed, taking her turn at being incredulous. "I've heard those are pretty cool.

"Definitely pretty cool, wanna come see?" Lindsay had invited.

"Absolutely, I'm there yesterday, girl."

* * *

"And the rest is history," Lindsay finished to herself, with a grin, as she climbed back into her SUV with three fresh copies of the letter and the original, which she carefully placed into the glove compartment. *What a history it's been*, Lindsay thought as she pulled out of the Kinko's turning left down Washington. She mentally clicked on the highlights of her ten-year plus relationship with her best friend as she made the short trip to the restaurant. They had become roommates within days of their first meeting. Sisters from some earlier life, Gaby would often say with genuine conviction, "What else could explain our soul sister symmetry?"

Gaby stayed on with Lindsay even after graduating with her bachelors in psychology. She had remained at Washington University, where she attended graduate school earning her master's in counseling psychology. Lindsay finished her bachelor's in business and completed her master's in advanced computer technology.

Lindsay had met her ex-husband, Bruce, in graduate school, and two years later, they had married, with Gaby as her maid of honor. The wedding had marked their separation as roommates, though they had maintained regular contact in spite of busy schedules. Gaby had taken a position as a therapist in a residential treatment center for emotionally disturbed children while Lindsay had found a position at a local computer firm. Gaby had been a major support during Lindsay's cloudy pre- and post-divorce days and was also there to share the joy of her recent success in the landing of her new position with Data International. They had been through many adventures during their years together, from hiking and skiing with her family in Colorado to several visits to Gaby's birthplace in El Salvador, but since the discovery of the letter, Lindsay had sensed a strange excitement. It was as if the grandmother's words had awakened a mysterious hope deep within her. As she felt that hopes beckoning for her to follow, she somehow felt more alive than she had in a very long while.

* * *

KK's was short for "Kitchen Kae's," a trendy restaurant in Downtown St. Louis. The restaurant was one of the many new features along the face-lifted section of Washington Street. The area was enjoying its new vitality with a surge of new business and growing popularity especially among young professionals. Kitchen Kae's offers a spacious dining arrangement that features an open view of the restaurant's immaculate kitchen. Through a separate doorway, the establishment includes the intimate ambience of a modest bistro, enticing patrons with nouveau appetizers and a drink menu that includes both wine and specialty drinks. One of the bistro's unique features was the inclusion of the ideal drink choice with each appetizer.

Lindsay walked into the Bistro and found a table. She was greeted by a cocktail waitress dressed in classic black and white. She ordered the fruit, bread, and cheese plate accompanied by a bottle of Piesporter Riesling ideal for the fruity palate. Her selection was strategic in its homage to a ritual that the two friends had created many years earlier. Whenever Lindsay or Gaby sensed the coming or passing of a self-growth event, as Gaby had with her graduation and later her new job, and Lindsay with her engagement and later her divorce, they went through their own growth affirmation ritual. The ritual utilized the bread, fruit, cheese, and wine as symbols in a unique and personally crafted format.

Lindsay was deep into a review of the first pages of the letter when she sensed a shift in the energy at the crowded bistro bar. She smiled to herself knowing without looking up that her friend had just entered the restaurant. Familiar by now with the magnetism of Gaby's exotic beauty, Lindsay had grown accustomed to the commotion that her friend's entrances generated. Confident with her own beauty, Lindsay had never felt the need to entertain the wiles of envy or resentment. In truth, she rather enjoyed her relaxed second-tier position in the orchestra of feminine beauty. Gaby, of course, being as graceful as she was beautiful, would adamantly disagree with Lindsay's genuine appraisal. Many women, Lindsay thought, given the same extraordinary measure of beauty, might well become dependent on that beauty, developing a need for the specific kind of attention that such a beauty naturally brought out in others. This attention, ranging from gratuity and entitlement all the way up to worship and grandiosity, may seduce women of lesser character to foster a dependence on their beauty and forgo the life task work of self-trust and self-awareness. This dependence over time produces female souls bound by the fear of beauty loss and the demands of beauty maintenance on the one side and a developed reliance on others for care of worth and identity needs and catering to entitlement needs on the other.

If a beautiful woman who is both self-aware and self-reliant could be called an anomaly, then Gaby was indeed an anomaly. Gaby owned her beauty; it did not own her. Her character simply would not allow it. Void of value judgments and entitlement expectations, she lived as though she could see and actually visualize the soul worth in each person. She would often find, without premeditation, the single physical property on the other that connected specifically to that person's internal worth place. She would then lavish the subject or object with genuine attention and at times, to Lindsay's amazement, would draw tears and warm hugs in a single meeting from a total stranger. She met and treated each soul with a fierce loyalty toward equality and never left a room without acknowledging, in some affirming way, the worth of each soul that had crossed her path.

As Lindsay looked up to watch Gaby's approach, she remembered telling her friend as much not so long ago, "Have you ever realized, Gaby," she had asked, "just how well you carry your incredible beauty?" Lindsay could count on one hand the number of times in their ten-year relationship that she had seen her friend cry. This time had taken Lindsay by surprise.

As two tears traced symmetrical paths down her cheeks, Gaby had replied, "You have no idea how much what you just said means to me. I know that every divine gift comes with a weight and measure of responsibility, but sometimes this mantle of beauty can actually get heavy. When you said that just now, Lindz, it's like you really touched the woman in me that carries that mantle, and then you saw her strength."

"That's it," Lindsay had returned, "that's exactly what I was seeing. The word *mantle* really says it well too. I also see that your strength does not just bear the weight of that beauty mantle, but it also masters the mantle as if you've told the beauty that it will not be allowed to alter or overpower your identity. You won't let it become more important than who you are. I believe that's why your beauty is so radiant." Lindsay's eyes took on a shine, as she recalled their warm embrace, and how after some moments she had pulled back and said, "I want to thank you for one thing, Gabriella Carmelita Menendez. I want to thank you for not entering the 1993 Miss Silverton Colorado beauty contest 'cause I would've had to kick your beautiful El Salvadorian ass, and then we might not have ended up being best friends." The memory of Gaby's laughter brought a wide smile to her face as Gaby herself walked up to the table and gave Lindsay a warm hug.

"So what's the big smile all about?" Gaby asked, flashing her own smile as she slid out of her long black wool overcoat.

"You know me, just reminiscing," Lindsay replied.

"So was it a full-featured DVD or just a back road memory?" Gaby asked as she carefully hung her coat over the chair back.

"Just a memory," Lindsay returned as she admired her friend's casual ensemble. Gaby wore Claiborne cashmere. The black V-neck sweater was accented by a silver necklace featuring at its end a petite, inverse pyramid, silver, with a black onyx stone at its center. Her dark denim Claiborne jeans were cinched with a silver strand belt secured by a round black buckle. Her boots were classic black Western with medium heels.

"So where is this incredible letter?" Gaby asked, sitting in the tall chair across from Lindsay.

"Gaby, you are not going to believe how 'you and me' this letter is," Lindsay said as she handed her the copied pages. "I also brought these," Lindsay added, handing some tissues to her friend with a sheepish smile. "I've got a feeling you might need them soon."

"So you really think it's going to take me to 'the Well' huh?" Gaby asked, referencing the word they used for their crying place.

"I think so. I know that it brought me there in less than two pages, and it's a twenty-one–page letter. That's why I called in reinforcements. There is something extraordinary about this letter."

"Wait a minute, is that a bottle of Riesling I see coming?" Gaby asked.

"What perfect timing," Lindsay exclaimed as the waitress approached with her order.

"This really must be special if it merits a growth affirmation ritual," Gaby said as she eyed the letter with anticipation.

The Dreamwatcher Diaries

"Go ahead and read the first eight pages," Lindsay urged. "I was thinking you could catch up with me before we do the ritual, and then we'll read the rest together."

* * *

Gaby was quickly swept away to another place as she read the grandmother's heartfelt prose. She was amazed to feel the tug on her heart grow with each paragraph. The letter seemed to flow with a rhythmic nurturance, coaxing her down the path of an endearing enlightenment that was both soothing and exhilarating. Gaby did not sense her tears until she felt the approach of the tissue in her friend's hand. Gaby took the tissue, looked at it for a moment as if it were an alien artifact, and said with a soft smile, "You know, Lindz, I think I just want to feel my heart on my cheeks right now. It's sentimental, I know, but these tears came from that girl in me, the one who still believes, the one somewhere in my own 'Hope Palace.' It's been so long since I've been touched so… just right….in here," she said, placing her hand on her heart. "I can't believe how these words spoke, my deepest thoughts, how they spoke right to that believer in me. It's like that incredible feeling you get when you finally feel understood after thinking for so long that no one would get it, that no one would ever really see, the person inside. I mean, I know that you see, and my family sees, but you can't help but hope that you'll someday find the man who can see.

Manolo sure didn't," Gaby added, referring to her most recent boyfriend of five years, "and my last five dates haven't even come close. The tears feel so right because now I know my hope is still alive."

"I love what you just said," Lindsay said. "It's exactly how I felt especially when she described Faith's sweet dream. Can you imagine finding a man who knows when to embrace and how to give space? Gaby, how can this be happening? How can it be that we would find the very words that could touch our deepest hopes, by accident?"

"I don't know, Lindz, I really don't, but I think it's safe to say neither of us believes that it's an accident.

"It's just so amazing, that we were both sitting on the brink of romantic hopelessness, and then this letter comes around and touches off an energy the equivalent of hope times joy squared!" Lindsay exclaimed.

"The timing is extraordinary," Gaby agreed, "but I say we follow our instincts and see where this energy leads us. So let's do some growth affirmation, take the letter back to your place, and take turns reading the rest out loud," Gaby finished.

"To the perfect plan," Lindsay said, raising her glass in a toast.

CHAPTER FOUR

The Letter Continues

One hour, one bottle of wine, and one growth affirmation later, Gaby and Lindsay, both dressed comfortably in old college sweats, were sitting on Lindsay's couch amid a cozy arrangement of pillows and blankets. Lindsay had whipped up a couple of "fragile babies," a coffee drink made with Baileys, Frangelico, and topped off with whipped cream in cinnamon-ringed mugs.

"Lindz, this is so good," Gaby remarked as she took another sip from her steaming mug.

"It really does hit the spot, doesn't it," Lindsay agreed as she licked the cinnamon from her lips. "So who wants to read first?" Lindsay asked as she set her mug on the coffee table and picked up the letter.

"That would be me," Gaby replied, setting her drink beside Lindsay's and finding her place in the letter's pages. "I'll read until something stops me, kind of like when something stopped you, and we'll go from there."

"Sounds great," Lindsay agreed, sitting back in the cushion while she hugged a pillow to her chest. "I'm ready whenever you are."

"Here goes," Gaby said and, in her musical Latin American accent, begins to read.

* * *

That precious moment also gave me an important clue to something that would secretly become very important to you as a woman. I knew from that day on that strong but gentle arms would become a significant feature in the man that you someday chose. I know that a man who has your father's arms will have the potential to reach in and touch the heart of that four-year-old, in that place that is deep and bittersweet. I just wanted you to know that just the right arms, on the right man, for that moment in your life, will draw you in, Faith. You will find yourself doing almost anything to keep such a man. You may become upset at yourself for falling so hard for the right man who turns out to be the wrong man. You may even choose the same kind of wrong man over and over again. You may begin to think that there is something wrong with you, but don't, sweetheart, not even for a moment. It's just that little girl in you trying to bring Daddy back for a little while longer and you have to know, Faith, that there is certainly nothing wrong with that. You must give yourself time to learn, and learn you will of that I am certain. Someday you will discover, Faith, how to dissolve the fear of loss for that little girl inside. She will heal to a place where she will even realize that she can feel "that way" (the way you felt within your father's embrace) without a man's arms around you. But that learning journey, honey, may well include the wrong man for a time or two or three... The important thing is to stay the course, enjoy the journey, and listen close to your wisdom angel. She will help you grow to that place where you will own all that you are in your father's eyes, and then there's more...your sweet dream.

When you meet your sweet dream, Faith, he will not need his arms to touch that "father's arms" place within you. He will touch that deep place with just one look and then take you beyond. You will see a deep and warm intelligence in his eyes coupled with a spirited intensity. That warm intelligence will take in all that you own, and unlike the wrong man, your sweet dream's soul container will not overflow or trap you within. You will find that he can flex and bend with the contours of your soul's shape. Like smoke around a flame, he will have the capacity to surround your being with a warmth and wisdom that includes the element of space. Held for a time within his intelligent energy, you will lose the sense of where he ends and you begin. Yet he will not alter or imprison you, as you will discover, some moments later, when you return to your sense of self, with your soul shape intact, but now aglow with the sweet residue of your union. Later still, in a moment of soulful vulnerability, he will find you doing the same for him. But it is the spirited intensity that will make you dizzy and leave you feeling more than just a little bit like the constitution of Jell-O. Regarding this moment, my advice to you, Faith dear, is breathe deep and find the nearest chair. I've been there before. It was the first time I caught your grandfather's "look." Speaking of breath, why don't we take a little breather. Sip some coffee, munch on your roll, and collect your thoughts. I'll meet you when you're ready at the next paragraph.

Well it's time for the third and fourth courses of your four-course gift. But, Faith, I must ask you to please finish reading before rushing off to the place where these gifts lie waiting for you. Let's begin with this introduction to the third course of your gift.

While it is a wonderful thing to have this knowledge of your sweet dream, it can also become a source of worry. Many years ago, when my great-great grandmother Hope passed on the tradition of the sweet dream and the wisdom angel to my grandmother Angel, she knew that she would need the blessing of divine destiny to address the worry that may come with the knowledge of the sweet dream.

The story goes that in the early morning, the day after her prayer and meditation for the aid of the divine, Hope was awakened by the sound of something, just outside her bedroom window. She pulled the curtain back, and there sitting right on her windowsill was a snow-white dove. It is written, in the letter that Grandma Angel gave to me, that when Hope opened the window, the dove did not fly away but rather continued to sit there watching her. That is when Hope knew that her prayer had been answered. The dove was to be the divine link between the wisdom angel and the sweet dream.

The Dreamwatcher Diaries

The dove was to be the "dreamwatcher." It was in those moments when Hope watched the dove and the dove watched her that she was given the words to the dreamwatcher prayer. Hope, keeping one eye on the bird, picked up her diary and pen from the bedside table and wrote down the words of the prayer. Smiling at the bird as she wrote down the last words, Hope whispered, "Thank you, dreamwatcher."

Then with a flutter of its wings, the dove took flight. As she watched it fly away, it is written that she looked down and saw a single snow-white feather. She picked the feather up, kissed it, and placed it carefully in her diary. With that feather, Hope rewrote the words of the dreamwatcher prayer along with the three missions of the dreamwatcher. The first is to find the sweet dream, the second to protect and watch over the sweet dream, and the third to create a link between the wisdom angel and the sweet dream that would eventually lead the dream to the angel. As the dreamwatcher leads the dream closer and closer to the angel, the angel will have increased sightings of the dreamwatcher.

Faith, just before I met your grandfather, I saw a snow-white dove five days in a row! It was on a Thursday that I last saw the dove (I'd swear it was the same one) perched on the pier at the beach café called Old Memories to New Moons. Some moments later, in that very café, I saw your grandfather's eyes for the first time (and yes I am proud to say I did find a chair before my Jell-O legs gave way). I know it all sounds a bit like a fairy tale, but I also know that sometimes hope believes in you whether you believe or not. You taught me that.

I wanted to especially note, how it is, that the dreamwatcher serves balance, peace, and contentment. This is found in the purposes of the dreamwatcher missions, which are to dissolve the doubt that your sweet dream exists, the fear that your sweet dream might be harmed or lost and the worry that you may never find him.

Your dreamwatcher, Faith, is at this moment in a vented box covered with a green cloth, on the nightstand, in the guest bedroom. There you will also find a second box. You may go look at your dreamwatcher dove, but don't open the second box . Carry this letter and the two boxes out to the front porch, and I'll meet you at the porch swing in the next paragraph.

It seems not so long ago, Faith, that I was there in the very place that you are now. Like you, I was sitting in front of my own house reading this same letter in the company of two very magical boxes, wondering what was to happen next. Here is what you need to do.

First, take the cloth off the dreamwatcher dove box. Next, give yourself some time to make a connection with your dreamwatcher. As you do this, think about your wisdom angel and your soul journey. Take all the time you like, and listen for a sign (could be a feeling, a word, or a symbol only you and your wisdom angel will know for sure) from your wisdom angel that she has made a link with your dreamwatcher.

The Dreamwatcher Diaries

Second, after you receive the sign, open the second box that is labeled "The Dreamwatcher Diaries." You will find Hope's original copy of the dreamwatcher prayer. Take the prayer out carefully as the feather used to write the prayer is just underneath.

Next, say the prayer to your dreamwatcher, then open the box and release the dove (allow your dreamwatcher to move as it will and to fly in its own time).

Third, once your dreamwatcher takes flight, look inside the diary box and take out the small bottle of ink. At the bottom of the prayer, you will find the signatures and dates made by Hope, Angel, and me. Using Hope's feather from the first dreamwatcher, sign your name and the date in the space just under my name.

I think that I would give just about anything to see your face right now, honey, but this is your moment, yours alone, and so it shall be forever.

The fourth and final part of the gift (you may have already guessed) is the box of diaries. I have just a few words of direction before you look them over. There are seven diaries (four green diaries and three blue diaries).

The green diaries are to be used to write to your wisdom angel about your soul journey experiences. So long as you begin each entry in the green diaries with "Dear Wisdom Angel," when, what, and how often you write is completely up to you. The purpose of specifically addressing your wisdom angel is twofold. One is to affirm that there is a being within you that truly does love and care for you more than tongue could ever tell. The special thing about this being is that "she" has a direct link to the original intention of "you." That is like having a direct telephone line to the designer of your soul who has all of the answers to all of the questions about you. (As you can see, we grandmas don't mess around when we give a gift.) Two is to increase your trust in "her" (I can't wait to hear what her name is once you've discovered it) as you share your deepest fears, dreams, and hopes with your best friend who always travels with you.

Before I tell you about the three blue diaries. I want to say a quick word about your soul journey.

Sweetheart, I want you to know that our "tea talks" over the past seven years have made my life far richer than I ever dreamed a life could be. I always smile when I remember the day that you introduced the idea. You were just eight years old when you phoned me and invited me to have tea, on a Sunday afternoon. It was on that day that you asked me if we could have tea talks every Sunday. I told you it was a wonderful idea and that I could bring some goodies to go with the tea. You flashed me one of those famous smiles of yours, hugged me, and then whispered in my ear, "And we can talk about Daddy." Of course those whispered words led to another hug and a few little tears. I will always hold that moment precious, my little Fay-Fay, as well as all of the soul journeying miles that we have traveled together from that day to this one.

I've been waiting, with anticipation for this mile of your maturation, for this moment of your readiness. You are ready to hear the answers to your constant questions about the soul journey. After so many times of hearing me say "when you're ready," I can truly say today you are ready and I am proud of you, granddaughter. It is time to answer your question, what is the point of the soul journey? Why travel inward? Why not travel outward and see new people and places? What is the value of this soul journey? (This is a collection of your versions of the same question, what is the point of the soul journey.) The answer, Faith, is, to free yourself, to be yourself, to reach that milestone where you see your "self" so clearly that no power nor persuasion could keep you from simply being the divine intention of you.

Remember when we read the Scarlet Letter together and you wondered how anyone could stand up against so many negative opinions. That's how, Faith. You can reach the place where you have enough "you" where you can see the truth, the truth that you cannot add to your self nor subtract from yourself, nor can anyone else. You are decidedly whole. All that you truly can do is uncover that which is already whole and complete, and seeing its shape discover all that it holds for you. That's it, honey, that's what the soul journey is all about. It's like when I gave you that ball of clay and I asked you to make a shape that no one has ever seen before. I told you to see the shape inside the clay first, and then uncover it. You did not add clay to the ball to make the shape that you saw. Instead, you peeled off the inessentials until the shape you saw was revealed and that, my dear, is the essence of the soul journey.

Faith, your personal vision of the unique shape of your own soul is the first of three soul journey milestones that you will need to attract (your sweet dream will be looking for someone who has enough of herself just as he will have enough of himself) and someday meet your sweet dream. To my delight at the age of fifteen, you already have a clear vision of your soul's shape. As the owner of the first "jewel of you," you have but two milestones to complete before you will have what you need to attract and meet your sweet dream.

The second milestone is to believe in what you see, to believe that the soul shape in your internal vision is really you. This milestone will take you through many tests and trials. It will teach you about the nature and power of illusion. In the end, you will discover that only faith (your name is no coincidence) will endure.

The third soul journey milestone, as you might expect from the nature of any growth process, has the highest degree of difficulty. This milestone requires that you not only see "you" and that you not only believe in the "you" inside, but that you now also own the worth of "you." Owning the worth of your soul is an astounding accomplishment. This third jewel of you completes your circle of balance. Sitting there, at that place just beyond this third milestone, you now see yourself with clarity (this is balance against illusion), you believe in that clarity with conviction (this is focus against illusion's power to distract), and you own the worth of your conviction (this is contentment). In the position of contentment, the power of all that you are intended to be is poised in a creative position. It is there, at the center of your creative energy, that you will find there is nothing that you cannot bend to your will. All things are possible, and dreams really do come true. Imagine reaching this third milestone and then meeting the man who has accomplished the same.

There will be days during your soul journey when you may feel a sadness at the loneliness of your journey. You may long for the warmth and security of just someone. Should you one day awake to find yourself with this someone, your soul (with clarity) will tell you that while the body is warm and most probably, in your eyes, beautiful, he may well be a stranger to his own soul and in turn unfamiliar with the nature of intimacy.

Strangely, intimacy attempts with strangers are a critical part of the soul journey toward your sweet dream. It is most important that safety always comes first; however in this event, do not be upset with yourself or the other for this is an inevitable element of soul journey growth. Stranger still is the truth that you will not encounter a single soul that divine destiny did not intend for you to meet. Each of these souls that pass in and then quickly out of your life are actually significant while unwitting teachers and messengers with important information regarding your current location on your soul journey path. While there will often be the impulse to imagine that these souls are or could be your sweet dream, you need not give in to the charms of illusion. Instead, stay the course, enjoy the moment, and listen most carefully to your wisdom angel.

As to the matter of the three blue diaries, allow me to enlighten you in the next paragraph.

* * *

"I think I need to stop for a minute," Gaby said. "My heart is pulling in one direction, and my analytical brain is in overdrive. I'm tracking thought streams along about ten different highways, but the streams keep crossing.

"How about you write out your thought streams, and I'll write out a quick summary of my feelings so far," Lindsay suggested, getting up for paper and pens.

"That is the best idea, but, Lindz, I don't want to lose any of what I am feeling. Maybe I should write my feelings first. It feels like I'm right on the verge of finding out something that is really important."

"Ten to one that after you write out all your thought streams, what you are looking for will be standing right out in the middle of one of those highways with a big neon sign," Lindsay predicted as she returned with pens and legal pads.

"You know what," Gaby said with a pensive frown, "I think you are right."

"Of course I'm right," Lindsay said, handing Gaby a pad and pen. "Have I ever steered you wrong?"

"Well, there was that stock broker in Clayton, some months back," Gaby returned with a mischievous grin playing across her mouth.

"How could I know he was a wolf in sheep's clothing? Very expensive clothing I might add. So OK, he had a great disguise, but you gotta expect a screwup now and then, right, and try to tell me he wasn't hot."

"Lindsay, the guy was a letch, he was all over me. I mean this guy had more hands than the 'We Are the World' video. I don't even remember his face. All I can see when I think about him is one big hand."

"OK, OK, enough said," Lindsay surrendered with a laugh. "Let's write down our thoughts and finish this letter before we both pass out from exhaustion."

The two women scribbled furiously as they poured out the melee of impressions, and feelings, stirred up by the letter's deep message. Gaby finished first and took the coffee mugs down to the kitchen for refills.

"So can I just say one thing," Gaby asked upon her return as she handed Lindsay her mug.

"No way, Gaby, not one word. I just now got my brain cleared enough to take in the last few pages. Please do not speak because when you do, I'll have a thousand more questions than I have already. Let me finish reading the final pages, and then we'll sit down and share reviews because I really do want to hear your analysis almost as much as I want to finish this letter."

"How can I say no to that?" Gaby submitted, settling back in her nest of pillows and blankets with her drink. "I'm ready for more. Let's find out what the story is with the three blue diaries."

Lindsay read on.

* * *

You will find that each of the three blue diaries is entitled the Dreamwatcher Diary. The first diary is Angel's, the second one is mine, and the third is yours. Here is how the Dreamwatcher Diaries work.

First, you do not write in your dreamwatcher diary until the day that you meet your sweet dream. You may address whoever you like as you write about him and you. (You could address your father, mother, best friend, wisdom angel, dreamwatcher, grandparents, great grandparents. Grandma Angel even included one of the soul strangers that she had met along the way.)

Second, you log forty days and forty nights, no more and no less. The forty days and nights may not be consecutive as it may take even several months to have spent exactly that many hours with him. (Just to let you know, that means that you will have spent approximately 960 hours together.) The format that Grandma Angel and I used was a total of eighty entries (forty day entries plus forty night entries). It took Grandma Angel seven and one half months to complete her eighty entries while my first forty days with your grandfather took only four months. Another format, which you might consider, is to make your entries by the dates that you go on with him, and then log the dates' time span at the beginning of each date entry (some dates may be just one night while others may go one whole weekend). The significance of the forty days and nights is twofold. One is to give you and your sweet dream time to sense your "us" and the potential for its birth into this world, and two, to express the joy and hope of your sweet dream experiences with a chosen few, with whom you wish to share those moments of rapture and romance.

While I have much hope that you and your sweet dream will sail smoothly toward the harbor, of the birthing place, of your "us," intimacy's nature is far more mysterious than it is predictable. For this reason, it is best not to reveal to him his meaning to your soul until sometime after the forty days has expired. To tell him about the dreamwatcher prior to that time may interfere with the natural progression of your fondness for each other. Once on the path of true intimacy, you will find there are no shortcuts to an "us" that is true and reliable. Intimacy will not be deceived into a closeness that is more an illusion in the mind, rather than a vulnerability of the heart. Intimacy in her natural state is her own person. The moment that you try to possess her, she will slip away, and the day that you think you have her under your control is the day that she will vanish from your life. Remember always that intimacy's air to breathe is freedom, her food to grow is trust, and her wings to fly are balance and equality.

At the end of the forty days, listen close to your wisdom angel, and she will give you a sign when the time is right. When that day arrives, how you tell him is up to you.

It was on the beach, under a full moon, when I shared grandma Angel's letter with your grandfather. Micheal read the letter by candlelight. I remember watching his face, at the letter's end, and how the moonlight caught a single teardrop that shimmered in a luminous path down his cheek. He pulled me close and held me, somehow knowing that no words could touch the magic of that intimate moment. It was there, in those moments, of that embrace, when the only sounds were the rhythm of our heartbeats and the soft music of the lapping waves, that our "us" was born into this world. Our intimacy journey had begun.

I believe, Faith, that such a moment will be yours and that you will someday find yourself in a similar place with your sweet dream.

As to the other two Dreamwatcher Diaries (Grandma Angel's and my own), they are yours to read at your leisure. Keep them safe, warm, and dry for they hold much wisdom and wonder both for your growth and enjoyment.

These final thoughts that I must share with you are the most difficult as they involve the possibility of a broken heart. As I mentioned before, intimacy's nature is mysterious, but stranger yet are the ways of divine destiny. Part of the wonder of divine destiny is that its nature is greater than anything else in your soul's universe, alas even your sweet dream. For this reason, should it come to pass that after the bliss of your early days together, you sense a growing distance from the heart of your sweet dream, do not be alarmed. Though it may break your heart to feel the loss of his warmth, that just moments ago seemed so near, do not lose faith. Sometimes true intimacy cannot be found until the illusions of intimacy are dispelled. Ironically the shattering of the picture of the "us" that you envision in your mind makes way for the "us" that aligns with the truth of your divine destiny.

The illusions of bliss mark the borderlands of intimacy. Bliss illusions are primarily founded in fantasy. These fantasies will hold the beliefs of what your sweet dream means to you, or more precisely the ways in which you believe your sweet dream serves you. The truth of your divine destiny will not be found in the illusions of how your sweet dream serves you but rather in how your destiny serves the universe. It is within this intimacy with your destiny that you will discover the reality of your intimacy with your sweet dream. Your being, just the simple truth of the freedom to be the divine intention of you, will bring you a bliss that does not depend on the arms of the one who at last adores you in just the right way. This is a bliss that is supported by the wings of a hope that lives within you.

Bliss illusions will suggest the achievement of an intimacy that has yet to be learned. While this bliss is true nectar from the universe and is due the honor of savoring every drop, the nature of bliss serves more to provide the soul a flight over the island of intimacy rather than signify the soul's actual arrival at the shore of intimacy's hidden cove. While it would seem that your "soul ship" is sailing toward a dream destination, once the last breath of bliss is spent, you will wake to find yourself at the birthing harbor, where you sit with your soul ship still in dry dock. There will be great pain in the discovery that your passion and bliss are not announcements of the arrival to your "us" island. For all the exhilarating moments in your first days together will most surely make your return to the earthbound realm seem like the very end of the world. While there is truth to the flight of bliss and the places that you have felt and seen, bliss can only show you a truth that you must discover within yourself. For this reason, it is important to see the limits of bliss and to not rely on its rapture as the sign of true arrival at your island of "us." It is a most difficult task to balance your being while in the grip of bliss. The key is to trust bliss only for its purpose, which is to show you the experience of oneness. The loss of balance occurs when you lose yourself to these powerful emotions. This submission to those emotions may cause you to trust bliss to carry the weight of your soul's purpose. If bliss is given the burden to define your life's meaning, then your courtship will be with illusion rather than with your sweet dream. Which is to say your courtship would be with the beliefs about how your sweet dream serves you. Those beliefs are like pictures in which you appear whole only because your sweet dream is beside you.

It is a strange truth to find that the pursuit of intimacy includes this season of illusion. It is however a truth that lives all around us. Why does the woman give her heart to the man she believes needs changing? Why does the gentleman devote his life to the woman who can never be pleased? Why does it seem that there are so many coconspir-

ators in intimate relationships, seemingly trapped in a revolving plot to sabotage their own intimacy? This is the season of illusion. For if you are living in a relationship within your mind, it is probable that like you, intimacy is not present in the room.

If your sweet dream is to fit into a plan that you have in mind (a picture in your head), you must ask yourself these questions: What is it that is most important to me the plan in my mind or the soul of my sweet dream? How much will my plan alter the genuine shape of my sweet dream's soul? If the shape of the plans in my mind determine my view of the shape of his soul, how will I ever see the true shape of his soul?

The answer will be found in the letting go of the plan. This act frees the mind to see not only the true shape of your sweet dream's soul but also that of your own.

It will be somewhere beyond the land of illusion where you will find the destiny of your being and the reality of your romantic dream. In order to get to the other side of the smoke and mirror ways of your illusions, they must be exposed and shattered. It is during this painful season of change when the warmth and comfort of your illusions evaporate that you will experience the cold winds and desert flatlands of the broken heart. Strangely, Faith, it is there, in the desert where you will discover a wonderful truth. It is a truth that will free you and give your soul a depth of the deepest blue. It is the truth that the nature of illusion cannot bear the weight of your being. To complete this journey and arrive at this truth, you must go through the land of illusion and across the desert of disillusionment to discover the oasis of your authenticity. Ironically it is only through the loss of illusion and its offerings that you will embrace the true hope of your destiny.

Not far from this desert place where you find this truth, you will suddenly see your first flower. The unexpected beauty of this fragile bloom standing up proudly in the desert sand marks the beginning of new growth that you will gradually realize is yours and yours alone. You are now entering new country. You are discovering for the first time that place within you where you were meant to live. It is there down the back roads of this strangely familiar land where you will find the spring from where the hope of your destiny flows.

So it seems that this season of illusion and bliss is as vital to the nature of intimacy as is the sweet reality of the realized (real eyes) "us" that is revealed, in the wake of the inevitable winds of change. For illusion is the "what is not" that will always give way to the substance and truth of simply "what is." It is intimacy's plan that your relationship would be the integrity of the palace stone that can bear the weight of your being rather than the beauty of the sand castle that will someday let you down.

This remarkable journey from reality places that reach for dreams...to illusion's bliss that somehow seems...to broken heart deserts of cost and loss...and finally to destiny and paths that cross...is to say the least a bewildering odyssey. Faith, I must tell you that many a soul will forsake this arduous journey toward their true destiny. Many will cling desperately to the security of their physical and material realm and all the comforts that the illusions of beauty and possession afford to them. Many others will remain fixed within the compensations of illusion's chemistry and the consolations of pleasure's principles. These souls may spend their entire existence during their moments of life here in the earthbound realm lost in the land of illusion, never quite sensing nor realizing the true meaning, nor the simple singularity, of their destiny. I feel that it is important to tell you, my little Fay-Fay, that you are, for one, a woman who will not forsake this journey. For alas, your connection with your destiny is too strong and your soul ship has long since left the pseudo-security found in the harbor towns of power and control illusions.

Dearest granddaughter, I know that I have just taken you on a mystical journey of words and meanings. It is true that you have many life miles to travel yet before my word clouds dissipate to reveal their horizons of truth. I have taken this seemingly strange discourse to provide for you a ray of hope should you one day awake to find yourself in the desert of the broken heart.

The one worry that is not quite addressed here, one that I know has placed an urgent call for your attention, is you, your sweet dream, and the hope of together forever. For this worry, there is one final truth I might share before I trace for you a healing path. It is a saying handed down from our own grandma Hope. She wrote it during a stormy day of loss when it seemed the rain would never end. Grandma Angel wrote that Hope held the words to her heart after writing them on the back of a colorful menu that she had secreted from a sidewalk café. It is said that as she held the menu to her chest, the words that she had written soaked into her heart like a soothing balm. I bring Hope's words to you now so that they will be here for you if you need them later.

How extraordinary is the paradox of forever.
How it is that forever's seemingly linear constant
Is actually an endless chain forged link by link.
Each link has a beginning and ending,
with each beginning marked by season's change,
and each ending reached by the natural rhythm
of embracing and letting go...

So, it seems that forever's line is more
a curve on which we learn
and its single constant is
the change through which we grow...

I will then let go of forever, my love
so that I might greet my new season.
But this I know... I will begin...
with the memory of your sweet face...
as I savor the timeless moment...of our last embrace.

The Dreamwatcher Diaries

Hope Asher
November 1, 1906

While the events behind this disclosure in Hope's poem, which weaves a strange thread of comfort through its layers of meaning, are as yet cloaked in mystery, Hope's words really do soothe as they bring home a calm reply to the question, what about forever?

It is like the story of the young maiden who left her home in pursuit of "that which lasts forever." Early in her travels, "forever" himself appears on her path. "Go home, my child," says Forever. Your forever is there at the here and now of your home and hearth. You already have forever's waiting for you there. For forever is meant as much to look back on as it is meant to look forward to. Each moment your life force forges a choice made by you, just you, really you, you will have begun a forever link in the chain of your existence here. Those links marking your time at this place have already begun to form. You are, even as we speak, forging a historic link. Remember always that it is your destiny chain that gives weight to your purpose here, increasing in measure and wisdom with each link that marks your path as you discover the course to your destiny. So go tend to your links, my child, and I will meet you again on the path for I believe our destinies will one day cross again.

I believe that's the best I can do on the nature of forever, sweetheart. I do enjoy the maiden story, but I must confess that I for one do tend to be preju-

diced in favor of looking north toward the links not yet forged.

Sweetheart, you may want to take some time to allow your mind to settle as it measures the weight of this lengthy passage. I will meet you soon at the next paragraph where I will share some healing direction should you find yourself in need of a broken heart remedy.

The secret to crossing over from what you desire, you and your sweet dream to be (sandcastle), to the place where you can have the destiny of what you and your sweet dream really are (palace stone), is the fourth soul journey milestone, the ability to let go. Should you find yourself at this place where you need to set your sweet dream free, I am including three steps that will help you reach this fourth soul journey milestone. This "let go" process should begin only after your forty days and nights with your sweet dream have passed. For example, if he separates from you after only thirty days of togetherness have passed, you should wait ten more days before you begin to let go. Completing the initial forty days is important to allow yourself time to heal from the initial disappointment and to gain perspective on just what it is that you are planning to leave go of during the coming forty-day process. Here are the steps to letting go. First, in order to gain entry into the rhythm of let go and let grow, you must leave your Dreamwatcher Diary and a copy of this letter behind (keep the original letter in your wisdom angel diary). Place it somewhere safe and hidden, but also someplace outside of your reach and access. This step is not about denigrating or minimizing your sweet dream and the time that you have shared. Its purpose is to clear your soul container and increase your sense of your "self" in your own space. Magically in a shorter time than you might imagine, honey, you will meet a "Faith" you never knew. Second, find and release a second Dreamwatcher dove saying the fifth and last verse of the "Dreamwatcher Prayer" first and the fourth verse last. The purpose of the releasing the second Dreamwatcher is to set your sweet dream free, placing the future of your dream into the hands of divine destiny. This act of faith and surrender to the will of the divine will give you a feeling of freedom and relief from the burden of attempting to control that which is beyond your will to determine. This is the path that will free your mind from the false comfort and misdirection of illusion (the now-shattered pictures in your mind that you believed would make you whole). Third, wait forty days and forty nights for a sign of what to do next. With each day that passes, you should let go of one of your sweet dream's charms and take back one piece of your heart that you gave to him in trust. This process of reclaiming your heart piece by piece, as well as letting go of "jewels of him," upon which you had begun to rely, will restore your balance and increase your peace of mind.

As for the hope that your sweet dream might still be yours, and someday return, allow your heart to hope, as it will, as you learn about letting go. Your heart will know the hour of that hope's last breath. Should that day come to pass, trust, as always, the guidance of your wisdom angel and hold close, my little Fay-Fay, all the precious jewels of you.

There is an unopened letter in the back pocket of my Dreamwatcher Diary, written by your great-great-great-great grandmother Hope. The letter came with the instruction that it was to be opened only in the event that a sweet dream did not stay. To this day, that letter has not been opened. Both Grandma Angel and myself did not have to go through the letting go process. I hope with all my heart that you, too, will be able to pass the Dreamwatcher Diaries on to your grandchild with that letter's seal intact. However, should this hardship occur, Hope's letter will be there for you to provide additional direction and encouragement.

If and when the troubled winds blow, know this, there are other worlds than the one in which you find yourself. These unfathomable and largely undiscovered domains are alive within you. There in the deepest level of the soul is a whole country created by divine design and ruled by the Virtue Angels. The purpose of this sacred place is to establish a link between you and the divine. This hallowed land along with its resident angels is supernatural and cannot be touched nor altered by the mortal soul. No matter what the human intent or agenda, the sacred will not be mocked nor reduced in any form or fashion. Even in the event of violence, like a sexual violation event, they remain untouched and alive. As you might have guessed, this is the home of your Wisdom Angel who, like the other angels, is able to travel up from that mystical depth to be with you in your conscious mind. I just wanted you to know that your Wisdom Angel has many relatives, like Worth, Hope, Charity, Patience, Reverence, and Contentment, to name a few. It is important for you to know that they believe in you and your soul, Faith, is their singular, fierce, and tender purpose.

Faith, it is important for you to know that much of the world will not hear about the Dreamwatcher easily. Many will not believe it possible. Others will think it quaint, like an Amish horse and buggy amid the commerce of Rodeo Drive. Still, others will maybe want to believe but will have forgotten how. The majority of marriages today are like your grandpa says "sparring protection collections." Just people who are human and would like to be themselves but in the process of surviving have become dependent on a collection of protections that end up under the same roof, sparring with the protections of a significant other. Love, faith, and trust have become hopes to guard against rather than harbors in which to live. The Dreamwatcher is not a fairy tale. It resonates with the three elements of hope (life, growth, and contentment) and is a far cry from the primary element of fantasy, which is the illusion of desire. So take special care of your Dreamwatcher gift and share it only with those who have earned your special trust.

Be sure to make at least a couple of copies of this letter and put them in a safe place. Keep the original in your Dreamwatcher Diary. I realize that there are many passages in this letter that will not mean so much until later. Don't worry if you don't get everything that you've read right now. This letter is yours to read as often and as much as you like. In the early days of receiving my letter from Grandma Angel, I must have read it every day for a month straight. What amazed me was reading the same passages years later and discovering new "wisdom pearls" that I had somehow missed, when reading, years before. I still have my original letter tucked away in my own wisdom angel diary. Somehow even after all these years, I still find joy in revisiting those magical words.

Well that's all, sweetheart, that's my gift to you. I hope and pray that your Dreamwatcher days will bring you as much excitement and passion as mine did for me. I can say with no doubt that this gift has changed my life many times over, and I have so much more of me because of the Dreamwatcher Diaries.

* * *

"Love always, Grandma Grace Adams, November 2, 1988," Lindsay finished placing the final page on the table.

"That is the most extraordinary prescription for a broken heart that I have ever heard!" Gaby exclaimed. "There are striking similarities to the clinical steps for grieving, like the shock stage, which Grandma Grace allows for in her direction to wait until the end of the forty-day period before letting go. The first step of letting go of intimacy hope evidence is a critical step toward balance. The intimacy hope evidence in this case is the letter and the diary in which Faith had focused that specific energy. It is not until after letting go that Faith is referred to redirecting focus to sense of self, which is, by the way, almost impossible to do unless you have cleared your space. The second step to release a second dove is remarkable as it would accomplish the release of a problem that she cannot nor was ever meant to solve the problem of 'why didn't we work?' Within the single event of that dove's flight, she would feel the weight, worry, and anxiety that come with placing yourself in the helpless position of trying to control something beyond your control, transfer to the power that does have control. The key word in that step is *surrender*, one of the most potent healing words we have. Imagine, Lindz, letting go of that problem in one fell swoop. That's the one that most broken hearts spend decades trying to solve."

"I agree with the first part of what you said," Lindsay said with a furrowed brow, "but I don't quite get the part where we don't have control. Are you saying that there is nothing you can do to make it work? No changes that could be made to make the relationship stay together?"

"That's exactly what I'm saying," Gaby returned. "Just like Grace wrote earlier, intimacy will not be deceived. The act of forcing, coaxing, bribing, or manipulating someone toward intimacy are the very acts that attempt to change the true nature of intimacy and ultimately are the very behaviors that will make intimacy go away. Intimacy either is, or it is not, and that is a divine determination, not a human one.

"OK, that clarifies, but does that mean that you don't have to work in an intimate relationship?" Lindsay queried. "You just meet, you know, and you go?"

"Not exactly, Lindz," Gaby replied. "Just the achievement of intimacy, accepting an invite requires the work of freedom, trust, balance, and equality. There is also work initially in that both partners will need developed self-awareness, self-trust, and self-worth to even be aware of the existence of true intimacy much less appreciate it's nature with another. There is also discovery work initially in that both partners who have grown eyes to see intimacy must now look for it using a specific focus as they feel for an "us" while feeling their way together."

"So the bottom line is," Lindsay summarized, "if you really want true intimacy, grow eyes to see it, learn how to listen to its nature, and then learn to care for it with the work of achieving and maintaining freedom, trust, balance, and equality, then and only then will intimacy stay."

"My God, you amaze me when you do that," Gaby said admirably.

"Do what?" Lindsay asked, popping her head up from her note-taking.

"Take such incredibly abstract information and put it into a neat little sentence like you just did," Gaby complimented.

"Thanks, Gaby," Lindsay said with a proud smile, "but look at who's talking. I'm sitting here trying to figure out how you, not only grasped what

Grace was saying to Faith, but you also applied the information and then ran with it."

"Thanks right back." Gaby smiled and then slipped quickly into a studied seriousness. "I'm a little stuck on the third step, but I've got some ideas. The waiting, while allowing the hope to stay alive as it will, is pretty self-explanatory though also strategic in its position as the third step. The strategy is focus direction. Most broken hearts will focus directly on the hope of reunion and either try to kill the fire or stoke it. Friends of the broken heart will inadvertently do the same, giving direction to 'cut the bastard loose' or encouragement that 'he'll call, honey, you just wait he'll call.' This places the broken heart in a perpetual state of imbalance and further serves to confirm that the broken heart's balance depends on the significant other. Grace has given Faith balance plus. Check this out, Lindz, not only will Faith have the hope of reunion in a focus position that serves balance, but Grace also has Faith rebuilding her soul supports by giving back little pieces of him and taking back little pieces of herself that she had entrusted to him. Like with Manolo and me, this letter helps me see that I still need to give him back his smile and his incredible voice. I really grew to depend on it, Lindz. It made me feel so safe, so cared for. When he would tell me how much he cared or how he missed me, it was always his voice that mesmerized me and filled this need to be held inside. Grace is saying give the voice back, I no longer need it to feel held. I will no longer need it because I will take back my faith in him. I will take back my faith in him as an expert or an authority, on holding and appreciating me as Gaby. I really depended on him for that. I really believed that only he could do it the special and specific way that I needed it to be done. I had never felt that before with anyone, Lindz, not in my whole life. I felt so worthwhile. Grace is saying that just because he is the one who helped me find the 'feel' of my worth does not mean he is the giver or the expert of the worth. The worth has always been there within me waiting for me to discover. Sure thank him for being the one who helped me see and feel, but I do not need him in order to own and enjoy my newly discovered worth. I do not owe him my soul for the ways that he helped me find my worth. My feeling like I owed him was another reason why he could hook me back in with his little guilt trips. Owning my worth is only something I can do for me. After taking back my faith in him as a necessity for my own worth, I relocate that faith and place it in my own self-trust in my own self-worth, for you cannot know your worth without first accomplishing trust. This brings me closer to balance. It also brings me closer to being a Gaby who can very much appreciate a masculine smile but will feel no need to depend on it because that need has already been met by me, within me. That's what Grace was telling Faith when she wrote that she would meet a Faith whom she had never imagined. When you look at the world with eyes that simply do not need, you see a whole new universe, and you experience a whole new self."

"Well I guess I won't have to say I told you so about that neon sign in the middle of the highway." Lindsay giggled.

"Touché," Gaby acknowledged with a smile. "You were right, Lindz. I think those last pages were like the missing pieces to a puzzle."

"I can't believe you put all of that together so quickly," Lindsay said with respect. "I mean everything that you said just seems so true, so real, real for me and Bruce too. I can see how I have assigned him the responsibility to increase and maintain my sense of worth. I know I have worth. I sense it but I tend to give it away to see if someone else will hold it and care for it, almost like a test to see if my worth has competitive value within the soul worth market. I can see how I wait for someone to acknowledge and respect my worth rather than finding the way to do that for myself. Though now from what you just said, I can see some of the logical consequences of relocating my worth with someone other than my worth's owner, which of course is me. I actually have a stronger sense of my current imbalance, and I can also feel the displacement of my worth responsibilities to Bruce. It seems so crazy when I look at that now. It's like I have this ultra-expensive heart made of china and I have all this internal knowledge about how to care for and appreciate my beautiful china heart, but instead of owning and caring for what can only be cared for by me, I give it away to someone thinking that this is the way to secure my worth. Then I am surprised when I find that someone neglecting the care of my china heart or maybe even dropping it and breaking it into pieces. A someone by the way who on his best day could not care for my china heart as well as me 'cause I am the only one with the technology. I can really sense how much better I would feel if I could bring my worth home. Tell me again, Gaby, how exactly does that part work?"

"You begin by seeing the truth, Lindz, like Grace told Faith you cannot add to yourself nor subtract from yourself and nor can anyone else. You are decidedly whole. You can only uncover the true shape of your character. You cannot make it more or less. The first step is declaring yourself to be the sole expert on your soul and realizing that there is no greater authority on you than you, at least not on this planet, not even Bruce. When you see that he could not possibly see or care for the shape of your soul as well as you can, it's not so hard to take your soul responsibility back, not to mention what you already mentioned so well with your china heart metaphor, that only you can complete that which belongs to you. Which is to say that Bruce really couldn't have completed your worth tasks even if he had wanted to, even if he had been good at it, because those tasks have your name on them, not his. Only you can secure your own worth"

"I can do that," Lindsay said more to herself than to Gaby. "I can definitely do that."

"Of course you can, Lindz," Gaby encouraged. "No problem."

"My God, Gaby, this wisdom actually offers a reality-based solution to the broken heart syndrome. It really breaks the cycle. It actually takes what feels like the end of the world and reduces it to a growing pain, and then makes that pain a temporary predictable event on a soul journey path. No more long crying spells while feeling like everyone else is in control. Everything comes back to having and being more of who you already are."

"It's a system of thought," Gaby explained, "that is based specifically on internal locus of control. *Internal* in this case refers to within the soul, and *locus*, Greek for 'location,' implies that true control is found within the soul, in one's internal universe versus the opposing view, the external locus of control, which breeds thinking systems that look to the external universe for control. Western civilization particularly North America is predominantly raised on the notion of external locus of control. Internal locus of control is generally taught more in the East. With external locus of control, the thinking systems are generally focused on manipulating the external universe to bend to the will of personal or group agendas. The result is faith in the illusion of a control that in truth does not exist."

"I'm not sure I get it, Gaby," Lindsay said with a puzzled look.

"Let me break it down for you," Gaby offered. "If I am a parent and my child is making a noise that I want them to stop because the noise makes me anxious or irritated, my agenda as the parent is to reduce or extinguish my feeling of increased anxiety or irritation. I want my balanced emotional state back. If I choose external locus of control, I will look to the external universe to solve the problem. I will seek behavior change in the child. I will accomplish this by giving the child a cookie, yelling at the child to stop, maybe even spanking the child. The intervention works and the child stops the behavior. Ah, yes, wonderful balance again. If I choose internal locus of control, I will look in and find the origin of the increased anxiety. I trace the anxiety to an unmet need and I, for example, find an unsolved money problem, that if solved would have placed my current anxiety level so low that I would not have even registered the child's noise as irritating. I choose not to give my unsolved problem to the external universe. I solve the problem with a temporary budget solution and refer the final solution to my faith in the divine. My anxiety plummets. I look over at my child and see his happiness as he plays with his toy making his redundant airplane noises. I smile thanking myself for choosing to look in. I sense my faith in myself increase, and as I return my son's smile, I sense a deposit in our relationship, of one thousand jewels of worth."

"My God, what a great example, Gaby," Lindsay said enthusiastically, that really clarifies the difference, "but what did you mean when you said that the external control is an illusion? How can it be that the giving of the cookie or the spanking is not real control if the child stopped the behavior?"

"Great question, Lindz," Gaby replied. "Control implies the independence of the position of regulator or director. This alleged independence however is questionable. Number 1, as an external control parent, I am dependent on my child to regain my emotional equilibrium. Within this dependence, I will begin to assume the belief that I cannot achieve equilibrium without the child. Two, I am dependent on the actual behavior change to retrieve my balance. Three, I am dependent on the child's desire for the cookie or the child's fear of my anger or spanking in order to lever the child toward my desired behavior change. Fourth, what if the child is the one doing the regulating? What if my child knows that making the noise will result in a cookie? What if my child just wants to see me blow, even if it means a spanking, because even the spanking doesn't hurt that much if the child premeditated to make the spanking happen? That is especially true if that child just wants to win a control game, which is how many children view power struggles, a power and control game that they are supposed to win? Or the child may thoroughly enjoy the entertainment of an adult doll that comes with predictable behavior buttons. So I ask you, where is the control in external locus of control? External locus of control actually fosters a dependence on a myriad of persons, places, and things in the external universe. Where is the control in all this dependence?" Gaby paused for a moment, and then asked, "Does that make sense, Lindz?"

"A lot of sense," Lindsay said, slowly nodding her head as if she could see the pieces coming together in her mind.

"Well if you got all that, Lindz, you are only a couple sessions away from graduating from the advanced Self-Awareness Parenting class. That was just a part of my little internal locus of control lesson for that parenting class."

"That's impressive, Gaby, and so clear," Lindsay said. "I understand now why you said it's a system of thought. I can see several areas where I use external locus of control, not the least of which is in my relationships. So in the letter, without coming right out and saying it, Grace is teaching Faith about how to look in."

"Exactly," Gaby said, "straight A's, Lindz."

Lindsay stretched and yawned, prompting a sympathetic response from Gaby. "Uh oh, look what you've started, Lindz," Gaby said as she attempted to stifle her yawn. "I feel like we're pulling an all-nighter or something, except I'm loving this feeling of growth and hope, and there is definitely some part of me that wants even more."

"Well there's plenty more," Lindsay said, grabbing her mug and heading for the kitchen.

"What are you talking about?" Gaby asked, grabbing her mug and following Lindsay's lead.

"You must have forgotten in all the excitement about the letter," Lindsay replied, yawning again as she rinsed her cup.

"Forgot what?" Gaby yawned back as she handed Lindsay her empty cup.

"The third Dreamwatcher Diary, you know, Faith's diary about finding her sweet dream," Lindsay replied in a tired voice. "It's in my window box."

"Faith's diary is where?" Gaby asked incredulously.

"Don't even think about it, Gabriella," Lindsay admonished. "My brain is cornmeal right now, and if yours isn't, it will be soon. Besides, its 3:00 a.m. It's just too late. Don't even think about opening that diary right now. Tomorrow, or I should say today, is Saturday. I was thinking we start reading it over a nice breakfast, say at the Majestic, and then spend the rest of the day reading to each other at some of our old college haunts in the Loop."

"There you go making the perfect plan again and even while you're running on empty," Gaby said, secretly anticipating the coming dawn. "But, Lindz, since you're the late sleeper and I'm the irrepressible early riser, would it be OK if I took a peek if I wake up?"

"Of course, Gaby, please feel free," Lindsay replied.

"I can't believe how tired I am," Gaby said gratefully as they made their way to the bedroom.

Exhausted but inspired, Gaby and Lindsay fell onto the soft bed. Like new best friends at summer camp, they talk in low tones about their discoveries until the light in their motivation fades to a soft glow. They link pinky fingers as their eyes grow heavy and their bodies submit to the warm weight of weariness earned. Sleep's invisible arms pulled the two friends down through the bed's deep cushion and into separate dream worlds. Some hours later, they share a moment together in a dream as grandmothers walking barefoot along a sandy shore, watching their granddaughters play tag with the surf, and trading stories of romance, long since past. Outside the loft, the dove is back standing on the window ledge like a small white sentinel.

CHAPTER FIVE

The Diary

Gaby is dreaming. She is walking with her mother and brother down a burning street in civil war-torn El Salvador. She is five years old. The death squads, unwitting servants of hate, had completed yet another traumatic imprint on yet another young mind. The neighbor's warning, coming on an early morning in late September 1982, the jerk to wakefulness from the peaceful sleep of a well-loved child, the flight to the hiding place under the burned out van down the street, the stifled screams as she watched her father executed, the whoosh of heat as her house exploded into flames, the hours of waiting in their cocoon of safety that reeked of oil and burnt metal.

Gaby's right hand registers the fierce squeeze of her mother's grip as her mother walks down the street's middle with her head held high as if in defiance to anyone who might seek to cross her path. Her mother's right arm cradles her eleven-month-old brother, Eduardo. Gaby looks up at her mother worrying about her prolonged silence and wondering how she could walk so far without taking time to rest. There is a strange look on her face, one that Gaby cannot recall seeing before. She is accustomed to her mother's beautiful face, smiling, adoring, and seeming to bring light to all those that she looks upon. Now her face is smeared with dirt and grease. Her blouse is torn, and her hair needs combing. Gaby, who is determined to find her smiling mother within the woman holding her hand, tries hard to read her mother's eyes.

Before she can, she hears the voice of a soldier, yelling orders in Spanish to her mother. Her mother's curt retort seems to confirm at once Gaby's unspoken fear, the woman who holds her hand is not her mother. It is instead some stranger who has taken over her mother's body. The woman pauses in her retort and looks down at her. She smiles and says, "What a brave little angel you are, Gabriella. We'll be stopping to rest soon."

"Yes, Mama," Gaby said, her mouth breaking out into a wide smile of relief, marveling at the realization that it had indeed been her mother who had spoken to the soldier. Her mother had told the soldier that yesterday these streets had been hers, "today they are yours, and tomorrow, you will die on this street and the wild dogs will eat your face."

"Or," Gaby's mother continues, in her address to the soldier, "you can allow us to walk on, and you, Roberto, can go home to Espiranza, the one who is most taken by your face, for on this very day, she will find that she is with child. Go now, Roberto, that the child would have a father and that the father would have his life." Gaby watches as the soldier's face go from anger, to confusion, through bewilderment, to awestruck, and finally settled on resignation as he waves them on down the street.

Just moments after passing the young soldier's post, Gaby looks back over her shoulder. The soldier is walking north toward a thick curtain of smoke and fog. He turns and for the briefest of moments locks eyes with Gaby. He smiles, gives a quick wave, and then disappears behind the opaque cloud. Slowly pulling her gaze back, she sees the soldier's gun lying on the road. As she turns her eyes back toward her mother, Gaby wonders if the soldier will be happy in the new life that he has chosen, his new life without the gun. She feels a brief tug on her left hand, something pulling on her little finger. Simultaneously she feels the protective squeeze of her mother evaporate.

* * *

Gaby looks up toward her mother questioningly, and sees the luminous green numbers on the clock telling her that the time is 5:30 a.m. Looking left, she saw her friend sleeping peacefully on her back, their pinky link broken now as Lindsay's hands rested comfortably on her stomach. Moving silently, so as not to wake her friend, Gaby slid out from under the bed clothes and felt her way to the bathroom.

After freshening up, she tiptoed to the kitchen and started the morning java. As she listened to the pop and gurgle of the brewing coffee, Gaby relished the solitude exclusive to the voluntary predawn riser. Gazing out at the darkened, St. Louis skyline, she made a mental note to call her mother at first light to ask her about the dream. She carried her coffee, strong and black, to the little nest where she and Lindsay had been deep in contemplation just hours before.

Setting her cup on the marbled surface of the coffee table, Gaby walked up to the window box and, taking a deep breath, opened the lid. She removed the pillbox containing the diary and placed it on the coffee table. Sitting, she leaned forward on the couch with her elbows resting on her knees. Gaby stared at the box for a moment as she held her cup in both hands. There was a stirring deep within her, one that she sensed was much stronger than the usual pregrowth flutters of the past. It was an energy that was both pleasant and mysterious, one that she could feel but could not seem to read. There was something special about the moment, and Gaby took the time to allow the magic of the romantic journey waiting within the box to touch the hope within her. "OK, I'm ready, Faith," Gaby said sincerely to the diary's absent author. "My heart says this is no coincidence, and like you, Faith, I love hope and want so much to believe. My heart is open to your words. Take me where you will." Opening the box, Gaby carefully removed the diary. Leaning back, she sank comfortably into the nest's soft layers and began to read.

The Dreamwatcher Diaries

* * *

Faith's Dreamwatcher Diary

The Dreamwatcher Prayer

Dreamwatcher, Dreamwatcher
find my sweet dream,
Guard it and keep it
'til I know what I mean.

Angel inside me
help me find "my" way
Help me get closer
to my "me" every day.

Dreamwatcher, Dreamwatcher
keep my dream whole.
Lead him to discover
my dream in his soul.

When come the morning
that I am enough me
Dreamwatcher, please bring
my dream destiny.

If come the night
I need let my dream go.
Oh, my wisdom angel
please help me grow.

Faith Adams
November 2, 2003

Lawrence Gabriel

Introduction

It's him, my God, Grandma, it's really him! I've finally found my sweet dream! How I wish that you were here so I could throw my arms around you and thank you ten times over for all your love and grace over the years. While I cannot have the hug I miss so much, I can share each moment with you on these pages, for your name is the one that I have chosen to address in, now at last, my own Dreamwatcher Diary. I want to call you by name as I write like we used to at Sunday tea. Like it was yesterday, I remember the Sunday that you told me you would like for me to call you Grace so that we could, for those moments, talk like "school chums," girl to girl. It is a memory, Mamaw, that still spins gold. Though I cherish my memory of you each Sunday by continuing our tea talks at my favorite café (And I'm sure they think I'm crazy there when I order, "Tea and crumb cakes for two please."), I promised myself I would not write you until I had arrived at this page, at this milestone in my Dreamwatcher journey. Before I begin to share the details of the universe and circumstance of our first meeting, I wish to share with you, Grace, the scenes and feelings that played out within me during that moment when at last we first met. I have kept in close touch with my "heart castle" and send you, wrapped in a spirit wind, a special granddaughter kiss for helping me discover this world within me and all the family that I have found in residence there. Of course, you and grandpa have a little cottage in the little kingdom within my heart. It is located some miles south of my heart castle along the white sand of the sunny shoreline. I saw a picture of

The Dreamwatcher Diaries

it once at a flea market in a small Indiana town. It is one of my most precious possessions, purchased for just seven dollars, and hangs as always in a place where I see it just before I close my eyes at night. So now, my beloved Grandmother, meet me at the lighthouse that marks the halfway point between your cottage and the castle. There I shall tell you of the stirrings within my heart during the single moment of my first "sweet dream" encounter. I can't wait to see you there, Grace (sweet angel of my childhood), in the next paragraph.

It was a chinook, as you used to say, Grace, an unseasonably warm day in the kingdom in my heart. The kingdom had been going through a cold spell brought on by a winter wind of which I may speak of at another time. The castle was closed to what little light was able to peek through the dark curtain of clouds that had surrounded the kingdom. A warm fire burned within the castle, and my heart was prepared to endure some days of frigid dark. Then suddenly there was a knock on the castle door. It was a dear friend who was quickly ushered in and upon her entrance brought a welcomed light and warmth to the castle's interior. From the magic of her presence, the semislumbered castle clan sensed the grim lines of determination on their faces, giving way to sighs of relief and from there to full-fledged smiles. Grandmother Patience opened a few of the castle's bolted and shuttered windows and leaning out was surprised to find the cloud curtain disintegrating before her very eyes, revealing growing patches of clear blue sky. Just as Grandma Patience decided to check on the children, a ray of light pierced through the bedroom window of her Granddaughter Hope. (It was at that very moment when I saw his face.) Hope, awakened by the brightness of the light, jumped from her bed with excitement and ran through the castle toward the bedroom of her mother, Faith. Running with the boundless energy of anticipation nurtured, she hurried to ask her mother the burning question, is it really time to fly or still time to learn and watch the sky? While Hope dearly loved learning, flight was her deepest passion, as only her wings and the sky could fulfill the grand purpose of her divine design. Hope burst into Faith's room to find her mother smiling at the light as she turned to face her beautiful daughter. Mother Faith nodded knowingly and said the words that her child longed to hear, "Time to fly, sweetheart, yes, it's time to fly."

Hope jumped into her mother's arms. As mother and daughter joined their energies in a celebratory hug, Mother Faith heard the footfalls of Grandma Patience walking along the south hallway.

Faith whispered to Hope, "If you wish to wake your sister Joy, you'd best hurry down the north hallway as Grandma Patience is about to wake up Aunt Constance, and she may try to shut down this sudden turn of events. If you go now, you might just make it, and as you well know once Joy is awake, the entire kingdom will be inclined to pursue the Bright Knight of Happiness whose light helps us see and feel so many new and exciting things. Hurry now, Hope, my love, go to your sister."

Hope raced down the length of the north hallway straight to her fraternal twin's door. Hope threw open Joy's door and was greeted by her sister's glowing smile as she, too, had been awakened by a visit from the light.

Moments later, Hope and Joy were holding hands, bouncing up and down on the bed chanting, "Time to fly, time to fly, time to fly."

The sight of Grandma Patience and Aunt Constance in the doorway brought the children's exuberance to a sudden halt.

"We just have something that we would like to say, children," Grandma Patience said purposefully.

"Yes, just a quick word," Aunt Constance added.

Mother Faith approached and stood behind her mother and sister, giving a quick wink to Hope and Joy as she took in this divine development.

"We just wanted to tell you," Grandma Patience continued, "and I think I can speak for Constance here."

"Oh, absolutely," Aunt Constance affirmed.

Mother Faith rolled her eyes at the children, who were standing on the bed holding hands and listening attentively.

"It is most definitely," Grandma Patience finished, "time for you to fly."

The children simultaneously jumped into the arms of their grandmother and aunt and with Mother Faith joining, in it was Hope and Joy, hugs and kisses all around. (This is when I went looking for the nearest chair, and yes, Grace, I found one in time.) While Grandma Patience and Aunt Constance fluffed and fussed over the children's wings, Mother Faith opened Joy's enormous bedroom windows. The now cloudless sky was a gorgeous, deep sea blue, and the brilliant morning sun sent its golden river of light into and throughout the castle's inner chambers.

Giving each child a final kiss, Mother Faith said, "Remember always, my children, I believe in you. You are free to fly with confidence, for the sweet dream is found, but before you go, I wonder, could you tell me his name?"

"Oh yes, Mama," the children replied in an excited chorus. "His name is Gabriel."

With that, Hope and Joy took wing as the three elders stood at the castle window hugging and watching with smiles of delight.

Grace, before I get to the first entry, I have to tell you the most extraordinary thing. I was born, as you well know, on November 1, 1973, at exactly 7:07 p.m. In your letter, you told me that I would meet my sweet dream sometime before my thirtieth year. I struggled mightily on this day, to keep the faith. In truth, the fact that your wisdom and sight have never steered me wrong helped me more on this day than tongue could ever tell. I watched the timepiece on the café wall strike the seven-o-clock hour. Within me, like the runner who has somehow kept the pace in spite of reaching a place already well beyond her physical limits, I felt my faith buckle. Yet before it could fall to its knees exhausted and spent, existing only on the fumes of the hope of oxygen, he walked into the room. As our eyes met, my eye also caught, just outside the closing café door, landing on the signpost, with wings widespread, a snow-white dove.

Grace, in the future, just in case it makes a difference, you and the divine have my permission to be right, much earlier. I thought you might enjoy the story of my heart castle's stirrings along with this short excerpt on the extraordinary reckoning of your sweet dream foresight. I'll see you soon in my first entry.

November 2, 2003
When at Last We First Met at the Venice Café
Sweet Dream Time: Five Hours of You and Me Together

The Dreamwatcher Diaries

Dearest Grace,

Before the telling begins, I wanted to mention that I will be using much the same format as you did in your sweet dream diary. I especially like the heading sequence of date, memory title, and elapsed sweet dream time, and I will of course be continuing the narrative, storytelling prose that is the hallmark of each Dreamwatcher Diary entry.

Settle in, Grace, for the 960-hour journey from my sweet dream and I's, "you and me," harbor to the island of our "us" has begun. My telling begins with the welcomed entrance of a dear friend.

Grace, do you remember the story I told you about Iris, the little girl down the street that I used to babysit. The time when Violet, her mother (what an extraordinary mother she was even at the tender age of twenty-one), had to get stern with her and told her to "get over there and sit in that corner and think about what I told you." On the day I told you about Little Iris, upon hearing her mother's words, she paused and turned her face up toward her mother with a look of deep thought. Violet had told me some days earlier that this was the hardest time for her as a parent, this being stern and serious about rules and directions. She had further confided in me that it wasn't delivering stern that worried her so. It was the moment right after the delivery, when she had to wonder what she would do if her direction were not followed.

"Though sometimes," she had said, "I have to pinch myself to keep from laughing as I watch the wheels spinning behind my four-year-old girl's eyes."

It was in that post-delivery moment, on that day, that Iris's face broke out into a wide and infectious smile.

She gave her mother a quick squeeze, as if to say, "You did good today, Mommy," and hurried over to the chair in the corner. She turned the chair to face her mother, still smiling with that smile of someone who is so tickled and so secretly pleased by something that it's taking all of her concentration not to bust out laughing. It was a smile that posed and queried, "Everything's peaches, you do know that, don't you?" My friend Layla is that smile.

Layla is the cool breeze visit on a hot summer's day. She is the feeling that comes with the welcomed second wind arriving just in time with the message that you'll be finishing your journey with energy to spare. Layla is the disarming wink and twinkle in the seductive smile of the adolescent girl, who with just that "look" shooshes the grumbling of her adolescent guy. The girl knows it is not the promise of sex that smooths out the ruffles of his resistance but rather the truth behind the smile that bids him to follow a higher calling. The calling to be a nobleman in the land of love's resolve. Not a nobleman enslaved to a passion but more so just a man grateful to have found this shore where he will discover what happens after love is certain. Layla is the light at the end of the tunnel that, rather than waiting, moves toward you, dispelling darkness as she approaches and bringing the message that hope believes even when you can't see it. Layla is my dearest friend.

I realize that I probably could have just said that Layla was unconventional, but I really wanted you to see the heart of the woman who has become my closest friend.

We met at a flea market in a small southern Missouri town. I had a booth there and was selling some of my workpieces (mostly the early work that was beginning to develop into a clutter problem in my St. Louis loft space).

Layla is the lead singer of a little rock band called Gypsy Rain (on another day, I must tell you the story about how the band got its name). Her band had a gig at the flea market that day, and during a break, she came by the booth to check out some of my work. She's a tiny thing, standing only about five feet, four inches and weighing in at about 105 pounds, soaking wet. Long, raven-black hair surround her compelling features that are sculpted with a natural beauty and covered in a creamy-white complexion. Gypsy Rain is an all-girl band, well mostly all girl, except for the drummer. They do a lot of '70s, '80s, and '90s tunes like Linda Ronstadt, Joan Jett, Cher, Heart, and even a few Stevie Nicks classics. Grace, Layla's Stevie Nicks is off the charts. Close your eyes and your mind will swear Stevie's in the room. Open them and you will wonder what that little girl in front of the microphone is doing here in little big town St. Louis.

It was a spiritual experience from the first with Layla and me. As it turns out, her grandmother was a gypsy in the truest sense of the word. Blessed with a foresight of uncommon clarity, she earned the title of fortune teller when she was just twelve years old. On Layla's eleventh birthday, she told Layla that she would marry young and that her husband would be a songbird who was afraid to fly. "With you, little Layla," she had said, "he will find his wings."

She was so extraordinary that first day. She had been browsing around my booth for just a short while when she walked up to me.

There was a light mist in her dark-brown eyes as she said, "Your work touches me and takes me to places in here," putting her hand upon her heart. "It's like you see those places and then recreate them with stone and light.

You've made it possible to actually hold the deep places, in my hands," she finished with a shy smile.

I smiled back at her not so much with gratitude as with understanding. "You see much more than many," I replied sincerely. "You honor my work with your words, and somehow I'm sure that we've met before at one of those deep places. I think it might have been that mountaintop café, you know, the one we go to for solitary celebration, when a dream comes true. As I recall, it was your singing that brought the angels to our table that day, angels I might add that were applauding and fighting off an emerald-green envy."

She smiled a delighted, full-mouthed smile and said, "Hi, I'm Layla, and you are coming with me to meet my gypsy sisters."

Linking her arm with mine, she pulled me toward the bandstand. I hung out with the band that afternoon and had the most wonderful time. Not really wanting to part ways, I accepted Layla's invite to join the band at a roadside bar for their nighttime gig. It was a night filled with music and merriment. Damp and glowing from my exertions on the dance floor, I stepped outside at one point in hopes of feeling a midsummer's night breeze against my skin. I could hear the outdoor band of crickets and locusts as they played their soothing country sounds. I felt the euphoria of one who has stumbled upon a long-lost sibling. The missing sister, who with her embrace quells a deep and unspoken yearning for family that you've dreamed of but never held, and all the while within my heart's kingdom, I could sense Joy leading the pursuit after the Bright Knight of Happiness. (The band's drummer, by the way, is her husband of seven years, gorgeous, painfully shy in the *absence of her presence, and brings the house down with his rendition of Eric Clapton's song of the same name.)*

That was three years ago during the first summer of the new millennium. I was twenty-seven, and Layla was twenty-four. In that time, our bond has grown in leaps and bounds. Her soulful presence in my life has held me up during some dark and lonely miles. Some weeks ago, I was met with a loss (the one of which I will speak at another time) that had me curling up in a cocoon of grief. I had not called nor talked with another soul for seven straight days. It was late morning, birthday morning, I was wrestling with my discouragement while lying on my comfy couch listening to Billie Holiday on the record player (which, like you, is the only way I will listen to Billie as she is definitely an LP-only artist). I heard the phone rang, and as I expected, it was Layla. Actually it was Brandon, her husband, but really it was Layla. When she gets all "fretted out," as she calls it, she talks to me through Brandon, not because she's too busy or otherwise involved, but rather because like with just about everything else, Layla worries with an "industrial strength" intensity. By the time she's filtered her worry messages through Brandon, whose down to earth, go with the flow, personality is the polar opposite of his adoring wife, not only is the message itself more clear, Layla's "fret meter" has dialed down to a more manageable degree. I also believe that she does this because she does not want me to worry about her worrying. She takes great pride in her ability to own her own emotions. So she protects me from her mother-like anxiety by using Brandon as a buffer. This all secretly pleases the both of us, and what's more I find it incredibly adorable.

"Faith, its Brandon," he speaks to the answering machine. "Layla says don't bother picking up the phone

even though she knows you're not doing anything other than lying on the couch beating yourself up. By the way, do you use whips or riding crops for that 'cause Layla and I just got a new catalog of whips and chains off the internet. All you have to do is go to wippentyme.com."

I can hear Layla in the background giggling and shooshing him, and then I'm giggling myself.

"Layla says you're coming out for your birthday tonight, like it or not, so don't even think about punking out. Besides, I just got my new handcuffs license and can now use them legally, so it's really not a good time to say no to the girl. She says we'll be there in about forty-five minutes, and you don't have to do anything except buzz us in."

I hear muffled conversation. "Oh and Layla says you better have something more chezzy than Billie playing when we get there, or she'll break your record player. See ya soon."

After a few giggles, I closed my eyes and with the first smile in days sank slowly into the perfect catnap. The buzzer woke me, and while in the semi-fog of the grudgingly awakened, I turned off Billie and unlocked the door. Moments later, the gloom in my loft began to cower as Layla and Brandon entered, bringing with her the irrepressible spirit of unbridled hope. After warm hugs and smooches, Layla, tired of reigning in her mothering nature, began to fuss and nurture.

"Ok, dear heart, what's with the cigarettes," she asked, holding up the half-smoked pack of ultralights, with raised eyebrows.

"Hey, I thought maybe it would help you know," I replied a tad defensively.

The Dreamwatcher Diaries

"How'd you make out," Brandon asked smiling but genuinely curious.

"Not too good," I said smiling sheepishly. "Kind of made me a little sick if you want to know the truth."

"Oh, Fay-Fay (Layla is the only one who calls me that and only in mothering moments like this one. Strangely I never told her about my childhood nickname. It just came out one day to my pleasant surprise), why didn't you call?" Layla asked.

"This sounds like girl talk time to me, so I'm gonna go run some errands," Brandon interjected. "Need anything, Faith?"

"If you could pick out a nice leather riding crop for me, I would be eternally grateful," I returned, grinning at the wide smile that broke out across Brandon's face.

I smiled at Layla who was looking at her man with a beautiful mix of love and pride. Brandon kissed Layla before heading out and with a "see ya soon" was out the door. It was never goodbye with Layla, and she wasn't even kidding. It was "see ya later," "see ya soon," or even just "see ya," but goodbye had long since been banished from her vocabulary. I believe that Layla's prejudice against goodbyes was inherited from her grandmother, who in her final days would not allow even family members to say goodbye. Layla firmly believes that goodbye arrests the flow of energy within the lines that connect others together, and Layla is all about keeping lines open.

"So," Layla asked, "are you ready to move down the road apiece from this bad spot on your highway, or are you required to spend more time there?"

"I think I'm ready to move on a little, but the loss of it all cuts real deep," I answered reflectively.

"I know, honey," Layla said, giving me one of her wonderful hugs, "and I would never push you to move an inch if you didn't think you were ready because I know it doesn't work that way. I only ask, Faith, because I know how much this particular birthday means to you. It's just that you're probably the strongest person I've ever met, and I can't stand to see you lose hope. I mean, I know that you are probably a little worried about whether your sweet dream will show up like your grandma predicted, but either way, Fay-Fay, we are going to make this an unforgettable birthday," Layla finished huskily. I allowed a few tears to fall and wrapped my arms around her in a tight hug.

"I really needed to hear that," I said gratefully. "Thanks, Layla."

"But wait, Faith," Layla protested. "It's still before noon. The gifts haven't even started yet."

"So what's the plan?" I asked, starting to smile as I felt the energy of Layla's excitement.

"Well," Layla said her eyes beginning to sparkle, "first, you shower and I tidy. Second, you prepare to be seriously pampered, and third, happy birthday, Faith."

Layla's birthday roller coaster is what I called the next twelve hours, a perpetual high of anticipation and delight. The first surprise came just after she led me out from the entrance of my loft blindfolded. Upon removing the blindfold, my eyes were greeted by the sight of a white stretch limousine. The driver opened the door for me, and there was Brandon dressed in a gorgeous Kenneth Cole suit, classic black and white, with dark-red tie.

"Cocktails, anyone?" he asked, giving us both that charming smile of his. "Sorry," he joked, "my Porsche is in the garage. I hope this will do in the meantime."

The Dreamwatcher Diaries

Giggling, Layla and I climbed in, and we were off. We made a total of five stops in the next five hours, including hair salon where we primped and partied, nail salon, Finola's Facials in the mall, Saks Fifth Avenue, where I got this gorgeous birthday dress in my favorite color, a sleek and simple basic black, and finally an early birthday dinner at the Seven Gables Inn. At each stop, we picked up another band member who presented me with a little gift and a card. By the time we left Seven Gables, I was traveling with the six gypsy girls and one boy drummer of Gypsy Rain.

The last stop, as you by now may have guessed, was the Venice Café. If there exists a bar in St. Louis that one might construe as bohemian, the Venice Café might well be that place. The café is a reputed safe haven and watering hole for free spirits seeking kindred souls and minds that live and think outside the box. The bar features a rustic interior papered with photos and memorabilia that incite a charming and pleasant nostalgia. Out back, there is a garden patio constructed of brick and stone, complete with fountains and birdbaths. In the front room, there is a sound stage, which upon entering I noticed was filled with Gypsy Rain's instruments. I shot a look at Layla, who smiled back and mouthed the word "surprise"! Layla had decorated the best seat in the house, front and center in honor of my birthday. Brandon escorted me to my chair. After taking my drink order, in his shy baritone, he said something that made my eyes moist.

"This little concert is dedicated to you, Faith," he said. "You are the big sister that I never had, and you will always be family. Happy birthday, Faith."

Brandon kissed my cheek. I took his hand into my own, gave him a kiss, and just before I could wipe at my misting eyes, Layla was there with a wink and a tissue.

She gave her husband an affectionate nudge and said, "Warm-up time, drummer boy."

I was so happy in that moment as I watched Layla and Brandon walk arm in arm toward the stage that my sweet dream anxieties all but vanished and I was overcome by an extraordinary feeling of peace and contentment. I took a deep breath and surveyed the exquisite final touch on the birthday gift to beat all birthday gifts. The café's front room was teeming with friends and family of the band as well as local patrons. The room resonated with a family reunion ambience, which included an element of openness that seemed to sweep even newcomers and strangers into a growing circle of warmth, freedom, and equality. Then suddenly, my sweet dream time clock pulled my eyes toward the timepiece on the wall. As I watched the clock strike seven, I experienced a sense of fleeting panic and made an anxious scan of the room. Coming up dry, I resigned myself to my drink when I felt the chill of the mid-November evening announce the entrance of yet another surprise.

Grace, as a student of light, which is so essential in my work, I have learned much about light sources and their relationship to shadow and position. It is sometimes said that the light plays tricks on the mind, and while I, too, believe that light is indeed a brilliant illusionist, I am uncertain as to whether my senses in the next few moments registered magic or truth.

The wind had caught the café door, which hung open offering a porch lit view of the masculine figure that entered. It actually appeared as if the light surrounding the visitor moved with him as he walked up the steps to the café entrance. In those few moments while his identity waited behind a double veil of light and shadow, it truly seemed as if he was the lights source. In that solitary silhouette, I could see shoulder-length hair haloed in a white light. The long coat that draped him stopped just below his calf, and as time seemed to stop, I could almost hear the sound of his boot heels changing octaves as one struck stone while the other wood just across the café's threshold. It was then that a flutter of white pulled my focus. I blinked twice in disbelief, but there it was, landing on the café signpost, a snow-white dove, my dreamwatcher. As if on cue, the wind's invisible hand released the door, and with its closing, the visitor's features were revealed as the shadows seemed to fly from his face. His hair was the color of dark honey mixed with occasional straw-colored strands. His face was strikingly handsome, drawing the eye with chiseled and angular features. His mouth was wide with generous lips, and his chin has a cleft (what you used to call an "angel kiss"), just like Daddy's. His walk was lithe but purposeful, catlike in some ways, like one who has learned to place his confidence in muscle memory and in that knowing exudes a comfort from the discovered union of mind and body. He stands about six feet tall with square shoulders and an athletic build that suggests flexible and fluid much more so than muscle and might. In a few words, Grace, I would have to say that he moves like a kung fu man. Very close in general movement and physique to Bruce Lee's late son, Brandon. His most extraordinary feature however was his eyes. They were a deep sea blue that appeared lighter on the outer edges, graduating to darker shades as they approach the iris. The reason that I know the depth belied in those darker shades is because those eyes were looking right at me. A strange certainty stole over me as our eyes locked and I thought (before I could think), "Oh my god, it's him."

At some point during his entrance, I must have stood, though I did not realize this until I registered the tremble in my knees. Not willing to trust my legs, I lowered myself back into my chair. His eyes, which had seemed casual in their initial glance, had doubled in their intensity. In one moment, he was looking at me taking in my image, and in the next it seemed as if he was looking right at the "me" inside. As I returned his gaze, he suddenly stopped and backed up against the memorabilia wall. He shyly lowered his eyes and seeming to realize that he had been caught staring made a studious effort to turn his attention toward the band. It was all I could do not to race across the twenty-some feet separating us and throw my arms around him. I believe it was the recipe of hope, fear, excitement, and incredulity (which all, to my surprise, when blended together with fifteen years of anticipation, really do make Jell-O) that kept me in my chair. I could feel this smile on my face, the dizzy giddy smile of the high school girl, alone in her room, just after hanging up the phone with the guy who asked her to the prom. I couldn't stop smiling. I had this overpowering urge to cover my mouth with my hand, but instead I snuck another glance toward him, and just like that, he smiled back. I swear I almost fell off the chair.

That's when I felt her, Grace, that's when I felt the presence of my "lady in waiting." The woman within who is alive with "forever love." The woman within that I have always been but had not yet arrived at, the woman who whispers sweet and steady truth about the shape of my character, the woman who knows exactly who she is and with the strength of that solemn conviction owns a natural resolution to the search for identity and worth. I could sense in that moment the strength of her resolve and marveled at the realization that the woman was me. I could actually feel her presence moving up toward the opening of my soul's conscious. I was heady with the knowledge that her natural shape had the potential to cover and comfort every crevice and corner of my soul. As she rose within me, I could feel her smiling from her true shape at the past shapes of me, the ones that never seemed to fit, the ghost women of relationships' past. I felt her glide past the woman I could have been with Brad in a marriage of convenience, past the woman I should have been with Trent in a marriage of security, housed in a shelter of religious roles, past the woman I might have been with Charles as a trophy wife with wealth and privilege, past the woman I would have been with Martin in a marriage of companionship, settling for a kind compromise to fend off the fright of forever lonely, and finally past the woman I had been just moments ago, the woman in a marriage to the hope of forever love with my sweet dream. Now at last, I was experiencing the actual being of my hope. Grace, I have never felt as alive as I did in that moment of genuine fulfillment. I felt like I could fly but at the same time knew that I could land with both feet on the ground. It was like having a connection with both heaven and earth.

The lady in waiting, the woman who I am, took my eyes and looked again for the man whose smile had beckoned her rising. He was gone. The spot where he had stood was empty, save the fading, faces of the past that papered the wall.

Before I could think to worry, Layla's familiar voice pulled me back into the universe of others in my here and now. She was singing the birthday song with the band jazzing it up along the way. I was looking at her when she gave me a secret smile and a little eye roll back and then up all without dropping a note. She was cueing me to turn around, so I did, fully expecting to find a birthday cake and candles. Suddenly there he was, looking at me with that boyish smile that somehow seemed so familiar.

"You're the one" were the first three words he spoke to me.

"The one?" I questioned back.

"The birthday girl, all this," he replied, gesturing with his hand at the grand ambience of my birthday finale.

"Yes, I'm the one," I came back, looking directly into his eyes as I spoke those four words. "The real question is, who are you?" I asked purposefully, my eyes not yet willing to release his.

"I'm Gabriel," he replied, looking back at me with his blue-eyed intensity. "I don't want to intrude, it's just I..." His voice trailed off for a moment. "I wanted to hear your voice to find out if I would like it as much as I did that smile I saw a minute ago from across the room. Now that I've heard, I should probably go. This seems a bit more like a family celebration, not the best time to meet a stranger."

"So how did my voice rate?" I asked with a smile.

"Let's just say that 'angelic' would be an understatement," he said with a soft but unflinching look of sincerity.

"You did not just say that. There is no way you just said angelic," I exclaimed.

"Too much?" he asked, feigning disappointment in himself with a little pantomime of knocking himself on the head "I do have a tendency to overstate things now and again, but I've got to tell you, I don't think this is

one of those times. I think I'm going to stand by my choice tonight if there are no strenuous objections."

"Not from me, there aren't," I came back, smiling softly. "Actually I'm a firm believer in the angelic presence. I was just so amazed that you chose a word that held such special meaning to me. I'm Faith," I said, offering him my hand, which he took and gave a firm but gentle squeeze. "I do think you might be wrong about one thing though."

"How extraordinary a mistake, detective," he said, sliding easily into an English accent. "I've heard about you detectives going around from village to village bringing enlightenment. I should like to hear your deductions. Please carry on."

I giggled and then said, "It's just that you referred to yourself as a stranger. I mean, who's to say you're not someone familiar? Think about it. What would you say if I told you that you are in exactly the right place at exactly the right time?"

"I would say," he replied, speaking now in his own unique timbre, "that your mind sounds like an interesting place to be. Happy birthday, Faith."

"Thank you," I said, feeling a slight blush at my cheeks.

We looked away simultaneously as if we both sensed the moment was becoming too much or maybe we just wanted a moment to savor the flavor of our first words and breathe for a heartbeat the fragrance of our first impressions.

We took in the Mediterranean mystique of Natasha, the newest member of Gypsy Rain as she performed Sade's "The Sweetest Taboo." During the song, we snuck a couple of looks at each other, and on about the third "sneak peek," we caught each other looking. As wide smiles split our faces, we laughed as much with unexpected joy as we did with mild embarrassment at our unexpected timing. As the band played on, I sensed that he still felt like an intruder of sorts, and I felt his silent urge to fade to the outer fringes of my spotlight. I wanted to do something to make him feel more comfortable, something that would melt his need for distance.

It was then that I heard my wisdom tell me to leave the tender moment alone, to let it be, to flow where it will. I smiled to myself and wondered at my resolve to do this. I wondered even more at the vision of my newly arrived presence as my "lady in waiting" discovered the intimacy proximity of this moment. Through her eyes, I could see with clarity this proximity of being close enough to touch the knowing of a closeness that you have not yet arrived at. To be in the knowing place and not yet the having place was more wonderful than I ever thought it could be. In this knowing place, I found that while having the closeness that I sensed we had the potential to achieve was milestones away, simple touch was turned up to full volume. It was as if some static atmosphere surrounded just the two of us, and within that magnetic moment, just the idea of touch was an invitation to unbridled rapture. I felt the impulse to touch him, to cross that boundary, to test the reality of that closeness, just one touch…just one…I wanted to…I needed…to just…so I did.

Gabriel was standing beside me with his right hand holding his drink and his left hand at his side just inches from my hand that was resting on my knee. I reached up, and without looking at him, I softly placed my hand into his. I lingered in this intentional touch for some time, floating on the intoxicating ripples within this single wave of passion. I memorized the warmth and texture of his hand before I squeezed with a restrained intensity that I hoped communicated, "Gabriel, I see you and you are not a stranger to me." I felt him squeeze back as he, too, kept his eyes on the band as we allowed the language of touch to express heartfelt sensations around that words had not yet formed.

Some moments later, I released my grip, not so much following conscious decision so much as an unconscious surrender to intimacy's rhythm. Gabriel's response to my slipping away from the moment when first we touched was a sweet surprise.

He squeezed my hand, firmly stopping my slow retreat. He pushed his hand purposefully against mine until our palms were pressed together. (Remember, Grace, all of this was happening without eye contact. I was amazed at his ability to read and flow with the tender moment. I mean it really takes a developed level of sensitivity that utilizes both self-possession and empathy to speak so clearly in a crowded room with just touch.) He laced his fingers with mine and with a gentle pressure folded our link into a cozy clasp. He held me like that for how long, I'll never know. I was being held by my sweet dream's initiative, and in those moments, the romantic proverbs of "Time stood still" and "Be still, my beating heart" most certainly ruled my universe. I thanked God for Gypsy Rain's music, which I then believed was the only noise that could mask the island drum sound of my beating heart. When he released my hand, we turned and looked at each other with a new intensity. It was as if the expressions from our touch had somehow given birth to the new affection that we now discovered in each other's eyes.

We looked back toward the band where Layla was just finishing out Cher's gypsy song (one of Layla's absolute favorites). Gabriel briefly excused himself and stepped off toward the bar. I wanted to watch him walk but instead forced myself to concentrate on the stage. My task was made easier as Brandon took center stage to the introductory chords of Clapton's "Layla." He gave me a wink with a raised eyebrow smile just before sliding smoothly into his spectacular vocals.

Gabriel returned just as the band went on break. "Listen," he said, looking intensely into my eyes (Grace, I could almost swear that the darker blue shade in his eyes turned lighter when he looked at me that way. The words that come when I think to describe that look are "fierce tenderness"), "I really need to go, but I wanted to say something to you. It's just," he paused, "I'm afraid that you might think I'm strange, so I wrote you a little note."

He took my hand, turned it palm up, and placed the note in the center. He gently used both of his hands to close mine around his message. He turned my closed hand back to the palms down position and, for just a precious moment, held it there. Then he did the most romantic thing. While maintaining the intensity within our eye contact, he kissed the back of my hand.

"A kiss for hope," he said softly. He kissed my hand a second time and said, "And a kiss for hope's angel." He released my hand and gave me a wink and a smile.

"Did you know that you've already been kissed by an angel?" I asked, squeezing his note tightly in my hand.

"Really and how would you know that?" he asked.

"Because you can see it right here."

On impulse, I kissed the index finger on my left hand and pressed it softly to the cleft in his chin. His response was the smile of a boy under the Christmas tree just after opening the gift that he dared not dream he would get.

"I like that," he said with a grin as if he'd discovered a hidden treasure within himself. "I like that a lot. I'm glad your birthday was happy, Faith." He began to step away.

"How do you know it was happy?" I teased.

While backing slowly toward the door, he put his index finger up to his lips and said, "Shhh, it's a secret. All I can tell you is a little bird told me. Hope to see you again soon." As he turned to walk out the door, he turned his head toward me for one last look and added, "And, Faith, sweet dreams."

As the clock struck midnight, my lower jaw almost struck the floor. I had to fight off the impulse to run out the door after him to ask him to repeat what he'd just said. That's how Layla and Brandon found me as the band returned from refreshing themselves. Layla mentioned something about flies being out of season, referring of course to my openmouthed expression. She swore me then and there to a "tell all" session over Sunday brunch.

The final surprise of the night was an old song that the band had been working on for the past seven months. (Layla and Brandon expected near perfection before they would add a song to their performance list.) Brandon stepped up to the microphone and in a surprisingly precise English accent said, "With great pride, Gypsy Rain would like to debut our tribute to the rock 'n' roll genius of Sir Elton John." Then back in his own voice, he looked at me and said, "This one's for you, Faith." Layla, now on keyboards, blew me a kiss and then blew me away as she played the introductory chords to Elton John's "Tiny Dancer." Brandon nailed it, and the close knit audience *begged for an encore. Brandon encouraged the crowd to join in on the lyrics, and there we were, all of my favorite people singing along with my all-time favorite song, making the perfect ending to the perfect birthday.*

Exhilarated but exhausted, I sat back in the limo alone enjoying my short ferry ride home. After, about a thousand thank-you hugs and kisses to all those who had made my birthday so wonderful, Layla had packed me into the limo with my gifts and packages. In her nurturing way, she had intuited that I would want some time alone to ponder and introspect.

As she kissed my cheek goodnight, she whispered into my ear, "And you better memorize every word of that note because I'll tear your loft apart looking for it if you don't tell me every word tomorrow."

I giggled my consent. Then with a tear in my voice, I told her that she was much more than a best friend and that to me she would always be the sister of my heart. I hugged her tight and then pulled out a small gift wrapped box and handed it to her. "This is for you, Layla, and for all that you mean to me."

"What are you doing, Fay-Fay, this is your birthday," Layla said affectionately as she took the box.

"Yes, it is, and this is my last present to myself," I told her as I pulled out a second box identical to hers.

"Go ahead, open it, gypsy girl," I urged with a smile of anticipation as I opened my own.

Layla opened her gift and pulled out a silver chain at the end of which hung a silver locket in the shape of half a heart. She opened the locket, and there inside was half of a picture, the face in the picture was me. It was one we had taken some months ago at the very flea market where we had first met. I showed her my locket, which was the twin of hers and opened it to reveal her beautiful face.

She pulled me out of the car and hugged me tight again, then pushed me back in and said, "You make me so happy I could cry, so please leave before I start. I'll see you tomorrow, OK, I love you, Faith."

So there I sat surrounded by the cozy energy that emanates from gifts given by familial friends, honoring the arrival day of a loved one's existence. It was in that ambience that I opened Gabriel's note and taking a deep breath began to read. I smiled pure joy as my eyes pored through his script, and I held it to my heart until the moment I arrived home.

After putting a few of the gifts in their proper place, I felt a pleasant weariness overtake me. Curling my hand around Gabriel's note, I fell into my bed and, under the soft luxury of my covers, gave way to a rapturous sleep. I dreamed of Hope and Joy riding horseback, galloping past the lighthouse, along the white sand beach while snuggled close to the smiling figure of the Bright Knight of Happiness.

P.S. Grace, I know you are crazy to know what the note said, but I had to give you a cliffhanger ending the way you always did with your stories at Sunday tea. Like you used to say, I must give you something to look forward to for tomorrow. God, how I miss you, Grace. To this day, I have never found anyone who spontaneously created anticipation the way that you did. I want you to know that in this process, you secretly passed to your little Fay-Fay precious pearls of wisdom, about the nature of hope. I will see you soon in the next entry.

CHAPTER SIX

Eggs, Enchiladas, and Explanations

Like an avid diver needing air, while reluctant to leave behind the mysterious beauty of the deep, Gaby rose from the depths of the enchanting spell cast by the diary's first entry. Carefully placing the diary back into the box, she laid back in her nest and hugged herself. Closing her eyes, she enjoyed a brief playback of the diary's vivid scenes.

The lingering residue of the diary's spell was broken by the soft thump of the pillow that landed on her face.

"Sorry, Gaby," Lindsay giggled. "I just couldn't resist."

Gaby grabbed the pillow and sent it sailing back toward her friend. "Well look who's up," Gaby said, giggling back as she watched her friend try to dodge the pillow while holding on to her coffee. "I'll get something to wipe up that spill," she laughed good-naturedly as she stepped quickly down to the kitchen. "You know, Lindz, we just had the most amazing development this morning," Gaby said as she came back with a wad of paper towels.

"I'm hoping that means that I'll require a cup size at least three times larger than what currently resides in my lingerie collection. Oh my god, Gaby," Lindsay feigned amazement as she looked down at herself, "my prayers are answered, but I think I'm going to need a walker to maintain any semblance of balance."

"Stop being silly," Gaby giggled as she mopped up the coffee. "I'm talking about the diary, not your delusions of grandeur."

"Oh, so we're talking about delusions now." Lindsay smiled at her friend as she took Gaby's place in the couch nest.

"No," Gaby insisted, "seriously, Lindz, you've got to read this first entry. It is so extraordinary!"

"Wow that good huh," Lindsay replied, beginning to connect with her friend's enthusiasm.

"You don't know the half of it," Gaby exclaimed as she walked the sodden towels down to the kitchen trash can. "I mean, Lindz, you have really stumbled onto something remarkably spiritual here. What did you call it last night, hope times joy squared? Just wait till you read Faith's words, she'll take you there in zero point two. I swear, Lindz, she pulls you into this world. It's just so beautiful."

Lindsay leaned forward and took the diary from the box.

Gaby picked up the phone. "I've got an idea, Lindz," she said as she dialed her mama's number. "A little adjustment to our 'diary day' schedule."

"No complaints here," Lindsay replied easily. "Spontaneous is my middle name."

"Don't I know it," Gaby came back with a smile. "Olah, Mama," she said into the phone.

Lindsay opened the diary and, allowing the lyrical litany of Gaby's native language to fade into the background, began to read.

* * *

Gaby placed the phone back into its cradle and poured two cups of coffee. "OK, here's the plan, Lindz," Gaby said as she walked up from the kitchen and placed a fresh cup of coffee on the table in front of her friend.

"I'm listening," Lindsay said, raising her eyes from the diary with visible effort.

"I've got to run some quick errands, including making another copy of this letter so Mama can read it. I know she'll have some good interpretations on the passages Grandma Grace wrote on illusion. I've got some ideas about what she is talking about, but it's not really clear yet. Listen to me, Lindz," calling her Grandma like she is family or something.

"Yes, you've caught the fever alright. The amazing thing is how the rhythm of her writing pulls you in so quickly and by letter's end, she really does feel like family."

"So, Lindz, why don't you finish reading the first entry, which will catch you up with me, and then meet me at Mama's say around nine thirty for eggs, enchiladas, and explanations."

"Awesome idea, Gaby. That will give me time to wake up before I wade back into the energy stream we left last night."

"Forget about wading, Lindz," Gaby said as she scurried toward the door, slinging on her shoulder bag as she went, "Those first twenty pages have a current that will grab you, sweep you downstream, and have you seeing white water before you take your first bite of breakfast. See you soon."

* * *

Inspired by the romantic wind of Faith's poetic perception, and refreshed by the hot spray of a leisurely shower, Lindsay pondered on the swirl of emotions that the diary's first entry had stirred as she drove the familiar route to the house of her friend's mama. The wonder and depth of the letter and diary had left her feeling strangely but not unpleasantly disoriented. It was somewhat like stepping into a dream where you get everything you've so wanted to have but not quite in the way you expected to get it. It was like going on a trip and finding that everything you had packed was inessential because everything you need and want is already there. So now you're looking at all the stuff you had packed and wondering what you should hang on to. You still feel a strange loyalty to the items in the suitcase even though the items at your destination are not only new but also the exact items that you would have chosen had you discovered the way to that choice. "Strange disorientation indeed," Lindsay said out loud, pleased with the way she had pinpointed her current state of mind. She was looking forward to hearing the insights of Gaby's mother. If anyone could find her way through a psyche turned upside down, Gaby's mama was that one. As Lindsay took the on ramp to highway 40 west, she smiled at her mental picture of the face that Gaby and her brother called the true princess of El Salvador.

Margarita Violeta Menendez possessed something mysteriously more than her natural charisma and exotic beauty. Lindsay had never quite been able to put her finger on this ethereal element. The closest that she could come to describing it was a word that she had conjured as a frequent bather in the light of Margarita's smile. Lindsay called this element (to Gaby's delight) "lovewise."

To Lindsay, *lovewise* meant being able to go to the exact "when" and "where" any given person is currently sitting within that person's own psyche. Sort of like the expression "he will hit you where you live," Margarita will sit with you where you live. Upon arriving, Margarita would just sit there with you, respecting even with reverence your current place, space, and time, exuding all the while the singular vibe "It's OK. We are supposed to be here."

At some point, you arrive at the realization that you are not alone, that somehow someone is actually in your inner experience with you. You begin to sense that this safe and comforting presence not only had the wisdom to find you but also has the wisdom to see things that you need to see. Then just before you could begin to form a dependence on the warmth and wonder of her just being with you, she shines her light upon the thing you needed to see. You then go to the thing you needed. Once there, you find delight in the discovery of this thing. You experience joy in the knowing that it is exactly what you needed. You marvel that it had been within you all along, awaiting your discovery. You look back to thank her, but she's gone. The only evidence that she was ever there at all is the light that still shines.

Sometime later, you find that the light that remains is actually your own and that her presence had just increased your awareness of that which had always been yours. This truth evokes a love for her that goes far beyond any sensation of mortal bonding that you can recall. For now, you realize only one way of life makes any sense at all, and that is to let your light shine. You somehow realize that it is also the best way to appreciate the light that found you and showed you the way to the light within you.

* * *

Born in 1954, in San Miguel, El Salvador, the oldest child in a family of seven children, Margarita's light of hope and innocence began to reveal itself at the early age of five. Lindsay's mind slipped away to a little village in El Salvador as she recalled a story that Gaby had told her from one of Margarita's earliest childhood memories.

When Margarita was just an infant, her father, a political advisor, moved the family to Santa Ana. There, her brother, Pedro, was born and for a while, as it was just the two of them, they became inseparable. At the age of four, Pedro had fallen completely in love with a rabbit that he named Elvis. One morning, when brother and sister went out to the rabbit's cage to feed him, they found Elvis lying down with his eyes closed. A snake was in the cage with him. The children ran to their mother, who came out and killed the snake.

Margarita's mother, the daughter of a San Miguel farmer, was raised in an unforgiving patriarchal home that served a severe loyalty to family and religion. Consequently, she tended to lean more on practicality than nurturance in the raising of her children. She told Pedro that the rabbit was dead and would have to be buried. Margarita hugged her crying brother and then ran after her mother, who was halfway to the shed where she kept a shovel. She begged her mother to wait just one day before burying the rabbit. She begged her to allow just one day for a miracle to happen "because miracles sometimes do happen, don't they, Mama."

"Yes, child," her mama replied, "but you must know that miracles are very hard to come by."

The appeal to her mother's religion worked, and she gave the children one day. Margarita ran and got some candles from the house. She made a little altar out of stone upon which her brother could pray. She made Pedro swear that he would not look in the cage until morning. Margarita then went to the church less than a mile from her home and said a prayer herself. She knew the rabbit was dead and would not come back to life. She told God that she knew this and that it was OK because there was another way for the miracle to happen. She prayed that she could find Elvis's twin brother.

A farmer who was in the church and happened to overhear the little girl's prayer told Margarita that he had seen several rabbits from time to time out behind his barn. He told her how they might be trapped with a box, a string, a stick, and a carrot. After getting directions, an encouraged Margarita set about collecting these items while she puzzled over the problem of how to get to the farm, a distance of more than three miles down the road from her house, without stirring up the *no* word that she was certain would come from her mother. She decided to bear whatever punishment she might receive in order to make this miracle happen. The thought of Pedro's happiness tomorrow morning when he saw Elvis alive and well in his cage was worth whatever price she might have to pay for the miracle's success. Margarita had also reasoned that she could not lie to her mama to make the miracle happen. Lying would just change the miracle into a common sin, and who wanted that. No, the only way to complete the miracle was to not go home until the work was done. She had gotten the necessary permission to go pray at the church, and that would have to do for the time being.

By the time she had gathered all the items that she needed, it was well after noon. Carrying the items in a small milk crate, which included string, stick, burlap bag with holes poked through to scoop up the trapped rabbit, four carrots, three potatoes, and an old canteen filled with water, Margarita made her way toward the farmer's barn. Having missed her lunch, she munched sparingly on one of the potatoes as she walked. The journey took well over two hours as she carefully avoided the sporadic traffic, somehow realizing that passersby may try to interrupt her urgent errand.

Once there, she scouted the area behind the barn and was rewarded with the sighting of three rabbits. She set up the box, placing one potato and two carrots in the trap and unraveling the string she strategically stationed herself behind a tree where she could keep watch. Margarita waited, hoping the rabbits would come soon so that she could get back home before she was missed. She ate another carrot and drank some water, keeping watch all the while. Fatigued from her long walk, Margarita found herself fighting the weight of her eyelids that seemed to resist her every effort. Losing her battle, sleep took her under the shade of the tree with her unfinished carrot resting in one hand and the slack string tied around the index finger of the other.

Some hours later, she awoke with a start when she detected something wet and prickly moving on the palm of her hand. She looked down to find one of the rabbits scurrying off with her carrot. Checking the box, she quickly noted that the trap had been sprung. Further inspection detected movement, and she leaped up, clapping her hands, doing a little dance of joy as she hurried to scoop Elvis's brother carefully into the bag. Securing the top of the bag with the string, Margarita made her way quickly toward the road. What she saw alarmed her enough to stop her in her tracks. It was dusk. Her errand had taken far longer than she ever imagined. She could not travel this road after dark. If the trek through the dark did not lead to harm, the arrival home to her anguished mother surely would. She would need another miracle to complete this miracle.

Before she could even open her mouth to pray, she heard a truck pulling out of the farm's driveway. She recognized the denim-blue cowboy hat that the farmer at the church had been holding in his hand. She ran toward the truck, waving vigorously with her free hand. The farmer popped the passenger door open and said, "Well, if it isn't my little rabbit hunter."

Some twenty minutes later, she was putting Elvis's brother in the cage after first removing the original Elvis and placing him carefully on the ground. Margarita used the shovel from the shed to dig a shallow grave. She used the potato sack as a makeshift bed and placed the dead rabbit in the grave. After filling the hole, she marked the grave with some stones. She was careful not to use too many to prevent attracting her brother's attention. Finally, she said a fervent prayer of thanks to God for answering all her prayers.

She walked into the house and without fear walked right up to her mother and gave her a fierce hug. Her mama kneeled down, embraced her daughter, and asked in a voice half relieved and half scolding, "Where have you been, child?"

Margarita replied, talking into her mother's wet cheek, "You were right, Mama, about miracles being hard to come by, and now I know why. It takes a whole day and a whole village just to make the miracle work," and with that, little Margarita fell asleep right there in her mother's arms.

She awoke the next morning to the face of her brother who was looking down at her with a combination of worship and awe. "Thank you for the miracle, Mygreeta (Pedro's four-year-old way of saying her name)," Pedro said gratefully.

"I think you need to thank God, Pedro," Margarita said, yawning and stretching as she sat up in her bed.

"I already did, many times, but then I still feel more thank-yous, so I think God wants me to give one to you too, Mygreeta," Pedro replied solemnly as he gave his sister a tight hug.

"You are most welcome, Pedro. It is a good thank-you that you give. Today, we will build a better cage so the snake cannot get in," Margarita said, brightly looking up in time to see her Mama's smile just before she covered it with her hand and called them to breakfast.

* * *

Taking the exit for highway 141 south, Lindsay smiled to herself as she recalled the mixture of love and pride in Gaby's voice on the day she had heard that story. They had been vacationing in Gaby's birthplace when her friend had fondly recounted the highlights of her mother's life.

When Margarita was ten, the family moved to San Salvador, where she graduated from Guadalupe's high school at the top of her class. Fluent in French, English, and Italian as well as several Spanish dialects, she worked for a short while as a translator for her father. Growing restless with her developing passion for the study of spiritual growth and healing, Margarita left her family's village just short of her twentieth birthday.

Margarita's mother had been courting high hopes that her daughter would marry a prominent political figure and begin to take decisive steps to join the small but privileged Latin American aristocracy. She took every opportunity to express her severe disapproval with Margarita's decision. So it was without her mother's blessing that she moved to Guatemala to study metaphysical science with a native shaman.

Three years later, she returned to San Salvador with her husband, Ricardo Raphael Menendez. Much to her mother's disappointment, Margarita came home not only with husband but also with child, unintentionally but effectively derailing her mother's hopes that she might yet be able to "fast-track" her daughter to a higher station. The birth of Gabriella in early November of 1976 and then Eduardo in late November of 1980, to Margarita's deep dismay, did little to soften her mother's severe judgment.

After the death of Ricardo, a casualty of El Salvador's twelve-year civil war, Margarita fled her native country for Cancun, Mexico, where she developed her painting, a latent gift that she had discovered with her late husband. It was there that her gift blossomed as her art grew with both depth and maturity. She even began to attract a modest group of fans and was especially known for her theme paintings that featured Latin American children depicted as angels bringing aid to would be victims in civil war-torn El Salvador.

The most famous of these paintings was that of a boy angel who possessed a deep, ethereal, Latin American beauty that seemed to pull the observer right into the picture. The boy angel hovering just above the head of a soldier appeared to be whispering through his cupped hand into the soldier's ear. The soldier was standing on the road with his discarded rifle lying at his feet. He was staring at his hands with a look of wonder, almost as if he had just discovered them for the first time. A woman carrying an infant while holding the hand of a little girl was portrayed some steps beyond where the soldier was standing. The little girl, whose measure of beauty was no less than the boy angel's, was looking back over her shoulder. She was flashing an unmistakable smile of recognition toward the angel. The face of the little angel was none other than five-year-old Ricardo Raphael Menendez. A few of the many who saw the painting at Margarita's first art show would comment that the little girl bore an uncanny resemblance to a girl who had made a brief entrance during the show to give Margarita a bouquet of roses. That girl was Gabriella.

The revenue, from the paintings, that seem to fly off the walls of Margarita's debut, led to a nest egg that birthed the arrival of the Menendez family to the American Midwest.

* * *

Turning right on Oakside Avenue, Lindsay brightened as she drove slowly down this now familial avenue that her best friend had dubbed Serenity Lane. Gaby, who like Lindsay possessed a passion for running, described her high gear kicks to the finish line (which was marked by the mailbox in front of her mama's casa) as "serenity sprints."

Lindsay chuckled to herself as she recalled Gaby's explanation given several years earlier during one of their many cool down walk and talks.

"Ok, Gaby, I give up. What's your secret? Where are you getting the rocket fuel for that finish of yours? Even when I try to save a little gas for some semblance of a kick, you leave me in your dust. How can you do that after almost six miles?" Lindsay queried breathlessly.

"No big secret, Lindz," Gaby replied as she pulled up on her ponytail to expose her moist skin to the cool air. "I call it serenity sprints. What it really boils down to is making a connection with a source of spiritual energy and then surrendering to that source. While I run the first five and a half miles, I link with that energy source, sort of like in the back road of my mind. In the case of this run, which I consider my home course, I link with my mama's love for me."

"I don't get it. How does that translate to running faster?"

"I know it sounds strange, but have you ever really thought about the strength of a mother's love for her child? I'm not just speaking of how a mother nurtures and appreciates her little one. I'm talking about fields of energy, fields of a specific divine design, fields filled with the vigilance of the lioness and her cubs romping safe within the ferocity of her love. I'm talking about oceans of adoration, teeming with baby dolphins swimming in their mother's wake."

"OK, so you mean that there is a metaphysical source that feeds a mother's love for her child. Sort of like a hidden reservoir of strength."

"Exactly, it is an underlying world of energy that exists and endures far beyond any mother's mortal strength or imagination. If you were to ask a mother, she would most probably tell you that she somehow knows that the source of her love for her child is much larger than herself and that many times it seems that she is far from in control and is somehow only along for the ride. It is through the mother that the child is drawn into this world of wonder and substance to which each mother is inextricably linked."

"OK, so you're saying that the child's connection to the mother and in turn that energy reserve is sort of like a familial gravitational pull."

"That's it, you know, like the specific magnetic energy that pulls you toward your family. So what I'm saying is by the time I hit the five and a half–mile mark at Oakside Avenue, that 'mother-love magnet' is revved up to love times joy times gravity to the tenth power. Lindz. I swear I can almost hear it hum."

"I never imagined looking at love as an energy source, but it totally makes sense."

"So I take about seven steps into that hum, and then I completely let go. I surrender to that energy with complete trust. I actually leave my body and that's when I feel her."

"Feel who?" Lindsay asked, momentarily puzzled.

"Serenity," Gaby said with a smile. "She takes my body, and the next thing I know, I can hardly even feel my feet touching the pavement, which is why I really can't take credit for the speed. I mean that girl can fly once she gets going. It's kind of like the bird to the nest energy you know? It's like the surrender is the serenity, like a complete freedom, like how the bird surrenders to instinct. It just trusts the instinct with all of its weight. Then the sprint is the magnetic pull of familial love drawing me into its center, which I located at Mama's house, you know, the finish line," Gaby finished.

"So what you're saying is your mama's house is like the mothership, and it kind of beams you up?" Lindsay asked, furrowing her brow innocently.

"Well sort of, but there is not much of a spiritual element to your metaphor. Hey, wait a minute, did you just go Treki on me. Why is it that everything has to be explained by Captain Kirk and company?"

"Sorry, Gaby," Lindsay said, forcing back the smile that threatened to break out into laughter, "but contrary to popular belief, there is a truth that goes far deeper than the 'six degrees of Kevin Bacon,' and that is the three hundred and sixty degrees of *Star Trek*. I'm talking about a truth that is all around us, girl."

"Oh my god, you're impossible," Gaby said, throwing her hands up in resignation. "The next thing you're going to tell me is that Scotty was actually the one responsible for parting the Red Sea."

"Well now that you bring it up, it is a well-known fact that *Star Trek* actually produced the template responsible for the archetypal gods and goddesses of Greek mythology."

"Are you trying to tell me that Homer was on the *Enterprise*?"

"Of course not, silly," Lindsay came back with the straightest face that she could manage. "I'm saying that Homer was the *Enterprise*. Where do you think he got all his ideas from?"

"Lindsay, honey," Gaby gently put her arm around her friend's shoulder and said with the authoritative air of a doctor about to give her patient really bad news, "you are beyond help, dear. I mean you need the help of a really good doctor. Something like, three times a day, seven days a week, should get you started. I'll be sure to have them drop off a truckload of medication for you. Do you know the name of like a really good doctor, Lindz."

"Well," Lindsay began appearing to ponder seriously, "do you suppose Dr. Spock might be available?"

* * *

Lindsay's face held a wide smile as she recalled the playful shove she had given her friend and the footrace that ended in breathless laughter in the very driveway into which she now turned.

Lindsay's knock on the door to the Menendez residence was answered almost immediately by Gaby's brother Eduardo.

"Welcome, Lindsay-san, how nice to see you again," Eduardo said, giving Lindsay a reverent bow.

"Oh, Eddie, puh-leeze," Gaby said with affectionate sarcasm as she made a sudden appearance from the hallway, "must you exercise your new religious preference in the company of my best friend?"

"Ah, Gaby-san, so much humor from one so beautiful is almost too much for me," Eduardo replied with a ghost of a smile showing from under his solemn features. He closed the door and smoothly turned to follow the two women toward the kitchen.

"Eddie just recently began his adoption process with Buddhism," Gaby explained, linking arms with her friend as they made their way to the Menendez kitchen. "It's his fifth religion within the past decade. He really believes that you cannot truly appreciate a religion unless you have actually adopted its walk and its ways. He says to really know it, you must really live it by walking its path. Mama and I agree that his current choice is such a refreshing change from his 'American Gothic' days. Wouldn't you agree, Eddie-san?" Gaby asked, throwing a teasing smile over her shoulder toward her younger sibling.

"Oh yes, Mama-san, she loves the light," Eddie replied with boyish delight.

Lindsay giggled and flashed her own smile back toward Eduardo, catching the gorgeous eyes and dark good looks that affected most women with what Gaby and Lindsay called the swooning sickness.

Eduardo gave her a wink and a smile as they continued down the hall toward the delicious aromas wafting from the breakfast buffet of El Salvadoran cuisine that was currently under construction.

The Menendez kitchen was located toward the back of a spacious, two-story Mediterranean-styled structure that faced east. It was in the space to the west, at the back of the house, where the majority of the memories in the Menendez family tapestry were woven. The living room, dining room, and kitchen were all designed into one large room. The design was inspired by Margarita's childhood wish for a home that combined the nourishment of the food from her homeland with the nurturing spirit of the Latino familial rhythm. The kitchen was separated from the dining and living areas by a long service island that ran parallel to the southern wall that held two ranges, two tall ice boxes, as Margarita still called them, and large double sinks and dishwasher. The serving island several feet to the north of the appliance wall looked out over the cleverly designed dining area and gave the enormous room the look and feel of a warm and homey Spanish restaurant. The north wall was constructed with a series of thick sliding glass panels and doors that looked out onto a flagstone courtyard surrounded by shrubs, blooms, and vines. The courtyard held the siesta ambience of an outdoor Spanish café. The dining table was a custom-made, cherrywood piece that could be connected to winged extensions that covered the width of the west wall and half the length of the glassed north wall. The table when full could seat well over fifty people. A fireplace sat along the east wall, which like the west wall was adorned with colors and scenes of Latin American art. Comfortable sections of lounge seating faced the flagstone fireplace. These sections could easily be moved to make space for the many impromptu dance parties, which at the Menendez residence were more of a rule than an exception. It was no surprise to Margarita's many neighbors to find Eduardo or Gabrielle on their doorstep in the early morning with a colorful invitation to a spontaneous "Margarita Mood Night." This mood that would sometimes greet Margarita at the odd hour of three in the morning would often lead to a twenty-four-hour mood marathon. This spontaneous celebration would always start with cooking that would begin in the wee hours of the morning. Mouthwatering scents would begin to usher in the first guests arriving around noon, and the gathering would often stretch out into the early morning hours of the next day.

Lindsay breathed in the fragrant nostalgia of her Menendez "memory room," her heart smiling as she joined the threads currently weaving on the family loom.

"Lindsay, my child, it's so good to see your face. You have been away too long," Margarita said as she pulled Lindsay from her brother and sister escort.

Lindsay allowed herself to fall into the light and warmth of Margarita's embrace. Lindsay gave herself to the hug, waiting to feel the energized effect that Margarita's hugs usually transmitted. To her surprise, she felt instead the steady hum of her own energy passing through her and into her friend's mother. Gaby and Eduardo looked on with seeing smiles as Margarita released Lindsay from an energy exchange that shimmered with a perceptible alteration in their mother's aura.

"Looks like Lindsay brought the 'orangeade' with her huh, Gaby," Eduardo said, giving his sister a nudge.

The Dreamwatcher Diaries

"Oh my god, Mama," Gaby exclaimed, "I can't believe your halo is—"

"Shush, Gabriella, and let the universe be," Margarita interrupted in a firm but reverent tone.

Eduardo smiled wider as Gaby's hand flew up to cover the foolish smile that took over her generous mouth.

"What a wonderful surprise you have brought me this morning, Lindsay. The creative color is strong with you today. In passing me your beautiful orange, you have just changed my day plan of shopping and fun into a day of painting and the joy of visits with visions as yet undiscovered. You are finding many doorways opening inside you right now, yes?" Margarita asked with a delighted smile.

"Oh yes, Margarita, it's as if all the rigid lines in my brain have become flexible. Like watching concrete walls dissolve before my eyes, or waking to find all mental barriers and boxes vanish without a trace. I can't say that I have ever experienced this before," Lindsay replied, surprised at how accurately she had verbalized her feelings. "Usually I'm spending most of my time trying to keep the lines rigid, believing that the walls would keep me safe somehow or that they would be my guide and keep me from messing up my life. But the biggest surprise is that even though those age-old lines are getting soft and blurry, I'm not afraid. I'm not afraid even though I don't know what is going to happen next," Lindsay finished, smiling through a teardrop.

Gaby gave Lindsay a hug and said with a smile, "Welcome to Serenity, the land where the river of trust dissolves the barriers of control."

"It seems as if this letter you found carries a strange magic," Margarita said, nodding in understanding. "The letter spoke to me also. There is much wisdom in the grandmother's words. I found her passages on illusion very enlightening."

"Did you hear that?" Eduardo said suddenly.

The three women with effort pulled themselves from their emotional communion. They looked questioningly at Eduardo.

"It was a voice, Spanish speaking, quiet but distinct. It said come and get me before I get too cold. I'm pretty sure it came from a couple of enchiladas on that plate over there," Eduardo said with a smile that broke the serious look on his face.

"Yes, mi amore, I hear it too," Margarita said, smiling fondly at her son. "Let's eat now and save the talking for hot cups of Colombian coffee after the meal."

Eduardo led the way to a cozy round table covered with a thick white cloth. The table, set up especially for the occasion, sat just in front of the flagstone fireplace.

"Well, I will say this for you, Eduardo-san," Gaby jibed her brother, "you do set up a beautiful table."

"Oh, a compliment," Eduardo said with surprise. "I must write this down in my memoirs so that someday I can relive this rapturous moment."

Eduardo gave Lindsay a wink and a smile as he pulled out a chair for his sister.

Lindsay giggled. "You two are too much," she said as she allowed Eduardo to pull her chair out. "Don't you ever take a break?"

"Only when his mouth is full," Gaby came back.

"Which it will be as soon as you give thanks for the bounty we are about to receive," Eduardo finished, rubbing his hands together in a gesture of anticipation.

After a short prayer of thanks, hot platters were passed and plates were heaped with a mix of eggs scrambled in an assortment of breakfast meats, coated with a rich covering of cheddar and Colby-Jack cheese. The mix was peppered with hot spices and covered in a secret hot sauce that Gaby had yet to pry from her mother's collection of secret recipes. Breakfast enchiladas and platters filled with an arrangement of fruit and crisp cinnamon sticks followed close in their quick procession around the white-clothed breakfast table. Light breakfast banter ensued, and Margarita was showered with accolades that evoked from her silver screen smiles of appreciation. Eduardo, who secretly held his mother's smile as the measure for all things beautiful, kept the shower going until she finally had to shush him.

Pleasantly full, the cozy group retired to comfortable lounge chairs arranged in a small circle in front of the fireplace. Basking in the warmth radiating from the crackling flames, they sipped rich coffee as they waited for their stomachs to agree with the portions which they had allowed.

"OK," Gaby began, "are we ready for some for some serious discussion, or do we need additional recovery time from that feast of a breakfast?"

"Why am I not surprised that you are the first one who is ready," Lindsay said with a conspiratorial glance in Eduardo's direction.

Eduardo smiled back and added, "Mama, wouldn't this be a good time to bring out the home movies? I'm sure that Lindsay would love to see the one where Gaby shaved her head."

"I did not shave my head, and we are not going there," Gaby said with growing exasperation.

"Mama, could I please have a little help here?" Gaby pleaded.

"Well let me think." Margarita paused in a gesture of contemplation. "I think we have time for a quick story about your brother's first lesson in metaphysics."

"Excellent suggestion, Mama. The perfect story, short and sweet."

"Oh no, not that story. I surrender," he said, frantically waving a white napkin. "I am so ready to talk about the letter. You know I read it too, Lindsay, and I've got to tell you—"

"Not so fast, Mr. Home Movie Man. Time to face the music."

"Sorry, Eduardo, I've got to hear this," Lindsay said enthusiastically.

"Alright, alright then, tell the story if you have to. Just try to make it quick and painless will you, sis?"

"I'll be quick, but there's not much I can do about the pain, bro," Gaby said with a giggle. "OK so we're living in Cancun right, Lindz, and Mama, Eduardo, and are just finishing up dinner. I was about eleven then and Eduardo was six. I had just asked Mama the definition of metaphysics as I was developing a real curiosity about her studies. Her exact answer was…" Gaby nodded toward her mother.

"Looking for that, which lies under," Margarita said, covering her smile before it could become a giggle.

"Well, Mama and I didn't really think that Eduardo was paying much attention to our conversation, but then early the next morning, Mama comes rushing into my bedroom all frantic because Eduardo is not in his bed and appears to be missing. So we're running around like headless chickens in this panic when I return to his room for one more look. I'm looking down at his bedclothes when I see one of his little shoes poke out from under the bed.

"He had been under the bed all night fully clothed. He'd fallen asleep, and when Eduardo sleeps, it takes an entire marching band to wake him. So Mama asks him, 'What were you thinking, Eduardo?' He answers with this serious face and that cute little six-year-old voice of his, 'I was looking for the witch that lives under like you do, Mama. I look all night under my bed, but I do not find her. I wear my shoes so that I can run fast to find you if I see the witch. Today, maybe I look under the house.' Well I bust out laughing, and Mama pushes me out of the room so she can set him straight without the distraction of my belly laughs."

Lindsay laughed, "That is the cutest story."

"Yes, but not really that funny because my sister's laughter is a trauma from which I shall probably never recover," Eduardo said, drying imaginary tears. "It is only through the miraculous power of forgiveness that I am able allow her presence at this table today."

"Well, would you and your forgiveness be so kind as to go and refill the coffee pot?" Gaby asked, smiling supremely.

"Yes, that would be wonderful," Lindsay added.

"Certainly, but only for you, Lady Lindsay," Eduardo said, taking the coffeepot from the table and giving Lindsay a humble bow. "Don't start without me now."

"We won't," Lindsay assured him.

Moments later, Eduardo returned to find the three women, studying their copies of the letter. They had again lapsed into a deep, introspective communion. Silently, Eduardo marveled at how quickly the weather could change across the complex geography of the feminine mystique. With respect to the rich change in the room's energy, Eduardo quietly refilled coffee cups. He placed the pot on the center table and, picking up a fourth copy of the letter, retired to his chair. Enjoying the atmosphere of focused feminine intelligence, Eduardo watched the group for a moment. A ghost of a smile played with his lips as the trio blew lightly, in unison over the surface of the aromatic blend in their cups. Scant seconds later, his smile widened as he witnessed the three women take a discreet sip as if on cue.

"Mama," Gaby began, "why don't we start with the paragraph that starts 'The illusions of bliss mark the borderlands of intimacy'? I want to bounce some theories off you and then get your interpretations on that passage. I count one, two, three themes that I hope to clarify. First, we have the illusions of bliss, which seems to allude to what we frequently call addiction, second is the influence of illusion on romantic love, and third is Grace's brief reference to what she calls a sexual violation event and the immortality of the angels that live within each human soul."

"Yes, very good, mi amore," Margarita replied, making notations on her pages.

"What do you think, Lindz?" Gaby asked.

"Sounds perfect, but let's also include some interpretation on the passage that ends with the part about the flower in the desert."

"Eduardo?" Gaby asked, pausing in her note-taking to look up at her brother.

"This is your show, sis," Eduardo said. "I'm just along for the ride."

"Well buckle up, Eddie-san. The train is leaving the station," Gaby said with a smile. "OK," Gaby said, taking a breath. "Here goes. I believe 'the illusions of bliss' is a reference to consumption fantasy.

We know that consumption fantasy is supported by desire. We know that the authentic inner self, what Grace calls 'the divine intention of you,' cannot be found in fantasy, and that in turn fantasy cannot lead you to the authentic self. We also know that fantasy contracts the external universe of persons, places, and things to serve the individual. Fantasy expects that some subject or object in the universe will serve to fill the void or the empty space inside. Fantasy suggests that the possessing of this subject or object will bring about a wholeness and happiness that is virtually guaranteed to dissolve the emptiness of the void."

"OK," Lindsay said, "so what your saying is that we hopeless romantics are just chasing 'paper moons.'"

"That's part of what I'm saying," Gaby said with a smile, "but chasing paper moons only answers the question of what we are playing at. I believe that Grace's letter actually tells us why we are doing that."

"This I've got to hear," Lindsay replied.

"I think the answer to the question why is found in the passage where Grace writes about appearing whole only when your sweet dream or soul mate is beside you. The message is that the primary motive for chasing romantic hope stems from the somewhat universal human sense that we are not whole. This suggests that we may be primarily driven by the absence of something. It also suggests that the heart of desire is hollow with a wanting too deep to access. Like an itch that can't be reached, or scratched, or an ache that can't be held or soothed."

"I not only understand what you're saying," Lindsay said, "I feel it. So you're saying illusion and fantasy are human attempts to relieve the ache or fill the void."

"You got it, Lindz. It's like having a container that cannot be filled from the outside in, but you keep trying anyway."

"But it doesn't work. Why would we keep doing something that we know doesn't work?"

"Because of our tendency to look outside of ourselves for control over the things that we feel on the inside, and because it does work to distract us from the ache."

"OK, let's get this straight. My understanding of external locus of control refers to the human tendency to believe that persons, places, or things in the external universe have the qualifications and authority to solve and resolve internal shortfalls or aches. Is that right, Gaby?"

"Exactly right. If we choose to rely on external control to solve internal disturbances, then we tend to believe that someday it will work. We have to believe that someday the fantasy comes true and will make the ache go away. Essentially, that means that the fantasy subject's value is not found in what that subject adds to an individual soul like we might think. The value is found in the subject's ability to distract the individual from the ache, not to fill a void but rather to hold onto a prolonged distraction form the ache. Which is to say the value of Mr. or Ms. Right is more about the way they make the void fade into the background. This leads to the question, is it the potential mate's presence that is valued or is it the mate's ability to distract the individual from the internal sense of emptiness?"

"OK, I'm with you so far," Eduardo said with a furrowed brow, "but can someone define this ache for me? What is it exactly?"

"Great question, little brother," Gaby replied. "In simple terms, the ache of the void is essentially the need for meaning, the need for a connection to something that is both bigger and more important than you are. This truth makes the ache more of a calling to take the journey toward authenticity rather than being perceived as an inner irritant from which you seek escape."

"Well done, Gabriella," Margarita said. "I could not have said it better."

"So," Eduardo asked, "how do we determine which subjects to employ for these fantasy ventures?"

"The French philosopher and psychoanalyst Jacques Lacan, who did some very compelling work on the unconscious nature of fantasy, shares a theory that is a close parallel to Grace's words. A rough interpretation of his work on fantasy suggests that we project personally specified attributes and characteristics onto the fantasy subject, attributes which the subject in truth does not possess. In other words, we distort the subject into a shape that fits our needs. This puts us in pursuit of a subject whose genuine shape is overlooked in favor of the shape of what is known as the animus."

"So you're saying," Lindsay concluded, "that the potential mates that we are so ardently pursuing exist only in our minds?"

"Exactly, Lindz, this animus that resides in the unconscious mind is known as the beloved. It is formed and fashioned from attachment principles that are internalized during those early developmental years. We project the beloved's specific attachment characteristics onto a subject and then proceed to relate with that subject as if they were the beloved."

"Alright, so how does this ache and the distraction of the pursuit of the beloved," Eduardo asked, "relate to what we know as addiction?"

"Great question," Gaby replied. "The key to understanding addiction is found in Lacon's suggestion that the subject being pursued is not nearly as important as the action of the pursuit itself."

"How is that possible, sis?" Eduardo asked. "How can the subject of your heart's desire not be the most important thing?"

"Well, according to Lacon, it's because we need the fantasy subjects in order to perpetuate the sensation of desire. We are desiring as long as we are chasing. This truth makes the acquisition of our desired subject anticlimactic."

"I get it now," Eduardo exclaimed. "It's like the saying 'the hunt is sweeter than the kill,' like how a hunter needs a prey or the way a traveler requires a destination. Desire is hard-pressed to maintain a state of excitement without a fantasy subject to pursue. It's like desire's state law dictates that if you are not in pursuit, as is the case when you get what you want, then you must find a new fantasy object to pursue, and if you finally do get what you want, you are doomed to not want it anymore. You must find something wrong with your acquired subject of desire in order to continue a lifestyle of pursuit. Essentially this means that individuals become dependent on this cycle of pursuit."

"I couldn't have defined addiction better myself, but let me give it a try," Gaby said, giving her brother a wink. "Addiction pathways," Gaby began, "in simple terms are landmark events within the brain that we might call overwhelming states of consciousness. These states of consciousness construct a neural stream within the brain that is psychologically perceived as an emotional state that cannot be regulated. This creates a sense of insatiable desire coupled with a psychological need to control this overpowering emotional experience. This perpetual hunger employs fantasy to create the illusion that the individual is controlling that emotional state that cannot be contained. So the addicted individual, no matter what the drug, whether it is sex, food, cocaine, or hording, will go from consumption episode to consumption episode in the mindless pursuit of more. In this progressive process of consumption, the individual becomes blind to the truth that in reality, it is their very life that is being consumed by this unregulated emotional state."

"OK, OK, I surrender," Eduardo said with a grin. "The resident PhD is the hands down winner."

"Well, Eddie, it is not a fair contest. Addiction was after all the subject of my dissertation."

"OK, let me get this straight," Lindsay began, "so what your saying is, we chase beloved paper moon subjects to distract ourselves from the inner ache that is actually a doorway to our authenticity."

Eduardo's mouth dropped open in awe. "How did you just do that?"

"Do what?

"Summarize such abstract information so quickly."

"Focus, Eddie-san," Lindsay replied solemnly. "The focus that comes with necessity and desperation."

"Very well done, Lindsay," Margarita said with a wink and a smile.

"Thanks, Margarita, but there is one thing that I want to clarify. This idea about no longer wanting the subject of your desire once you get it, which supports the saying that 'the grass is greener on the other side of the fence.' Is it fair to say that this had something to do with Bruce and his infidelity, like once he had me, he was no longer in pursuit?"

"You've got it, Lindz," Gaby said softly. "That's why I keep telling you that it really wasn't about you no longer being desirable. It was about Bruce's dependence upon the excitement of the chase."

"Wait a minute, I think I just figured something out," Lindsay said more to herself than the others.

"What's that?" Gaby asked.

"My desire, or more accurately my fantasy, is to be the irresistible subject of my dream man's desire. Though I dream that the desire is adoration and a love-based inspiration, I still aspire to be the subject that the man of my dreams will forever need to hold and appreciate. That has always seemed so logical and imperative. It's so strange now to find that I have never realized that my desire to be a subject of desire is, not only an illusion, but more importantly, a distraction from the truth. The truth that Grace wrote about that my being cannot be defined as a subject of some man's desire, no matter who it is that desires me. The truth that this ache was not meant to be filled by a suitor's adoration but is rather a beckon call to take the journey inward toward my authenticity."

Lindsay looked up from her introspective trance to find three smiles nodding in understanding. "So," Lindsay asked, "what happens if you choose not to play in the state of desire any longer? What if you just refuse to find a new fantasy object to pursue, or in my case refuse to be an object to be pursued?"

"Then the illusion of desire begins to break apart, and you enter the land of disillusionment," Gaby replied.

"So based on what you're saying," Lindsay speculated, "happiness cannot be found within the state of desire, or in simpler terms, our wants cannot make us happy."

"Bingo," Gaby said, "chasing your wants cannot tell you who you are nor what you are worth, which are rather critical elements when you consider a recipe for happiness. In other words, desire simply does not have the technology to make you happy, or in Grace's words, 'Illusion cannot bear the weight of your being.' The popular belief that you should be happy when you get what you want puts even more pressure on our expectations of desire's illusions. Getting what we want is determined to fail in the 'happiness department' primarily because desire is based on the nature of consumption or the idea that more is more. That is why I called desire a treadmill going nowhere because perpetual pursuit gives the illusion of movement toward happiness when in truth, no linear progress is accomplished. All that is accomplished is desire's endless cycle of wanting to consumption to gratification and back to wanting again. Basically, this cycling leads to a perpetual distraction from the truth that awaits discovery on the other side of ache."

"When you put it that way, the land of disillusionment almost sounds like a sweet relief," Lindsay said thoughtfully. "Hey, I just realized something. The land of disillusionment is Grace's desert, isn't it?"

"I was thinking the same thing," Eduardo interjected.

"That's right," Gaby replied, "the desert of the broken heart."

"OK, we got that, but what's up with the flower?" Eduardo asked.

"May I?" Margarita asked her daughter.

"Please, I'd love to hear what you see, Mama."

"I believe that Grace is referring to what we tend to call the authentic self. The flower in the desert is the authentic self, reaching out to touch the conscious self. This undiscovered country deep within where the authentic self lives is filled with fields of the very same flower, possessing the same unique color and scent. Imagine this beautiful place within, awaiting your discovery. Imagine your authentic self, walking along a road that winds its way through the fragrant blooms. Content, you breathe in the perfume of the divine intention of you. Suddenly you feel a stirring as a gentle wind, cool and sweet, caresses your skin. You smile and as you watch the flowers dance, a single tear of joy traces a path down the slope of your cheek. You are happy because you know that the conscious self has just let go of another illusion. The wind, like an affirmation, is the conscious self reaching out to you. The wind sings, 'I choose you. I'm looking for you now. I believe that you are, that I am, and that being me is enough.' You reach out to the conscious self by picking a flower and holding it up. The flower, responding to the wind's kiss, releases a seed. The seed moves toward the conscious self and settles on the desert floor. Sometime later, the conscious self discovers the flower and, resonating with a heartfelt connection, waters the bloom with a single tear."

"That's just the most beautiful picture," Lindsay said. "You see it so clearly."

"OK, Mama, I get the concept, but I'm still trying to wrap my head around this idea of the authentic self in more tangible terms." Eduardo asked, his brow furrowed in focused concentration, "I mean, what might be a way to identify the presence of the 'deep self' in daily life?"

"One sign of the deep self can be found in friendship connections. Sometimes we meet someone who somehow, without trying, touches the deep self. What will always be different about this person is how he or she will not try to define, edit, or alter you. You will remark quietly to yourself that you feel so much hope and life when you are around them. But the telling quality about this person, the one that evokes a fierce passion, one that cries out for familial descriptors, is how they will set you free. In that experience lies the evidence that the deep self has been touched and the birth of a longing discovered. Another proof on the other end of the spectrum is the man or woman pushing for personal growth and then waking up in a marriage of many years to find a stranger. The stranger they come to find is not so much about their mate being unfamiliar but more so about an awakening to the existence of the deep self and how that connection makes it impossible to go back to the illusions of the conscious self. There are few things stranger than waking up to find yourself being someone, whom you have always somehow suspected, you are not. This is the nature of the deep self breezing in with hints and clues about the self's deeper nature that cannot be determined nor defined by any external authority nor contained by any collection of beliefs. The deep self creates within the conscious self a yearning for both a freedom from our illusions and a hope for a self that is yet to be discovered."

"Never underestimate the resident shaman," Eduardo said, smiling at his mother. "Gabriella, are you still with us?"

"I was miles away, thanks to Mama's gorgeous picture story, but I'm on my way back. So where are we?"

"We're at the place where I need a summary," Lindsay said, "something that will put all the pieces together for me in a neat little package. Also, we still need to clarify Grace's point surrounding a sexual violation event and the immortality of inner angels."

"That's right, I'd almost forgotten," Eduardo added.

"A complete summary will be no easy task. Any volunteers?" Gaby asked, looking directly at her mother.

"I think I just might be able to accommodate you, but I'm afraid Eduardo gave me more credit than I deserve. Most of that gorgeous picture story comes from this," Margarita said, holding up book bound and covered in a deep purple.

"I can't wait to hear what you found, Mama, but I think I need a short break first," Eduardo said.

"Why is it that the only male in the room has the smallest bladder?" Gaby asked teasingly.

"Well, you know what they say about men with small bladders," Eduardo replied with a smile as he collected the china.

"No, what do they say?" Gaby challenged.

"I have no idea. I was hoping you knew. When you figure it out, please get back to me. I believe you have all my numbers, or you could just text me if you prefer," he teased back, making his way to the kitchen.

"Here we go again," Lindsay said with a giggle.

"Mama, lets finish up in the front room," Gaby suggested. "The couches are more comfortable, and I have a strong feeling that siesta will be calling sometime soon."

"Very good, Gabriella," Margarita replied. "We'll meet in the front room for summary and siesta."

CHAPTER SEVEN

There Are Other Worlds than These

Refreshed from their break, the group filtered in one by one to the sitting room. While Eduardo and Margarita sat in comfortable lounge chairs, Gaby and Lindsay chose to stretch out on the two soft cushioned sofas.

"Is everyone comfortable?" Eduardo asked with a smile as he tossed a pillow at his sister.

"That's the second pillow I've been hit with today. If you know what's good for you, there will not be a third."

"That sounds like a challenge," Eduardo said.

"Mama, please start before Eddie-san ruins this delicious, intellectual momentum we've got going here."

"Oh yes, let's get started, Mama," Eduardo said, flashing Lindsay a wink and a smile. "I think you were going to tell us about that purple book."

"Actually, it's violet," Margarita began, smiling at the familiar repartee of her son and daughter. "I found the book several months ago while browsing at a little secondhand bookstore in Alton, Illinois. It's an allegory of sorts written by an author from a town in Vermont, although I cannot seem to determine where. The title of the book is *Hope's Journey through the Forest of Illusions*. The author's name, by some strange twist of irony, is Hope Aaron. I did a little research and discovered that the book was published about one year ago by a publisher in Vermont. It is a small publishing company called Word of Mouth Publishing. To my surprise, after an exhaustive search, there is no Word of Mouth Publishing, not in Vermont nor anywhere else for that matter. It's become a bit of a mystery that is quite puzzling, as the writing and the story are quite extraordinary."

"Wow, that it is puzzle," Lindsay said, her brow furrowed in consternation. "I would love to help you solve that riddle."

"Seriously, Mama," Gaby said with sincerity, "if you need to solve a mystery, Lindsay is your girl."

"You're hired," Margarita said, nodding at Lindsay with a wink and a smile.

"So what's the story, Mama?" Eduardo asked.

"The story surrounds the strange truth that we, as human souls, are not born with a conscious knowledge of our authentic self, which is to say that we don't know who we truly are, what we are truly worth, nor why we are truly here. The story suggests that this knowledge must be learned. The author poses that to earn the conscious knowledge of the deep self, the conscious self must journey inward toward the center of the soul. This leads to the idea of the conscious self as the Traveler. In turn, the deep self, often called the authentic self, reaches out to the conscious self from the universe within."

"I think I'm with you so far, Mama, but could you give me a better feel for the conscious self?" Gaby asked.

"Certainly, mi amore, the conscious self is the sum of the collected information about the self that one has received from a host of external sources in caretaker positions such as parents, guardians, peers, teachers etc. The conscious self has no control over the formative messages received surrounding the identity and worth of oneself. The child does not get to choose the parent, or caretaker, nor the messages inherited from these significant others who reside within the child's external universe. These core beliefs accumulate throughout the developmental years of the conscious self, also known as the Traveler. The author uses trees to represent the core beliefs that grow within the mind of the Traveler. She clarifies that each tree is given substance and volume from the faith of the child within who embraces those beliefs one by one as they are handed down to the child from these others. The author gives the example that if a child embraced four core beliefs per day over a twelve-year period using this equation ($4 \times 365 \times 12$), that child would have 17,520 trees in his or her core belief forest."

"With an inner child at the exact age and time that the core belief was embraced sitting under that tree, staring up at the tree with the mesmerized faith of a child," Gaby finished incredulously at the thought.

"Exactly," Margarita continued, "then in an effort to find choice, the free will of that child begins to design a way to claim independence from that forest. This pursuit of autonomy will occur whether the core beliefs radiate light or darkness, whether the energy in that forest is positive or negative. In an effort to accomplish this independence, the individual designs a compensatory thinking system to push back against the core belief thinking system. The author poses that in this way, the conscious self busies itself with the task of proving or disproving those oppressive core beliefs by redefining the Traveler's identity and worth in compensatory terms. These pushback efforts are driven by the force that we call free will."

"Could you give us an example?" Eduardo asked.

"Sure, let's say that the general theme of an individual's core belief forest is that the individual is just not good enough. Let's call her Jane. So somewhere around just postpuberty, when the free will in each of us tends to rise up, Jane decides to leave the 'I'm not good enough' identity, and she finds a compensatory belief to push back against the designs of the core belief forest. She employs perfectionism. The idea is that if she is perfect, then 'I'm not good enough' creatures from the core belief forest must leave her alone. So she gets on her perfection treadmill each day, and at the end of the day, when the creature knocks on the door, she opens it, shows him her registered perfection treadmill mileage for the day, and then she slams the door in his face. The creature must then return to the forest. Her accumulated mileage on the treadmill fashions a system of resistance, which gives her shelter from the oppression of her core beliefs. She begins to develop a sense that she is freeing herself from the confining notions of her youth."

"Oh, Mama, that is so true on so many levels," Gaby exclaimed, "but let me add a wrinkle. What if Jane's core beliefs were entirely positive like kind and loving from caring, nurturing parents?"

"Yes, great question and from such a surprising source," Eduardo said, giving Lindsay a wink.

"Do please get over yourself, Eddie-san."

"The point the author makes is not whether the core beliefs are positive or negative but rather that those beliefs originated from external perceptions. She clarifies that these perceived external authority figures who initially delivered these core belief messages simply do not have the depth nor the qualifications to know in its entirety the truth and worth surrounding the divine intention of you. Thus, the compensatory city is not about the battle of good versus bad, nor right versus wrong. It is rather about the determination and drive of free will and the individual pursuit of autonomy from the influence of the trees in the forest. If, for example, Jane were a preacher's daughter who embraced core belief themes that held to messages that she was a good girl, precious, and an angel, she may one-up 'good girl' by pursuing divine chastity, maybe even becoming a nun, to free her will from these positive definitions of her youth. If, on the other hand, she defied the good girl core beliefs, she may seek bad girl pathways in order to claim independence from those good girl core beliefs."

"So, Margarita, what does the author say about how this battle between the city and the forest ends up?" Lindsay asked.

"Yes," Eduardo added, "what she said."

"Over time," Margarita continued with a laugh, "the individual builds a compensatory belief city with each building in the city designed to show autonomy from each tree in the core belief forest. This suggests that while the conscious self is inclined to rely on some external authority for definition and worth, it is also restless for a truth and wisdom that is independent of this reliance on an external authority. This is true because the conscious self somehow knows that these core beliefs and their value estimations are somehow false or incomplete. Although it must be said that the Traveler is hard-pressed to believe this truth. The Traveler's doubt stems primarily from the sheer faith of those inner children who believe so blindly in the authority of those significant others who authored their core beliefs. So the direct answer to your question, Lindsay, is that the battle never ends unless the individual discovers the truth."

"I think I know what that truth is," Gaby said, her eyes lit up with excitement. "If we're saying that all the core beliefs are not really true and the compensatory beliefs are designed by notions that give the illusion of freedom from our core beliefs, then the author is saying that we spend a major portion of our days here in this life using illusion to fight illusion. This suggests that the software of our minds regarding identity and worth is primarily programmed with illusion, and most of our tasking tends to surround the frustration of cycling and recycling illusion rather than engaging the hope of journeying down a linear pathway toward a divinely independent authenticity."

"I don't think I have ever been this far down the rabbit hole," Eduardo said, "but you really nailed that one down well, Gaby."

"I'm way over my head," Lindsay said, "but strangely eager to go deeper."

"Now," Margarita paused, smiling at the pensive faces of her young audience, "the author introduces three themes that are woven together in this storyline. The themes include the two that we have just been discussing, the journey toward authenticity and the role of addiction as a barrier to that journey, and the third theme, in a surprising turn of events, the impact of a sexual violation event on the soul."

"Oh my god," Lindsay said, "now this is really blowing my mind all the way out."

"This is unbelievable," Gaby said. "How did she approach this, Mama, while still including the other themes? I mean sexual trauma is so heavy, how could she possibly tie it all together?"

"Well, Ms. Aaron, accomplishes this by choosing the perfect narrator to tell the story about what happens in the soul before during and after a sexual violation event. This narrator then tells her story to the most receptive audience imaginable"

"Ok, I give up, Mama," Eduardo said, his hands in the air. "Who pray tell is the perfect narrator?"

"She is a being both divine and mortal who lives within each and every soul."

"I think I know who the audience is," Gaby said, "but I'm not sure on the narrator. The audience has to be survivors of sex abuse."

"Exactly right, Gabriella," Margarita said, giving her daughter a proud smile.

"It seems like such a strange direction for the author to go when talking about the complexities of authenticity."

"Who knows, little brother, maybe surviving violation is what it took for the author to find the path to authenticity."

"I can't argue with that."

"So how does Hope introduce the story, Margarita?" Lindsay asked.

"She begins," Margarita continued, "by introducing the idea of the inward journey toward authenticity. She then lays out what we might call a map of the soul, with the suggestion that our souls, by divine design, possess a natural infrastructure. She uses ocean depths as a metaphor to help us gain some insight into the layers of our souls. Hope then uses the notions of country and kingdom to describe the systems that govern each of those levels."

"Here is an excerpt of the author's description of the journey along with a portrayal of the soul with its layers and kingdoms. The author begins her story as I had mentioned by specifically addressing Travelers who are surviving the impact of any form of sexual violation. The narrator, as yet unrevealed, alludes to her identity as a hallowed being who lives deep within the soul."

Opening the violet-colored book to her first marker, Margarita began to read.

* * *

I come to you now, dear Traveler, as you walk that survivor path. I must reach you with this message, may your brave heart hear my pleas, may you hear Epiphany's whisper, "There are other worlds than these."

I come to you, dear child, from that deep country, that sacred place, from the deepest realm within your soul. I will share my identity with you in good time, but this I will tell you.

I am the one who walks there down the pathways, along the streams, and up those secret lanes through the wood. I send you light and warmth from that region of the soul that is called the borderlands. I have but one purpose, to show you the truth about just how beloved you truly are. Mine is a difficult task mostly because of the strange truth that the real truth seems so unbelievable. As if this mission to shine a light on this profound certainty of your singular significance were not hard enough, there is now within you a terrible disturbance that is taking so much of your energy to survive. My hope is to clarify that disturbance and lead you back to the path toward that self that we call authentic, that place that you never knew, you never knew.

I must also tell you that I am now a refugee, secreted to this inner sanctuary. It is from this place of wondrous solitude that I send you a message so imperative that it is nothing less than divine intervention. I have so much to tell you, so many secrets of the soul. So it is with great urgency that I endeavor to reach you. I pray now that you will listen and somehow hear me with all your heart and mind.

This is the story about one woman's journey, the journey toward authenticity. Imagine if you can, the divine intention of you, that original thought embryo that evolved into the full maturation of your inner being, giving you a significance so irreplaceable that the universe is irrevocably altered by the absence of your presence. The notion that the sense of this personal meaning of our lives is elusive and the voice of our purpose, more a whisper than a shout, certainly seems to be a common experience. The echoes of self-doubt, the feeling of being a bit lost at times, maybe even disoriented like waking up in a mystery without any clues. How mysterious that we are born in this condition so estranged from the truth of who we are and why we're here.

It's been said that we are like travelers in a strange land and that here at this place, we are as far from home as we ever shall be. What if home is not so much a place as it is a being, a being that radiates the warmth of home and hearth? What if there is such a being residing there in the deep inner country of our souls, a being rich in the knowledge of our singular purpose and worth? What if this being is whole and complete, even pristine, a being that cannot be added to nor subtracted from? What if our primary purpose here in this life is to take the journey to find that being and walk side by side with our authentic self?"

In order to begin this journey, we must first have a vision of the terrain. What if it were true that similar to using only a fraction of our brain that we, too, have discovered only a fraction of our soul? Imagine that the human mind, like the ocean, is multilayered and multidimensional. Imagine that each layer is a country, a literal kingdom in your mind, complete with king and queen, custom and castle, forests and streams, village and common folk, magicians and knights with creatures, and magic emanating from both the dark and the light.

Using the ocean layers as a gauge to mark the depths of the soul's layers, we will attempt to map the multifeatured territory of what is sometimes called the Ghost in the Bio-Suit.

The first layer is the Epipelagic soul level, also called the sunlight zone because it is the most visible layer of the soul. Compared to the other regions of the soul, the sunlight zone is shallow. This layer contains the Compensatory City, which is comprised of the specific images that we seek to present to the outside world. This city where resides the conscious self, or Traveler, consists of compensatory beliefs that are purposed to establish independence from the core beliefs that determine our initial impressions surrounding our identity and worth. For each core belief tree, there is a corresponding compensatory belief building designed to challenge and override that core belief."

The compensatory layer is built on the notion that free will gives us control over past influences. This is confirmed by the idea that doing things your way is evidence that your mind is free from core belief influence. The Compensatory City will offer a showcase of one's independent colors. These colors may embrace or defy the colors handed down to us from those in whom we so believed. This compensatory thinking system also seeks to alter the external universe in an attempt to resolve disturbance and dissonance ceaselessly echoing from the core belief forest. Thus, if the forest echo's with "I'm not good enough," the shout back from the Compensatory City is "Oh really? Just look at my perfect city. Perfection proof that I am good enough and I will prove it again tomorrow." Above all, this city must confirm and endorse the belief that that you are in control.

The second layer is the Mesopelagic soul layer, also called the twilight zone because this region of the soul holds the illusion of both darkness and light. The twilight zone is said to hold both the promise of the light of hope and the judgement of the darkness of despair. This layer consists of the core belief forest, also known as the Forest of Illusions. The conscious self, or Traveler, also has access to this region of the soul and is able to travel in both the forest and the city.

This ancient primordial forest is comprised of identity and worth definition trees (beliefs). A belief tree appears each time that a child embraces a belief about their identity and/or worth. It is not the child's faith in the belief that gives the tree it's substance but is rather the child's faith in the authority figure who handed down the definition. Over time, as the trees are nurtured by the blind faith of the children who sit under the trees, the beliefs themselves become absolute. It is in this way that the children gradually lose all sense of where the beliefs end and they begin.

The forest is considered ancient because many of these characterization trees are handed down from generation to generation. These hand-me-down beliefs supported by generations of blind devotion wield enormous power in the vast expanse of this region of the psyche. Consequently, these beliefs become living, breathing organisms running loops of circular thinking systems that are both closed and self-sustaining. Thus, the Core Belief Forest is destined to become one of the most compelling forces within the human mind, and yet these belief trees that are held there by the steadfast loyalty of the children who embrace them are founded upon illusion.

The beliefs are illusion primarily because the perceptions of external authority figures whether negative or positive will be tainted and distorted by the lenses through which they view the child. These lenses are tainted because the authority figures' view will be influenced by their own core beliefs. Which is to say external sources cannot tell you who you are. You must look within yourself to find the divine intention of you.

The southernmost part of this land mass that holds the Illusion Forest serves as a sanctuary for those sacred beings that are spirit guides to the divine intention of you. There are guides that live in the shadow and those that live in the light. These virtuous characters that inhabit this area that lies between the Forest of Illusions and the deep valley of the unconscious provide a sacred presence that can be sensed by the conscious self. This presence may take the form of both great comfort and great sorrow. This region is separated from the Core Belief Forest by a mountain range known as the Alps of Illumination. The area is divided by the River of Divergence with the Shadowlands and the Kingdom of the Fates to the east and the Province of Prosperity and the Tranquil Forest to the west. Children have a keen sense of these beings who, in those early years, travel across the alps for frequent visits with the conscious self. As the child grows, the visits become less and less regular. This tends to occur because the child has become absorbed with a devotion to the illusion trees in the forest.

The landscape in these borderlands is serene with rolling meadows, shallow brooks, flowered hillsides, and lush green woodlands. Just one mile north of the plunging cliffsides that lead down to those unfathomable depths of the psyche unawares, there is a small cottage in the woods. The Maiden Worth lives there, where she holds and cares for all the treasures of the soul. Her parents, Mother Serenity and Father Wisdom, visit often but tend to reside in the region of the soul known as the Sacred Realm. Her twin sister of whom her parents rarely speak ran away one day long ago. She lives now in the Shadowlands, somewhere to the west of the River of Divergence. Just where, Worth does not know, but every so often her estranged sister sends a flock of crows who bring chatter about how it is she might be fairing.

Worth dearly loves her life of solitude and her daily communion with the nature of the borderlands, a nature that holds the divine promise of original shape. "The mold was broken, indeed," Worth would scoff at the saying, "There never was a mold, only a wild untamed artist."

This maiden within you holds a beauty so raw, I cannot find words in your world that might describe her countenance. This I can tell you, there is magic in her and a light that has the power and intensity to reach each and every crack and crevice of the soul. Her cousins Hope and Innocence are frequent visitors as are her aunt Destiny and uncle Contentment. They do so enjoy those early days when the clarity of the soul's original shape is as yet unspoiled by distortion. The best days are when the Traveler believes in Worth's existence within her and a connection is made in the conscious mind. As the Traveler allows the Maiden to hold her hand, there in that first layer of the soul, remarkable transformations race across the landscape of the psyche. Generally, however, the Traveler is only able to maintain this faith for short periods of time before her faith in her illusions reasserts itself returning her to the soul-scape of the Traveler's distorted perception of self.

As the illusion trees grow and the conscious mind begins to step further and further away from its authenticity, the Traveler gives less and less attention to those guardians in the borderlands of original shape. Even so, as the conscious self pursues that autonomous path, Worth shines her light on her beloved Traveler. Wrapping jeweled worth sensations in mystical spirit winds, she sends daily messages north in hopes that the Traveler might discover the immeasurable fortune within her soul. Moving about her cottage and the hallowed woodland trails, Worth would often think about her estranged sister and what she might be thinking there in the Shadowlands to the east. She sends out loving kindness to her sister each night in her prayers and throughout the day, often wondering what her sister's purpose in this soul might actually be. "It is not as if," she sometimes thinks out loud, "she does not have some purpose too, but that is a truth and telling somehow beyond my grasp."

The third layer is the Bathypelagic soul layer, also known as the midnight zone primarily because it is shrouded in darkness but also because it communicates to us through our dreams. The midnight zone, also known as Midworld as it is the middle layer of the soul, houses the unconscious, which serves as both a guardian and healer. The conscious self generally cannot access this dark and hidden layer of the soul. The unconscious serves as a protector in the event of threatening emotional disturbances or forbidden acts that might threaten the sanity of the conscious mind. These memories are concealed and stored there in the midnight zone until the conscious mind is able to process the event without damage to the soul. The unconscious also holds information surrounding significant attachment principles that are formed during those critical bonding moments in childhood. The unconscious is also the home of the animus, sometimes called the beloved, which is the individual's notion of the ideal partner or soul mate. The beloved is the product of attachment principles that plant indelible footprints on the white sand beaches of romantic hope.

The primary task of the unconscious is to resolve disturbance and discord within the conscious mind using dreams. Where the Compensatory City addresses conscious discord from the outside in, attempting to actually alter the external universe to accommodate the internal views, the unconscious attempts to solve cognitive dissonance from the inside out by altering internal resolutions with solution-focused dreams.

The fourth layer is the Abyssopelagic layer of the soul, also called the abyss primarily because of its depth from the surface of the soul. It's been said that when we look into the abyss, we will finally see our self as we actually are. This layer of the soul is comprised of that deep inner country of the authentic self. The authentic self is that deep inner being that is completely independent of all the beliefs and illusions that reside within the conscious mind. This deep self is whole and pristine and cannot be added to nor subtracted from. One of your deep self's remarkable gifts is balance. There is no situation in which your authenticity cannot find the precise equation for balance in any single moment nor season of your life. There is no power nor persuasion that could alter nor deter this magic sense within the being of your authentic self.

This fourth layer of our souls holds everything that surrounds the divine intention of you including your identity, your purpose, and your worth. While the conscious self does not have access to the fourth layer of the soul, the authentic self has access to the all layers of the soul except for the fifth layer.

One of the primary tasks of this life is for the Traveler to discover and journey toward the authentic self. This is a journey that is sometimes called the Self-Growth Pathway. This journey involves the work of moving from a survival gratification state of consciousness to a growth state of consciousness. This work requires the conscious self to identify, discredit, and discard illusions surrounding one's identity and worth that obscure the truth of one's authenticity.

Should the Traveler take a step toward the authentic self, the deep self will take one step back. This is true not because the deep self does not wish to embrace you but rather because all those illusions that you believe in more than you believe in your own authenticity stand between you and your deep self. It is your illusions that push the deep self back a step. When the Traveler begins to believe in his authenticity over his illusions, the authentic self begins to move toward the Traveler and vice versa. Each time the Traveler exposes and surrenders an illusion, he steps closer to the state of disillusionment. When the illusions in the forest fade to a shimmer, the Traveler begins his journey through the desert of Whoami. This is a journey that must start with the three words "I don't know," a condition otherwise known as the empty cup. It is there in that desert of disillusionment where the Traveler first meets the authentic self.

The fifth layer is the Hadalpelagic layer of the soul, also called the sacred realm because it it's the divine within us. This is the spirit place, a domain within our soul that is both sacred and supernatural. The hosts that inhabit this the deepest of all realms cannot be altered nor even touched by human will or intention. This is true because the inhabitants are both mortal and divine. These beings in human terms are generally known as the virtues. It is said that the virtues live there not as a set of morals and codes to live by but rather as a literal family of sacred beings and angels. These spiritual guardians, living there within this mystical domain that resides in each and every soul, have the ability to travel into any and all layers of the soul.

Each character of virtue also has a twin, like two sides of a single coin. One side is in the light and one in the dark, the twin for Reverence is Depravity, Charity's twin is Defilement, Hope's twin is Despair, and so forth. These characters in the dark are not in and of themselves evil. Evil is a supernatural force that uses this inherent darkness to desecrate the sanctity of life. Overall, dark does not mean bad but is rather more about the meaning of suffering and the role that it plays in our lives. Dark in its natural state surrounds the absence of the revelations of the light. Dark is the veil that covers the secrets that are as yet unknown. The personalities in the dark are simply the characters of contrast created to give light its vision and darkness its mystery. While the characters such as Despair, Doubt, and Blame live in the Shadowlands, the characters of Hope, Wisdom, and Charity live in the Lands of Illumination. The Shadowlands and the Lands of Illumination, separated by the River of Divergence, run through each and every layer of the soul. Thus, there is shadow and light in each and every layer of the soul.

The ideal for each soul is to maintain a state of balance. Balance is achieved and maintained by the primary muscle of the soul, which is generally known as Faith or one's ability to believe. Thus, the saying "We live where we believe." The secret to balance is to believe in the being of authenticity more than any belief. To do this, we must go on the journey to surrender our illusions and free our mind to see the truth of our authenticity. In the absence of this knowledge, individuals generally abide by the supporting characters of those beliefs that they have embraced.

However, in the event that the conscious self believes with exaggerated fervor in one character in the light or some contrasting character in the dark, a grave imbalance takes place within the kingdom of the mind. This imbalance may lead to internal distress such as a crisis of Despair or Doubt, or a crisis of Arrogance or Martyrdom. This condition within the soul, sometimes called cognitive dissonance, alerts that psyche that there is a power differential in the kingdom that is causing disorder.

Among the experiences that may generate alarming disturbances within the soul is what is known as a sexual violation event. Amid all the experiences, borne from the external universe that may collide with the foundational elements of the soul, few rival the tornadic impact of sexual violation. I wish to attempt to give you a vision of this event and hope to bring to you some enlightenment surrounding the ways in which the sacred has anticipated this horrific happening. There is magic within you, child, a magic wiser and a warrior fiercer than the most profane of predators, healers with balms that will stagger your imagination, and spirit guides that will call you by name, embrace you with the strength of your purpose here, and lead you back to the path, the one that goes to that place you call home.

I should note that in the event of a soul disturbance, the authentic self may summon a virtue being, should the conscious self become lost or overwhelmed with distress. Sometimes the virtue being may be called from the Shadowlands or at times from the Isle of Illumination. The deep self summons this aide from the sacred to make an attempt to restore some semblance of balance to the soul. Balance is an important prerequisite to self-growth as it is difficult for the distressed soul to focus on anything more than the next breath of survival.

I will share with you one final note on soul infrastructure. This information surrounds the functional elements of the psyche, what we might call the muscles of the soul. I impart to you now, my valiant survivor, this deep and specific intelligence to help you understand just how heroic your heart actually is.

We could spend hours on the nature of each soul element, but in the interest of brevity, I shall just name them and frame the significance of the mass and volume of these elements in the briefest of descriptions. There are ten operational elements in the soul, five running from east to west latitude and five from north to south longitude. The elements running east to west through every layer of the soul include free will, social, sexual, relationship, and physical and north to south include worth, identity, emotional, cognitive, and spiritual. Each element is comprised of approximately seven to nine features that cover the specific operational features of each element.

I share this information to bring some clarity to the reasons for the level of disturbance that is generated by a sexual violation event. This means that the ripple effect of the violation may well have impacted up to seventy different regions of the soul, giving us a scope of the wound's mass. The depth of the wound is measured by the number of incidents. Should an individual have survived ten incidents of sexual violation, using our geographic metaphor of miles, the wound would measure to be seventy square miles in mass times ten miles in depth. This, my dear, not only makes your survivorship courageous, it also makes you a living miracle.

Here in this brave beginning, dear Traveler, I have cast some light on the vast and mystical world within you. Now that you have a vision for the terrain within the soul, you are ready to hear my story, the story of Caroline. By story's end, my fervent hope is that you will see the courage and purpose of my sister and the vital role that she plays in your survivorship.

Before I begin, I must tell you that even now as you read this message, I live and breathe within you, yes, this is a truth, I am the Maiden Worth, untouched and alive.

* * *

"Oh my god," Gaby exclaimed, "talk about thinking outside the box! I'm not sure how the author hopes to support this, but the very idea that Worth could come through a sexual violation alive, let alone untouched, seems to defy imagination."

"I just know," Eduardo said with uncharacteristic ferocity, "that it would just be so cool if she can. If it could really be true."

"Yes, mi amore," Margarita said, looking down quickly to hide the shine in her eyes, "so cool."

"So," Lindsay began, "Caroline's story must be about how a sexual violation experience led to an addiction that is keeping her from her journey toward authenticity."

"There she goes again," Eduardo said, giving his sister a wink.

"Yes, that's correct, Lindsay, and if you can find yourself some pluck, we can explore one final passage to clarify this idea about how addiction is founded upon the laws of consumption. I am afraid however that the story about Worth and her sister must for now remain a mystery."

"I think I've got one more in me as long as you do, Margarita," Lindsay replied with a smile.

"Maybe, just one more."

"I can read for you, Mama," Gaby said, standing up and kneeling to give her mother a kiss on the cheek. "Just a quick powder room break and a good jolt of espresso, and I'll be good to go."

"You get the powder and I'll get the espresso," Lindsay said, collecting empty cups and following her friend to the kitchen.

"Mama, can I get you something?" Eduardo asked.

"Yes, a tall glass of iced tea with lemon and a little honey."

"Coming right up."

"Hey, Mama," Gaby called from the kitchen, "Lindsay had an idea to move out to the deck for the final passage, what do you think?"

"I think she is psychic. I was thinking the same thing."

"Hear that, you're psychic, Lindz," Eduardo said. "What do you think, you could like maybe start with a phone line, you know, 1-800-4-sights."

Margarita chuckled to herself as she heard Lindsay giggle as she replied, "I don't think so, Eddie-san, but I will predict that you don't have much of a future in advertising."

"Good information, Lindsay. I will definitely give it some thought."

CHAPTER EIGHT

Hope's Journey Begins

The group took some time to refresh themselves. Taking a moment in their separate spaces, they appreciated the simple magic of a splash of cool water. Toweling off, they lingered in that moment of cleanliness as the sensation of white cotton cleared away hazy horizons to reveal clarity's crystalline view. They relish the comfort of woolen sweaters as they head out to the patio, appreciating how the fabric's weight was able to fend off the mild chill of the damp March wind. The sky was overcast, and the air held the weight of the moisture that may yet become the rain that had been forecasted to fall in the early morning. In spite of the cloudy weather, there was a mood of budding inspiration amid the group as they went about their preparations with a quiet and even comforting resolve. There was an unexpected communion; they were going somewhere, to a place that they intuited held a singular importance. They seemed to share this quiet determination to savor each and every step.

Eduardo started up the outdoor firepit as his mind wrestled with thoughts and concepts that had long since ripped to shreds the proverbial edge of his mental envelop. Lindsay came out and began to arrange cushions and blankets on roomy patio chairs though her mind, too, was elsewhere. Constructing and reconstructing lounge chair nests as her mind attempted to assume command over thought soldiers that refused to follow orders, constantly stepping out of their columns and confounding any semblance of formation. Gaby came out with a tray of hot chocolate laced with espresso and whipped crème. Eduardo placed miniature tables next to each chair and carefully placed a cup on each of the tables.

Margarita came out to find the three absorbed in their reveries as they took thoughtful sips from fragrant steaming mugs. Marveling at their energy, she settled into her chair.

"Do you want me to read, Mama?" Gaby asked as her mother got comfortable

"No, I think I would like to be the guide to the next milestone on our quest."

"Sounds good, Mama, we are ready to follow your lead."

* * *

The Dreamwatcher Diaries

The story is about Caroline, a woman in her late twenties living in the City of Angels. Caroline, gifted with both uncommon beauty and intelligence, is the child of techno wizards who tend to love their life in the cyber world a bit more than their existence in the real world. As parents, they tend to rely on the creeds "you can always do better" and "the world is not enough." As you can imagine, Caroline is quickly baptized in the notions surrounding conditional acceptance. Being a good student, she quickly becomes an expert on the pursuit of approval by process of performance perfection. Standards of excellence hold sway in a core belief forest that is overrun with judges and critics.

Amid her pursuits at the tender age of twelve years old, she is molested by her mother's older brother, who is forty-five years old at the time of the abuse. Uncle Gregory, who moved to LA around Caroline's eighth birthday, lavished her with his full charm and attention. Surviving for many years now the emotional unavailability of her parents, Caroline took to her uncle's attention like a bee to honey. The first incident of abuse occurred on Caroline's twelfth birthday at the carnival, which comes to town in the fall of each year. They were on the Ferris wheel the first time and then again when they rode the car through the House of Horrors. These sexual violation events carry on for more than two years before Caroline finds the courage to tell one of her teachers at school. At first, her mother does not believe her, accusing Caroline of making up stories to get attention. Her father however supports her claim, but then remedies the situation by sending her to a boarding school more than one thousand miles from her home.

The combination of the sexual abuse and her striving for perfection take their toll on Caroline as she strives to find a way to survive this private world in which she finds herself. It was in the midst of this striving that she discovers the power of seduction and promiscuity. She begins to develop a sense of tenuous control over that helpless girl within her, the one who was betrayed. By the time she enters her late twenties, Caroline has perfected her skill sets in the game of seduce and conquer. She uses drugs and alcohol at times to escape her body and to help transport her to a place of numbness where the judges and demons could not reach her.

Caroline's authentic self, Violet, observing her conscious self from her home there in the fourth level of the soul, becomes alarmed at the reckless nature of Caroline's lifestyle. She watches as Caroline steps further and further from her purpose and her path. Violet fears that the current level of Caroline's sense of hopelessness is bordering upon despair. Distressed by these developments and by Caroline's growing dependence on consumption states of consciousness, Violet summons Hope and Destiny to engage divine intervention. The authentic self requests that Hope and Destiny might make the journey north to the conscious self and help Caroline to free her mind from her dependence on the pursuit of desire and the lifestyle of chasing fantasy states of consciousness and the bliss illusions therein.

This brings us to our next passage, which surrounds our earlier discussion on both illusion and the nature of addiction. This rather ethereal episode also includes some surprising insights into the impact of sexual violation events on the human soul. As the author navigates these captivating occurrences playing out within Caroline's soul, she switches strategically from the physical world of Caroline's conscious self (the Traveler) to the world deep inside Caroline, where Destiny and Hope, responding to Violet's (the authentic self's) summons, begin their journey north. As Hope travels with her mother, Destiny, from the deepest and southernmost layer of the soul, that level called the Sacred Realm, she is instructed by Destiny on the nature of each layer of the soul. Hope also receives instruction on the nature of the sexual consumption lifestyle (sex addiction), the nature of desire coupled with fantasy, and the outcome of being consumed by sexual consumption, which is the state of consciousness known as "becoming the wanting."

Meanwhile, in the conscious mind, the author follows Caroline as she is struggling with the sense that she has lost control of her life. She feels the hollowness of the great void within herself as she chases desire no longer in the driver's seat of the fantasy vehicle that she has leased to own. It has been many years since she has felt any semblance of meaning or hope.

Just before leaving on their sacred mission, Destiny imparts an urgency to her daughter surrounding the three primary pursuits of this ethereal endeavor. Destiny specifies that Hope must first free Caroline's mind from the oppression of sexual consumption, second, she must show her the spirit guide that has the wisdom and power to help Caroline recover the Worth that was taken on her twelfth birthday, and finally Hope must guide the Traveler to the path, the path that leads to that deep Violet country, to that place of authenticity.

The passage I read now begins with Hope and her mother deep inside Caroline's inner universe. Hope takes the form of a twelve-year-old girl, the age when Caroline felt some semblance of wholeness in spite of the harsh judgments of the conditional acceptance trees in her core belief forest. Hope is both mortal and divine and is approaching that day when she will find her wings. This is symbolic with a happening that is typical of most coming of age girls as they discover the promise and the dream of realizing their feminine potential. Hope is excited about this momentous milestone, and it is all she can do at times to keep her feet on the ground. It is early morning, and having left the pasture lands of the Sacred Realm, they are just now passing through the borderlands into the fourth layer of the soul called the abyss, the country of authenticity.

* * *

The Dreamwatcher Diaries

Margarita paused and, smiling at the rapt expressions of her youthful audience, began to read.

* * *

Hope looked over at her mother to ask about where they were exactly when she saw the determined look on Destiny's face. Knowing that look, Hope held her tongue and concentrated instead on matching her mother's powerful stride. The excitement of walking this path that wove through the meadowlands in the country of authenticity was more than enough to persuade her to keep her silence. She did know that the path wound its way toward Midworld, the layer of the soul that the external world calls the unconscious. Hope thought to herself, *I might as well just enjoy the view*. Putting her stride on cruise control, Hope allowed her senses to breathe in the vision splendor that stretched to the east and west of her. The meadows are covered with violets stretching as far as the eye can see. The blooms bow as they pass, creating a vision of violet-covered velvet quivering under the gentle stroke of an unseen hand. The blue sky complimented by the rising fire of the sun bathes the violet fields in a warmth that gently persuades the release of their perfume. Hope smiled as she felt the breeze, for this was a moment that she had been dreaming of, the moment when the breeze picked up the scent. Like a personal messenger, the wind carried the fragrant package to Hope's waiting senses. As the messenger delivered the delicious scent, which seemed to envelop her body, in a caring caress, she could almost taste the color of violet. She heard her mother's contented sigh as she, too, took in Violet's gift. Hope wondered at the mystery of the tickle that filled her belly as the color's scent swam through her. Her fingers rose to press against her face to feel the heat of the blush that had blossomed on her cheeks.

"It's such a beautiful gift, isn't it, Mother?" Hope asked, smiling at her mother's face lifting toward the sky.

"Yes, it is, Hope. Yes, it is," Destiny replied with a smile of her own.

Hope watched her mother's eyes suddenly take on the deep shine of familial recognition. Destiny's arms open and close around her waist, with her body moving in a rocking motion in the gesture of a warm embrace. Hope turned to see who it was that had caught her mother's eyes.

It is Violet herself standing in the field of flowers just to the west. She is a vision of beauty. Her dark hair, that falls full and luxurious around her shoulders, is flowing in the breeze, framing the allure of her striking features. In spite of her moderate distance from the road, Hope can still see the clarity of the smile in the almond shape of her deep-brown eyes. She traces the curve of Violet's full lips and wonders at the rich texture of her cream-colored complexion that pours so evenly from her forehead and prominent cheekbones over the china of her delicate chin. Her neck is long and elegant, even fragile in contrast to the square strength of her shoulders and the sudden swell of her breasts. Her white gown flows with the exquisite curves of her body undulating in the breeze, clinging and releasing her shape like two lovers lost in the steps of a ballroom coupling. Hope looks down at her own body and smiles at the thought of having some curves of her own someday. Looking up, she watches as Violet bends gracefully and plucks a large bouquet of violets swaying at her feet. Pressing the flowers between her palms in a prayerful pose, she closes her eyes and looking skyward blows out, sending the petals toward her and her mother in a musical swirl. The violets of the field respond joining the airborne petals showering mother and daughter with sensations of violet kisses from petal lips. The violets sing while they move in a rhythmic ballet. Although the violet dance lasts for only a few minutes or so, it seems much longer to Hope who feels as if she's been lifted heavenward and transported to a place so beautiful, she never wants to leave. It's as if she has fallen through a hidden window into the universe where the music goes when the instruments take their sleep. When Hope feels her feet touch the ground again, she finds herself swaying in the solo dance of the music fan, who having soaked up every note, continues to be the music's instrument long after the band stops playing. She opens her eyes to find her mother watching her with a look of adoration.

"I see you enjoyed Violet's blessing on our urgent journey," Destiny said with a smile.

"Yes, Mother, it touched me so deeply, and her beauty leaves me breathless."

"Yes, child, I know exactly what you mean," Destiny replied, looking out at the violet field and returning Violet's wave.

Hope waved herself and watched Violet's graceful walk as she headed back toward the inner country. As she watched, Hope carefully pulled at a violet petal caught in her hair. She released it to the wind, following its flight with a quiet reverence as it joined its sisters who were moving toward Violet like ducklings in headlong pursuit of mother duck's wake. Mother and daughter kept vigil until Violet was but a vague shape fading into the southern horizon.

As she disappears, Hope cannot hold back the creative energy stimulated by Violet's inspirational blessing. She begins to show her excitement by stepping effortlessly from a one-hand walkover into a backflip.

"So it's going to be soon right, Mother?" Hope asked, bouncing on the balls of her feet.

"Save your strength, sweetheart. We have lessons on the road ahead," Destiny replied, smiling at her daughter's enthusiasm.

"Yes, Mother," Hope replied, falling back in step with Destiny.

"It seems so pointless for Caroline to have traveled so far from her center. She has become so lost in the forest of her illusions, so disoriented. How can she let herself drift so far from Violet, her true self? Can't she see how extraordinary she is inside?"

"Caroline is chasing Desire, dear, and she can see little else than the fantasy just over the next horizon.

To reach her, you must understand that she will soon reach the place where she may become the wanting."

"The Wanting is the child of Consumption right, Mother?"

"Yes, Hope, and up ahead is the place where you will take your lesson on the ways of Consumption and Desire, so you must go now to that learning place within you, where your mind is open and your anticipation is still."

"Yes, Mother, I shall go there at once," Hope replied, slowing her step as she turned her focus inward.

Walking now in a measured silence, Destiny and Hope continue their trek along the path toward Hope's their next destination. As the sun reaches its peak, they stop for a quick lunch along the edge of a cozy brook. While Destiny laid out a simple lunch of fish, bread, and water, Hope closed her eyes and took in the music of the water's gurgle and babble. She tried to imagine where Caroline might be at this very moment and wondered if any part of her might sense the rhythm of this stream within her. Using all her concentration, she tried to connect with the Traveler's locale.

"Eat now, child," Destiny interrupted. "There will be time enough for connecting with Caroline. You must keep your strength up, even Hope needs her energy," Destiny finished, winking at her daughter's sheepish grin. After a short rest to allow their food to settle, Destiny and Hope resume their brisk pace toward Midworld.

Lawrence Gabriel

The road toward their destination gradually leaves behind the deep violet country of Caroline's center toward the place where the fields, meadows, and streams of the creative self give way to the dark gray sands of Whoami.

As the sun begins to dip into the western horizon, Hope begins to notice that the violets have become sparse over the past mile or so, and just ahead, she sees the last flower, tiny and fragile, standing boldly in the gray sand. Destiny calls for a short rest, and Hope walks over to the lone violet. Sitting cross-legged, she dips her head and inhales hoping to collect its scent. Surprised at the strength of the bloom's fragrance, she blows it a kiss and looking up to the heaven sends up a little prayer toward Caroline. It is the same prayer that she says each evening in hope that the Traveler might one day hear and awaken from the spell cast by the illusions of bliss.

"Wake up, Caroline, won't you, dear, will you come awake.

This could be that moment, oh what a moment you could make.

For another summer day has up and gone away.

With you in that place, where you think you have to stay.

So here I am to tell you if you did not hear before.

The truth is you don't have to live there anymore.

You've come upon the time the day is here to seize.

So baby let your hair down, feel it blowing in the breeze.

I'll be waiting for you even when you feel alone.

Oh, babe, I know you feel it, it's time that you come home."

"It is a beautiful prayer, Hope," Destiny said proudly as she pulled her daughter to her feet.

"Thanks, Mother," Hope whispered, "but there is one thing I must do before we go."

Hope gently pulls the flower from the desert floor and, pressing the stem between her hands in the same prayerful pose, pushes the tender petals skyward with a long sweet breath.

"I asked the violet to keep flying until it finds Caroline, Mother," Hope said, her voice becoming husky. "I also asked the scent to whisper in her ear the name of my sister," Hope said as twin tears rolled to the corners of her mouth, disappearing with an unconscious flick of her tongue.

"Innocence," Destiny said, releasing a single tear of her own.

"Tell me again, Mother, tell me why Innocence was taken so suddenly by the Dark Knight of Violation. It seems to be such a harsh and dire consequence for someone who did nothing but be herself."

"Caroline did a very human thing, sweetheart. She placed the weight of her existence into the hands of a man she trusted. It is a terrible fate that her uncle is an offender of children. There is no way for any soul to change the ways of Fate, least of all a child who seeks to be loved and watched over."

"I will never forget that night, Mother. The night that Innocence was taken, the skies were so dark. I tried to reach out to Caroline, but I could not seem to reach her. She just wouldn't let me in. Each and every entrance was closed off, even my secret entrances. I was shut out from the back door to the attic window. It rained inside of Caroline that whole day. I didn't think Violet would ever stop crying."

"Yes, she cried longer because Caroline stopped crying when her mother who did not understand her sadness scolded her for her tears."

"Mother, that was the year 'Innocence Walks' came to be, wasn't it?"

"Yes, dear, the tears from the emotional injury brought on by a sexual violation event are a critical part of the soul's healing process. During the sexual offense, deep within the borderlands of the Core Belief Forest, in the landmass that sits just north of the Unconscious and east of the Divergence River, violation trees begin to appear. The trees reach full growth over a twenty-four period, and by the morning of the second day, they cover an entire region of this shadow world that has come to be known as the Woodlands of Insult and Injury. The trees appear full grown because these are ancient timbers, filled with rings that can be traced all the way back to that first defilement of the sacred nature of the womb, the first seizure of the dignity of feminine beauty, and the first attempt to deny feminine intelligence. Like all other regions of the Forest of Illusions, a being sits under each tree. The being may be an adult or a child depending on the age at the time of the violation event. The violation trees, reverberating with the authority of the offender surrounding the message of the diminishment of the survivor's worth and meaning, gain strength from ancient echoes that this message is supported by the ages."

"It is such a force of strength, Mother, but I remember how Violet was determined to help Caroline push back to help her begin to believe that there was a way, a way forward to her authenticity."

"So, dear child, what'd she do?"

"Well, as you know, a violet grows for each tear Violet sheds. So she cried tens of thousands of tears until she had one thousand violets for each violation tree. The tear count was enough to fill the stretch of land in Authenticity Country that sits to the north, creating what we now call the north meadowlands. Violet herself named those violet fields Innocence Walks in honor of my sister. It sits right next to the fields where Innocence and I used to run and play. The meadows of Innocence Walks are my favorite, Mother. The flowers there seem to stand so proudly. Their color seems to light up as I pass by, and when the wind is just right, I can actually hear her whispering the words she used to say to me. I would chase her around the meadow, allowing her to get away as I feigned frustration. Her laughter was like music," Hope recalled with a sad and wistful smile. "Then I would finally catch her, pulling her down squealing with a tickled delight as I cushioned her short fall to the meadow grass. We would lay there breathless for a moment. Then she would say, 'Isn't not knowing wonderful, Hope? Having nothing ahead but the delight of the next discovery?' I would say, 'Knowing isn't so bad, sis, you might really like it.' She would look at me like I was crazy or something and say, 'What, and ruin the mystery? No way, big sis, why would I go and do a thing like that when I've got you to do it for me? You're my cushion, Hope, my unicorn-drawn carriage that ferries me to my next destination of joy.' She finished with a sweet hug and a kiss on my cheek. At times on nights when the moon is full, I can still feel her there just ahead of me, waiting to be caught, but somehow I never seem to be able reach her."

"She could not stay a child forever, sweetheart. All souls must let go of Innocence in order to grow. But when Innocence is taken before her time, before the natural order of her passing, Caroline herself must reclaim her free will in order achieve the self-growth milestone of self-reliance. This milestone will help her discover the path to her authenticity."

"How does it work, Mother, Caroline's recovery of her free will?"

"Caroline must find her way to the truth that the human soul was not designed to fight the Kingdom of Fate. The will of the sentient being has no control over the Fates. Humans cannot alter the path of lightning and whom it chooses to strike. In their hubris, however, and due to their leaning heavily on a blind faith in the illusion of control, humans have a strong tendency to storm Fate's castle gates with little regard for this inevitability. What I'm saying, Hope, is that human will cannot be free within the Kingdom of Fate. Its freedom lies elsewhere. Caroline must find that elsewhere. She must take back her will from that fated kingdom. Having surrendered that futile battle with the fates, she will discover a sweet freedom. This is the freedom to refocus her will on a healing journey, one that leads to that authentic country where her true destiny might be realized."

"I think I understand, Mother, but if humans do not have control over the fates, then what is it that the sentient being is able to govern?"

"Response, Hope, that is where human will holds dominion. They cannot control the fates, but they do have the ability to choose their response to the fates. Caroline will recover her sense of potency by rediscovering her freedom to choose how to respond to the violation and the resulting wound."

"Yes, I see now this is what is called response-ability."

"You've got it now, Hope."

"But I wonder how will Innocence survive there, in the Kingdom of Fate? I mean, how do you think she is fairing?"

"I get messages now and then. They come from a maiden who lives near the castle in a village called Resilience. The maiden sends messages when she can. She writes that there are spies everywhere, so she sends the messages by way of dove. I have learned that your sister is held captive in the Castle of Desolation. King Profane sees her as a jewel in his crown. His son Prince Blame visits her nightly. The prince, a boy frequently called the High Chair Tyrant by villagers, relishes his persecution pursuits, and he thoroughly enjoys plying her with his guilt-ridden speech. I hear that Queen Loathing also passes daily judgments on her, trying to break her spirits. I also learned that there is a maiden who works there in the keep. She secrets messages passed from Resilient villagers who bring her words of comfort and solace. This maiden is the one who brings her food and whispered direction about how to grow within those gloomy walls of accusation and doom. Even as we speak, she is learning to find spirit food in even the smallest things around her. She is becoming aware of an energy far greater than what she found in the cradle of dependence. Yet her capacity to believe in herself has suffered profound damage."

"Is the Maiden Worth at the Castle of Desolation too?"

"That is a question for another time, dear. We need to pick up the pace. We still have several miles to go, and the hour grows late."

"I feel much better knowing that Innocence is growing and discovering that she is more than she thought," Hope said, quickening her step in an effort to match her mother's long and graceful strides. "Mother, the maiden that whispers to her, what is her name?"

"Reverence," Destiny answered, increasing her speed as her face took on a look of focused determination. "Now less talk and more walk."

* * *

Some moments before Hope finds the last flower and sends up her prayer, a woman with a face identical to Violet's walks up to an LA bar and grill. This familial establishment holds a special meaning for her and is one of the few places in her world that she considers sacred. Morgan's Bar and Grill was a place that she and her best friend Marlee had discovered one day when they were seeking shelter from a sudden cloudburst. The owners, Jacob and Agnes, had named the place after their only daughter, who had gone missing at the tender age of thirteen. Her and Marlee had entered the restaurant on the anniversary of the day that Morgan had gone missing. When the couple discovered that Caroline had the same birthday as Morgan, a serendipitous connection was born. The couple had provided such warmth and hospitality that her and Marlee had toasted the bar and grill as their official home away from home. While the woman relished the warmth and connection of this nourishing establishment, she secretly felt a kinship to the missing girl sharing with her that sense of innocence lost. There were times, however, that the familial energy of the restaurant's homey atmosphere fed the urgency of the caged Tigress that paced inside of her. There was something about the sense of family that somehow triggered her insatiable hunger to seduce and conquer. Once awakened, all that the woman really wanted was to let the Tigress take her, body and soul. She both loved and hated the singlemindedness of the dark cat's hunger. Once freed from its cage, it sometimes took her to places that she never thought she would go. This concerned her more and more lately, but she thrilled to the Tigress's prowl. The excitement of chasing the eye candy that she knew she could taste was a powerful indulgence that compelled her to live out fantasy after fantasy regardless of risk and maybe even more so because of it. She fought back against the urge to give and lose herself to those ravenous appetites. Besides, Marlee needs me now, she thought as she opened the door to the restaurant.

The woman was greeted by a chorus of hellos from regular patrons and appreciative glances from what Jacob called the wolves in wolf clothing. Pictures of Morgan papered the bar along with pictures of other missing children. The pictures were not the kind that you would see on a poster or milk carton but were professionally remastered photos that seemed to capture the life and spirit of each child. Agnes scurried around the hostess stand.

"It's my Caroline," she said, adoringly pulling the woman into a warm embrace.

"She is at the bar, honey, and in a very fragile state. Jake is nursing her now with his fatherly advice and some industrial strength piña coladas, but I think she's going to need your genius to get through this one."

"You're the most, Agnes," Caroline said sincerely. "By the way, if we ever figure out a scheme to market those hugs of yours, you'll be a millionaire in a week."

"Oh, what a dear you are," Agnes responded, her eyes shining with pleasure and pride at Caroline's words.

"I'll go see what I can do," Caroline said as she gave Agnes a peck on the cheek.

As Caroline made her way to the bar, heads turned and necks craned to follow the long-legged woman in the lavender summer dress. It was a gift a suitor had once told her, that nonchalant grand entrance of hers. There was the sensual sway in her walk, coupled with the harmonious rhythm of head, shoulders, and hips moving together in a suggestive synchronicity. She smiled as she spotted her friend's petite figure. The curly locks of her thick brunette hair fell over her shoulders, cascading down her back, nearly covering the back of the barstool. Caroline now within earshot could hear the stress in Marlee's voice. She pictured the furrow that was certain to be between her eyebrows and the grim line that took over the pout of her lips when worry took its toll on her features. Stepping up behind Marlee, Caroline blew a kiss at Jacob.

"Well, Marlee, it looks like the cavalry has just arrived," Jacob said with a wink and smile at Caroline.

"I'm sure my Marlee will be just fine without the cavalry, Jake darling," Caroline said as she wrapped her arms around her best friend in a tight hug.

"Oh, Caroline, thanks for coming," Marlee said, returning her friend's hug with a fierce squeeze of gratitude.

"Where else would I be, girlfriend? How often do I get the chance to be there for you? Besides, I think you're way ahead in the rescue department," she said with a secret wink as she took the chair next to her friend.

"It's just that you're so good at reading men, and I am in desperate need of an expert reading," Marlee began.

"The usual, Caroline?"

"You're a sweetheart, Jake, but let's go easy on the chocolate and heavy on the martini."

"Coming right up, angel heart."

"OK, start at the beginning and let's see what we've got."

"Well, Abbott and I as you know have been dating for almost two months now. He starts calling me girlfriend within six weeks, which is fine by me because as you know package-wise, he was scoring in the upper eights, almost a nine, gorgeous, financially secure, southern charm, even romantic in a 'surprise gift' kind of way. So I'm starting to fall a little for the guy right, and as you know I fall pretty hard when I let go of my self-preservation instincts. So there I am on the precipice, sitting on that fence, looking at the one side where my heart had been shattered, not once but three times in the past eighteen months. Then looking at the other side where Romantic Hope is building a house with three beautiful children, and suddenly my phone doesn't ring for six days in a row. I don't get it right? So finally I *can't take it anymore, and I call. Do you know what he says?"*

"I don't think I'll hazard a guess," Caroline replied, rapt with respect for the hurt in her friend's blue eyes.

"He says, 'I was waiting for you to call me. I wanted to see if you were really into me as much as I was into you.' By the third day of no calls, he says, 'I started to think that maybe the interest was a one-way street.'"

"What did you say?" Caroline asked, accepting her drink, mouthing a silent thank you toward Jacob.

"I told him that I cared for him so much that I had packed all of my emotional hopes and dreams bags and taken a flight from my beautiful Self-Preservation Island to Relationship City, where I was staying at the I Think It Might Be You Hotel. After the third day of waiting for you to call, I had repacked my bags, hailed a taxi, and headed straight for the Get Out While You Can airport, where I booked the first plane to Deli. Then I say, 'Why Deli you might ask, Abbott? Because no one knows me there. I just want to drop off the face of the earth for being such a romantic fool again.'"

"What did he say?"

"He said, where are you now?"

"I said, 'I told you where I am. I'm in the Get Out While You Can airport where I waited as long as I could for you to call, but my plane is leaving now, and it's last call for boarding. I switched destinations five times. My plane isn't going to Deli, Abbott. I'm not really sure where it's going. All I know for

sure is you won't be there when I land, and I have all the miles between that landing and this airport to make that okay.'

"So he says, 'Why do you always talk in metaphors?' I said, 'Because I keep choosing men who don't understand the language of my heart, and I seem to have no choice but to translate what I'm feeling into a language that you might understand.'

"'Oh, I see,' he says, 'you expect me to read your mind.'

"No, I was just hoping that you might find a way to listen to my feelings."

"What then?" Caroline asked.

"Silence on the other end for what seemed like an hour but was probably all of half a minute or so, and then he says, 'Well I guess I'm not sure what that means.' That softened me a little and I said, 'Thanks for your honesty, really, I think you're wonderful, but I finally realize I need someone who does know what that means.' And that was it, we both seem to let go in that moment, no residual blame or faultfinding. I even sensed that we were somehow both relieved."

"So why the sadness, I mean besides the loss of someone to go places with and the major loss of a reliable lay?" Caroline said with a wink. "It seems that you've broken even here."

"Thanks for that eloquent summary, Caroline, you really do make an excellent love doctor," Marlee said with a playful sarcasm.

"No charge, girlfriend."

"I don't know what it is exactly. It's not really sadness, more of a disorientation with a dash of *hopelessness. Like what am I doing wrong, and how do I correct it if I don't even know what it is?"*

"Well, you're not really asking for a reading on the man because you've already read him quite well. He is at the very least emotionally unavailable with a dash of emotionally clueless. That generally means that the man doesn't really know what he wants primarily because he probably defines himself by his consumer identity, you know, his interests, his career skills, and measures of financial security. But it seems to me that you already know that because you do know what you want, it's just not him. Bottom line, you just jumped the Titanic pre-iceberg."

"Now that summary is hitting much closer to the mark. I guess I did pick up on unavailability, otherwise I wouldn't have broken things off if I thought there was a hope or a prayer. You're right, I don't need a reading on the man."

"So ask the right question."

"Why do I feel so lost right now?"

"You've already answered that question. It's right there in your metaphor."

"Please, Caroline, no riddles. Just tell me what I need to know."

"OK, let me ask you the real question. Looking at your current location in your metaphor, where are you now at this moment."

"I'm in a plane flying at ten thousand feet, circling the state of disorientation."

"Good, now where did your trip begin?"

"Self-Preservation Island."

"You said, my beautiful Self-Preservation Island."

"OK, OK, so what's your point?"

"Why is it so beautiful there?"

"Well, I feel safe there and so comfortable, so emotionally at ease and connected to this sense of hope. Yes, that's it, hope. That's what makes it beautiful."

"So here's the last question. Why would you ever leave a place like that?"

"To find a man of course."

"At what price? The loss of comfort and peace makes you not entirely you, doesn't it? Have you ever thought that if you stayed on the island that maybe the right man would come to you, the balanced you?"

"So you're saying I am unhappy in my relationships because I keep leaving my self-appreciation place and trying to be what someone else wants me to be?"

"Exactly."

"Wow that's really hitting me where I live or more accurately where I haven't been living."

"So where's the plane headed now?"

"Back to me, I think, back home, but with a new understanding about how important home really is."

"Perfect, and might I be the first to say it's great to have you back. Now let's go out and celebrate your return to happy and single."

"Whoa, wait a minute, slow down a little, Caroline. I don't have the high-speed Internet insight that you do. I mean what you said helped a

lot, don't get me wrong. Somehow you always seem to know just what to say to make me feel better, but I don't know if I'm ready to go out. My head's still spinning from where this conversation has taken me."

"Well, there's nothing like a little drink and dance to set you right again," Caroline said as she gave the cute guy at the end of the bar a coy smile.

"You mean there's nothing like a manhunt to set you right again."

"OK, OK, you've got my number," she said, and as the man returned her smile, adding a wink and a nod, she felt the Tigress growl.

"No, it's more like you can't wait to dangle your number, and please stop multitasking. Besides you said you wouldn't do that here."

"What's the harm? I'm just looking. You know what they say about the color purple, well it goes double for the color cute. I'm just noticing."

"Yeah right. Really, Caroline, I still don't get how someone with as much sensitivity and intelligence as you have can still be into the chase. I mean you are my role model when it comes to toying with men, but sometimes I just wish you would stop before it all comes back on you."

"No worries there, gorgeous, but I will promise you that if you can find me a man who doesn't think like a toy, I'll stop toying," Caroline quipped, raising her glass in a mock toast. "Please, Marlee, just be my wing girl for an hour, one little hour."

"OK, I give in but just for a drink or two, promise me, Caroline. I'm desperately in need of some

clarity here, and that will require more than a little solitude."

"You got it, girl, just a drink or two to take the edge of your blue, and then a smooth landing at camp solitude. A toast to solitude, the mother of clarity," Caroline said, raising her glass.

"I'll drink to that," Marlee said with a smile as she touched glasses with her friend. Looking up at Caroline while she sipped her drink, Marlee noticed that her friend's glass had paused at her lips. Her eyes were trancelike, staring at the picture of Morgan hanging on the back wall of the bar.

"What is it, Caroline, not enough gin?" she teased with a smile.

"No, it's just, do you smell violets?

"Violets? They're really not in season, Caroline, and you know how I loathe flowery perfume. I think you're having an olfactory hallucination.

"I don't know. It seems so clear," Caroline's porcelain nostrils flared in an attempt to capture the ghostly scent. Quite suddenly, she sensed a surge of sobriety; a sweeping swell of quiet reverence washed over her. This wave of peace and promise held both a potency and a knowing. She was held in this sensation, and in that moment, she felt a strange resolve that she actually was good enough and somehow always had been. Caroline looked back at Morgan's picture, and yes, it was unmistakable the lost child's eyes held the color violet. It was the color she had chosen for the bedroom of her childhood, the color of innocence lost.

"Caroline, Caroline, are you okay? What is it?"

"It's, I don't know, I'm sure it's nothing. I just… had this feeling and I…I think I just need to get some rest or something. I'm sorry for the sudden change. I just feel like I need to find…I mean I just feel like I want to go home."

"Are you sure you're alright? Jake have you got a tissue back there?"

"Sure, sweetheart, but hey, I thought you modern girls were ready for anything."

"Most of the time, but anyone can get caught unawares by a sudden cloudburst."

"Yes, Marlee, I know exactly what you mean," he said, handing her a box of Kleenex.

"Do you want another martini, Caroline?"

"No, I'm good. I just got hit with a hurricane force mood swing. Who knew, right."

"Not a problem. You just take care of you."

They lavished Jacob with warm hugs and a generous tip and made their way out of the bar. Saying their goodbyes to Agnes, Caroline received a secret thumbs-up sign from Agnes, who silently mouthed the words "she looks much better." Releasing Agnes from her own hug, Caroline asked, "Agnes, honey, what color are Morgan's eyes?"

Agnes paused at the unexpected question, her eyes taking on a brief shine.

"Oh, Agnes, how clumsy of me. I didn't mean to take you to a bad place."

"Nonsense, dear, actually I was feeling grateful to you for using the word are instead of were. It allows me to dream a little dream that she is still here somehow, somewhere. Her eyes were hazel

with a touch of green. Little flecks of jade, a bit more in her right eye than her left."

"Thank you, Agnes. Your words mean more to me than you could know," Caroline said as she took the woman's hand, giving it a warm and parting squeeze. "Until next time, be well."

"Namaste to you as well," Agnes said, returning the squeeze.

Marlee and Caroline step out into the cool breeze that accompanied the sun's descent. As Caroline gazed at the red sky edging toward the fading pink of day's end, she felt a strange sense of serenity drift over her. The Tigress had fallen into an unexpected sleep, and she wondered what mysterious force had the power to stay the cat's insatiable hunger. As she walked silently down the street with her friend who was still watching her with concern, she sensed a new presence enter her consciousness—one that had not visited her for many years. She felt hope.

CHAPTER NINE

The Carnival of Consumption

Margarita paused, and then looking up at the expectant looks of her audience, she smiled and took a sip lemon laced tea.

"We are ready for our final passage," she said, opening the book to the last marker that she had placed in the book several hours earlier.

"Before we begin, I just want to briefly map the progress of our travelers. We just completed the excerpt regarding Hope and Destiny's trip from the Sacred Realm, the fifth layer of the soul, through the Authentic Country, the fourth level of the soul. The next chapter in the book called the Bridge of Truth and Lies takes Destiny and Hope over the bridge that crosses high above Midworld or the Hidden Valley of the Unconscious. This is the third layer of the soul, which connects directly to the Forest of Illusions, or what is also known as the Core Belief Forest. Let me share just a few words about the Bridge of Truth and Lies. The crossing of the bridge occurs in hours rather than miles. The bridge takes seventy-two hours to cross. The only mode of transport is walking. You can walk fast or slow, but either way you must walk for seventy-two hours. Walk fast and the bridge may seem shorter in time when it is actually longer in miles. Walk slow and the bridge may seem longer in time when it is actually shorter in miles. The three-day walk must be done in absolute silence."

"There is no way," Gaby and Lindsay said, giggling at their impromptu chorus.

"Every three hours, there is a statement posed to the travelers by a voice coming up from the dark depths of the valley. The travelers must step to the right if they believe the statement to be true and to the left if the statement is a lie. If they choose correctly, they must travel on that side of the bridge for the next three hours. If they are incorrect, they will fall into the unfathomable depths of the gorge."

"Yikes, I shall pray that if I ever encounter that bridge that I am with a very wise man," Eduardo remarked.

"As it turns out, no one could be wiser than you as all the questions pertain to your own soul. The questions are not surrounding a test of intelligence but rather a test of self-accountability. The questions test you on whether the beliefs you have embraced are authentic or illusion."

The Dreamwatcher Diaries

"Extraordinary," Lindsay said more to herself than anyone else.

"I thought you might like that," Margarita said. "It really makes you wonder how you would fair."

"And now for our final story," she said as she pulled out the final marker and began to read.

* * *

Had someone been standing there staring at the mists that rose from the depths of the subconscious gorge, it would have appeared as if Destiny and Hope had materialized out of thin air. Stepping onto the terra firma of the Mesopelagic layer of the soul, mother and daughter slowly allowed their unyielding focus to unwind. They found the path that would take them toward the Shadowlands, and Destiny called for a short rest as they reached a stream at the foot of a sloping hill. Hope took a long drink and then sat for a moment on a creek bed stone. She closed her eyes, listening to the wind song when she heard the distinct sound of the calliope and the barker whose voice defied both distance and obstruction.

"Can you hear it now, Hope, less than a mile off to the north just over this hill?" Destiny asked, watching her daughter's face closely.

"Yes, Mother, it's the carnival," she replied, her eyes widening at the sight.

"What do you know of the carnival?" Destiny asked, smiling at the thoughtful repose that had replaced the youthful enthusiasm of the early morning.

"Only the stories Father told me," Hope replied spellbound at the pitchman's sing-song rhythm designed to draw its mark.

"What did your father Contentment say about this carnival?"

"He said that I would never find him there. But tell me, Mother, what is the name of this carnival, and why does it seem to pull at me so? It's as if I'm about to be pulled along by some force, but then its grasp on me cannot find purchase and the pull slips away, but then it starts all over again."

"What is the primary distraction that Caroline has contracted to escape the pain of the violation that she survived?"

"Let's see, that would have to be sexual consumption and the pursuit of the illusions of bliss, otherwise known as Desire."

"Top marks, child, and absolutely correct. You see before you the Carnival of Consumption. The pull that you feel that cannot seem to get a grip on you are the consumption fantasies reaching out for your energy. They hunger for you to believe in them because they know that without the energy of your faith, without your spiritual muscle that has the capacity to embrace a choice, they are nothing and will soon dissolve and dissipate like cotton candy in a summer rain."

"Yes, I think I see fantasy can't get a grip on me because it senses that I cannot believe in something that is not real."

"Exactly, Hope, yours is a nature that so beholders you to reality that all things unreal will wither in your light. Now let's get a bit closer so that we can bring some clarity to the carnival's existence."

Standing now on the precipice of the final dune that rose above the carnival, Destiny put an arm around her daughter's shoulder as they enjoyed a bird's-eye view of the carnival. Hope caught her breath as her eyes took in the full scope of the carnival. A warm desert breeze pulled at a wisp of her luxurious mane splashing the raven-colored hair across her face. She pulled the hair back and, tucking it behind her ear, turned to look at her mother. She, too, was taking in the spectacle of the Carnival of Consumption in full swing. Her mother's beautiful face framed a smile so sad that it tugged at Hope's heart. Impulsively, she pulled her mother close and wrapped her arms around Destiny's waist in a close embrace. Destiny squeezed her daughter back, cradling Hope's head against her bosom.

Mother and daughter carefully negotiated the steep downhill slope and stepped onto the shady lane that serviced the entrance of the carnival. Spying a bench set back from the path Destiny, motioned for Hope to sit down with her before stepping into the carnival's madness.

"You will take five lessons once we enter the carnival," Destiny began. "These lessons will give you the wisdom you need to navigate the darkest region of the Illusion Forest called the Woodlands of Insult and Injury. But first, I must layout for you the meaning and importance of the carnival's existence and why it holds such prominence in Caroline's soul."

"I was thinking," Hope said, "that because the carnival is the place of betrayal and lost innocence that it must hold great significance for her."

"Yes, that is a truth but something more. The carnival has become for Caroline both the problem and the solution. The problem is that in the wake of the sexual violation, she feels a loss of her own free will. She feels an absenteeism where her will to make choices independent of the violation used to be. Caroline believes that her free will is here at the carnival."

"So what is the solution?"

"Caroline believes that if she can control sex, which is to say to use sex on her own terms, she can recover her freedom of choice. Her acts of promiscuity give her the illusion that she is reclaiming her free will in a sort of 'I'll get you before you can get me' effort. The idea is to be the consumer, not the consumed. What she does not understand is that control and free will are not the same thing."

"So her solution doesn't work."

"No, it doesn't and what's worse is that in the process of pursuing this solution, she has developed what is called an addiction, something Caroline calls the Black Tigress. She is being consumed by the two primary elements of the carnival."

"Which are?"

"Fantasy and consumption."

"So how can I help her, Mother?"

The Dreamwatcher Diaries

"Let me show you."

Leaving the bench behind, Destiny takes Hope through the gate that leads to the turnstiles. A pitchman perched on an actual soapbox is plying all comers with price deals and summer specials on admission bargains. There is a huge sign to his right with big block letters in alternating silver and gold. The letters sparkle, reaching out to the marks glittering with pomp and promise. The sign reads,

Hold out the six coins
Apportioned to the pocket
Of each and every soul.

If you want my
Fantasies of Bliss
You must pay the toll

30-Day Admission	—	Your Hope Coin
3-Month Admission	—	Your Hope & Power Coins
6-Month Admission	—	Your Hope, Power, & Freedom Coins
1-Year Admission	—	Your Hope, Power, Freedom, & Purpose Coins
5-Year Admission	—	Your Hope, Power, Freedom, Purpose, & Dignity Coins

Lifetime Admission   —   Your Hope, Power, Freedom, Purpose, Dignity, & Destiny Coins

"These prices are impossible," Hope said, her forehead wrinkled in consternation. "No one would be foolish enough to give away the power and promise of their very life for a bunch of illusions, would they, Mother?"

"People who chase their wants tend to let their feelings do the shopping. So yes, Hope, more people than we would like to think will pay the price. They are riders on the fantasy carousel reaching for the brass ring of bliss. They believe that they have found Eden in that feeling. They have little regard for the fare they must pay to board that transport in the arms of bliss and the weightless warmth she so reliably brings."

"Where to first, Mother?" Hope asked as they stepped through the turnstiles.

"Head straight down the fairway. Turn left at the center where you will see the cage of the black tigress."

Striding down the fairway with her mother, Hope's senses are assaulted by the seductive appeals of the many illusions that vie for her attention. The air is heavy with the carnival smells, and she tries to identify each fragrance, a game that quickly loses its appeal as the odors too numerous to count seeming to blend together, eluding identification. They pass a countless variety of game booths. Each booth featured an attendant casting out a strident pitch in hopes of catching a mark. The attendants were clad in jeans and T-shirts with rolled up sleeves that accented sinuous arms displaying colorful tattoos. The urgent pace that her mother had set caused the different pitches to go in and out like a radio changing stations. Pulling her focus away from the cacophony of pitchmen, Hope turned her eyes toward midfairway and came to a sudden stop.

There not twenty steps in front of her was the Black Tigress. The big cat's coal-black coat seemed to gleam. The cat's muscles and tendons shivered and rippled as she prowled looking much like snakes squirming within a black satin wrap. The Tigress paced in her confinement, growling at passersby and clocking their proximity to her cage with luminous yellow-green eyes. Hope focused on the almond shape of the cat's eyes, tracking their gaze until suddenly those eyes were staring straight at her. The eyes seemed to be growing, and then she realized that she had somehow moved closer now just an arm's length from the Tigress herself.

The Tigress blinked and made the sound of a muffled growl as if she should be upset with this intrusion but for some strange reason found a grudging acceptance of Hope's presence. The cat retreated to the far corner of her cage. She circled and shifted the way that cats do when they are seeking a comfortable position. Settling herself, she rested her head on paws that approximated the size of an average car tire. The cat stared at Hope with eyes that seemed to be waiting for something. Looking back at those eyes, Hope sensed what it was the Tigress wanted. She wanted Hope to leave. It was as if Hope's presence denied the cat's prowling restlessness. The desire to prowl was still clearly alive and well within the Tigress, but Hope had somehow reduced the cat's supremacy. In Hope's presence, the Tigress had found a fence line, a limit to its influence over Caroline. In that moment, Hope learned that in this world of natural forces, Hope eclipses Desire. Hope sensed that the cat somehow knew that it's authority would return in Hope's absence. Hope turned questioningly toward her mother who was smiling at this silent interchange.

"Yes, Hope, your light has the power to bend and even alter the consumption energy of the Tigress. Your presence arrests the flow of energy that feeds the cat's hunger. This is another effect that you have on Caroline's psyche, the ability to redirect focus, to change the importance of the forces within Caroline's soul. You have the power, Hope, a power decreed by natural design to pull energy away from gratification illusions in favor of the enlightenment found in dreams and imagination."

"But I sense, Mother, that I do not have the power to defeat the Tigress to make her release Caroline from the terrible power that she has over her. I have never even imagined such a power. I have never felt such a fierce strength. The enormity of this creature's force is so constant and compelling, it must dominate her every waking moment."

"Your assessment of the cat's power and strength is both fair and true, but can you tell me where the power of the Tigress comes from?"

"Yes, I think that the cat's power comes from Caroline's faith in the feeling she gets when she is consuming bliss illusions. She believes in that feeling with such ferocity because it has been so reliable, always there ready to transport her to a world of pleasure and weightlessness outside of her body. In that world, she feels both safe and secure, wrapped in the floating warmth of Eden's embrace. The Tigress is just the image that Caroline has conjured for that feeling, and the cage is Caroline's endeavor to contain that all important feeling. What I can't figure out is how does the Tigress get out of the cage?"

"Close your eyes, Hope, and count slowly to ten. Now when you open your eyes, focus on the tree line just past the back wall of the carnival."

After counting, Hope opened her eyes and found the tree line just beyond the end of the fairway.

"Next, I want you to slowly enlarge your focus to include both the far sight of the tree line and the near sight of the cage."

As Hope opened her focus to include both the tree line and the cage, the bars of the cage began to wink in and out of view. Shocked at this discovery, Hope brought her hand to her mouth as she watched the Tigress and the cage become a shimmering mirage. Just a slight eye movement to the left and the cage vanished completely, taking with it the image of the Tigress. There in its place, furious with its exposure to the light, sat the true form of Consumption. The unmasked face of Consumption glared at Hope with a rage that strained against a leash.

"Oh my stars!" Hope gasped in surprise. "That creature thing is Consumption."

"Yes, child, and now you know the secret to seeing through illusion is focus and surrender. The focus on the possibility of seeing truth and the surrender of letting go of past illusion. This skill, sometimes called 'the observer in the empty cup,' will be an important one as you travel through the Forest of Illusions. Now that you can see through the illusion, can you describe the creature for me?"

"Yes, Mother, the creature has no form because it is constantly changing form. It stands on four legs but may rise up to stand comfortably on two. It is both male and female and is both beautiful and ugly. It is seductive in both frightening and exciting ways. Its allure appeals to you in ways that make you want to run from it and touch it with an excruciating urgency all at the same time. Its eyes are the only things that remain constant on the creature. They are cold and empty but at the same time smolder with a restless hunger. The creature does not scare me, Mother, but the creature's power concerns me greatly. I cannot seem to imagine a force that could overcome the chameleon nature of Consumption.

"There is one force, Hope, that makes Consumption cower, that makes it bleed power, changing its form in much the same way that a puncture renders a tire ineffectual. The force of which I speak, Hope, resides within a particular virtue angel who lives there in the Sacred Realm. She travels with some regularity to that sanctuary in the Tranquil Wood. She is frequently accompanied by her companions Wisdom and Courage, and she is often called the *author of acceptance*. I wonder, can you tell me her name?"

"You gave me too many clues. This one is too easy, Mother. Of course it is Serenity. But tell me how is it that Serenity can overcome a force as powerful as Consumption."

"It is not Serenity's brute strength that disarms the fire of Consumption's hunger. It is rather her nature. Serenity is like the nature of water. She, too, can change forms. She can be soft but she can also shatter stone. She can be calm but can also quench fire. Where Consumption is blinded by its single-mindedness to feed, Serenity is guided by a divine intelligence, one that flows to a place where there is no want or need."

"I think I love her more now, Mother. I love Serenity even more than I ever did before."

"Yes, I too love her spirit, and she grows more remarkable with each day that you know her, but the light is fading fast, child. We must move quickly now."

Leaving the cat behind, Hope and Destiny continue their walk down the Midway. Hope tires quickly of the pitchman's appeals to her hunger and desire. She wonders how anyone could stay in this place for any more than just a little while. A darkness creeps in as they advance toward the back corners of the carnival. Hope notices a sign reading "Out of Order," blocking the entrance to the House of Horrors. There on the side of the structure, she sees a disarray of the now derelict cars that used to transport consumers along the track through those attractions designed to curdle the blood. Hope feels a chill as a misty fog rolls in from the Shadowlands. She quells a fleeting sense of anxiety shaped by the murky shadows, but she is grateful when Destiny slows her walk and comes to a stop at a booth. The booth is poorly lit and rickety in its appearance. In spite of this, there are a surprising number of patrons waiting in a line that snakes around the booth and extending deep into the shadows. Hope could see several men in the booth who all appeared to be engaged in completing tasks along some sort of assembly line. All of the men had the same face—the face of Caroline's uncle. The men appeared to be dismantling large dolls that featured sexualized body parts that were exaggerated and designed to induce sexual excitement. The face on all of the dolls was Caroline's. The body parts were placed in cellophane packages with labels and price tags. The packages were then put on display in a series of glass cases that ran along the sides of the shop.

"This will be your final lesson here, Hope," Destiny said in a low and reverent whisper. The whisper commanded confidence and a hush of deep regard for the victims of a secret infliction of a deep and silent wound.

"This is the Booth of Reductionism. The process that takes place within this structure is designed to reduce sentient female human beings into sexual products. This reduction ritual is a primary element of Caroline's sexual violation wound."

"So part of what Caroline is surviving is this reduction ritual."

"Exactly."

"Why does the feminine have to be reduced in the first place, Mother?"

"Primarily because the sentient being is whole and cannot be consumed. Sentient being implies that there is an intelligence in our design that is undeniably present. This divine intention surrounding our original shape intends that all sentient beings are self-aware and intelligent with a soul whom possesses human rights, human worth, spiritual purpose, and free will. This wholeness cannot be consumed in its natural form. It is literally too big to swallow."

"That seems so elementary, it is hard to imagine how a soul would not recognize that simple truth. But I must ask you, Mother, how, pray tell, does this reductionism process work?"

"Reducing sentient human beings into sexual products requires the use of a systematic reduction process that includes sexualizing, objectifying, depersonalizing, and dehumanizing. Sexualizing gives the being a sexual definition while ignoring all nonsexual qualities. Objectifying is a critical step that defines the being as property designed for consumption. Depersonalizing intends to deliberately remove the soul and personality from the sexualized body. Dehumanizing means to deliberately strip the human rights from the being to facilitate the use of the being for gratification appetites."

"And the reason that all the steps must be used is because there are so many qualities that must be removed in order to manufacture a sexual product."

"Exactly, well done, Hope. Oh my, the darkness has crept in far more quickly than I thought. We must make a quick exit behind this booth. Make haste now, Hope. We must find a safe place to camp for the night."

* * *

Pulling herself from the author's enchanting vision, Margarita stopped. Raising her head, she found a bewitched audience hanging expectantly on her last word.

Choosing a tone that seemed in sync with the room's pensive atmosphere, Margarita spoke, "I'm hoping that these passages give you a summary about how the existence of our internal universe might work. The visions painted here also give us some pictures describing what events might take place within the soul that is surviving the injury of sexual abuse and also the soul events surrounding an individual's struggle with addiction. At the very least, the book seems to unveil a host of mysterious and unseen events going on within us, events of which we are not entirely aware."

"OK," Lindsay said with wonderment, "that was a summary supreme."

"Supreme deluxe," Gaby added.

"Deluxe with a cherry on top," Eduardo chimed, "and so beautifully read. You really brought us there."

"It was my pleasure," Margarita responded warmly.

"A couple of questions though," Eduardo said.

"Wow only two, count yourself lucky," Lindsay said, half-serious.

"Not necessarily lucky though, Lindz. When talking about the unknown, the greater number of questions indicates the higher IQ," Gaby said, smiling teasingly at her brother.

"Oh, uh, thanks for that, sis. Now if we could just get back to my questions," Eduardo said, winking good-naturedly at Gaby. "OK, the first one goes back to Hope's discussion about her sister Innocence. What did Destiny mean when she told Hope that the young maiden who whispered to her was Reverence?"

"Innocence is never truly lost for those who learn how to learn rather than how to blame," Margarita replied. "Innocence matured is much like the nature of reverence. This maturation process marks a remarkable spiritual transformation. Innocence in the sense of its beginning, glowing from the wonder of truly not knowing and holding with the fierceness of a child's faith, that all the world, carefree, like her runs with horses through Elysian Fields. Then comes the shock of the growing pain of her soul's weight no longer cradled, falling on her shoulders, demanding the skills of independence, the skills of learning. Then finding the skills and the courage to shoulder her survival, she takes great joy in the return of innocence as she makes the discoveries of self-awareness and the confidence that comes with learning how to learn. Loving to learn, she discovers the way to appreciate, the here and now outside the state of consciousness that we call Dependence. Living in this way, she finds nourishment from the worth in each moment. As each new moment unfolds, she holds it as she would a treasure because it is hers, and it is now because it is her 'now.' So I think the author is suggesting that without realizing it, the lost innocence of our childhood is, rather than lost, actually just changing forms."

"Yes, that makes sense," Lindsay said. "The maiden Reverence is teaching Innocence how to free her mind even while living within the walls of blame. She's teaching her that by appreciating each moment as her own, not even blame can stop the power of learning, nor can it take away an appreciation for the worth that lives all around us. Like with me, how sometimes before I can remember to start my worrying ways, there's this feeling that breezes through me. A feeling that I am so worthwhile, not in a prideful sense like I'm all that, but more so in the sense that I belong somehow in some important way. In that moment, I see worth materialize all around me, jumping out of the background like one of those children books with the figures that pop up when you open the page. I see things like a painting on the wall that never registered before, a person in my office building with a heartwarming smile, an elm tree stretching to provide shade from the summer heat, just effort and energy all around me. It's energy that does not expect recognition nor payment. It just loves being and that is what makes it worthwhile."

"Ah," Margarita said, "so you have been listening to the whisper of that maiden."

"Yes," Lindsay said more to herself than to anyone else, "I suppose I have."

"That was really good, Lindsay," Gaby said genuinely.

"That's a wonderful way to sum it up," Margarita said warmly.

"And now," Lindsay said, stifling a yawn, "I think that my need for a siesta is critical. I actually think my brain needs the downtime to digest even more than my tummy does."

"You said it, girlfriend," Gaby said, stifling a yawn of her own.

"How can you think about a nap after hearing all that? I feel like running, biking, dancing, or something."

"In the words of our beloved mother, it sounds like the universe has other plans for you, Eddie-san."

"Yes, I suppose you are right about that," Eduardo said, smiling at his mother. "Hey, but what about my last question?"

"I already have the answer for you, Eduardo," Margarita said, suppressing a smile.

"How can you know the answer when I haven't even asked the question?"

"Just a little lesson that I learned in the old country."

"OK, so what is the answer?" Eduardo challenged.

"The answer is, read the book."

Gaby and Lindsay smiled.

"And what is the lesson that you learned?'

"Never give shortcuts to those who seek them."

"Well there is no doubt that she has your number, little brother," Gaby said.

"OK, OK, but I really was curious," Eduardo said, feigning defensiveness.

"Well, I'm off to my siesta, ladies and gentleman," Margarita said, rising from her seat. Margarita gave each of them a warm embrace, and as she went to her place of replenishment, her mouth pulled up in a secret smile as she thought about the potential of youth seriously considering the power of wisdom.

Eduardo stood and gave Lindsay and Gaby a kiss on the cheek. "I've got to do a run, but I wanted to say that well…" He hesitated.

"OK, Eddie, what is it?" Gaby asked gently. "You can say it."

"It's just that it's nice to meet women who see the importance of pursuing meaning the way that you both do, and it's been well…it's been refreshing. Speaking of which, you two look like you could use some beauty sleep," Eduardo finished, winking at Lindsay.

"How can anyone be so sweet and sassy at the same time?" Gaby said, giving her brother an affectionate hug.

"Alright I'm out of here. Nike is calling. Dream a little dream," Eduardo said with a wave as he exited the room.

"He's definitely a rare man," Lindsay said as she went to grab a blanket from the closet, "and such a sweetheart."

"Yes, he can be that, but don't tell him I said so," Gaby said, snaring the blanket that Lindsay tossed to her.

"Your secret's safe with me," Lindsay said as she made herself comfortable.

"OK, so let's map out our diary-reading plans before we crash. There are twenty-one entries, I figure seven entries per setting, meaning we need to come up with three settings. Any ideas on where we should start?"

"Lucky for me, that's a no-brainer. We'll start at the point of origin, the place where they first met."

"Ah yes, the Venice Café," Gaby said, curling up on the sofa. "Perfect."

"I can't believe that I feel this tired," Lindsay said in a voice fading toward sleep. "It's not like I ran a marathon or anything."

"Feels like we did," Gaby said tiredly. "See you in dreamland."

"Not if I see you first," Lindsay said as she yielded to the enticing warmth of a midday slumber.

Drained from the energy spent on the pathway to enlightenment, the two friends slept. They dreamed of finding doorways in walls that in their conscious world had seemed impenetrable, doorways that led to that inner country and the place where Hope and Destiny whisper.

Part Two

Diary Dawn

CHAPTER TEN

Sweet Dream Believers at the Venice Cafe

Feeling rejuvenated from their nap, Lindsay and Gaby took a moment to freshen up. After a quick splash of water to wash away the residue of sleep, they applied hasty facials and hurried tweaks to hairstyles. Beginning to feel energized by the renewed anticipation of immersing themselves into the diary's pages, they stood in Gaby's closet and deliberated on clothing selections that might prove equal to the moment.

"Something that fits a late afternoon but flows seamlessly from early evening to late night," Gaby said, shaking her head again as she sent yet another choice down the rack.

"Wow, that really narrows the field for me," Lindsay said with good-natured sarcasm. "Why don't we just bring a suitcase and run into the bathroom for a quick change about every two hours or so."

"Hey, what a great idea. I've got the perfect suitcases, and I'm sure they wouldn't mind if we just stashed them behind the bar."

"Still the quickest wit in the Midwest," Lindsay said with a giggle.

"No, but seriously, Lindz," Gaby said as she held a dark blue dress up to the light. "I don't know why but I feel like something special is happening here and I just want to do it justice."

"OK, OK, I think it's special too. Hey what about this one?"

Christian Dior and Halston having won the day, the two women dressed quickly and made the drive to the city. The Venice Café sits in a shady neighborhood in south St. Louis. The location is just minutes away from the Soulard district famous for its Mardi Gras celebrations and just across the highway from the Anheuser-Busch plant.

Turning right off of Arsenal down a tree-lined side street, Lindsay began to scout for parking spaces.

"You know, Lindz, I've been thinking about this whole 'soul mate' thing," Gaby said as Lindsay swung the SUV into a spot several blocks from the café.

"Well, you've got about six blocks to tell me about it 'cause once we step inside that café, it's nothing but diary time, girl," Lindsay said as she turned off the engine and set the parking brake. "I'm just about dying to know what Gabriel wrote in that note."

"That would definitely make two of us," Gaby said as she grabbed her bag and exited from the car.

"OK, here's the thing," Gaby said as Lindsay shut the car door and bleeped the car alarm, "it's this whole soul mate idea. It just doesn't make sense anymore after reading Grace's letter."

"What doesn't make sense?" Lindsay asked as the two women fell in step with each other.

"It's just that the traditional view of soul mates follows the tradition that there is that unique someone who completes you, you know that whole he or she's my better half theory. I mean I get it, the man gratefully appreciates what his woman does for him, it's sweet but that is exactly what Grace was talking about when she spoke of illusion."

"How so?"

"Well for one thing, one or both partners are cast into the role of better half."

"So what's your point?"

"My point is, how can I be me when I'm serving as someone's better half? I would be a picture in my mate's head, and at some level, I'm allowing that to define me. I would be relying on someone else's picture to tell me who I am rather than taking the journey myself. A journey that includes a period of not knowing, a season of mystery, and wandering as I look inward to discover a truth that no one outside me could ever know."

"Whoa, that is a good point."

"It's like my entire sense of purpose would be defined by the ways in which I complete my soul mate. Like for example, maybe he is a little bit unsure of himself but the way I adore him buoys his self-confidence. He relies on me for that self-esteem boost. This is not so terrible especially because I love him, and boosting his self-esteem helps me feel purposeful and needed. Yet at the same time, he is not learning how to discover his own worth and I am not discovering the purpose of my being. It seems more as if we are in a play in which we both see the other as responsible for filling in the gaps in each other's psyche."

"What you're describing sounds more like 'role mates' than 'soul mates.'"

"That's exactly what I'm saying, playing a role rather than just being a soul."

"I can see how the awareness of illusion leads to questioning the whole soul mate phenomenon, but it's hard to give up on especially considering my parents' relationship."

"Actually, your parents' relationship precisely makes the point that two wholes make a 'soul relationship' and two halves more of a 'role relationship.' My point being that your parents had the wholeness thing going on when they met."

"OK, I'm with you, but then why don't I have the wholeness thing down when both of my parents have it?"

"Well it's not like its inherited, Lindz. Even the children of exceptional parents with marriages of the soul have to go on their own journey."

"Yeah, that's true. I guess we're both living examples of that."

"No doubt about that. Hmm, role mates versus soul mates. I really like the way you qualified that, Lindz. I'm going to have to write that one down when we get inside," Gaby said as they reached the café entrance.

"OK, you jot notes and I'll study appetizers. I can't believe it but I'm actually famished," she said as she pulled open the café door.

Situated in a booth nestled in a cozy corner surrounded by '80s memorabilia, Gaby raised her glass of Merlot in a toast. "To the diary, best friends—"

"And the perfect appetizers," Lindsay added, referring to the generous helpings of smoked salmon, calamari, and beer cheese soup that filled the booth with stomach-growling aromas. "OK, who reads first?"

"That would be me," Gaby said, opening the diary to where they had left off. "Off we go," she said with a smile and began to read.

November 3, 2003
The Boathouse at Forest Park
Sweet Dream Time: Seventeen Hours of You and Me
Epiphany's Whisper

Dearest Grace, I know you must be going crazy to hear what the note said, so I won't make you wait any longer. His writing already seems to have cast a spell on me. It really seems to have a magic about it. I mean I know it was just a note, but it really reached into my heart, and as I read it, I kept seeing his eyes and the way he first looked at me. It was certainly what he wrote that moved me, but the deeper touch, the one that reached my heart, was more about the way he wrote it. Here is what he said along with its heartbeat.

Dear Faith (woman of uncommon countenance),

I think it was the traveler in me, that familiar yet mysterious presence, that sometimes breezes in moving you with some quiet urgency toward your center.

On this night, that sense of purpose was compelling, like hearing the voice of an epiphany that waits for you just around the corner.

Surrendering myself to this mystic intelligence, I set out under the watchful eye of the winter moon. I journeyed without the familiar guides of time or destination, trancelike yet still mindful.

It was the wind that woke me, nudging me with a gust of cold air that was just trying on its winter teeth.

Pulling up the collar to my coat, my eye caught the sight of an unfamiliar café. I thought to walk on, but the wind was pushy and persuasive.

Walking into the café, I felt surrounded by light and warmth. It was a familial warmth, the kind you might feel when you happen upon singers at a campfire after long days of solitude in the wilderness.

It's been said that in moments of sweet clarity, time actually stops, past memory fades, and future vision blurs, leaving only the face of now.

The Dreamwatcher Diaries

It was like that when I first saw you. Just a look in your eyes, one that murmured that if we could just be still, just be here in this moment…we might hear Epiphany's whisper.

I would love the opportunity to share with you what she whispered. Please meet me if you might tomorrow afternoon at noon at the Boathouse at Forest Park. I'll be by the bench across from the flagpole. I would be most honored if you would come.

Genuinely Yours,

Gabriel

P.S. What you said about me being exactly where I was supposed to be was a simply remarkable truth.

Layla showed up of course at the crack of dawn with Brandon in tow, bearing gifts of lattes and pastries.

As Brandon set the lattes down on the table in my cozy breakfast nook, Layla pulled out plates and mugs from the kitchen cupboard and brought them to the table.

I settled into one of the comfortable chairs that sat beside the tall widows looking out on the St. Louis skyline. I wrapped the wool shawl that you used to wear more tightly around my shoulders as my eyes adjusted to the morning sunlight.

"OK," Layla said as she pulled the lid off of her latte and poured the steaming liquid into her favorite mug, "where's the note, gimmee, gimmee, gimmee."

You know you might have given me a couple hours more beauty sleep," I said, giving Brandon a conspiratorial wink. "It's not even seven o'clock yet."

"You don't know the half of it, Faith. If not for the famous Brandon stall tactics, we would have been here at five o'clock in the morning," Brandon said, returning my wink.

"Note please," Layla said, holding out her hand.

"Alright, alright," I said surrendering the note, *"but don't you want to hear my thoughts about what he wrote?"*

"Absolutely, right after I finish reading it," Layla said as she opened the note.

"Why is it so wrinkled already? What did you do, sleep with it?"

"Well, I might have fallen asleep with it in my hand," I said sheepishly.

"Hmm, good information," Layla said as she began to peruse the note.

"I think I'll check out the newspaper while you two work out the details, but I definitely want a summary on your thoughts later," Brandon said, giving me a peck on the cheek and taking his latte, and went to the couch on the lower level.

"My God, this thing is almost lyrical, even poetic."

"Yes, I thought so too," I said, sipping my latte.

"So do you really think its him?"

"I'm inclined to say yes."

"Is it a cautionary yes or a throw caution to the winds yes?"

"It's a I have my wits about me yes."

"Wow, even better."

"Be careful though, honey, this one could hurt you in the worst way."

The Dreamwatcher Diaries

"Thanks, Layla, really, but somehow while I realize the risk of hurt and how deep that hurt might run, it is a risk that I am willing to take."

"OK, now for the really important question."

"What could you ask that could possibly be more important than the risk of being hurt?"

"What are you going to wear?"

Grace, I swear that girl must have gone through every shred of clothing in my wardrobe. She cracks me up. I got the feeling that she was even more excited and anxious than I was. Brandon kept poking his head in prodding her to give me more space.

"Layla sweetheart, I just got a call from my guitar, she says that I'm late for my appointment, and if I don't hurry, she may quit the band."

Oh, Grace, I've got to tell you this story about Brandon's guitar. He named his guitar Jade after his twin sister who died from complications just seven hours after she was born. He holds an amazing bond with her and talks to her as if she were right there beside him much the same way I do with you. One day, just a few months after they had first lived together, Layla overheard him talking to someone in their music room. She walked into the room expecting to find someone, but it was just Brandon with his new guitar. His eyes were wet, and he quickly wiped them, giving her a weak smile.

"I guess I never told you this but I talk to my sister," he said, handing her the guitar. "I sort of project her into my guitar. I know it sounds a little crazy, but I believe that she is the music in me. So whenever I buy a new guitar, I listen for her while I look, and when I hear her, I know I've found my songwriting guitar. On our first day together, I talked to her to let her know that she will *always be a part of me, the best part, and then we write a song together."*

"Oh yeah," Layla said in a soft voice. "What's the song about?"

"It's a song about the woman I'm going to marry. Would you like to hear it?"

Layla looks reverently at the guitar and says, "I'd love to hear it, Jade."

My god, that story makes my eyes water. So Layla gives me this exasperated look and says, "He did that on purpose, I just know it. He knows I'm a sucker when it comes to a session with Jade."

"I think I'll be OK, gypsy girl. You've given me a real head start on narrowing down my final selection."

"Of course, you'll be OK. It's him I'm worried about."

Brandon appeared with Layla's coat and, draping it over his wife's shoulders, gave me a wink and a smile.

"Enjoy, Faith, and remember to just have fun."

With that, Brandon in one deft move hoisted Layla across his shoulders in a fireman's carry.

"You tell him that if he breaks your heart, he has to deal with me," Layla said, gesturing emphatically with her arms.

"I will, I'll tell him that first thing," I said with a giggle.

"Call me," she yelled as the door closed.

The Boathouse at Forest Park sits just north of the entrance to the zoo. The structure is constructed of white stone pulled together under a sloping shingled roof. The annex that overlooks the lake was originally built as a boat storage facility. The dining room that sets in the woody interior offers a rustic yet cozy ambience. This quaint eatery is often referred to as the comfort food restaurant, referring not only to the home-style cuisine but also to the massive fireplace where, during the chilly months, patrons warm themselves while dining. Boathouse sports include paddle boating, duck feeding, and the simple pleasure of people watching. Pets are welcome, as are warm hearts and bright smiles.

The plan was to meet in front of the boathouse by the park bench that faces the flag. I parked on the street and followed the signs toward the entrance. The air was crisp, beckoning the bloom of roses on my cheeks as I walked down the leaf-strewn lane. The cool breeze seemed to applaud my wardrobe choice of white cotton blouse, under a dark, peach V-neck cashmere sweater by Ann Klein. Along with jeans, boots, and a lined brown suede jacket, I felt draped in casual comfort. My heart hit a sudden high note at the sight of him. He was standing there dressed in a forest green cardigan, jeans, boots, and a long brown coat that reminded me of a gunslinger in an old western.

"Hey, it's you," he said.

"In the flesh.

"I'm glad that you came."

"Well, your note was so gorgeous. I mean how could anyone say no."

"Speaking of gorgeous, you look wonderful."

"Thank you, kind sir," I said with a quick curtsey. "You're not so bad yourself."

"Would you like to walk for a bit or maybe ride in one of those?" he said, pointing to a horse and buggy clopping down the stone path.

"I think a walk sounds good."

"Perfect."

We walked down the lane toward the Jewel Box, crossing a bridge, passing the horse and buggy station, then heading down one of the paths off the beaten track.

Grace, what happened next was unusual for a first date. My first date experiences have generally started with rounds of Q and A that have ranged in flavor from the mellow taste of a hopeful interview to the bitter tang of an outright interrogation. But here in this beginning, we both chose without deliberation to trust in something other than words.

We walked together in a silence that bordered on intimate. It was a silence common to those who are certain of the other's affection. It was as if our souls were contemplating the shape of the presence beside them, and somehow we knew that words would interrupt this intelligent communion. In those moments, I sensed that we both knew that something about our meeting was uncommon. A welcome calm overtook me, giving me the liberating consent to just be. Surrendering to this deeper sense, we let our emotions feel their way, and as that hush magically went from leisure to comfort to a building sigh of contentment, our hearts like our strides fell into a mysteriously familiar rhythm.

Somewhere during that tranquil stroll, his hand linked with mine, an eventuality we did not seem to register until we were both standing at the entrance of the Jewel Box. We both cast quick glances at our link, and shy smiles formed on our faces.

"Want to go in?" he asked gesturing toward the turnstile.

"Sounds good, but first I want to take a closer look at this statue."

The Dreamwatcher Diaries

Grace, the Jewel Box is an art deco conservatory featuring cantilevered vertical glass walls that delight the eyes and inspire the imagination. Dedicated on November 14, 1936, the conservatory was designed and built by the city of St. Louis. The Jewel Box has been described as an outstanding example of greenhouse design. Recently renovated to the tune of 3.5 million dollars, the Jewel Box is once again referred to as the Jewel of Forest Park. The enchantment that awaits you inside the box is a veritable feast of organic growth. One step inside and you become a believer in Eden's garden, with colors and green life that celebrate the senses. Life inside the jewel radiates that greenhouse warmth and displays the richest tones and tinges that nature has to offer. You can almost taste the green and feel the complex textures while you listen to the music of the water trickling from the alabaster fountain. Each spring and summer, there are flower shows, with a chrysanthemum show in the fall. The conservatory is also a frequent site for weddings. The front of the structure is guarded by a statue of St. Francis of Assisi, which is one of the four great works of art created by the sculptor Carl Christensen Mase.

"Oh, Gabriel, he is so brilliant, I wonder if I will ever be that good," I said, looking up at the statue.

"Well, you've set your sights high. St. Francis here took altruism to a whole new level."

"Not him, silly," I said, covering my mouth to smother a giggle. "I'm talking about the sculptor Carl Christian Mase. Just look at the clarity in his attention to detail."

"Would you show me?"

"You really want to see?"

"Yes, I would like to try to see what you see."

I watched his face closely to see if he was teasing, but his look was earnest and his eyes were already trying to pick out the details that I had mentioned.

"Well, OK then," I began. "See these grooves right here?"

So I got into some sculpture appreciation with him enjoying more than I realized the telling of my passion and the spelling out of why it held my favor. His questions showed surprising insight for a beginner in the medium. At times he would point excitedly at the sight of a new discovery much like the triumphant child who finds the hidden object in the picture. As we circled the statue, I would catch him at times watching me, his blue eyes measuring both my ardor and my intelligence. In those moments, I would have to look away, lest my eyes belie the fluttering of butterfly wings in my tummy. It was the grumble in my stomach that pulled me out of our teacher-student reverie.

"I'm suddenly ravenous. Any thoughts on food?"

"Well, I'm for it of course, but I do think it's a bit overrated."

"Yes, but that's only true for chefs, children who live above bakeries, and ravenous women everywhere."

"Yes," he laughed. "Your point is well made."

"Would you like to go overrate some food with me?"

"I would be honored."

"Shall we say goodbye to St. Francis?"

"I'm not crazy about goodbyes. How about a 'We'll see you later'?"

"Works for me. See you later, Francis, and thanks for watching over the Jewel of the Forest."

As we headed back toward the boathouse, I commented, "I don't know much about saints, me being more of an angel person. I'm afraid the only thing I know about St. Francis is that he founded the Franciscan order."

"I might be able to help with that. Let's see, St. Francis of Assisi, born in Umbria around 1181 to his wealthy parents, Pietro and Pica. Died in 1126 at the age of forty-five. Dubbed the patron saint of animals and the environment, it was said that Francis took great delight in the little things. He could pull the wonder out of each moment like pulling jewels from a treasure chest. He was also said to be a bit of a pleasure seeker and, due to his parent's wealth, wanted nothing. He had little interest in his studies and chose instead to chase distraction and merriment, though they say that even in his youth, he paid homage to the poor. Much to his father's dismay, he never developed a taste for the business of a cloth merchant. Yet in spite of his youthful wanderings, it is said that young Francis seemed to be reaching for something higher, something deeper, something beyond the landscape of his father's world. They write that much like the poets of that time, Francis was a romantic soul dreaming youthful visions of chivalry and knighthood. At first he thought the 'something beyond' that he yearned for would be found in glory, the glory found on the battlefield, but the universe it seems had other plans for him. Before his twenty-first birthday, he was struck twice by sickness. Contracting some viral affliction prevalent among the commonwealth of that day, health fled from his body. He suffered through long days and nights of intense fever and respiratory distress. It is written that he survived this experience with surprising patience and grace, almost as if it was some strangely anticipated rite of passage. Coming out on the other side, he embraced health like a brother coming home from the war and from the day of that embrace took

his first steps toward a bold new vision. It was as if the fevers that he endured had had somehow divorced him from his marriage to a life of surplus, freeing him to discover the beauty of scarcity. Dante wrote that it was in those days following the sickness that Francis began his love affair with Lady Poverty. At one point during this intense transformation, he went on a pilgrimage to Rome. Arriving at St. Peter's tomb, he was angered at the poor offerings there, and he immediately emptied his purse onto the sacred stone. Then searching at the door of the basilica, he found the beggar with the poorest clothing and exchanged clothes with him. Dressed in those borrowed rags, he stood for the day holding out his hand with the other beggars. This was an extraordinary act for a man who had direct access to riches and affluence."

Grace, I was rapt. He had this rhythmic storytelling cadence that made you feel like you were right there in the story. His eyes were alive while he spoke as if he were watching the events unfold scene by scene in his memory.

"Not long after this, his outraged father brought him before the city council with orders to forgo his inheritance. Only too happy to do so, Francis went before the bishop and stripped himself of his clothes and gave them to his father. Having liberated himself from the final trappings of wealth, it was then and there that Francis made his nuptials with his beloved spouse, Lady Poverty. Confident in the knowledge that he had at last reached the birthplace of his new beginning, he surrendered all of his worldly goods, honors, and privileges and at some level in this process shed the very skin of his ego. Trading in zest for zeal, Francis committed himself to charity and nurturance. His devotion to Lady Poverty was so devout that on the eve of his death, it is written that he was overcome *by a heartfelt desire to get as close as humanly possible to his spouse. To get closer to his love, the very child of Scarcity, he removed his habit and lay his body on the bare earth covered Spartan-like in a borrowed cloth. To him, this was the truest intimacy with his bride, to have nothing between himself and the bare bosom of Lady Poverty, save his connection with the bare earth. That's the basics,"* he said with an almost apologetic smile, *"at least according to what I've read."*

"Well, that was rather beautifully told, but what's the significance of scarcity in his story?"

"Thanks for the compliment, and I will tell you exactly what the significance of scarcity is if you tell me what the significance of angels is to you," he said with a smile.

"It's a deal but only if I get a bonus Gabriel question in addition to my St. Francis question."

As it turned out, the wait for a table was close to thirty minutes, so we decided to have ourselves a little paddleboat competition.

"And no letting me win," I said as we marked the finish line.

"The thought of such an insult never entered my mind," he said as we settled in our boats, familiarizing ourselves with the controls. *"OK, are you ready?"*

"Ready to leave you in my wake, handsome," I said, feeling the surge of excitement that comes before the start of a race.

"OK, we'll see about that, gorgeous. On your mark, get set, go."

We stayed pretty even at first but stealing glances at his progress, I could see him inching his way ahead of me. He had a two boat-length lead as we circled the halfway point. Coming down the homestretch, we both noticed that we had attracted a small audience, some standing on the pier and a few peering out from the dining room windows.

"Looks like the pressure is on now, Sir Gabriel. Don't muck it up."

Enjoying his lead, he looked over at me and smiled. He put his hands behind his head in a relaxed pose and gave me an exaggerated yawn. This little performance caused him to slow a little.

I gained about half a boat length, and then suddenly in a shrill tone, I yelled, "Gabriel, lookout!"

He straightened suddenly, causing his foot to slip. Losing his balance, the boat began to tip and he was forced to take some time to right the craft. This is what I had been waiting for, and I punched it. By the time he got his balance back, I had moved two boat lengths ahead. Some ten boat lengths or so from the finish line, our small audience began to cheer me on. Now only a boat length behind, Gabriel was peddling furiously to regain his lead. I could feel him pulling up even to me. Ignoring my burning quadriceps, I gave it one final burst of energy. It was a photo finish with Gabriel, winning by a few short but convincing inches. The spectators gave us a round of applause. I blew them a kiss, and Gabriel gave them a little bow. Then we both fell back in our boats laughing and breathing in deep helpings of crisp fall air.

Moments later, our name was called and we were seated at a table located a cozy distance from the white stone fireplace. We ordered red wine and steaks with all the trimmings and settled back in our chairs sipping water and enjoying the warmth and crackle of the fire.

"OK, Speed Racer, you owe me your thoughts on the significance of scarcity."

"Ah yes, scarcity, it is that time, isn't it? Well, my thought about scarcity's significance is that it is a doorway, a doorway to reverence. It's almost like a portal, like how those time travelers in the movies couldn't bring anything with them in the time machine. They had to be naked and void of all possessions. If we were to sit there in that means and possession void with something akin to surrender, just accepting this generally unwelcomed state of being without, we would find, after traveling though that gray and cloudless desert, something waiting for us on the other side. We would step into a new country, a sacred place that we did not know existed, a place where we discover a simple truth. The truth that just being is enough. The truth that each living thing has worth, an authentic worth that simply is enough. The dawn of a realization begins to rise in you, the realization that you are OK without your possessions, all those things that, for a time in the desert of scarcity, seemed so terribly important and so measured as a grievous loss. You're awake now, awake to the irony that it was scarcity that led you to this vision that all around you there has always been enough, and there within you, you have always been enough. A deep appreciation coupled with worshipful respect swells from your inner spirit. You breathe now in a rhythm with reverence and your finding with each moment that this reverence sustains you. So I imagine that maybe reverence was St. Francis's vision, his gift. The way that even in his early days, he could revel in the beauty of each moment because secretly he somehow realized that he did not need worldly treasures. He knew somehow that the earth was treasure enough and as well all those who live upon it. He found that to see this gift clearly and to hold it dearly, he must start with nothing. He must achieve bareness and

learn to embrace scarcity as a lover with whom he might spend his days in the contented sigh of reverence."

"Gabriel, that was wonderful," I said, placing my hand on his, "so beautifully put."

"Thank you," he said with a blush on his cheeks, "but I should have warned you that I tend to describe things the way I see them written on paper."

"I like it, and I have to tell you that as you described the idea of just being enough, I was thinking to myself that it described exactly how I imagine love is supposed to be," I said wistfully. "Not so task-like, obligatory, or work-a-dayish but more like the flow of a lifestyle, just a way of being."

"Yes," he said, "I think so too. It's more like a current that pulls you down the river of intimacy and whether you found the river or the river found you, you just accept its flow."

"Just a man grateful to have found this shore where he will find what happens after love is certain," I half whispered to myself.

"That was beautiful, something you wrote?"

"No, just something my father once wrote to my mother. He died when I was just a young girl. When I was around ten years old, I found a box of letters that he had written to my mother. There were more than one hundred envelopes in that shoebox. It was raining that day back home in Indiana. As my mother slept the day away, I spread cushions and blankets on the window seat in the sitting room, and I read every one of those letters. As I read, I felt as if I were bathed in the light of my father's eyes. That warmth caused me to shed the wraps and blankets in exchange for the passion fire that seemed to emanate from each letter. Some hours later, *when I came out of that visit with my father's spirit past, I found the sunlight smiling down on me. I blew the sun a kiss, and packing the box with the letters, I ran and hid it in that secret place in my room that only young girls know," I finished, coming out of my memory glaze, giving him a brave smile.*

He gently placed his hand on mine and said, "I'm sorry if I've caused you stumble upon a sad memory."

"All memories of my father are welcome friends, sad or otherwise," I said through the shine in my eyes.

"So what would it take to get you to tell me exactly where that secret hiding place is?" he asked in a conspiratorial whisper.

"An act of God," I said in the same whisper.

We laughed at that, and as if on cue, the waitress appeared with our food.

The steaks were divine as were the loaded baked potatoes and the asparagus spears seared in butter. We both ate like shipwrecked galley slaves who had stumbled upon a luau. Giggling at our mutual assault on our food, we managed piecemeal conversation between bites and gulps of wine, sharing tidbits about cuisine, eateries, and cooking aspirations.

Once the plates were whisked away, we settled back in our chairs basking in the warmth of the fire. We sipped Burgundy and watched the sun go down over the lake. Somehow we had slipped back into this comfortable silence. It seemed as if we were sitting in our own dining room at our own rustic lake house after a sumptuous supper. Gazing out our French pane windows, we watched memories dance on the lake's golden surface, enjoying the end of another day at our little corner of God's country.

"I would give quite a bit more than a penny to know what you're thinking," he said, suddenly pulling me from my reverie. "It's just that you had the most peaceful look about you."

"I may actually tell you someday," I said, feeling the heat rise to my face while at the same time thanking God that my flush from the fire hid my blush, "but for now that information is classified."

"Fair enough," he said with a smile, "I can wait, and when that day comes, I can tell you about how beautiful you were in that moment."

"I'll look forward to that," I said with an appreciative smile.

"I'm not sure I can move," he said, "but if I don't, I'm afraid that I will fall off this chair and fall into a deep and satisfying sleep."

"I'll second that, but I think I may have just the remedy."

"I'm all ears," he said, placing his hand over mine.

"Really," I said with a teasing smile, "I could have sworn that I saw a mouth with a fork in it just a few minutes ago."

"OK, you got me ears and mouth. What's your remedy?"

"Coffee, Kaldi's, you and me, after a quick trip to the powder room."

"QuikTrip has a powder room? I had no idea. Why am I always the last to know?"

"You're not the only one, hardly anyone knows," I said with a giggle. "It's available only to exclusive members of the QT Powder Room Girls Club. All we have to do is flash our card and they buzz us through this secret door. We even get free powdered sugar donuts."

"OK, OK," he said with a laugh, holding his hands up defensively. "This joke has gone too far. You go ahead and freshen up. I'll take care of our waitress and we'll meet up outside."

"See you soon," I said, squeezing his arm as I walked past.

Grace, I can scarcely describe the delicious tremors that coursed unbidden through my body, nor how, with just a single squeeze of his biceps, I could feel such blissful heat. I remember thinking, Oh Mamaw, I think I may be in trouble here. I thanked the stars that my face was turned away from him, lest he see the color of the fire that for the second time in one night had risen in my cheeks.

"How is it that a woman's body can betray her so when she has done so well with collecting the reins of her passion?" I wondered out loud as I splashed my face at the ladies' room sink. "If just one squeeze conjures this much electricity, how will I hope to survive a kiss?"

The sudden opening of the stall door told me to my dismay that I was not alone. A tall, blonde-haired woman, fiftyish, sculpted cheekbones, and stunning figure, looked at my reflection in the mirror as she stepped up to the faucet. I recognized her as the woman who had been sitting with her husband two tables away from ours. Turning on the water, she smiled easily in the mirror as I slowly lowered my hand from my mouth, realizing that my words like wild horses had long since left the corral.

"You'll be fine, honey. It's him I'm worried about. He is as smitten as they come. And yes, dear, he is mysterious with those deep blue eyes of his, but he is also a man who has 'fallen' written all over his face, just as you do," she said with a wink.

"As far as the kiss goes," she continued as she dried her hands, *"as they say, there is no sense in crossing a bridge until you come to it. But I can assure you, darling, you'll both be crossing soon. Ciao."* As she stepped toward the door, she blew a kiss and smile over her shoulder.

I smiled at myself in the mirror and was pleased to see that my dignity had returned and was smiling back at me. I looked heavenward and said, *"Thank you, Grace,"* and walked out the door toward my sweet dream.

Kaldi's is a rustic coffee house just a few doors down from Sasha's Wine Bar on Demun. In contrast to the larger chain coffee houses, which have an almost corporate feel about them, Kaldi's provides a more *"folksy"* experience. It reminds me, Grace, of the old country store down the road from our Indiana farm. You know, the one that had the old gas pump in front and sold ice-cold Coca-Cola from an old white refrigerated cooler that sat just beside the entrance door with the cowbell hung on the inside. Trending toward the health conscious, the emphasis at Kaldi's is organic. From the decor framed in rough, hewn timbers, to the brownies made from the purest of down-home ingredients, Kaldi's percolates the natural fragrances of warmth and comfort.

We sat at a window seat with our lattes, his caramel, mine vanilla, sipping and secretly sighing with some relief at the settling of our stomachs. We had somehow become shy again on our drive over, and there at the table, I could sense that he was wrestling with how to word something. I suspected or rather hoped that his word tussle had something to do with Epiphany's whisper, and in spite of this growing urgency to encourage him, I found the wisdom to still my heart and let the universe be.

"Do you remember what I wrote about time standing still and how I heard Epiphany's whisper?" he said softly.

"I've thought of little else since I read your note, Gabriel," I said, my voice somehow matching the softness in his.

"I need you to hear her, Faith. I need you to hear her whisper for yourself."

"I'm listening."

"To hear, I need you to trust me for just a short while."

"I can do that."

He leaned across the table and, gently placing his hand under my chin, pulled my face close to his. He gave me a soft smile as we paused there for a moment, literally looking through the eyeglass into each other's soul. He gently whispered, "Close your eyes with me, and just for a moment, listen with your heart."

I began to close my eyes, watching as his lids covered those blue pools of intensity. There was another small pause during which my sense of touch increased exponentially. In that vulnerable dark, I could actually feel the supple of his lips so close but not yet touching. And then "they" were there, a soft and delectable pressure murmuring a moist caress on my mouth. His fingers tenderly wrapped around my chin, and in that moment, he held our first lingering kiss in the palm of his hand. As our lips memorized shape and desire, giving and taking with a visceral intelligence, I listened to my heart.

I heard the woman there, that keeper of the lighthouse, the one who walks the white sand beach keeping watch for Hope, Joy, and the Bright Knight of Happiness. She spoke some words to me, that woman who believes *even when she cannot see. She smiled and blew a kiss as she slowly faded like a white sail over the horizon.*

Then I was back levitating in that sweet beginning, alive in that moment that held no boundaries, floating in some place that was not subject to space or time. But before the kiss could blossom, opening to release the honey that gives way to a more blissful urgency, Gabriel gently broke the bond. Our lips parted but still sang with the impressions of their recent joining. He caressed my cheek with his hand and held my gaze with his eyes. I was about to speak when he put his finger to my lips.

"Now that we've heard, I was hoping that we could write down our discoveries. I was thinking we could share our whispers later when our time has matured and there is no danger of turning the hope of an epiphany into the obligations of an expectation. It's not that I'm not eager to know what she said to you...I just—"

"Sshh," I said, putting a finger to his lips. "I think that your idea is wonderful, but I wasn't about to tell you what I heard."

"Don't I feel like the fool," he said with the cutest blush, "what was it?"

"The moment's sort of gone, but don't be too hard on yourself. I've got this feeling that it will come back around."

"Oh, you're good."

"You have no idea. Why don't you find some writing utensils?" I suggested, looking toward the front counter. My eyes caught the sight of the young woman who had made our coffee. It seemed that she had born witness to our first kiss. Her hand was over her mouth, and her right cheek glistened with a tear track. As her eyes registered our brief connection, her hand slipped from her mouth to her

The Dreamwatcher Diaries

heart, and she smiled at the wink I gave her before ducking back behind the cash register.

"Hold that thought," Gabriel was saying, "I won't be a minute."

He returned with pens and Kaldi cup sleeves. "Sorry about the sleeves they were out of stationary, but I did get a kind message from Rose, our coffee matron."

"I don't think that slender young woman would be very pleased with the word matron. What did she say?"

"That's a good point. Matron does not quite get it, does it? It's a bit too 'nuns at a Catholic schoolish,' isn't it?"

"Yes," I giggled, "just a 'bitish.'"

"OK," he laughed in that boyish way of his. "Let's see how about coffee steward, no, too proper. Coffee wench, definitely too vulgar. Ah, coffee technician, nope, doesn't work. Hmm, coffee stylist."

"Stylist will do. What did she say?"

"Actually, our Rose said something quite encouraging. She said, 'I'm sorry but I have to tell you that was some kiss you two shared back there. I swear I felt it all the way over here. Just promise me that you won't take for granted what it takes to make a kiss like that because whatever it is, you both got it.'"

"Well, our 'coffee Rose' is a very intelligent woman. What did you say?"

"You're right, coffee Rose is much better. I told her that she was very kind, and that it was the easiest promise that I would ever make."

I kissed him softly on the mouth. "That was for your promise."

"Then I shall promise more often," he whispered in a solemn voice. "So are you ready to write?"

"Definitely."

We wrote out our whispers on Kaldi coffee sleeves, which we tucked away for safekeeping. He drove me back to where my car was parked, and we lingered for a moment as we both seemed to feel a reluctance to greet the night's end. Sitting there in his Jeep, which held the masculine scents of car leather, cologne, and the faint smell of clean sweat, he put to me the question, "So what were you going to say back there before you were so rudely interrupted?"

"I thought you would never ask," I said, leaning slowly toward him.

He leaned toward me. I paused with my lips just inches from his mouth. I breathed his name, "Gabriel," and whispered, "think of Epiphany's whisper, and this time listen to your body. Listen to hear if your body does not already know that which Epiphany has just now made familiar. Listen closely."

Then I kissed him with a fever that shook and shimmered. The wet heat passing from my mouth to his came from the very sun in my soul. Oh my heavens, Grace, such a kiss I have never known. What made it so rare was that as that fevered desire coursed from my body to his, the same measure of fervent passion came back to greet my yielding lips.

He drove me back to the lot where I was parked, and after a final parting kiss, I made my way to my car, hoping all the while that he could not tell that I was walking on clouds.

See you soon, dearest Grace, in the next entry.

The Dreamwatcher Diaries

November 7, 2003
Dancing at the Viva
Sweet Dream Time: Twenty-Six Hours of You and Me
Salsa Serenade

Dearest Grace, I spent that Thursday in my humble warehouse studio, putting the finishing touches on my "best ever" piece, which started twelve months ago with a slab of alabaster stone that stands a little over ten feet high. Grace, it is my fervent prayer that you will look down one day and see what you inspired. It is your love for my soul that helped to discover my character's shape. So here in this space, bathed in your inspiration, I have carved and chipped away the inessentials to reveal my tribute to your spirit captured in stone and light. I have found the perfect spot for it in a place where those in sore need of hope gather. I had petitioned the city some months ago and just today received word that my proposal had been accepted.

I stopped work at about 3:00 p.m. and took a quick catnap. Layla gave me a wake-up call around 4:00 p.m. While she milked me for information about my plans for the night, I laid out what Layla calls my cha-cha dress. It's a deep sea blue with a plunging neckline and is designed to flare out when you spin, which I planned on doing frequently that night.

The plan was to meet up at the Viva for some salsa dancing an activity with which I was only vaguely familiar. Gabriel had promised me a quick lesson, which is why we had agreed to meet at 6:00 p.m. Layla was giving me a crash course on the basics of salsa stepping while I scurried around my room fumbling miserably with the fine art of accessorizing.

"OK, here's the basics. Salsa is a syncretic dance form with origins in Cuba. Today's salsa dancing is a rich blend of Latin American and Western influences."

"Syncretic dance form? Layla, please, we're pushing here. I need basic movement information right now, not dance history lectures."

"Right, right, good point," Layla giggled. "Sorry, wait, here it is, styles, rhythms, movements. OK, wait, what style will you be dancing?"

"Layla, you've got to be kidding me. How could I possibly know that?" I said with the exasperation of the totally incredulous. *(Grace, at that exact moment, I happened to look up and caught myself in the mirror. I had that look on my face. You know the one that arrives when I get so impatient because my expectations are spiraling out of control. My hand was out in suspended aggravation, accenting my tense facial features. I smiled at my consternation. I suddenly remembered your words about the illusions of bliss. So I took a deep breath and began to let go of that perfect picture in my head.)*

"Faith, earth to Faith."

"Layla," I asked with a little catch in my voice, "I think I'm really falling here. Am I going to be OK?"

"Of course you are, Faith," Layla said evenly. "You have yourself, which as we both know is more than enough, and you have me to catch you. Faith honey, your bones will never touch the ground." Thanks, gypsy girl. You don't know how much it helps to hear you say that."

"Faith, you are doing it right, you know? You have to jump. It's not real if you don't jump. Just as long as you jump with your eyes wide open."

"They are open, Layla, but God help me if all I can see is his face."

"I don't think God would blame you, Faith, as I remember he's got a pretty awesome face."

"Yes he does, doesn't he?"

"OK, salsa movement, and I'll let you go. New York style mambo, the beat is on two, and the Los Angeles style is on one. Either way, he'll be following you before the night is over. I've seen you in your cha-cha dress with your Jimmy Choos, no worries there, girl, and don't try to curl those blonde locks of yours. Straight and natural, that's your best look, tall, blonde, and gorgeous. He won't know what hit him."

"You're the best, Layla. Thanks for being there."

"Always, besides, you know it's going to cost you all the details that I can squeeze from you."

"For you, those will always come free of charge. Ciao, gypsy girl."

Grace, as one who was born and raised on the coast, you may not possess a deep appreciation for what attracts us Midwest folk to the realms at the points furthest inland. For me, just a simple Indiana girl born in that place, that is somewhere between city and country, I will always have a soft spot for the neighborhood. There is something so endearing so freshly all American, about those neighborhood memories woven into my childhood. Just walking down the streets of my locale, waving to most everyone who would call out a greeting, and I would shout out a "hey, you" with their name, which always seemed so immediately familiar. Riding bikes with friends down shady tree-lined streets while listening to the staccato of the clothespin-secured playing cards clip-clacking against our spokes, visiting private haunts, and building backyard tent cities where secrets ruled and dreams were spun. That's what endears me to this place, Grace, the magic of the little universe that we call neighborhood.

St. Louis is a city of neighborhoods, seventy-nine magical mini universes, woven together with both comfort and character, like patches on a homespun quilt. The Viva is a Latin American dance club located in an upbeat, progressive district known as the Central West End. The vibrant energy of this village with its fresh air attitude, sidewalk cafés, and wide cultural and sexual diversity welcomes and invites. It is a free spirit community, one that actually broke the glass ceiling on the conservative tendencies of Little Big Town. The streets of this neighborhood include preserved avenues of cobblestone that go back to the turn of the century. You can almost imagine the bustle on those streets during the 1904 World's Fair hosted by St. Louis and held on the grounds of Forest Park located just a few blocks to the west. You can walk down those same cobblestone streets, smell the fragrance of pastries and pasta dishes, watch the people enjoying their lunch at the sunny sidewalk cafés, then browse and maybe buy at Left Bank Books. You could take your purchase down the street to Bar Italia, where you can sit at the patio bar, drink Italian wine, read, relax, and just breathe in the singular spirit of that neighborhood. Should you choose to stay on as the evening shine gives way to the saffron glow of the village lamplight, lingering there well past the time when the rhythm of the street commerce transforms to the sound of music, you may feel the desire to discover dancing in St. Louis. You need only cross the street where you will see the Viva in pink neon. Once inside, you walk down the stairs and magically it's almost as if you were entering the roomy basement of a close Latin American friend who has invited you to an exclusive Dirty Dancing party. Which I have to tell you, Grace, is pretty much how I felt as I descended those very stairs myself. That is until I saw him standing there at the bottom of the steps and absolutely forgot everything about the nature of walking.

I felt myself trip, but somehow he caught me. Grace, I have to tell you I do not know how he got from the bottom to somewhere in the neighborhood of ten steps up in the nanoseconds that he did, but there I was, safe, secured, and staring into his dreamy blue eyes.

"So you're glad to see me, and while I certainly appreciate that, I would much rather walk down these stairs than be carried," I said, grabbing my dignity by the collar before it could flee the building.

"My thoughts exactly," he said with a telltale twinkle in his eyes. "I did neglect to tell you that the entranceway here is not exactly compatible to high-heeled shoes," he said, releasing his hold on me.

"Entranceway," I said, straightening myself while flashing him a sarcastic smile, "I think a negotiated descent down the north face of Mount Everest would be a tad more accurate."

"My humble apologies, fair maiden," he said, slipping again into that English accent as we made our way down the steps.

"I'll think about…" I said turning toward him, but he wasn't there. He had stopped a couple of steps above me. I looked up at him and found his eyes taking in my dress. "What?" I asked frantically examining the fabric. "Did I rip it?"

"Faith, you look stunning."

"Oh," I said, feeling suddenly bashful and pleased all at once. My hand went up to cover a smile that pulled at the corners of my mouth.

"Really," he said with a soft sincerity, "what a beautiful dress, and what you do for it is just delicious."

"OK, you're forgiven," I said, melting toward him.

"Forgiven or not, I have never been so struck by a beauty as alluring as yours, Faith. You do have a magic about you."

"Thank you," I managed while pulling back on the reins of my passion who, in her growing urgency to respond to his compliment, threatened to slip from her bridle.

"So are you ready for your dance lesson?" he asked, linking my arm with his as he escorted me past the check in booth toward the main room.

"More ready than I would be if you hadn't caught me," I said, giving him a quick peck on his sculpted cheek. "Which reminds me, I do have an urgent request."

"Anything, name it."

"Don't ever stand at the bottom of a long flight of stairs watching a woman in heels walk down while you are wearing a black Armani suit with a soft white cotton shirt opened to the chest, looking like you just stepped off the cover of Gentlemen's Quarterly. I stopped him mid-walk, and sending him a smoldering look of sexual hunger, I finished. "Please don't ever look that indescribably sexy at the bottom of a stairway again."

"Yes, but that...that...how did you do that look?"

"What look?" I asked, coyly steering him toward the bar as I watched his "man temporarily lost at sea" look.

Walking up to the bar, we were greeted by a beautiful Latin American couple dressed to dance. The lady was a striking Brazilian woman whose warm smile exuded *the kind of warmth that elicited instant friendship. Her eyes were large, brown, and absolutely mesmerizing. Just underneath their inviting warmth, a passion fire radiated, projecting a will that could love and protect with equal ferocity. The shape of her body pulled at the eyes, and her legs conditioned and toned by the art of the dance had curves on their curves. The handsome man beside her was the picture of tall, dark, and handsome. His winsome smile flashed white teeth and activated a magnetism in his eyes that pulled you into his universe and made you want to stay. Just under six feet, he was a head shorter than Gabriel, but there was something about his exuberant personality that seemed to pull him up to an equal height.*

"OK, what's up, Gabe?" he said, flashing me a wink and a smile. "We don't hear from you in almost a month, and now you show up with the belle of the ball on your arm. What's your excuse? It better be because you've been shacked up in that poor excuse for a domicile that you live in, laying around and ordering takeout."

"Carlos," the woman said taking my hand, "you are incorrigible. Holla, I'm Maria, and that very rude man is my husband, Carlos."

"Maria, Carlos, this is Faith," Gabriel said, intercepting the introductions.

At the mention of my name, Maria put her hand to her mouth. I thought for a moment she may have found some humor in my name, but the look in her eyes was more an expression of shock or wonder.

"Pardon me, Faith," Carlos said, flashing me his brilliant smile, "I have a part-time job dishing out grief to Gabriel here. It does not pay so well, but watching him squirm is just too much fun. Where's my hug, compadre?"

The men embraced, and Maria and I smiled at each other. There was a sense of activity behind the curtain of our smiles as we engaged in the secret art of weights and measures. A distinctly feminine activity as you used to say, Grace, this woman to woman measuring of shape and constitution—like two women at a quilting exposition, studying the craft of the other searching, the landscape for both virtue and flaw. I must have passed the first examination because she put her arm around me and in the spirit of female camaraderie whispered, "I love your shoes." Then Carlos said, "Let's dance!" The next few hours sailed by on the ebb and flow of the salsa tide.

Gabriel taught me the basics, and with the help of Carlos and Maria, along with my years of jazz, tap, and ballet, I advanced from salsa's "bunny slope" to the "intermediate hill" in one night. Gabriel told me as much in the way he spun me around with increased confidence shedding the "kid gloves" and really pushing my learning curve. The energy of the club was exhilarating as the DJ mixed rhythm and passion with what seemed to be a psychic connection to the mood on the dance floor. I was swept through several revolutions of five fast and two slow songs with a ten-minute break between rounds. The density of the dancers on the floor seemed to increase with each rotation. Somewhere in the middle of the third cycle, Maria pulled me off to the ladies' room for a little primp and powder.

"You move like a dancer, Faith," Maria said as she dabbed at her high cheekbones with a tissue. "You're quite graceful for one so tall. What are you, about six-foot?"

"About five-eleven, which is...well, yes," I giggled, "about six-foot."

"Have you had training?"

The Dreamwatcher Diaries

"Just a little tap, jazz, and ballet, nothing terribly formal. Certainly nothing near your caliber," I said, splashing some cold water over my face.

"Thanks, but you learn so quickly, and you definitely look like you know what you're doing out there."

"Thank you," I said, flashing her a smile of appreciation.

"OK, enough about dancing. I want to hear about how you landed Mr. Beautiful and Mysterious."

"Well, I don't know about landed, but you certainly have the beautiful and mysterious right. To tell you the truth, I almost tripped and fell when I saw him standing at the bottom of the stairs tonight."

"Really," she giggled. "It's no fair God is not supposed to make men that beautiful. They already have too much ego as it is, but it's no matter. Karma has her own mind, and she has smiled on you, Faith."

"How do you mean exactly?"

She stood there for a moment with this look on her face as if she were having some internal debate. Then in a sudden show of resolve, she took my hand and said, "Come with me."

She pulled me toward our table. "Gabriel, I'm borrowing your woman. We're going down the street for a quick minute, for a glass of wine and some girl talk."

"Whoa there, gorgeous, don't you think you should clear this with us first?" Carlos said.

"I am clearing it with you right now. Oh, Papi, you…" And then let out a string of Spanish spoken exasperation. "It's just down the street. We'll be fine. Trust us, I mean look at this face," she said, putting her finger under my chin. "How can you not trust this face?"

"I don't think that is the face that worries him, Maria," Gabriel said with a wink.

Maria stuck her tongue out at Gabriel and, then giving Carlos a kiss, said, *"Be good, Papi. I see you soon."*

Gabriel took my hand and briefly kissed it. *"Watch this one,"* he said with a smile, *"she's trouble."*

"With a capital T," Maria said with a toss of her luxurious mane.

We walked the short distance to Café Balbans and sat at the bar. We ordered chilled glasses of Chardonnay, and for some silent moments, we just sat there relaxing and breathing in this change of disposition. We allowed the French café's ambience to wash over us, trading in the fever of the dance for a new mood. The mood that greeted me was a guarded apprehension that held hidden in its core a seed of foreboding. Ignoring that seed, I looked for Gabriel's face and found it nestled safe and warm in that picture frame that sits on the mantle in my mind.

Our drinks arrived, and we both took a sip of wine. *"Faith,"* Maria began, *"what I tell you now I say not to discourage you. I share my story because I can see that you are in love. Even a blind man could see what is written on your heart this night, when you look at him with your eyes. Faith, it is much beautiful, I can proudly bear witness to that. What you will hear this hour I tell you because I want to give courage to your love. It is amore, no, Faith?"*

"Yes, Maria, it's amore," I said with a blush. *"I guess it shows more than I thought. I have always believed that it could happen this way, but now that it is actually happening, I'm afraid that this love that I'm feeling will not mature into."*

"A true intimacy."

"Yes, that's it exactly," I said, hugging Maria impulsively. "I mean I have only known him for less than a week, yet my heart seems to be so confident that for me it's only him."

"Yes, Faith, this is the way of amore," she said with shining eyes. "To amore," she said in a toast.

"Amore," I said with a smile, and as I drank, I began to feel a cautious kinship with this exotic woman.

"First I…" (With a single Spanish expletive and a glare that could have melted cast iron, she stopped three would be suitors in their tracks. They retreated with mutterings about lesbians and laughter to restore their wounded egos.)

"Frogs I call them, men who have not yet found that their purpose here on this planet is not located between their legs."

"You are most kind, and because of your restraint, I will not tell you what I call them."

"First," she began again in that intense voice that touched the spirit in my soul, "I must tell you how I first met Gabriel, and second, I will tell you how your life has even now altered his."

"Three year to the past, it was a fall night," she said as her melodic voice fell into a storytelling timbre. "The trees were showing off with a riot of September colors, and the air was crisp with the arrival of Indian summer. I can still recall the smell of dying flowers and burning leaves sending their sad but clear message that summer was out of reach. It was this smell of season's change, which greeted me as I rose in a panic from the subterranean party below."

I'm sitting forward with my elbows resting on my knees, staring at her in fascinated rapt attention.

"It was Saturday night at the Viva, it was my cousin Rita's twenty-first birthday, and she was, how do you say, 'sowing some wild oats.' She was drinking like a fish, dancing with every man who asked, roaming the room like the very devil herself on holiday." (At this, Maria winked at me and added who's to say, "the devil is not a she.")

"It was her night, and as her self-appointed guardian, I drank nothing but juice and water. I pushed Carlos to do the same, but that push did little good. I swear that man was born to test me." (She sighed.) "My god, but I love him so. She made me work that girl, too gorgeous for her own good, that night. She had a reckless air about her, one that seemed to invite danger. You met her briefly tonight, the lithe little knockout who looks a little like Thandie Newton, you know the girl in that Tom Cruise movie Mission Impossible 2."

"Yes, I remember the one in the lavender dress. She had that little scar on her forehead. She gave Gabriel that big hug and that kiss that made him blush right down to his toes."

"That's Rita," Maria said with a laugh, "and after this story, you'll understand why you needn't worry about that kiss. So a little after midnight, I made a quick run to the ladies' room. When I came out, I noticed that the tall, red-haired guy who had been chatting her up all night was no longer at his spot at the bar where I had last seen her. I'd had a bad feeling about the guy all night. Like some kind of bad vibe coming from the way he eyed Rita when she wasn't looking. I did a quick circuit and came up dry. I literally screamed for Carlos. He came running up, well more like staggering up. I was so angry with him in that moment that I actually slapped him. 'Rita's in trouble!' I screamed and then ran straight for the stairs. With *each step, I became more certain that the blaring warning system from my instincts was right on point. I burst out the door and ran into the street. Looking right, I saw a commotion down toward Delmar Avenue. 'Rita!' I yelled kicking off my heels and running barefoot down the now nearly deserted street. Closing in, I could see the red-haired guy from the club with his arm around Rita. She seemed to be only half conscious, staggering toward a car that was angled from its parking space sitting half out in the street. I saw a head poke out of the car and heard a male voice say, 'Come on, Derek, get her into the car.' That stagger in her walk was what got me thinking that she was under the influence of something more than alcohol. I mean I've seen Rita drink before, and that girl has always been able to handle her liquor. So I started to speed up sprinting with everything I had with my mind trying to figure out what my next move will be, and then I see him.*

"He steps out from an alleyway just ahead of the car. From my position, I can only see him in silhouette, shoulder-length hair, long coat, boots, looking everything like a gunfighter out of some old western movie. His arm snaps up in a throwing motion, and the world around the car that Rita is now only steps away from seems to explode. At first, I thought it must be a grenade or one of those Molotov cocktails, but then I realized there were no flames. The would-be grenade turned out to be a garden variety rock thrown with such force and accuracy that it nearly took out the entire windshield. Suddenly everything around me seems to be moving in slow motion. Following his throw, covering the distance to the car with amazing speed, the gunfighter vaults over the hood of the car without even breaking stride. The driver's side door opens, a man steps out, cursing with threats of violence and death.

Lawrence Gabriel

The man is about six feet tall, bald, with tattoos covering the back of his skull, and built like a tank. He sticks his hand inside his coat. Still between the car door and the car, the driver begins to raise the gun in his right hand. Coming across the hood from his vault, the gunfighter slides feet first toward the driver's side of the car. As his feet hit the ground, he goes into a squat and does a neat somersault on the driver's side of the street. Then in one deft motion, the gunfighter back-kicks the driver's side door before the bald man can even raise his gun above door level. The gun goes off, the bullet striking and shattering the driver's left shin, causing him to fall into the street along with the gun. The gunfighter slides up to the fallen driver, picks up the gun, checks to see that the car is empty, and noting that the passenger door is wide open examines the driver's wound. I actually hear him say, 'You'll live but I do need you out for a while.' He applies a headlock to the guy and applying pressure to a specific spot on the man's neck causes the driver to pass out. He rips a strip off the bald guy's shirt and ties it around the wound to stop the bleeding. In a crouch, the gunfighter circles around to the back of the car. I'm probably less than ten feet from the back of the car where I'm standing half in shock and half trying to memorize the car's plate number. He gives me this grim smile. 'Nasty business,' he says almost apologetically. I can still recall how his brow was furrowed scope-locked in a focused concentration. It was like he was straining to hang on to some radio signal that only he could hear. Yet he seemed surprisingly self-possessed for a man in the midst of combat. 'You hurt?' he asks almost as if he is noticing me for the first time. 'No, just scared shitless,' I say with more than just a little tremble to my voice. He puts his finger to *his lips and motions me into a crouch where I can now see him face to face... Faith, it was Gabriel."*

Grace, at that point, my mind had still not truly registered that she was talking about my Gabriel.

"'Does the other one have a gun?' he asks.

"'Yes,' I say, 'I saw him pull it out, and the other man has a knife to my cousin's throat.'

"'Where's the man with the gun?' he asks popping the guns cartridge, looking at it, and then slamming it home again.

"'Last I saw, he was crouching behind the passenger front quarter panel.'

"'I'm going around toward the front, stay here,' he says, pulling something that resembled a silver star out of his boot. He moved back toward the fallen driver. 'Hey, dude,' he says, suddenly in a surfer sort of lingo. 'I totally screwed up here, man,' he said, standing up slowly. 'Here take the gun.' He popped the cartridge, which he placed in his left hand and tossed the gun to the man in a gentle arc. Peering through the back window toward the gunman, I watched his eyes follow the arc of the gun. In one fluid motion, Gabriel dropped the cartridge while sliding the star to his finger tips and said, 'I'll toss the cartridge over there,' pointing just over the passenger door. He slowly raised his right hand in the motion of a throw while at the same time his left hand snaked out, releasing the star in a calculated underhand pitch. He quickly ducked for cover and moving from the driver side front tire peered around the front of the car. The star had taken the gunman in the wrist of his gun hand, his gun clattering harmlessly on the pavement. Gabriel cleared the front of the car in a quick shoulder roll and one shoulder roll later was standing over the gunman. He was howling at the wound in his hand,

staring in disbelief at the star points winking at him from back of his hand and burrowing up through his palm. He stared at Gabriel sliding away as the fight winked out of his eyes. Gabriel picked up the gun, pocketed it, and pulled the bandana from the man's head. He jerked the star from the man's wrist, provoking yet another howl. 'It's best to remove the object quickly, slowly is much more painful,' he said as he bandaged the wounded hand. His focus was so resolute that he did not register the look of incredulity that replaced the gunman's screams as he completed the field dressing. 'That should hold you till the medic arrives. Meanwhile I think it's time you should join your friend in nap city.' Then applying the same pressure to the man's neck, the gunman lost consciousness. Gabriel stood, pulled out the gun, released the cartridge, and threw it to the ground along with the gun. He walked toward the man who still had the knife at Rita's throat. 'What's the point now, dude? Your boys are out. Why not just take them and drive away? No one is seriously hurt here. I help you load them up and you're out of here.'

"The man with the knife who I later find is one Derek Mason, a convicted serial rapist who is out on parole, pushes Rita toward me, who I catch in my arms but the force of the push sends us both sprawling. I get her up and lean her against the back of the car. The man is circling Gabriel with the knife, slashing at him but only finding air. Now Gabriel backs up to this low wrought iron fence, the kind with the little spearheads on the vertical rails to discourage would-be trespassers. The man drives the knife toward Gabriel's stomach. Gabriel does a full body spin away from the jab, and suddenly he is behind the man. He back-kicks Derek with such force that his body is almost impaled upon the fence. He would have been if Gabriel had not lunged at the last second, catching his jacket and pulling him back, avoiding the spear point by mere inches. Gabriel pushed him to the ground. Backing up toward the car, Gabriel, perhaps thinking that the knife had fallen during the struggle or maybe just feeling immense relief that he had pulled Derek from almost certain death, backed up against the car to catch a breath.

"Suddenly Derek yells, 'You're not the only one who can throw a knife, asshole,' and throws the blade toward Gabriel. With lightning reflex, Gabriel deflects the blade with a sweeping motion of his arm, which sends the blade in a new direction. The knife nicks Rita on the forehead just as I pull her down out of harm's way. Derek rushes toward Gabriel in a rage. Gabriel sidesteps and using Derek's momentum drives his face through the passenger window. He pulls him out and lets him fall to the ground.

"Just then, Carlos runs up with a group of friends on his heels, as Gabriel checks out the wound on Rita's forehead. 'It's just a nick,' he says, 'but she'll need some first aid.'

"Gabriel nods at Carlos and asks, 'Are you with her?'

"'Yes, but who are you?'

"'Nobody important,' Gabe says and then pulls Carlos to the side. They had a quick parlay. Carlos shook hands and shared a quick masculine hug with Gabriel and then went straight for the guns and cartridges while shouting orders to a few of the men in the group. Gabriel walked up to me, but before he could speak, I took his head in my hands and kissed him on the mouth and told him fiercely that he had a friend and ally for the rest of his days. He hugged me warmly and told me that the opportunity was a gift in itself, and that my gratitude was enough. I told him in a solemn Spanish phrase that my gratitude was just the beginning.

"'I better be going,' he says and took off at a trot down the street.

"'Meet us at the Viva next Tuesday night!' I yell over the sounds of police sirens. He flashed me a wave and then disappeared into the darkness of the alleyway. Carlos who had sobered up completely had brought a real crowd with him. He ushered several of his friends to stand guard over the three offenders who were just coming to when the police arrived. Rita was still out on her feet when the ambulances finally arrived. The paramedics sorted out the injuries and rushed them all to the hospital. Carlos followed in his car as I had insisted on riding in the ambulance with Rita, who still held my hand in a death grip. There at the emergency room, the police questioned me for hours. I told them that I had chased down Rita when I saw her leave the club with a guy who was up to no good. I said that when I caught up with her, I saw the man that she had been at the club with forcing her into the car at knifepoint. Then this guy came out of nowhere and overpowered the three men and then took off down the street in a red Mustang. I said it all happened so fast, and I didn't see much because I was busy trying to get away with Rita. Carlos had placed the guns with empty cartridges into the hands of Derek and the driver while they were still out. I'm thinking this is what Gabriel and Carlos discussed during their quick parlay. Derek got a possession charge along with assault with a deadly weapon and attempted rape. The police also found several tablets of Rohypnol in his pocket. Rita had the date rape drug in her system and could remember little of what actually happened. She could recall only fragments even after her release from the *hospital when I told her everything a day or so later and well…Faith…oh my god, honey, I'm so sorry here. I am just rambling on."*

Grace, I was so overwhelmed with so many different feelings, fear about what this meant about Gabriel and me, doubt about who he was and if I was safe with him, and wonder at how he could have done such a brave and foolish thing.

"Talk to me, Faith," Maria said, gently taking my hand. "I can see your mind spinning. Ask the questions. Just take them one at a time."

So I did, and she answered each one with patience and resolve.

Swallowing, I fought for composure as I felt the first droplets of virgin bliss beginning to leak out of the fault line crack in my maiden illusions. "So do you think he is safe?" I asked, a tear sliding down my cheek.

"Yes, Faith, I do," Maria said in a reverent whisper that seemed to wrap my fragile state in a warm blanket.

"You know the way that you begin to form a picture in your soul, a picture of how the one you want looks in your heart. I'm afraid now that my picture is not true. I feel this uncertainty, this splinter of doubt, and it is ruining the photograph in my dreams. Do you know what I mean?"

"I know exactly what you mean. I'll just say this and then you tell me what you think. I believe in him, Faith, even as much as I believe in myself. He genuinely has that quality. I want to share something with you. Since that September night when we first met Gabriel, Carlos has stopped drinking. I was happy at first, but later I worried. I told him that I didn't want him to change his ways, not even his drinking because he blamed himself and punished

himself with a straitjacket of guilt. He told me it was not guilt, my sweet Corazon. That's what he calls me when he is being that sweet and sensitive man that I see so clearly inside of him. He calls me his heart."

"*Smart man,*" I said with a smile.

"*He certainly was that day,*" Maria said, staring at the memory with her brown-almond eyes. "*He says it's not guilt, its aspiration. He said in his talks with Gabriel, he had found the way to uncover within himself a larger sense of purpose, something bigger than his wants and our needs. He told me that he was discovering a way of being more like his grandfather who had learned the secret of how to live happy even in times of poverty and struggle. He knew that his father had rebelled against his grandfather's ways. But strangely, he said, even as a child, he had always been drawn to them. He had always wondered how it was that his grandfather was always singing and giving what little he had to others as if he were rich without a care in the world. How he could live like that while his father who was much better off always seemed unhappy even in times when they had more than enough. I met Grandpa Manny only one time when I was seventeen years old during a visit to Brazil. I fell in love with him instantly, such a magical combination of humor, wisdom, and warmth. Like an old sweater wrapped around that radiates a comfort that everything is going to be all right. I was amazed at how he and his wife, Yolanda, could be so in love after more than fifty years of marriage. The way that they looked at each other, Faith, you would have thought that they were stepping into the beginnings of young love.*"

"*Oh my, there I go again off the beaten path,*" she said, putting her palm to her forehead.

The Dreamwatcher Diaries

In spite of the moment's weight, I had to smile at the sincerity in her frustration with herself.

"What I'm saying is that I would stake both my life and my love on Gabriel's honor. Faith, it is because of the way that he looks at you that I tell you these things because I can see that he believes in you the way that you also believe in him. The fear that you sense now is that he may be some thug in disguise, a boy who chases violence to feel like a man, but that is not Gabriel. There is honor in him, Faith, I know it, and I know that you have seen it too."

"I guess my doubt is healthy then," I thought out loud. "The doubt comes from a closer view of the picture, one that is more intimate. I can now see elements of his character that were not so visible in the distance. The crack is not in the picture but rather in the illusion that the picture must remain the same. My task is to determine if I can accommodate the new elements without losing myself and to accept that changes in the picture are the rule and not the exception."

"That was nicely put, Faith, and what would you say is the new element in the picture?"

"Violence not in him per se, but more like violence around him."

"Exactly and the truth is, violence is scary, and I can only imagine how shocking this all is to you. It is a good thing to question the presence of violence, but what Gabriel did was a brave and noble thing. He very probably saved Rita's life and maybe even my own. Your new vision can now see that Gabriel has warrior in his blood. I don't know, why he just does. What I do know is that he does not let the warrior define him. He knows that he is more than that, and so much more. I mean, I know that I have a *distinct advantage over you in having known him longer, and I would never expect you to just take me at my word having just met me. I just hope that you will consider that your few days, worth of knowledge, of this man that you are falling for is still true and still yours, unspoiled. It is so important that you see that the innocence of those early days of your heart's affection is still sacred and intact."*

Starting to feel better, I asked, "What did you mean back at the Viva when you said that karma has smiled on me and that already I have changed him?"

"He has chosen you, Faith, just as you have chosen him. It is karma's smile because I believe that choice was made long before you met."

"Yes this I, too, believe," I said with a faraway look in my eyes as I traveled memory's back roads, witnessing my Dreamwatcher take flight from that old porch swing back home in Indiana.

"As far as how you have changed him, I can tell you two things with certainty. In the three years that I have known Gabriel, there has always been a restlessness in his eyes as if he were on some quest and had resigned himself to some nomadic spirit. Beneath that cover of restlessness, there has always been another face, a face of profound hurt and sadness, one that resided so deep within his being that no individual soul could ever touch it. The first time that I saw him since you two met was Monday, the day after your first date. Faith, that look of restlessness and pain was gone. In its place was a peace and openness that I had never seen before. It was like he was letting us into this room in his soul that had been closed for a very long time. A room that he had just recently worked to clean out so that he might invite some trusted souls of his choosing."

"He feels like a traveler in a strange land, seeking a face that is more than just a stranger, but troubled by an ancient wound," I said in a whisper more to myself than to her.

"I'm sorry, what was that? I couldn't quite hear you."

"Oh, it's nothing, just something my grandmother once told me. You were saying."

"Faith, I've got to tell you in the short time that I have known Gabriel, I have never seen a man turn away so many advances from so many different women. He did it with grace and dignity, but he also did it because he knew exactly who he was looking for. He would always wink at me and say, 'I know what you're thinking, it's just that she's not her. You know what I mean.' 'Yes,' I would say, 'I think I do.' He was talking about you, Faith, you're her. Now tell me honestly," she finished with a wink and a knowing smile, *"that you were not also looking for him because you, too, knew exactly who you were looking for."*

At this, I remembered my *"Lady in Waiting"* and the resolve with which she had risen up in me. *"No argument there,"* I said with a shy smile.

"I can tell you that never once has he ever brought a woman for us to meet. Carlos was shocked when he called and told him about you, and I almost fell over when he asked for us to meet him at the club. He told us about his first date with you, but when we asked him about your name, he said, 'Not until you meet her face to face.' When I heard your name tonight, I was struck by the irony of these changes in Gabriel, and then I thought about what happens when a restless spirit finds purpose, a home, when it finds faith."

Feeling close to a complete resolution of my worries, doubts, and fears, I embraced her in a warm hug and whispered a heartfelt thank-you in her ear. "Maria, I've got to tell you, you are an amazing person. You're like a Buddhist nun helping me through this minefield of emotions, and here I am coming out on the other side feeling stronger and God help me," I finished speaking, now more to myself again than to her, "even more in love."

Maria suddenly laughed out loud, nearly choking on a sip of wine. "You're a sweetheart, Faith," she said, patting her chest with her palm, "but the nun part is a bit of a stretch."

"That's me," I said laughing myself, "always overdoing on the descriptors."

"Actually, an emotional minefield is a fair description of what we just went through, though the telling of it does impact the mood. I think it knocked the dance fever right out of me."

"I am so relieved to hear you say that. I feel the same way, but I could eat a horse."

"You got that right, sister," she said, letting loose again with that musical laugh of hers. "Let's collect our men and go score some pancakes and sausages."

"Let me run to the ladies' room and we're out of here."

So there I was, Grace, looking at myself in another mirror, in yet another ladies' room trying to regroup and take some accounting of what I had just learned. I listened closely for Camiel, my wisdom angel (so now you know the name of my wisdom angel, Mamaw, the same name my father chose for that name in the middle), and in those private moments she spoke. You are here, sweet Faith, you have arrived. You are no longer the Lady in Waiting. She has moved on. Her season of significance has passed. You are Faith, and you are here standing now in this moment of your existence where the wait is over. It is time this night to love your soul with the ferocity that you see in his eyes. Embrace your soul, Faith. Look closely at whom Destiny has brought into your universe, listen to the truth of him, and if your heart's affection be both true and in your bones all through and through, then you must jump!

Grace, I felt such exhilaration at this knowledge, and there was an ache in the deepest part of me to see his face, to wrap my arms around him and melt into his embrace. I smiled at the intense look on my face coupled with the strength of a resolve in my eyes, one that I had never truly felt for any man up to this particular moment. I took that smile and practically ran out the door.

Arm in arm with Maria running across the street back towards the Viva, a question suddenly crossed my mind.

"Hey, Maria, did Gabriel tell you to share all this with me tonight?"

"No way would Gabriel do something like that," she said so matter-of-factly. "That's just not his style. He's pretty much the polar opposite of a manipulator. He's more of a 'let the chips fall where they may' kind of guy. Don't get me wrong, he is guarded and about himself reveals only one layer at a time. As for how I ended up choosing tonight for my disclosure, I would chalk it up to karma. I didn't even know that I would tell you until we spoke in the ladies' room. I think it was your story about how you almost literally fell for him down the club stairway that led to my certainty that tonight was the night."

"Ahh here we are home sweet home away from home," Maria said as she pulled open the club door. She

teased me as I made my careful descent. "Don't fall now, don't trip on those beautiful Jimmy Choos."

"Quiet already," I giggled, "can't you see I'm concentrating here."

Reaching the bottom a few steps ahead of me, she said, "My turn for the ladies' room. See you at our table."

"See you there," I called after her.

I made my way to the bar hoping for a few minutes of introspection to collect my thoughts and consider what I might say to him. There was this moment of strangeness, Grace, strange in that, in spite of Maria's comforting words, I felt as though I were about to meet my sweet dream again for the first time, and then I saw him. He was standing on the edge of the dance floor watching Carlos and Rita dance. I swear he must have felt my eyes because he suddenly turned and, seeing me, looked again straight at the Faith inside me. There was this look of passionate affection in his eyes, but it was the sense of certainty behind that affection that caused my composure to break.

Grace, I imagined that I actually heard the hairline crack trace a path through the wall of my reserve. I had a scant second to think "oh no," and then I felt it shatter into a million tiny pieces. The only thing I knew in that moment when this flood of fluid's effect came pouring through the breach was that I wanted very badly to be in his arms, but my legs wouldn't move. So there I stood, all my feelings for him exposed, blazing like hot pink neon signs on my cheeks, paralyzed while being utterly naked in my vulnerability. But then I remembered what Camiel had said, "Honor my worth, see the beauty of my being, be here and now, and if my feelings be true, show your colors." So I breathed there in that moment, letting my feelings flow, allowing him to gaze at the silky under-skin of my passion, opening my heart with the resolve of its affectionate invitation. In that brief interlude, I found the courage to believe that while the universe held sway over the province of tomorrow, in the kingdom of "here and now," I was truly the queen. So I let go my string of morrow worries and chose to just trust in the wisdom of the Divine. As I watched those worry nuggets disappear round the bend, pulled now by the current toward the place where they belonged, I realized with a smile of discovery just how much energy it had taken to keep those beads of worry from their home. I felt a surge of refreshing energy, and in that moment of sweet surrender, I jumped.

Grace, I am not sure how I covered those few steps to where he was standing, but suddenly I was in his arms, melting into his embrace. My face was in his chest, and my head was dizzy from the masculine scent of him. There were no words in that timeless bliss, only a closeness that my imagination had never imagined and the whispering that comes, when heart is pressed to heart, about how they already knew what we had just discovered. I looked up at him, a certain shyness in my eyes one that seemed to say, "I wonder what you make of all this."

"Maria told you?"

"Yes."

"Are you OK?"

My reply was a soft kiss on his mouth.

Before he could reply, Carlos piped in. "The temperature is way too hot in here for that, and we have a vote on the floor for breakfast, so I say we make a mad dash for Uncle Bill's before the obnoxiously intoxicated people get there and lay waste to the ambience."

"We're right behind you," Gabriel said, mouthing a reverent thank-you to Maria. I smiled at her, still leaning into Gabriel's chest.

"Alright, see you there, and I want at least two feet of separation between you two at all times or you'll never make it there."

Gabriel gave him that boyish grin of his and said, "You're asking a lot, but I'll do my best, compadre."

"See you two there," Maria said, giving me a smile of approval. "Rita, you coming with us."

"Yes, I'm probably staying the night. I'm a little bummed Donte never showed."

"That's it, finito, no more, Rita," Maria flared. "One time maybe, two times maybe not, but three times and karma is screaming 'get out!'"

"Yes, you're probably right," Rita said, giving Faith and Gabriel a wistful look, "but sometimes, Maria, that 'karma' of yours can be a real bitch."

"Karma is not mine, Rita, and it doesn't serve us. We serve it."

"This sounds like a great discussion to have over pancakes," Carlos said, taking Rita's hand and pulling her toward the exit as Maria and Rita start chattering back and forth in Spanish. He, threw an exasperated eye-rolling, looked back over his shoulder. "Hey, call Dr. Phil for me will you? See you there."

I snuggled close to him on the ride to "Uncle Bills" which is by the way, Grace, a St. Louis landmark, friend to "all-nighter" creatures everywhere, whether study, party, or even chronic insomnia, the restaurant that never closes is there to get you through. I shared with Gabriel about the emotional minefield that I had walked through *during Maria's telling. I told him about my worry, doubt, and fear and relished the way his arm squeezed me closer in comfort when I did. After I had finished talking, we drove for a while, cocooned it seemed, for those moments in a warm and intimate hush.*

"*I planned on telling you about it,*" *he said.* "*I did not expect all this to come out the way it did, but I am grateful that you took it well. It's just…well…I mean there are some things that I want you to know about me of course. I just hope for that to happen as a matter of course, you know little by little, and not some big chunk that I lay in your lap, burdening you with a collection of unwanted expectations.*"

"*Well, you don't have to worry about that,*" *I said softly.* "*I don't believe in expectations, only hopes and wishes.*"

Something about that moved him because he kissed my lips with the sweetest sincerity.

"*But I am grateful to you for not putting big chunks in my lap. That really doesn't sound like much fun,*" *I said with a mischievous grin.*

"*You are so disgusting, chunks? I would never say chunks.*"

"*Hey, you chose the word, not me.*"

"*I said chunk, you know like a big glob of stuff rolled together, just sitting there in your lap,*" *he said, his hand digging into my side finding my ticklish spot.*

I squirmed and giggled, "*Oh yes, glob sounds much more appetizing than chunk. Let's go with that.*"

"*You're impossible, so hard to please word-wise. What am I going to do with you.*"

"*We'll figure something out,*" *I said as we pulled into the restaurant parking lot. We got out of the jeep, and he straightened my crazy hair saying he did not want anyone to think that anything untoward had occurred. I said I didn't care and mussed it up again. He laughed, took my arm, and walked me in, telling me that untoward was already starting to grow on him. I felt a little wild, a lot giddy, and more than a little certain that I was walking the foothills just below "Mount Bliss." I snuck a look at him, smiled, and promised myself that I would savor each and every moment.*

The breakfast was filled with food and conversation covering topics that bounced from romance to music and dancing to religion and back to romance again. The voices were passionate, the laughter musical, and the souls were kindred. Some hours later, we said our goodbyes with hugs all around and promises of "let's do it again." Gabriel brought me back to the West End, and parking a few spaces down from my Land Rover, he took me in his arms where for some minutes I levitated, hearing only the sounds of distant traffic, the ticking of the cooling engine, and the rhythm of his beating heart. He broke this peaceful stillness by gently lifting my face to his. He kissed me with his eyes wide open, just gazing through the brown iris glass into my soul, as if he were actually surveying some scenic countryside in that universe within me. I held his gaze while I myself dove into those blue depths with hopes of finding clues to mysteries that were even now just beginning to unfold. I swam in that lagoon for how long I do not know as my sense of time had vanished, pulled out with the tide of his embrace. My determination to find some revelation, testing my capacity to focus, pushed me to greater depths, and suddenly I saw a face. It was the face of a girl, a girl-child on the cusp of womanhood, but something bright and red was coming out of her mouth.

I shot toward the surface, but the girl swam with me, though giving me a safe distance. She suddenly put her hands together in a prayerful and reverent air, stopping me in my panicked ascent. She bowed to me, slowly backing away, and I watched in disbelief as she mouthed the words "bless you" and then slowly swam back down into those deeper blues.

I came to inhaling the cool November wind stream that was drifting through the crack in the opened window of his jeep. He pulled me close and said, "You are so brave, Faith, so brave to let your feelings show the way you did tonight. When you came back from your talk with Maria and you stood there by the dance floor looking so beautiful, looking at me with all your feelings, Faith, it was the most courageous thing. All of my life, I have never found the way to open myself like that. I just want to say to you before this moment ends that I see that in you, Faith, that courage and also a wisdom about the nature of grace. I feel that what you did in that moment was a precious gift, one I will always be grateful for."

Grace, when he said that about the nature of grace, I smiled the biggest smile but at the same time wondered how could he know to say such things after such a short time of knowing me?

There were no words, so I kissed him in response and was amazed at how that kiss said everything that I had wanted to say. We let go our embrace, and he with one final caress on my cheek said, "Let's get you home." He got out and let me out onto the sidewalk. He walked me the short distance to my car, and after a long final kiss goodnight, he saw me off down the road back to that space that I call home. I glanced in my mirror as I pulled away and to my joy found my sweet dream watching over me. I made my way back home where I arrived just before dawn.

As I prepared for bed, I pondered the question, who was that girl? Was she a projection from myself, maybe a figment of my imagination? Could it be that was there was some "seer" in me activated somehow by this budding romantic energy? Was it a soul from his past? Too many possibilities and while intriguing was not my chosen theme for my dream set this night. I chose to let it go and extended another invitation to Serenity. She arrived in her typical fashion like a welcomed summer breeze with her brother Peace in tow. There in their presence, I began to settle into a pleasant weariness.

I must sleep now, Grace, but I will be with you again soon to share more about these early days of my sweet dream journey.

November 12, 2003
Shopping in the Loop
Sweet Dream Time: Forty-Two Hours of You and Me
Gifts and Kindness

Dearest Grace, I awoke this morning feeling like a child, Grace, so fragile against this current that has swept my heart so swiftly downstream. The strength of this river's undertow leaves me breathless as I try to focus during these hours away from him. How strange to find with such consciousness that love is a force to be reckoned with, I mean I had always imagined it, but never anything quite like this. Never have I been pulled so from my rou-

tine stream, waking to find myself drifting again down that blissful river gazing at his face, cradled in his arms. I can still see that girl who, inspired by her Mamaw Grace's "Prayer Boat" story, set sail her own prayer for this day to come. I shall share with you the story of that girl who still walks there in that summer day down the back roads of my memory.

She stands there tall and tomboy, skinny in an Indiana creek with the water up to her knees. The late summer sun leaking through the camouflage of maple and oak trees that line the banks dapples the water's surface. The girl is dressed in cutoff jean shorts and a red checkered blouse tied at the waist. Her long blonde hair is pulled back in a ponytail secured by a band that features a small red butterfly. It is only days before her thirteenth birthday and she is just beginning to feel the stirrings of a pubescent yearning. It is a longing that greets all coming of age girls breezing in like an exotic new boarder, strange and exhilarating, like an adventurous woman child taken to larks in the sun and walks with the moon. The girl senses that the woman is settling in (to her delight), unpacking this very moment in some room in her soul with plans to stay (she hopes and prays) for more than just awhile. It was this boarder who had woken the girl that morning, whispering in her ear with visions of romantic adventure.

The girl just stands there for a moment, enjoying the feel of the water gurgling around her legs. She feels skeptical about the alien texture of the creek bed silt that seeps up between her toes as she tolerates the sensation of walking on the silky skin of some ancient reptile. She tilts her head toward the sky breathing in the moist summer air and allowing the sun to plant warm kisses on her face, *kisses that would blossom her cheeks and leave a splash of freckles across the bridge of her nose. Leaving her reverie, she looks down at the handmade sailboat in her hand. She had spent the early part of the morning looking for the perfect piece of driftwood; the rest of the morning was spent in furrowed brow concentration, carving and shaping the boat's hull. She feels a welcomed kinship with the determination that the boarder has galvanized within her. Early afternoon, as she munched on a lunch of cheese and baloney sandwiches and potato chips, washed down with a glass bottle of creek-chilled Coca-Cola, she completed the finishing touches. These included a mast and a sail fashioned from a swatch of cotton cut from an old shirt of her father's. She also included a small compartment in the hull where she could secure her prayer written on a small piece of paper that she had wrapped in plastic. Less than one hour before the afternoon gives way to evening, the girl is ready to launch her brave little prayer boat.*

She wades through the water looking for the best launch site. She giggles at the way the current plays with her balance and gasps at sudden drop-offs that send splashes of cold water as high as her chest. At the place where the creek takes a sudden turn, she spies a wide section in the stream, free of foliage and debris. She walks to a place midstream where the water reaches just above mid-thigh. The girl pauses to look skyward and then says a little prayer, the one that she has written and tucked securely in the little boat's hold. Kneeling in the stream, she cups the boat in her hands and places it on the water's surface. She feels the current's hand curl around the fragile vessel trying to pull it from her grasp though she is not yet ready to let go. Or maybe she thinks, it is the boat itself that is eager to sail, and the pull that I feel now is the spirit of the prayer boat's destiny that is eager to begin its journey. She smiles at this thought and suddenly remembers that she has not given the boat a name. "I shall call you Hope," she says out loud, "and I shall pray your sail is smooth." With that, she takes a deep breath, and gently releasing her breath toward the sail, she lets go. She watches for a moment, crossing her fingers on both hands in hope that the boat will sail. The craft remained upright, boldly sailing on the flow of the waterway. Impulsively, the girl jumped up and down, clapping her hands and giggling with delight. She blew the boat a kiss and waved as children sometimes do with places and things to which they have assigned a soul. As she watched the sky-blue sail bobbing downstream, she wondered how far will Hope go and will she weather any storms and overcome those obstacles that might seek to cross her path. Maybe someone will find you one day, she thought with an excited smile, as the prayer boat became a blue speck that disappeared around the bend, and maybe my prayer will be answered.

Feeling pleased with the successful launch of her prayer boat, she waded back to the south bank and collected her lunch pail and tool basket. She tied them in a neat bundle to the handlebars of her bike, which she had parked against a massive oak. Walking the bike up to the street, she pedaled toward home with thoughts of that exotic new boarder, marveling at how fluidly she could transform from child to woman and back again. She was woman now curled up in bed in that room, her soul sleeping with a smile of contentment and dreaming of Hope's adventures and the moonlight that shimmered across the sky-blue sail.

I know what you're going to ask, Grace. "What was your prayer?" "Give it up, honey child," you would say

with a wink, "old women should not be kept waiting."
How I miss you, Gracie, and I shan't make you wait. The
prayer went like this:

> Now, oh Lord, to you I pray
> That you might show me the way
> To find the one who sees me.
> The one who really frees me.
> Paint his face inside my heart.
> Keep his soul while we're apart.
> Whisper wisdom in my ear.
> Harp heart strum when he is near.
> Hold him safe and warm and dry.
> Bring him close when time is nigh.
> Lord, I pray because you see.
> Who I am, what we could be.

Though on this day, the words of the past seem a bit naive as I look back at the girl that I was. I want to hug her and tell her that she has no idea just how precious her heart really is, and please, honey, don't stop believing. I hope you enjoyed my "prayer boat" story, and I send you my heartfelt thanks for sharing yours.

The past few days I've been putting myself into some new pieces that I had been avoiding. My newly acquired inspiration proved to be a strong ally in this recent victory over Procrastination, the reigning queen of the Kingdom of Sloth. Of course, I gave Layla an update, and she agreed that the revelation of Gabriel's encounter with violence was not ample reason to jump ship just yet. She did say that it would be provident to proceed with caution. To that I asked, "How do you free fall cautiously?" To which *she said, "Very carefully." We laughed at that and made plans to meet later next week. I could sense that she was still worried, but I have known her long enough to know that her worry is a somewhat wonderful and natural consequence of being her best friend. Fortunately, she had helped me to learn to not worry about her worrying. I still laugh at her response when I told her that day in our distant past that I was beginning to feel responsible for her worry. She laughed and said, "Don't you dare try to carry my worry suitcase. It's got my name on it and my stuff in it. I don't pack it with my worry treasures every day to have someone else go carrying it for me. I earned each and every one of those worries, and I like their weight. It's what keeps me grounded, girl. So don't go messing with my anchor to reality, unless you want your best friend to go floating off to the never, never."*

"That's a deal," I'd said, giving her a hug of relief. The call ended with my announcement of my next date with him, which would be taking place in the Loop some three hours from this very moment. You'll be getting all the details, Grace, so stay tuned.

Let's travel for a moment, Grace, back to those turn of the century days when our own (several "greats" to the past) Grandma Hope walked the streets of Downtown St. Louis. It was that time of bittersweet evolution when the era of the literal work horse was coming to its end as the advent of machines enjoyed its beginning. Horse-drawn carriages and cobblestone streets gave way to rail systems and the innovation of the streetcar. Should we desire to see the sights in that St. Louis of the early 1900s, we might hop onto the trolley and travel the east-west thoroughfare along Delmar Boulevard. It would

Laurence Gabriel

take us to its turnaround some blocks away from Skinker Avenue. From there we would begin the trip back to the city, this historic turnaround was christened the Loop by St. Louisans. The Loop was destined from its beginning to be one of the most unique neighborhoods in the country. In the 1950s, at the height of its character development, the Loop was adopted by scores of teenagers. Some say it was the birth of rock 'n' roll that characterized the unique soul of this neighborhood. In the days of Chuck Berry, Buddy Holly, and James Dean, to name a few, this stretch on Delmar featured first and ran movies in both the Tivoli and Varsity theatres with Joe's Billiards sitting in between. Episodes at this pool hall, which was typically teeming with adolescent rebels without a cause, were the bread and butter of lunchroom chatter in high schools stretching from St. Louis City all the way to the southernmost counties. The restaurants up and down the Loop area during this tender age included drugstores on both Enright Avenue and Kingsland Avenue. The establishments were highlighted with old-fashioned soda fountains, complete with art deco counters and red barstools finished off with a record store all in the same shop. The district enjoyed a revival in the 1970s by inviting owner-operated shops and restaurants. One of the first businesses to establish itself was the now famous Blueberry Hill, a pub and music club that fueled a fire of inspirational commerce that would stretch for six city blocks. Shops like Vintage Vinyl, Headz and Threadz, the Star Clipper, and restaurants like Brandt's Café, Cicero's, and the Melting Pot keep the patrons coming back for more. Not to mention the St. Louis Walk of Fame, which features brass stars planted in the sidewalk with names like Tina Turner, Kevin Kline, Chuck Berry, John Goodman, and Sheryl Crow. In 2007, the American Planning Association named the Loop one of the ten great streets in America viewed as a neighborhood business ideal for towns across the country. With Washington University, a short walk away, the area is a major draw for college students who frequent the diverse boutiques and outdoor cafés. There is talk of revitalizing the streetcar with additions to its circuit, which would include stops at Forest Park. At the corner of Delmar and Price Avenue, the old car sits waiting for that day, and there just across the way from that restored vintage trolley sat my sweet dream and me in the early moments of our third date.

We had planned to meet Tuesday morning, elevenish, in the Loop at the coffee shop across from the old trolley. I had arrived a little early, one, to get a little coffee in me and relax for a moment and, two, to see if I could catch him strolling amid the Tuesday morning pedestrians. I wanted to see if I could pick out his walk before I saw his face. I wanted to sit there and just feel my affection flow out to this man who, in that moment, would be unaware that in the distance there was a woman falling for him. As it turned out, that moment had to be postponed because there he was walking toward me while flashing his broad boyish smile. He wore Calvin Klein jeans, a navy blue Nautica sweater with a brown bomber jacket, and of course the gunfighter boots. I, too, wore boots minus the gunfighter with my Claiborne jeans and V-neck navy blue cashmere sweater with a brown suede jacket.

"Looks like you got the navy blue memo," I said with a giggle.

"And what a memo it was, like a whisper in the back of my mind, or was it that I haven't done laundry in a month and this was the only item left in the drawer."

"I think I rather like the whisper memo," I said, looking into his eyes.

"Yes, me too," he said, softly kissing my mouth hello. "I was actually hoping to get here early so I could sit and look for your face in the crowd, but this works just fine," he said, taking my hand and steering me toward the java shop. "It gives me something to look forward to."

Grace, I wanted to say something about confessions and coincidence, but the sincerity of his sweet remark was so beautiful that I found the wisdom to keep silent. I squeezed his hand instead and leaned into him to show him my appreciation.

We took our coffees to a table outdoors, as the day was crisp but not cold. Sitting down, I noticed for the first time that he had two nondescript brown paper bags, neatly folded, which he placed on the table.

"Gabriel, you know that lunch should actually go in the brown bag before you leave the house. It works better that way."

"Well, actually I'm fasting, and the bags help remind me that lunch is on God," he said with a mischievous smile.

I laughed. "You're hysterical, but do explain how does fasting translate to lunch is on God."

"Well certainly, my child," he said solemnly with a bow in a prayerful pose. "I shall enlighten you."

"Please do," I said with a giggle.

"Fasting as you know is primarily about spiritual nourishment and a cleansing that comes from directly ingesting your faith like food from the spirit for the soul. Thus the expression 'lunch is on God.'"

"That's actually quite brilliant. Please tell me that you read that somewhere and that you're not that witty."

"I'm finding that I surprise even myself when I'm around you," he said, giving my cheek a caress. "Now let me tell you what I had in mind. The brown bags are for a little shopping expedition during which we both buy each other a gift, which will be placed in the bag and given at the end of the day. To determine what to buy each other, we will do two things. First, we'll browse and window-shop together, keeping a watch on those things that catch each other's eyes. As we shop, we will also be thinking of a story that best describes those things that we personally hold dear. It could be any story, one that you make up on the spot, one that comes to mind, whether fact or fiction, it need only contain the sentiments of what it is that you value. The gift we purchase should hopefully echo those sentiments. Over a light lunch, we will tell each other that story. We will then have two hours or so to separately shop for that gift. Of course if you need more time, just post a note on the bulletin board by the trolley. During our search, should the universe accommodate us, we will look for an opportunity to perform a single act of kindness for a stranger. Do not initiate or volunteer this kind act but rather allow it to find you. Just keep your eyes open for the opportunity, and let the universe do the rest. This evening over dinner, we can have a telling of our adventures and later over coffee back at this very spot, if it's not too cold," he said with his smile, "we can exchange gifts. So what do you think? Does that sound OK, or we could just play the day by ear?"

"No way, your plan sounds wonderful," I said enthusiastically. "Can we start now?"

"Now is good," he said with a laugh. "Now is definitely good."

Laurence Gabriel

So we did it, Grace, we did all of it. It was a day filled with discovery and anticipation. We shopped and browsed till about oneish and then took our lunch at Blueberry Hill. Over salads laced with Cajun shrimp and chicken, we told our stories, the ones that would capture our individual senses of both passion and contentment. I told him the "Prayer Boat" story and added the events of the evening of that day. It was a memorable moment of contentment. I was sitting in a rocker outside Grandpa's old country store across from the lake. I was wearing one of my father's old button-downs. It was sky blue and still held the faint odor of his favorite cologne, Grey Flannel. I sat there sipping Orange Crush while carving a piece of driftwood that would someday resemble an angel. As I worked the wood, I kept an eye on the sun waiting for it to turn the lake into liquid gold. I felt so warm and content in that old shirt, as if my father's arms were around me, giving me that sense that all is so very well with my soul. As the sun took its light leaving us under the care of sister moon, I whispered, "I love you, Father, and you should know your little Fay-Fay is well."

"My God, but you can tell a story well," he said sincerely.

"Look who's talking, and it's time to ante up."

"OK, here goes. It was some months after my sixteenth birthday. My father was working, and my mother was in town shopping with my little sister. I was staring restlessly out the window of our cozy wood cabin, the place I called home. I looked out at the naked trees, shorn from the comfort of their colorful fall jackets. They stood resolute, waiting to brave the first snow of the Vermont winter. I had just recently discovered the deep comfort of running. The simple pleasure of finding a stride and let-

ting it take you, where it will. Just feeling the drive of your own will moving you down a road through space and time leading you to a soulful communion with this new companion that goes by the name of Self-Reliance. In spite of warnings about the first winter storm, I felt compelled to commune with my new friend. That compulsion coupled with the hubris and the sense of indestructibility enjoyed by sixteen-year-old boys everywhere had me pulling on my running togs and heading out the door. I ran with wild abandoned smiling at the light snow that had begun to fall as if challenging the weather to a duel. There is an old eighties song by Chris Cross called 'Ride Like the Wind.' I had replaced the word ride with run, and strains of that song ran through my head as I ran down that old logging road like an animal, which had somehow escaped the confines of his cage. Never having much interest in measurements of time or distance when it came to running, I am not sure how far I ran before I came out of my hypnotic pace to find that the weather had taken my challenge seriously. I was on a secondary road that while far from busy was at least paved. I was thinking that I knew the road, but the usual landmarks on the landscape were now hidden under a thick white blanket. The temperature had dropped alarmingly, possibly in the neighborhood of the low teens with a wind chill somewhere in the nether regions. I discovered my face was numb with cold, and I stopped for a moment to poke some holes in my stocking hat, creating a makeshift mask to pull over my face. I also marked a tree by tying a strip of my shirt to a lower branch just in case I started to go in circles. As I headed back down the road I found that the wind and snow had tripled in force. The way ahead was a white blur, and I could see what seemed to be less than a foot in front of me.

Laurence Gabriel

I was, in a phrase, lost, blind, and freezing. Forced to a blind man's walk, I blundered forward, feeling less afraid than I did, foolish at my grave error of judgment. I marveled at how small and fragile my existence had become in the grip of nature's will. In that state of disorientation, I truly felt as if I had stumbled through a rip in the fabric of this earthbound dimension to be born on the other side, delivered to some alternate universe. For some moments, I wandered in that alien place, a barren wasteland, filled to the brim with a cold, opaque nothingness and a silence that together dared your mind to suggest even the concept of existence. It was as if I could feel the dissolution of my ego, not a shattering, but much more like a generous scoop of butter melting away on the surface of a hot skillet. My notions of self became squishy, and my will to look at myself a certain way lost its shape. As I walked on, they faded into vague impressions like a blurry photograph of someone I once knew. Somehow I continued on in the viselike clutch of this void so complete as to escape all conscious imagination. Having ceased to exist, I wondered what it was that kept me in motion and, even more so, who it was who was doing the wondering. Then I sensed a presence within me, the shape of that deep self, rising from the dark mist of the void to reveal himself. 'I am,' the presence said, 'and you are here to discover me. Let the journey begin.' Before I had time to contemplate those words, I saw before me what appeared to be a black hole. Though my mind was reluctant, my feet stumbled forward as if they knew something that my brain had not yet registered. The hole turned out to be the entrance to a covered bridge, and magically it was as if that alien world had spit me out through some portal to land back in that familiar universe from whence I had come. I lifted my mask and sucked in the air, which held the scent of aging pine, hay, and horse droppings. Surging up from the depths of that nether universe deep within me, I broke the surface of my conscious mind where I was greeted by the sound of howling wind and the protesting reply of straining timbers. I leaned forward against the wall caressing the wood like a lover in a gesture of appreciation for its sheltering strength as well as its existential reassurance. I took stock of my physical condition and spent some time doing circulation exercises. While the numbness transformed to a hot pain and itchiness, I knew that these were good signs. As I paced back and forth in my shelter that spanned about ten yards or so across the swift moving stream, I began to work out an exercise and rest schedule in my mind. As the light of day began to fade, I had resigned myself to spending the night in my peaceful shelter when I heard something akin to a train shatter the silence. A horse and sleigh had entered the structure startling me at near the same measure that my unexpected presence startled them. After a series of 'winnies' and 'whoas,' we made quick introductions followed by my rueful account of my adventure. The couple was Dwight and Evette Coogan, and they were returning from tending to their sick daughter who lived with her husband some miles down the road. They wrapped me in a blanket and brought me to their home where Evette tended to my frostbite. All my limbs were saved, but it took a good three months until I was 100 percent again.

"As it turned out, I was over twenty-five miles from home, and the storm was the second worst on record rivaling the epic winter storm of 1932. All the phone lines were knocked out, and Dwight, due to the force of the storm and the equal force of his wife's pleading, was persuaded to wait till morning before attempting to alert my

parents. My father, who is the sheriff of our district, collected me the next afternoon. He didn't say a word nor did he need to as we rode home in a deafening silence. Once home, I headed inside with my head down, but before I could reach the door, he grabbed me, embraced me, released me, and headed straight for the woods. The door opened, and my mother was there with her arms around me ushering me into the cozy warmth of our cabin. 'He's alright, Gabriel,' she said soothingly, 'you know Calvin, he just needs some time. You scared us all, silly, nobody slept a wink all night.' I apologized profusely, and she assured me all was forgiven. My little sister jumped all over me, hugging me and jumping into my arms where she stayed for just about the next twenty-four hours, never letting me out of her sight. I fell asleep that night on the oversize davenport in front of the fire. Little sis snuggled close fast asleep with her head on my chest. Mother sat on her rocker knitting as she often did. She must have been tired, but she just sat there watching us two as if she wanted to memorize every detail of that moment, believing that if she watched long enough, she just might be able to immortalize the memory. Father walked in and out, pretending to be busy with something until mother told him, 'You're acting like a fly hovering over a bunch of pies cooling on the window sill, so you best land somewhere, Cal, before I have to take that flyswatter to you.' To which he matter-of-factly replies, 'Well, do you suppose you could give that damn knitting needle a rest, woman, and sit here on this couch next to me?' 'Nothing would please me more, old man,' she would say. Come spring time, I ran that course again, and I looked for that tree that I had marked. The distance from the tree to the covered bridge was just under five miles, a distance that given my halting pace took somewhere in the neighborhood of two to three hours to cover. It seemed like a lifetime, which as far as I can say confirms the theory of relativity."

"I love the vision of you falling asleep with your little sister. How little was she?"

"She was six at the time. Her name is Jennifer, and technically she is my adoptive sister."

"No point in getting technical when it comes to family."

"You've got that right."

"The void that you described sounded ominous at first, but then it turned out to be something akin to a doorway."

"My thoughts exactly. So what do you think, is it time to shop?"

"Yes and to my surprise, I'm actually excited about this shopping adventure. You should know that contrary to popular belief, not all women love to shop. I'm the fly in the ointment on that one. I'm more of a dash in and dash out kind of shopper. There's something about the energy of the shopping phenomenon. It's like I can feel all these things reaching out for my energy, not to mention my pocketbook. What's the fun in being surrounded by shelves and shelves of things crying out the words "consume me, consume me"? But this is different. There is a spirit to it, yes, it's a spiritual shopping adventure."

"Well said," he laughed, "and exactly what I was going for. So were off then. Meet you in say two hours in front of the coffee shop. Just one last thing, but I have to whisper it to you."

I leaned across the table toward his face. Instead of saying anything, he kissed my lips.

He took care of the bill, and we went out to the street. He gave me my brown bag, telling me with a smile, "Don't lose this now. It's a very special bag, one of a kind."

"Absolutely," I said with a giggle, one more kiss, this time from my initiation, and then we strolled in separate directions off into the marketplace.

I calculated as I walked running his story through my mind and picking out the subjects of significance. Let's see, restless traveler, running, covered bridge, horse, comfort, by the fire, Mr. Desperado himself, I thought with a smile, just as I passed Vintage Vinyl. Perfect place to start. I got him the Hotel California album, which features "Desperado." I solicited the store clerk's help to find the Christopher Cross CD and hugged him with a squeal of delight when he came walking up with it. I'm certain that he thought that I was certifiable, but his smile told me he was not at all offended by the hug. Thinking next about comfort by the fire, I found a crafts store and browsed the quilts. I actually found one that featured winter scenes including snow-covered forests and cabins in the woods. There was no way the quilt would fit in my brown bag, but fortunately the store had large bags. They were brown to my relief, but they had handles. Nothing a little snipping with some scissors couldn't remedy, I thought, feeling very pleased with my adventure so far. OK, covered bridge and horse and maybe something that represents travel, and I could call it a day. I tried several shops in search for anything resembling a covered bridge to no avail. Following the advice from the shop owner at the Antique Attic, I walked with a determined step looking for a shop called All Things Wood. Woman on a mission, I thought with a giggle. I quickened my pace and almost ran into a little girl who stepped out from a doorway right into my path. I had to grab her to keep from knocking her down.

"I'm so sorry, honey, I didn't even see you."

She couldn't have been more than six years old or so. She had on a little jeans outfit and a brown winter jacket with a fur-lined hood. She was a brunette with big brown eyes that were wet with tears.

"What's your name, sweetheart?"

"Abbey."

"Hi, Abbey, my name is Faith. So where's your mommy at, honey?"

"She's losted and now I'm losted too. I'm not spose to be here cause Mom said I couldn't go, but I came anyway. I sneakded in the car, and the car was going but then I fell asleep. Then the car stopded and I woke up and Mommy was gone and I tried to find her but she's losted and now I'm losted too."

"I see, well, do you think we could call her? Do you know her phone number?"

"No, they won't let me have a phone even though my friend Casey has a phone, but Daddy won't let me have one."

"Do you know Casey's number."

"Yes, I call her from my daddy's phone at home all the time."

"How about you and me go to that diner over there and have a soda and maybe try to get someone to come and give you a ride home."

"OK, but I'm not spose to talk to strangers. Are you a stranger?"

"Yes, everyone is a stranger until your mom says they're not. So we two strangers are going to sit and have some soda and make some calls, does that sound OK?"

"Yes, but do you think my mommy will be mad at me?"

"Maybe, sweetheart, but I think mostly she'll be very happy to see you."

I took her by the hand, and we sat on stools at the City Diner where I made a call to Casey, who gave the phone to her father who, to my relief, was available. I explained the situation and could he maybe help out. He agreed to call Abbey's house and agreed to come to the drugstore to pick her up if he couldn't get an answer. He also agreed to bring Casey along for reassurance. Abbey chatted me up while we waited, telling me about her cat and her parakeet, about her school, and which boys were mean and which girls were nice. She told me about her friend Casey who lived a few blocks down from her. She talked about her mom and dad and how she didn't like it when they yelled and liked it even less when her mommy left the house crying.

Some twenty or so minutes after I made the call, I heard a woman's voice behind me.

"Abbey," she said with a cry of relief racing to pull her daughter off the stool in a tight embrace. "Oh my god, Abbey," she cried, pulling her daughter into her arms. "You're safe, baby, you're safe. Abbey, honey, you scared Mommy so bad. You mustn't ever run off like that again. No matter how bad things get, you must never leave without telling us. What if something bad had happened to you or we could not find you. You must be safe, Abbey, always safe, tell me you understand that."

"I do, Mommy, I do," Abbey cried into her mother's neck. "I just knew that you were sad, and I knew I had to find you to make the sad go away. Then I fell asleep and you got losted."

"I know you don't like it when I cry, but, Abbey, I wouldn't be able to stop crying if anything ever happened to you. You've got to be safe, baby, you've got to be safe."

"I'm sorry, Mommy, I just couldn't help it. You were crying more minutes this time, I even counted more than sixty, and I had to make you better like I did before. I just had to, Mommy."

Grace, it was at this point in the interchange that I almost lost it, but fortunately mother and daughter were so lost in the intensity of their conversation that they did not see me wiping the moisture from my eyes.

"You must help it, Abbey, you must be safer. I need you to promise me that you will never do anything like this again."

"I promise, Mommy," Abbey said, squeezing her mother's neck in her arms.

Abbey released her mother and looked up at me and with a smile said, "You were right. She's more happy than mad."

"Faith Adams," I said, standing and offering my hand in introduction.

She hugged me fiercely and said, "I owe you everything, and I'll never be able to thank you enough. Abbey is my heart. I just don't know if I could go on if anything happened to her. I've actually had to consider that for the past five hours. Thank you, Faith. It seems I'm on the receiving end of a miracle."

"You're very welcome, and I am grateful to have been in the right place and the right time."

"Mommy, is Faith still a stranger?"

"No, I think we can call Faith our friend. I'm Louise Stevenson," she said, offering her hand.

"Very nice meeting you, Louise," I said, taking her hand, "and nice meeting you also, Ms. Abbey," offering my hand to Abbey, which she ignored in favor of a full body hug and a whisper, "You've got to come see my parakeet, will you please?"

"I shall do my very best," I said, giving her a wink.

"I'd love to have the opportunity to thank you properly," Louise said, handing me her card. "Please call sometime if you would."

After some hugs goodbye, we went our separate ways and I headed back toward the path from whence I had come.

I was only five minutes into my browsing at the shop All Things Wood when I found it. I was still smiling to myself about how the universe had given me the gift of an unexpected opportunity to perform an act of kindness. I was thinking about Abbey's sweet smile when she saw her mother when my eye caught the covered bridge to beat all covered bridges, not to mention the most perfect centerpiece gift that brought all the other gifts together, fitting Gabriel's story like the proverbial glove. I actually gasp out loud, putting my hand over my mouth when I saw it. The shopkeeper poked his head around the corner and gave me a concerned look, which changed to a wide smile when he realized what I was looking at. It was a snow globe the size of a basketball. The scene in the globe featured a horse and sleigh that circled a track through the woods to glide through a gorgeous red-covered bridge and back into the woods again. By winding the knob at the bottom of the globe, the sleigh would actually move in a slow circle around the track. All the gears were made of wood; the only thing not wood was the glass surrounding the scene. According to the homemade label, even the snow *was made of splinters of wood that were painted white. I scooped it up like I had known where it was all along and had the man who had caught my gasp wrap it and box it. I introduced myself to the man whose name was Walter and told him about how he had saved my day. He started going on about the man who made the globes, but I was barely registering his words. My mind was miles away watching the scene of Gabriel's face when he opened the box to see the globe.*

"It's magic you know, Walter, this whole day has been absolute magic," I said with a wide smile as I collected my bags and headed for the door.

"I hope he likes it, Faith," he said, opening the door with a wink.

"He, how do you know it's for a he?"

"Something in your eyes, I think," he said, flashing me a warm smile.

"Thanks for the magic, Walter," I said, returning the wink.

"Wish my wife would say that every once in a while," he said with a rueful grin.

"Well, you never know," I giggled. "Thanks again, Walter."

"You're very welcome, Faith," he said, smiling to himself as he stepped back into his shop. "Come visit again soon."

I took off down the sidewalk in a fast walk that bordered on a run. Time had gotten away from me, and the daylight had stolen away without saying goodbye. Lamplights, storefront neon, and headlights now lit my way. It was that mixture of man-made light that altered my mood, filling me with a sense of gratitude and a connection with humanity. Our intelligent light sending a message that seemed to bring a strange comfort, a message that we are human, still here, together, connected in the same plight, each soul somehow selected for this sentient journey. I spied the old trolley car and looked across the street at our coffee shop table, but before I could register that it was empty, I heard a voice behind me.

"Hey, beautiful, could I help you with those bags."

And there he was, smiling at me with his grin, his hands also holding a variety of brown bags.

"Looks like your bag had some babies too," I said, standing on tiptoe to kiss him.

He set his bags down and put his arms around me in a warm hug. "You look cold. We need to get you indoors and get a mug of hot chocolate in you."

"I'm a little cold, a lot happy, and your arms around me are working much better than hot chocolate ever could, thank you very much."

"Your welcome very much," he said, his smile growing bashful. "I was thinking that the coffee shop isn't the best place for the gift exchange now that it's gotten so late," he said as he collected his bags and headed with me across the street.

"Yes, I was going to apologize for that. The time really got away from me."

"No worries there, it kind of got away from me too. It was cool how I would get these ideas and then chase them down. Speaking of ideas, I've got a few about where we might go next. How about you, any thoughts?"

"Well, I've got a proposal. How about we go to this great Thai restaurant downtown, get some takeout, a bottle of wine, and bring it to my loft. We could just share our stories and gifts there," I finished shyly.

The Dreamwatcher Diaries

"Well, that pretty much puts all of my ideas to shame."

"It's about time, so far your ideas have been magical, which is, by the way, my word for this day that I don't want to end."

"Then we shall make it last as long as we can."

He followed me downtown in his jeep to the Thai restaurant where we ordered takeout. While we waited for our food, I took him to the Wine Shoppe a few doors down where we picked out some wine. We laughed together in the elevator on the way up to my loft as we took in the sheer number of packages that we had amassed. Our arms were loaded to the hilt, and we kept juggling and shifting to find some semblance of balance. Once inside, we set our packages on the kitchen counter, and I took his coat and got him settled on my oversized sofa in the living room level with a glass of wine. I scurried around the kitchen, putting out silver and flatware while racking my brain trying to remember where I had put my recent purchase of candles and incense.

"What a great view of the arch, and the perfect spot for this little breakfast nook you've put together. You've really done the place up nice, Faith. It's got such a homey feel to it."

"Thanks, it was actually a longer process than I thought it would be. I would get a vision about how I wanted each room to look and then put it together one piece at a time. It was as if the pieces that I started with, like that sofa for example would actually tell me what they needed to keep them happy."

"Looks like you got some good advice because every piece looks like it was made for the other. Hey, Faith, do you need any help down there?"

"No, I've got it," I said as I spooned out the food, which emitted the yummy Thai food smells of noodles, veggies covered in a Thai glaze with spiced beef and chicken, and cups of egg noodle soup.

I brought up the food, which I set on my oversized cherry coffee table and went to retrieve the wine bucket. I was about to sit down beside him when I remembered, "bedroom closet," I said, popping up again like one of those old "jack in the box" toys.

"What was that?" he asked.

"Finishing touches," I said with a giggle.

So there in that cozy homespun ambience, we laughed and talked as we ate enjoying the food and each other in equal measures. Eating with chopsticks, we sampled each other's entrees, feeding each other and sipping wine that was sometimes gulped to dampen the mischievous heat of an unexpected measure of spice. Pleasantly full, we brought the dishes to the kitchen and brought up the gifts along with frothy expressos made by Gabriel himself, who was delighted by the choice of my home expresso machine.

We shared our gifts. "Me first, me first," I had said. "I can't wait any longer." He let out an OMG when he pulled out the Christopher Cross CD saying, "How in the world did you find this?" He laughed as he read what I had written on the "Hotel California" LP, which was "On my third date with a real Desperado." He really seemed to like the quilt and seemed to appreciate the intricacies of the needlework. Having saved the best for last, I handed him the last brown bag. I wished I could have had a picture of his face when he pulled out the snow globe, which showed a mixture of treasure, pleasure, and awe. He kissed me and hugged me tight, telling me that the globe scene *captured the memory with a mystical clarity that was both warm and mysterious.*

Then it was my turn. The first bag I opened greeted me with an unmistakable fragrance that immediately called up the face of my father. I pulled out a new sky-blue button-down shirt that had been sprinkled with Grey Flannel. A small box containing a bottle of the cologne sat in the breast pocket. My eyes watered a little at that, and I thanked him with a tight hug. The next item brought a warm laugh it was a six-pack of those little green glass bottles of classic Coca-Cola complete with the words "Creek Chilled," which he had scripted on the side. The next bag held a painting of a young girl walking along a tree-lined stream with fall colors bursting out from the canvas.

"I couldn't find one with the girl wading in the water, but I was hoping this one might still be close enough to trigger the memory," he said almost apologetically.

"Oh, Gabriel, it's wonderful and surprisingly close to the creek scene in my memory. It's as if she's walking down a different section of the very same creek some days later, looking for the boat."

"Well, I have some very good news for that girl," he said, presenting me with the final brown bag. "The boat has been found."

I opened the bag and pulled out a sailboat about two feet in length. Someone had sewn triangles of sky-blue cloth to the white sails underneath, and there in the hold of that nostalgic craft made from rough-hewn wood was a small blue envelope, which I pulled from its perch. "Prayer Boat Dreams" was written on the envelope.

Suddenly his mouth was close to mine. "That's to read for later," he said softly. He kissed my lips and with a soft smile said, "Happy Prayer Boat Dreams day."

"Gabriel, it's so beautiful," I said, kissing him back with a fever. "How in the world did you do this?" I asked, sitting the boat on the table and staring at it in wonder.

"Well, I found the boat at this place called All Things Wood."

"Oh my god, that's where I found your snow globe."

"Interesting," he said with raised eyebrows, "that place really does have a magic about it, and isn't Walter a riot."

"Yes, he is a charmer, and he knows everything about every piece in that shop."

"So then I got the idea for the blue sails, and I got an old button-down from Headz and Threadz and took it to a tailor down the street. I explained my idea to her and then made her an offer she couldn't refuse," he finished in a fair Marlon Brando impression.

We talked for some time sharing those intimate details of our shopping adventures and the excitement of how our visions came together as we hunted from shop to shop.

After hearing my story about little Abbey, he told me about his act of kindness, which took place as he hunted for the old button-down. A mother with three children in tow was struggling with her purse at the register as she paid for some for the small pile of clothing that she had picked out for her children. As it turned out, she did not have enough to cover the cost of the coat that her ten-year-old daughter wanted.

Giving her mother a brave smile, the girl said, "That's OK, Mama, my coat works just fine."

The girl's mother bit her lip and fought a tear as she watched her little girl return the coat to the rack. As the girl passed Gabriel, she dropped a glove, which he scooped

The Dreamwatcher Diaries

up almost before it hit the ground. He slipped a few folded bills discreetly into the glove and turned to the young girl. "Here, honey, I think you dropped this," he said, handing the girl her glove.

"Oh thanks. I'm always dropping them," she said with an apologetic hand over her mouth. "I just can't seem to keep those things in my pocket. I'm so clumsy."

"No," said Gabriel as he turned toward the door, "what you are is brave and full of hope," and with a wink at her youthful brown-eyed smile, he was out the door and down the street.

Some hours later, he saw them coming out of Fitz's, a family restaurant that was famous for its own brand of gourmet soda. The brown-eyed girl was bouncing along behind her mother twirling along the sidewalk in her new coat.

As the hour grew late, we fell into a contented weariness, which moved us to stretch out on the sofa, and under his new quilt, sleep took us as we lay there snuggled close in each other's arms.

I awoke several hours later to the feel of his tender caress on my cheek. He had gotten up and dressed somehow while I was sleeping.

"I've got to go feed my beast, an Akita-chow mix named Nikita, who will not be happy with my prolonged absence. She is by the way very excited about meeting you. I was thinking of maybe picking you up sometime before noon on Saturday to bring you out to my neck of the woods. Does that sound appealing?"

"Very appealing," I said, kissing him on the mouth while I fought the urge to pull him back down into our warm nest.

"Sleep, sweet beautiful, and I'll see you soon."

Lawrence Gabriel

So I fell back into that warmth, pulling up the quilt that still held the smell of him. I breathed in that fragrance, and smiling wide, I closed my eyes and returned to that place where sails ripple in the wind, where seagulls perch, and whales sing to women who have fallen under the spell of Prayer Boat Dreams. When suddenly I remembered the blue envelope...

November 17, 2003
Walking with the Eagles
Sweet Dream Time: Sixty-Four Hours of You and Me
River Road Romance

Dearest Grace,

Yes is the answer to your question, Grace. Yes, I absolutely popped out of my nest when I remembered the blue envelope with the words "Prayer Boat Dreams" written on it and practically ripped it trying to get it open. Thank God for Scotch tape huh. So you're probably wondering what it said, well here you go. (How's that for immediate gratification?)

Prayer Boat Dreams

*I met a girl who dared to dream
set sail a prayer upon a stream.
I wished to tell her from the start
how brave and beautiful your heart.
When came the night the heart the same*

The Dreamwatcher Diaries

I met the woman she became.
We danced into the night awhile
And wisdom whispered from your smile.
Whispered, "dreams really do come true,
Prayer boat dreams of me and you."

—Gabriel

P.S. Faith, I had the most memora-
ble time with you this day.
You are an amazing person.
I will tell you true that if I am not
with you now as you read this,
I am missing you. Hope to see you soon.

Grace, I'm not sure which I like best, the poem or the P.S. I must have read them at least a hundred (well maybe not one hundred) times, but they keep finishing in a dead heat. I actually called Layla at five o' clock in the morning and, after filling her in on the details of the third date, tried to get her take on it.

"Faith, it's a no-brainer he would have had to write that poem in the space of time between the shopping and the moment that you met back up at the trolley. I mean it's not Shakespeare but take it from a songwriter that's not all bad for someone putting words together to touch a memory that they have had all but a few hours to weave. I'm actually a little impressed."

"You're kidding me?"

Grace, just FYI, Layla tends to be very hard to impress. I mean, with the exception of feats of nature, acts of God, the great poets, and musical performances from a chosen few, Layla simply doesn't impress.

"Whoa," I said a little, "and I am becoming a little concerned that this guy is starting to sound a little too perfect."

"Too perfect? Is that like possible?"

"Oh my god, you're starting to lose it. Of course, it is, like the guy who tells you everything you want to hear and works his ass off to get you in bed. Please, Faith, don't be naive. I know that you know better."

"Of course I know that kind of guy, but Gabriel has not even mentioned the bedroom, not to mention that we spent the most of the night sleeping in each other's arms albeit fully clothed, and he didn't try anything."

"That's exactly what worries me."

"Oh my god, you're impossible. Now you're worried because he didn't try to get me into bed."

"Maybe," Layla giggled into the phone. "It's just that I've read your creek story, which in my book is one of the most touching coming of age scenes that I have ever read. I mean I could just about feel every nuance of that piece. I just never figured any man would relate to it as well as he did. I mean his gift ideas were right on point."

"Well, it's not like it's a competition you know," I replied a tad defensively.

"Not at all, Faith," Layla said, her voice taking on a soft sincerity. "I'm just saying it sounds like he's really sweet and he really gets you, and that's a little scary for me 'cause some part of me is afraid of losing my sister."

"That's simply not a choice. Our relationship wrote the book on forever. You will never lose this sister, Layla, but someday you may find that you have a new brother."

"Alright, Faith," Layla said with a soft laugh, "I can live with that for now. I'm actually glad that I said it out loud because it has been nagging at me a bit."

"I'm glad too because your presence in my life has given me the deep warmth of one who is so loved and a freedom that brings more comfort than I could have ever imagined. You are precious to me, and my plan is to treasure you all the days of my life."

There was a pause, and I could sense that she was in a struggle with her emotions. Grace, in that deep emotional moment, as our bond silently reaffirmed itself across the airways, a small smile formed on my lips as I pictured Layla confronting her heartfelt connection with me. As one who fiercely shies away from showing her emotions, I imagined that she wanted badly to hang up but was trying to be brave. My smile was much like the mother who sees her child struggling on the brink of learning something that the mother has already learned and is now quite good at. The mother is also smiling at the child's courage and at what she sees the child becoming, right before her eyes.

"OK," she said some moments later, "and of course I feel the same way, but I'm not going to do this all the time, not even once a year, so please don't get any ideas that I've changed about this whole feelings thing."

"Of course not," I said quickly, "I'll just say that you are courageous and I'm proud of you and leave it at that. So what's the Thanksgiving Day plan?"

There was a little sigh of relief on her end. "Looks like most of the band will be scattering to the four winds, so it's going to be us, you, and whoever you would like to bring of course. So have you asked him yet?"

"Not exactly. I'm looking for the right time to ask, I mean I don't want to just spring it on him."

"Faith, honey, it's not like you're asking for his first-born child. It's just Thanksgiving dinner with some friends. The worst thing is he says no, we have a fabulous time here eating turkey and talking about how well you two are doing, and then you go meet him at your place or his and screw his brains out, right?

"Well, when you put it that way, it does kind of sound like a win-win. OK, I'll do it today."

"Today?"

"Yes, today, he's picking me up in a couple of hours. He said he wants to take me to his neck of the woods."

"And where is his neck of the woods?"

"I didn't exactly get that information yet?"

"That's cool, just do a 'port of call' call."

Grace, Layla and I came up with a safety measure called port of call. In the rare event that I'm out with a new man, I call Layla on her cell and GPS her by saying, "Hey, girlfriend, it's your best friend calling from exotic ports of call like, the loop, the hill, along with street names in whatever area I'm riding through. This safety measure was created and designed by Layla who is my guardian angel deluxe.

"Port of call it will be, and I'll even put him on the phone. If I do, will you be good?"

"Maybe, it depends on my mood."

"Can I put in an order for a nice mood somewhere in the next three hours?"

"I will do my utmost to fill that order."

"Mucho gracias, girlfriend, see you soon."

He called some minutes after I hung up with Layla, giving a pickup time of around 10:00 a.m. and directions to wear warm outdoorsy apparel, which for me ended up being well-worn jeans, brown wool sweater, and thermal-topped hiking boots. I told him I'd be waiting in *front, which worked out grand as I spied his Jeep pulling up just as the elevator doors opened. It was a strange kind of timing thing that I had only rarely experienced. I jumped into the Jeep and took in his rugged outfit that included old jeans, long-sleeved army-green thermal crew, and hiking boots. I threw my tote bag in back and gave him a "so nice to see you so soon" kiss, and we were off for as it turned out all points north.*

As we drive, Grace, I will describe to you Gabriel's neck of the woods including some bits of history as we go. Strangely in the seven years that I have lived in St. Louis, I had never been as far north as I was currently being taken. What struck me first as we traveled down Highway 367 across the line that divides Missouri from Illinois, I saw on the distant skyline what appeared to be a tower made of gold. It reminded me of Dorothy's first view of Oz as her and Toto, along with her three friends, reached the end of the yellow brick road. As I moved closer, the solid gold of the steepled tower became the gravity-defying cable-stayed design of the Clark Bridge. The complex construction of the four-lane bridge was engineered by Hanson Engineers of Springfield, Illinois, and was opened in 1994 in spite of major obstacles like traveling barges, surging river currents, and the great flood of 1993. I caught Gabriel smiling with appreciation at my openmouthed awe at the sheer genius and beauty of this extraordinary feat of engineering.

Once across the bridge, I found myself in the town that I had once read about as a child, a child who was fascinated by the brave souls like Harriet Tubman who had traveled the underground railroad. It was said that if the passengers of this railway could reach the city of Alton, Illinois, the prospect of freedom would increase tenfold.

Laurence Gabriel

Here I was rolling along the river road through that very town. The actual city climbs an abrupt incline ascending from the waterfront inland like houseboats riding the swell of a wave. It was compelling to think of those inland homes, the homes of those long ago abolitionists that might still hold secret tunnels and hiding places. Shelters of kindness created by those civil war day souls who chose to risk their comfort and even their lives to make their personal spaces into actual stations, offering passage to those pursuing freedom along the underground railroad.

I remembered reading that not far from the riverfront along which we rode in the mid-1800s, the first penitentiary in Illinois was built right here in Alton. Around 1863, it was used by the Union Army to hold Confederate prisoners of war, and due to its size, which ran along several city blocks, up to twelve thousand prisoners were confined there. A Confederate mass grave along the north side of Alton holds many of the over two thousand men who died of the conditions of overcrowding and the smallpox epidemic of 1863–1864. Prisoners who were clever enough to escape would try to cross the Mississippi to find refuge in the slave state of Missouri.

I later learned that when the prison was dismantled, many buildings in Alton both public and residential used the penitentiary stone as foundation. At least according to paranormal experts, who have dubbed Alton as the most haunted city in America, this restless spiritual presence in Alton is largely due to displaced Confederate souls who sought escape to inhabit the porous rock of the prison's walls. This theory is somewhat supported by the theme of ghost siting after siting that feature men in Confederate uniforms.

The Dreamwatcher Diaries

We passed the large grain silos part of the ConAgra mill. One silo bore the markings of the flood levels over the past one hundred years. The 1993 mark continues to hold the number 1 spot as the highest flood level in the river town's history. Just past the last silo, you'll see a collection of barges and ferryboats docked for loading and unloading. Beyond that, you can gaze upon the sheer expanse of the Big Muddy herself rolling along her cavernous trench, almost docile enough to disguise the frightening strength of her current.

If you were to look inland, you would see the beginnings of Alton's famous limestone bluffs—walls of stone rising majestically above the road carved, etched, and layered by the stress of water, wind, and time. It was a haven for souls passionate about shapes trapped in stone, and suddenly I was a kid in a candy store. I tore my eyes away from the bluffs for a moment to look at him and again saw a wide smile on his face.

"Are you enjoying yourself, you sneak? You planned this whole thing didn't you? You knew how much I would like this."

"Well I hoped, but your face has been telling me that you're enjoying it even more than I hoped, which makes me very happy."

"So I gathered from that one-thousand-watt smile of yours. Any chance you could turn it down a little," I said with a wide smile of my own.

"I tried, I really did, but my mouth seems to be stuck in this position."

"Here, let me help you with that." I kissed him with a brief but heartfelt thank-you kiss and then whispered into his ear, "Thank you, but we are going to have to stop for a closer look, you know."

"Already scheduled in the tour package, miss," he said in that English accent of his.

Moments later, we pulled off the road onto a gravel lookout area. My mouth dropped open as I took in the sight of an engraved painting carved into the stone high on the bluff, which we currently faced. The carving depicted a birdlike creature that possessed a monstrous blend of animal characteristics. The grotesque array of features on the creature included the gills of a fish, the telltale scales of a reptile, the horns of a deer, the saber teeth of a tiger, the wings and claws of a bird, and a serpentine tail that was forked at its end.

"Extraordinary looking fellow, isn't he," Gabriel said as we exited the Jeep.

"It almost looks like a painting done by an amazing child artist who couldn't figure out which animal to draw so he drew them all together. Does the creature have a name?"

"As a matter of fact, it does. It's called the Piasa Bird, which means 'the bird that devours men' or 'bird of the evil spirit.' The colors used symbolize war and vengeance for red, death and despair for black, and hope and triumph over death for green."

"Thank God for green," I said, slipping my arm into his as we both looked up at the alien bird etched in stone.

"Yes and I believe the Illini tribe would agree with you. Would you like to hear the story on the way to our next destination?"

"Why yes, Mr. Tour Guide, I would love to hear the story," I said with a teasing smile.

So, Grace, as we made our way back down the Great River Road, my wonderful tour guide, who was by *the way very easy on the eyes as you would say, told me the legend of the Piasa Bird.*

In a primeval time tens of thousands of moons before man walked the earth, ancient glaciers pushed their way overland from the arctic north. Moving south, these behemoth islands of ice crossed into North America inching their way inland. After tracing a path over most of the land mass that would someday be called Illinois, these country-size ice floes ground to a halt.

The melting ice carved deep trenches and gullies in the bedrock, forming an intricate system of rivers and streams. The greatest of these rivers would come to be called the Illinois, the Missouri and the Mississippi. The weight of the shifting glacial ice ground tons of soil and bedrock, reducing this dirt to a fine silt. This dust blown by the winds of time collected along the hillsides. These ancient layers of airborne dust called loess (less) can be seen to this day along the upland hills and trails of the area's dense forests. These woodlands, which primarily featured oak and hickory, gave way to wetland plants and fertile prairie grasses that would someday cover up to two-thirds of Illinois. Rich with game and vegetation, the area became home to six different Native American cultures among which was the village of Illini. It is written that many millennia before, the first white explorers arrived in that area, a prehistoric bird flew over the great Father of Waters. The bird was named the Piasa bird, "the bird of the evil spirit," and is said to have ruled the skies in the primeval era of the mammoth and the mastodon.

The bird's legend was first recorded in 1836 by John Russell. A rough parody of his account begins with a description of the Illini village.

Laurence Gabriel

The big river rippled its way south in plain view of the village. The thick forests and high bluffs shielded the natives from brutal winds that would sometimes blow in from the north. Secure and happy, the Illini people led by their chief Ouatoga (Watoga) loved their home and their way of life. One morning, in the midst of preparing for a fishing expedition, Illini braves already on the river in their canoes heard the terrifying sound of an alien screech that seemed to move the very earth itself. Swooping in from the west, the braves stared spellbound at a gigantic flying monster. Its body was the shape of a horse, white fangs stabbed upward from its protruding lower jaw, and flames shot out of its nostrils. It had two white deerlike horns coming out of its head, and it's huge wings beat the air with such force that trees actually bent in its wake. Its stubby legs held knifelike talons, and its spiked tail wound around its malformed shape as many as three times.

Before the Illini could react, the bird pulled one of the braves right out of his canoe and flew away. Terror reigned in the village for several moons as the creature returned and more often than not pulled from the village another victim. When Illini arrows proved useless in the people's attempts to slay the monster bird, the village sought the wisdom of their chief. For nearly a full moon, Ouatoga prayed and appealed to the Great Spirit. Then in a dream, the chief was shown that the bird had a weakness. It was not protected under its wings. All the next day, braves sharpened arrows and painted them with poison while the tribe fasted and prayed. That night, six of the finest braves crept up to the highest bluff and prepared themselves for battle with the flying beast.

The morning sky was filled with shrieks of the bird's return. Ouatoga offering himself as bait stood on the bluff in plain sight. As the bird swooped down and hooked the chief with its talons, Ouatoga held fast to the strong roots of an oak tree. As the bird spread its wings wide to pry the chief from the tree, the braves shot six arrows that found their mark in the unprotected area beneath the monster's wings. Again and again, as the bird spread its wings, six more poisoned arrows hit that vulnerable spot. Finally, with a scream of agony, the bird released its hold on Ouatoga and plunged down the bluff to disappear forever into the churning waters below.

Tenderly, Ouatoga was nursed back to health. Upon his recovery, a great celebration was held. The next day, Ter-hi-on-a wa-ka mixed his paints and, carrying them to the bluff, painted a picture of the Piasa Bird in tribute to the victory of Ouatoga and the Illini. Every time an Indian passed the painting, he would shoot an arrow into the air in a salute to Ouatoga's bravery.

The first sighting of the painting was made in 1673 by the French explorers Pere Jacques Marquette, a French missionary, and Louis Joilet, a cartographer. The explorers were paddling down the Mississippi in search for a passage to the Pacific Ocean when they came upon the painted monster forty to fifty feet up on the limestone bluffs. After learning from the natives that the Mississippi emptied into the Gulf of Mexico, Marquette and Joliet turned back from their ocean run and returned to the area by way of the Illinois River. They stopped near what is now called Pere Marquette State Park.

"Hey, I just saw a sign for that park."
"Yes, you did because that is our current destination. See there's the large stone cross that marks their historic

landing site," Gabriel said, pointing to a cross some feet west of the lazy river.

"So why is the painting so far from their landing site?"

"I'm not exactly sure. I just know it's been relocated several times and is now on the bluffs about twenty miles north of here. That's the lodge there on your right. We'll check that out later. I thought we might hike some trails first."

"Sounds great," I said as he parked the Jeep in a spot across the way from the lodge.

The park features twelve miles of trails, many of which converge at certain scenic lookout points. So we hiked those trails breathing in the crisp November air and enjoying the woodland pathways that were once traveled by the Illini people.

The woods seemed to have an effect on Gabriel. It was as if the boy in him took over. He became almost bashful, smiling shyly at me from time to time, and then moments later would point something out and chatter excitedly about it. Whether it be the discovery of some loess, that ancient dust upon a stone, or a lone flower growing from a rocky crevice, his feeling for this woody cathedral held a poignant passion that bordered on reverence.

At one point along the trail as he flashed me that cautious smile, the subtle meaning behind his affectation occurred to me. It was the smile of a boy who has invited a girl into that special room within his soul, the room that leads to the door to his inner sanctum. A smile that while hopeful is also uncertain whether these things that please him will also please her. Then suddenly I saw myself showing him the sculpture in Forest Park. This is home to him, I thought, here he is the teacher, and he is giving me the *chance to learn about his soul. In that moment, I felt the beauty of affection's reverence wash over me. A sudden breeze swept the trail gently pulling at a wisp of my hair. It was as if nature itself had recognized this fragile beginning. A spirit wind marking the moment when the fondness between two souls grows to the place where heartstrings weave a bond like tendrils from a vine intertwining to form a single strand.*

I responded with a smile of my own one that said "I see you and I like so much all that I see." I took his hand in mine, and for a step or so, I rested my head on his shoulder. With these small gestures I thanked him for bringing me here and sharing with me this tender view. He acknowledged the sensation of the bonding that came with the growth of that first delicate strand with a firm squeeze of my hand and a brush of his lips across my forehead.

Truth be told, Grace, no man had made it to that room within my heart, that place deep within the walls of my heart castle where lived that exotic woman-child who had not so long ago taken up residence there. But now a man walked there, stepping softly with respect, this masculine presence had actually made it to that door where on the other side the woman-child smiled in wonder with her ear pressed to the door. She listens for those words that will, I sense someday soon, open that sacred door to reveal the secrets of my heart.

We climbed to that lookout point "where eagles dare," which featured a breathtaking view of cliffside heights that are favored by the majesty of the bald eagle. Sitings of the eagles and their nests are commonplace, and this location is spoken of in hush and reverent tones by birdwatchers everywhere.

We made our way back toward the lodge, laughing our way down inclines, letting gravity do most of the work. Gabriel would at times give me a tag, say "you're it," and run off into the woods. I would give chase, threatening dire consequences if I fell and broke a leg. Having the uncanny ability to dodge and weave through trees and brush, I would quickly lose him and just as I was about to feel a little disoriented, he would pop up behind me and lift me laughing and screaming off the ground. In this playful manner, we made our way down the trail back to the visitor's center.

"How about lunch?"

"Are you kidding, I'm famished," I said as I caught my breath. "I could eat a whole deer right now, antlers and all."

"I'm right there with you, but I think I will pass on the antlers. Could you settle for some beef? I'm not sure that I know any good venison places."

"Beef works for me. I'm not sure that I could find it in my heart to eat a deer anyway," I said, shyly laying my head against his shoulder.

"I knew you were a friend of Bambi's the moment I saw you. I thought she is a Bambi lover for sure," he said, pulling me close to him. He held my face in both of his hands. "A kiss for your heart, Faith, your brave and beautiful heart." He kissed me tender at first and then more urgent as he let his passion go. His lips and tongue were furious with desire that seemed to grow with my fevered response. The fire in that woodland kiss burned out slowly though at its peak, we were as breathless as we had been after our downhill run. At its end, we held each other swaying there at the bottom of the trail as if

we were both trying to find our way back down again from the dizzy heights where eagles dare.

"That was wonderful," I said softly into his ear. "I have to say that I have never been kissed like that before."

"That would make two of us then," he said with an easy smile, taking my hand and stepping again toward the lodge. "Let's go get some food before we both fall over."

Feeling energized and a bit giddy, I faked a yawn, then suddenly gave him a shove, said, "You're it," and took off in a sprint toward the lodge.

Grace, the Pere Marquette Lodge was originally built in the 1930s by the Civilian Conservation Corps on the former site of a Native American village. Although the lodge has undergone expansion and renovation in recent years, the rough-hewn timbers and aged limestone of the original lodge continue to give the building a unique character. The dominant feature of this impressive structure is the massive stone fireplace that stretches fifty feet from the ground to the roof and weighs a whopping seven hundred tons. As if this earthy castle of wood and stone were not romantic enough with its gothic chandeliers hanging from a timbered ceiling over forty feet high, the lodge is also said to be haunted. Housekeepers there have reported a man-size image moving through the lobby when no one is there. Nightstands have shaken violently in rooms where everything else remained still. A park ranger once witnessed a civil war soldier sitting by the enormous fireplace, a mystery that might be related to the fact that a small detachment of Federal soldiers were camped near the site with orders to protect access to the Mississippi and Illinois rivers. For no particular reason, the entity that haunts the lodge is affectionately named George.

Sitting not far from the very rocker in front of the fireplace where old George had been sited, we devoured an appetizer of cheese, deli meats, and crackers washed down with chilled Chardonnay. We finished just as the entrées of fried chicken and braised beef arrived. We ate and laughed, as we chided each other for our "piggishness," until we could eat no more. We paid the bill and took our wine and desert of cinnamon-apple cobbler into the common room that looked everything like the castle drawing room straight out of Arthur's Camelot. Well except for the modern furniture including oversize cushion-backed chairs and a life-size chessboard with chess pieces that stand three to four feet tall.

We nursed our wine and desert while making a noble effort at a chess match, but by the time our drinks and sweets were down to a sip and a nibble, we were overtaken by a pleasant weariness. We sat in one of the chairs by the fireplace with me sitting sideways in his lap with my legs hanging over the chair's arm, his arms around me, and my head resting on his chest. I'm not sure, Grace, whether it was the weariness, the wine, or just the intoxication of his arms around me that made me feel like we were floating in a boat, somewhere warm in a blue tranquil sea. I just knew that whatever it was, I sent up a prayer for the moment to last as long as was super-naturely possible. We drowsed there for a while, enjoying so thoroughly that feeling of closeness, the kind that defies both time and gravity, leaving the impression that we are the only two souls in the universe.

We were stirred to wakefulness by the excited laughter of a child, a not so unpleasant reminder that we are indeed not alone here. The mother gently coaxed her daughter who was staring at us as they passed to use her indoor voice. She was about five or six with dark hair and big beautiful brown eyes. She wore jeans and a white sweater, along with those sneakers that light up when you walk. She gave us a curious look and then asked, "How come you don't use two chairs. There's another one over there," she said, pointing at an empty chair to our left.

I smiled at her with my sleepy eyes and said, "We wanted to pretend that we were in a boat floating on the river."

Her brow furrowed. "Why would you want to do that?"

"Because we like boats and we love pretending," Gabriel said with a wink and smile.

"Sorry, this is Alyssa. She's my little realist," the woman said, offering me her hand. "I'm Cora."

We introduced ourselves as we slowly rose from our nest.

"Oh please, don't get up on our account."

"No problem, our boat had just pulled onto the beach anyway," Gabriel said, smiling again at Alyssa.

"You mean you're pretending this is a beach?" she asked with a sweep of her arm indicating the airy room.

"Yes, you should try it. I'll bet you could imagine it if you tried," I said, trying to smother a giggle at her adorable gesture.

"Can we try that, Mommy, do you want to walk on the sand with me?"

"Yes, precious, that sounds marvelous," Cora said, mouthing a thank-you.

"Bye, bye, Ms. Faith and Mr. Gabriel," Alyssa said, taking her mother's hand.

"Have a nice walk," we said in what turned out to be a smiling chorus.

"Well done, Ms. Faith," Gabriel said as we both yawned and stretched, working out the kinks that had developed during our snooze.

"Right back to you, Mr. Gabriel," I said as I clasped my hands and extended my arms toward the ceiling in a cat stretch.

"So what do we feel like?"

"Like I need a Red Bull or something," I said with a yawn.

"Let's try a more natural remedy," he said and kissed my mouth, nudging my desire to a wakefulness that brought the roses back to my cheeks.

"Yes, that is going to beat a Red Bull every time," I said, kissing him back.

"So what do you think, city or country?" he asked, taking me by the hand and steering me toward the exit.

"I'm afraid it's going to have to be city. I've got an appointment with a prospective buyer, and I need to do some polishing up on the pieces I'm showing. But I would love it if you would stay with me for a while back at the loft. I mean that is if you're free of course," I added quickly, not wanting to sound presumptuous.

"Well, I would have to check with my secretary and feed a certain beast," he said as he opened the passenger door to the jeep.

I jumped in smiling and opened his door for him. "So what did she say?" I asked, plying him with my smile.

"Turns out I'm free till midday on the morrow," he said, going British on me. "What say you, fair maiden, shall we ride to the dawn."

"Why yes, bright knight, I think we shall," I said in a feeble attempt at the accent to which we both laughed until our sides split.

So off we rode, trading in the sun and clouds for the moon and stars, we headed again down the Great River Road. Holding his hand that rested on my leg, I watched a tugboat, its cabin lights bright against the river's dark surface. The boat pushed a barge along the Big Muddy, and I marveled at how something so small could push something so big. I felt the energy of our past hours together swirl inside me, warming me and filling me with the hope that becomes such an endearing companion when braving the winding path on the journey toward intimacy. That hope moved me to put his hand to my lips and then press that kiss to my cheek, sharing in that moment a message from that companion within me. He put his hand on my cheek, his thumb moved softly across my lips in a caress, and he raised his arm in an invitation to snuggle. I moved to my new favorite geographic location, which was the state of "under his arm around my shoulder" and told him to let me know if he needed to downshift because I knew how to handle a stick. I giggled at the innuendo, which got us both to laughing again as we slowed to a small town speed limit.

We were approaching Grafton, a storybook archetype of small town USA. The town's origins surround a failed enterprise spearheaded by an association of St. Louis businessmen in the late nineteenth century. This venture took place during a time when the furious growth of Alton had even surpassed St. Louis. In an effort to curtail Alton's expansion, this group of businessmen attempted to build a city whose commerce might deter Alton's development and redirect business to St. Louis. The result was Grafton, Illinois. Through the years, the little burg had evolved into a tourist town, complete with quaint craft, wine, and candle shops, an old town bed and breakfast hotel, and old-fashioned ice cream parlor. At the town's outskirts, Grafton features a water park that draws patrons from neighboring towns and states. The city has also become an endearing oasis for motorcycle enthusiasts. Though newcomers often gawk, tree-lined streets teeming with Harley's is a common scene in this modest river town province nestled below its panoramic limestone bluffs.

As we cruised down the main street, I enjoyed the unique architecture that brought with it the comfort that comes with the souls of historic structures that have stood the test of time. I lay my head on Gabriel's shoulder, my cheek pressed against the soft leather of his flight jacket. I closed my eyes, allowing that comfort to take me on a walk down that dreamy lane through the flower fragrant meadows of contentment.

I awoke sometime later, in another small town, sitting in his Jeep in front of a small shotgun structure that turned out to be the home of my sweet dream. The name of the town is Elsah, the story of which I shall tell you at another time. The shotgun structure was one-third garage, the back of which was built against a small hill, and two-thirds living space, which comprised the second story, the back of which rested on the crest of the small hill. The back of the second story was swallowed by a dense grove of timber, essentially making those woodlands the abode's backyard.

"*Welcome to my little cabin in the woods.*"

"*It's actually quite adorable,*" *I said taking in a lamp-lit view of this idyllic dwelling.*

"*Would you like to come in? This will only take me a minute.*"

"*I wouldn't miss it,*" *I said as we got out of the Jeep.*

The Dreamwatcher Diaries

We climbed the stairs that went up the left side of the building to a small covered deck. The deck served as a landing that led to the cabin's main entrance. The cabin was constructed with oak timbers that covered both the length and width the building. The logs may have at one time comprised a small grove of towering oaks that, once vertical, now lie fallen in precise horizontal rows. Hanging from the deck's cover, about mid-ceiling, was a wind chime made of wood. As he keyed open the door, a zephyr swirled through that timbered space stirring the chimes as if in greeting. The melodious song made from wood and wind evoked in me a deep gratitude for this moment. I pulled him back from opening the door and kissed him, with my hands cradling the back of his head and my fingers running through his hair. It was the bark and scratch of his "beast" as he called her that pulled us from that kiss. He held me close for a moment and whispered to me about how much he appreciated the spontaneity of my affection and how it was a gift that he treasured more than tongue could tell.

Releasing me, he said, "Prepare to be evaluated."

"Any tips?" I asked as he turned to open the door.

"Just pretend you're being 'wanded' by one of those security guys at your local airport. Only you don't have to raise your arms."

Nikita practically jumped into his arms whining and yipping with excited greetings. Gabriel hugged her, showering the dog with affection. Only after she had consumed her appetizer, of well- deserved attention from her master, did Nikita begin her inspection of me. She sniffed curious circles around me, whining at odd intervals. Gabriel turned on lights and heat while he watched this process with that dimpled smile of his. Suddenly Nikita stopped. She sat in front of me and looked up at me with green-gold eyes that brimmed with intelligence. Then to my delight, she lifted her right paw in a gesture of greeting. I took her paw and knelt to stroke her dark-brown coat. Fawning over her and telling her how beautiful and clever she was, I gave Gabriel a big smile. He was watching us, with a mixture of pride and joy on his face. With a sudden jump, the dog's paws were on my shoulders. Losing balance, I fell on my back giggling as Nikita licked my face.

"Nikita, drink," Gabriel said, and just like that, she was trotting off to the back of the cabin barking with welcomed recognition of a familiar routine.

"I was thinking we could pick out a book or a movie to bring back to the city," he said, walking over to a large bookcase in the living area.

"You mean you're going to read me a bedtime story," I asked, walking over to the rows of books that lined the far wall.

"That's the plan," he said, scanning titles along the top shelf.

"OK," I said, running my finger along a row of DVD's, "you pick the book, and I'll pick the movie."

"You're on," he said, pulling a few books from the shelf.

Just then, Nikita pads in with a bottle of Coke between her teeth.

"Oh my, what a smart girl you are," I said, taking the bottle and hugging her.

"Good girl," Gabriel said, "one more now, Nikita, drink," and off she went back to the kitchen.

"OK, I've got my picks, how about you?" he asked, taking the Coke and opening it for me. Nikita came in

The Dreamwatcher Diaries

with a second Coke, which Gabriel took as he praised the dog, scratching her affectionately behind her ears.

"I've got three good ones I think, and one of them is even my favorite movie of all time."

"Bring them all, and later let's see if I can guess which one is your favorite."

"OK," I said, taking a long draw from my bottle, "but," I said giggling as a very unladylike burp escaped me, "you have to guess without me telling you which three I picked."

"What?" he said, advancing toward me as I hid the movies behind my back. "That doesn't seem fair."

"It's your collection, you should be able to figure it out," I said, backing away with a teasing smile.

He reached for me, and letting out a little squeal, I dodged away. Not wanting to be left out, Nikita started barking. She jumped between Gabriel and me and let out a playful growl, challenging Gabriel to try for me again, which he did, and up the dog jumped pushing at Gabriel with his paws.

"I can't believe it, you've poisoned my dog against me in less than fifteen minutes. And you," Gabriel said, pointing at Nikita who went into a low crouch, her eyes scope-locked on Gabriel's finger. "This is how you treat the man who has fed and walked you since you were a pup, no more beer and bacon for you. Beer, Nikita."

At this, Nikita barked and took off again toward the kitchen.

"The girl likes her beer, what can I say," he said, giving me his boyish smile. "Looks like you've lost your bodyguard."

"Don't be silly," I said moving toward him. "You're my bodyguard."

353

"You got that right," he said, giving me that look of fierce tenderness. He pulled me close and embraced me. "Are we ready?" he asked.

As if in answer to that question, Nikita whined and we both looked down at her sitting there with a Budweiser in her mouth and an inquisitive look in her eyes.

"Let's bring her with us," I said, winking at her, to which she turned her head and pricked her ears as if she knew that we were considering her. "I hate the idea of her being here alone."

"There you go again, Faith, making me even crazier for you than I already am. Just how much craziness do you think one man can stand."

"Darling," I said giving him a brief kiss, "we haven't even scared crazy yet."

"How about it, girl, you want to go on a trip to the city?"

The bottle dropped from her mouth, and she barked excitedly going toward the entrance where she pulled at the leash that hung from its hook by the door.

"You just said the one word that she likes even better than beer, trip," Gabriel said with a laugh. "You now have a friend for life."

We made quick work of loading up the Jeep, packing some essentials for Nikita along with our bundles of books and movies. The drive back to the city seemed to fly with the inclusion of Nikita, whose ebullient spirit brought to our universe the intelligent presence of watchful, unconditional adoration.

Once we were settled back in my cozy loft, sometime after Nikita had sniffed out every corner of every room, we laid out in a snuggle on the couch to watch my favorite movie. We had played the guessing game while we drove, *and with a few clues, he came up with the correct answer, which is of course Meet Joe Black. Earlier at his cabin, I had hidden my surprise that he had the movie had been destined to be my all-time favorite. I did not own DVD's myself but preferred rather to discover a movie moment on cable now and again when I was in the mood to step through the looking glass and just get away for a while.*

After the movie, we moved to the bedroom where on the bedside floor I made a doggie bed for Nikita with old pillows and blankets. Getting comfortable, we stretched out on the bed. I placed a pillow on his lap where I rested my head, and giving me a wink and a smile, my sweet dream began to read to me. He read passages from a novel, the title of which he said he would reveal to me only after I had heard the story. It was in this way he said that I could embark on a more pristine journey with the characters. The absence of a title, he theorized, pulled the story from the frame of "book," giving the reader rawer sensation of the character's experience.

Grace, I'm not sure if it was the hypnotic timbre of his baritone voice or the mystical allure of the story itself, but in no time at all, I was entranced with this tale of perseverance and hope. The plot surrounded the plight of Caroline, an abuse survivor struggling to find her way among the lost souls in the City of Angels. The arrangement of the story was so magical as the author (who suspiciously had the same last name as Gabriel) created a vision surrounding the deep inner workings of the soul. She wrote about angels within us that journey toward our conscious minds on a mission of hope. The Hope Angel's quest was designed to free Caroline from her illusions and reveal to her the true nature of her authenticity. The story was so delicious with detail, and I was transported to that place, losing myself in that idyllic yellow brick road.

* * *

Gaby gave Lindsey a look of openmouthed astonishment. "It can't be, it just can't be, I mean, can it?"

"I suppose, maybe…but we'll figure it out later. But let's just keep going, don't break the spell."

"Oops, sorry, you're right," Gaby said, unconsciously covering her mouth the way that she did when she caught an error in her way.

"Gaby, let me have a go. You've been at the wheel for quite a spell now."

"Thanks, girlfriend, that would be a most welcome proposal. I think I will take you up on that."

"Okay, let's see where are we. Oh here it is."

* * *

As fatigue crept in lashing invisible weights to our eyelids, we fell to slumber's invitation, traveling to the land where dreams whisper clues about who we are and why it is we might be here.

I awoke the next morning and took a moment to watch him sleep. In that intimate moment, I fell for him all over again, wondering to myself what it was that pulled so fiercely at my heart. I got up quietly, careful not to disturb the sweetness of his heart-melting vulnerability. I made some coffee and got some food and water for Nikita, who had followed me to the kitchen. I spoke softly to the dog as I sipped coffee. Playfully asking her to tell me all her master's secrets, she jumped up and put her front paws on my robe as if she were about to answer me. Then going back down to all fours, she padded back to the bedroom where I found her moments later curled up at the foot of the bed upon which her master slept. I got ready for my appointment and softly kissing them both quietly let myself out to greet the cold St. Louis morning.

Having forgot to ask him about his Thanksgiving plans, I had wrote him a note to that effect and placed it by the coffee maker.

His reply was found several hours later when I arrived home to find a thank-you note under a doggie snack from Nikita. His answer was a short and sweet, "no place I'd rather be" and a "can't wait to see you soon."

And I will see you soon, Grace, in the next entry.

~~~~~~~~~~~~~~~~~~~~~~~~~~~~~~~~~~~~~~~

November 23, 2003
Lark in the City
Sweet Dream Time: Ninety-Five Hours of You and Me
Intimacy and Desire

~~~~~~~~~~~~~~~~~~~~~~~~~~~~~~~~~~~~~~~

Dearest Grace, there is something pleasantly unusual about the interludes in this romance. The unusual thing is that there has been no formal exchange of cell phone numbers, landline numbers, work numbers, or even email addresses. Thus far, our meeting arrangements have all been accomplished with either the written word or word of mouth. I had not even registered that curious development until after this our fourth date. The fact that we have fallen into an old-fashioned approach of feeling our way toward each other seems to be an eventuality that we both naturally take in stride. There seems to be this strong unspoken trust that we will somehow find our way back together. There is no anxiety about whether he will call, or come around again, no push from him or me to make access demands or form schedules to meet "together time" expectations in the manner that past suitors have always seemed to require. There is instead a strange peace that emanates from an unspoken pact. It is as if our souls had already pledged themselves to a quiet and mutual understanding. It seems to be an understanding that has evolved over the course of our solitary journeys toward self-discovery forming within us a silent and sober resolve. It is the resolve that if we believe in each other in the manner in which we had come to believe in ourselves, we will find the trust, hope, and creativity to discover a bond that could be founded upon freedom and equality.

Knowing that he believed in me the way that I also believed in him made the hours away from him a different kind of wonderful, which brings me to the pleasant part of that unusual something about our interludes. This unexpected wonderful that I discovered in our hours apart surrounded the way that my memories of him took on a life of their own. It was as if my collected impressions of his presence on my soul began to shape themselves around my heart, forming within me a singular sense of his being. While this sense brought with it a strong craving to be close to him like a bittersweet ache both pleasant and painful, I began to realize that this extraordinary sense would not have grown at all without the necessary time and space that comes with separation and physical distance.

The Dreamwatcher Diaries

Grace, this profound insight reminded me of your words regarding intimacy's rhythm, how you described that a lover cannot know the face of the one with whom she shared her kiss until she steps back. How it is that the meaning of a loving embrace clarifies its message about that soulful bond only in those moments after you let go. How wonderful it is to experience your description of the ebb and flow of intimacy's rhythm in true living color. It seems strange to say that I am even grateful for these hours away from him without which the growing sense of him would not have swelled into the living being that walks now in that deep country within my heart.

I wonder at your foresight, Grace, as I recall from memory your description of my sweet dream, "he will know when to embrace and how to give space," and here I am with the man who seems to be doing that very thing. I've come to think that he, too, appreciates the way that intimacy requires space to breathe as well as closeness to thrive. With that understanding, I decided to initiate the ending of this longest interlude with a short letter inviting him to dinner and a tour of my neck of the woods. It was on the fourth day away from him that I wrote the invitation as I listened to my heart where resides that woman behind the door. She told me that time was nigh, and the health of our fondness again required the food of our togetherness. So I wrote to him, and having memorized his address from my visit to his cabin, I sent to him Express Mail that letter from my heart. Here is what I wrote.

Dearest Gabriel,
    Seeing as how you're a bit ahead in sharing yourself with the written word, I thought that I would make an effort to even up the score.

Laurence Gabriel

Speaking of the written word, how do I tell you just how deeply moved I am by the way you write? Your reply to my "Prayer Boat" poem made my knees weak and left footprints in the sand on those shores within my heart where no man has ever walked. Dare I tell you now out loud, right here on this page, that I am coming to believe in you, Gabriel? Dare I write that with that belief's fragile beginnings, I feel the birth of a hope in you, one that whispers to me in the night and evokes from me secret smiles throughout my day? Dare I share with you these reflections from my heart?

Yes, I dare…

I wanted to tell you how much I cherish our hours together on the Great River Road. I also wanted to thank you for letting me visit your sanctuary, not just your cabin in the woods, which seems to me both cozy and charming, but also just the woods themselves.

I wonder if you realize just how the trees in the forest affect you, and why it is that they stir within you an innocence, the innocence of that boy in you, the boy with the brave and open heart.

I miss you, Gabriel, and while I use these hours away from you to regain my breath, which you frankly tend to steal away, I do look forward to losing it to you once again sometime soon.

This brings me to the point of this express dispatch from my heart. I wish to cordially invite you to "A Lark in the City of St. Louis." This series of impulsive escapades may begin at any time after 5:00 p.m. on Friday night. I should tell you dress is casual, but please also pack "dress to kill" wear, and please feel free to bring your canine companion as I, too, in this short time have come to find her presence precious. Gabriel, should you both wish to attend, all you have to do is slip this invitation under the door of 707 Castleway and the door shall be opened to you. I pray that this message finds your heart.

P.S. Gabriel, when I think about what you wrote to me about clarity, about how "in moments of sweet clarity, you can only see the face of now," I am reminded of what happens to me each time we kiss. How it is that I don't know where I end and you begin? How it is that everything that does not flow with that moment is somehow sifted out, leaving only that feeling of oneness, only that precious jewel, that goes by the name of intimacy?

Grace, I finished the letter just before 5:00 p.m. on Thursday evening. When I saw the time, I was suddenly struck with the frantic realization that I must get this letter out tonight. I sealed the envelope and grabbed my purse as I flew out the door.

I was sprinting down the street to a Mail Boxes Etc. just around the corner from my loft when I had a sudden vision of Daddy smiling down on me. I heard him whisper the words "no worries, sweetheart, you'll make it just fine." Seconds later, I burst through the door, looking everything I'm sure like a crazy woman on a mission. The attendant at the window was just beginning to pull down the door to his window.

"Sorry, miss, were closing here, but we open tomorrow at 8:00 a.m. sharp, so we'll be happy to... ma'am are you okay? Ma'am? Please don't cry. I'm sure that whatever is happening here, it can be fixed."

Grace, I did not even realize that tears were coming down my face. What I did realize was that I was looking at the face of a man who bore an uncanny resemblance to your pictures of Daddy and the name on the plaque that *he was pulling from its slot was the name that you gave to your only son.*

"I'm sorry," I said breathlessly, "your name is William."

"Yes, dear, could I help you with something?" he asked as he allowed the door to slide back up on its track.

"I'm not crazy," I said before I could think. "I just...William, have you ever been certain that there are critical moments in every love story and maybe even in true love stories? You know that timing thing, that sense that universes could be altered if just this one thing got through space and time...in time...I mean on time."

"Have you been talking to my wife?" he said with a warm smile.

"No," I said with a soft smile of my own, "but I must tell you that the tears on my cheeks are not only due to the urgency to send this message to the man that I am falling for. They are also because you bear the name of the father that I lost as a child, and just before I stepped through that door, I was thinking of him."

"It is now required of you to tell me how it is that I can serve you, dear."

"I have to get this letter to this address by tomorrow," I said, sending him a gracious smile between great gulps of air. "The rhythm in my heart depends on it."

"Twenty-four-hour service is what you want, and I know just the carrier. No one is more reliable than Lawrence when it comes to matters of the heart."

I gave the letter to William who took it and began to stamp it with official markings in that deft and efficient way that all postal workers seem to possess. My eyes never left the envelope as I followed his every move until the let-

ter was at last placed in the bin marked twenty-four-hour service. I watched a wide smile cross his face.

"You're in good hands now, dear," he said. "Your message will arrive at its destination sometime afternoon tomorrow."

"Oh, William, bless you," I said, actually grabbing his head with both hands and kissing him on the forehead.

"Not at all, dear, you've just given me a wonderful memory as well as a good story to tell my wife tonight over our bedtime brandy. Love is in the air it seems," he said with a wink and a smile.

"Yes, William," I said with a wink and smile of my own, "and now thanks to you, it's about to be delivered."

I spent the night watching old movies a Cary Grant double feature, which included Houseboat and An Affair to Remember. I fell asleep on the couch with strange dreams of being a rider with the pony express trying to deliver a bag full of love letters with a thousand cupids dressed like Indians chasing me with bows and arrows down a dusty desert highway. I woke around 6:00 a.m. and remarked to myself as I headed toward the bathroom, "I have no idea what that means."

I spent the first half of the day running errands and engaging in those domestic chores that upon their completion seem to bring a refreshing sense of nourishment. I stretched out on the couch for a little snooze some time after midday and fell into a dreamless sleep. I awoke some hours later to what sounded like an urgent scratching on my front door. Feeling a bit fuzzy the way that you do when waking from a catnap that has truly bordered on perfection, I stumbled toward the door.

Laurence Gabriel

The first thing my eyes registered was what appeared to be a small snow drift at the foot of my door, except the snow was filled with creases and what appeared to be formations of ants. I was trying to make sense of it all when another white invitation breezed in under the door. Suddenly I was wide, awake. A big smile wreathed my face as I jumped for the door almost slipping on the pile white, which I now recognized as a growing collection of my invitation to Gabriel.

Feeling a giddy sense of school-girl jubilation, I somehow managed to get the door open without falling. Nikita was sitting there with a collar made from a wreath of my invitations strung together around her neck, and a long-stemmed yellow rose in her mouth. She sat obediently and, at the sight of me, actually seemed to smile and offered me her paw.

"Hey, girlfriend," I said taking her paw, "was that you I heard at my door? Is this for me?" I asked, carefully taking the rose from her mouth.

Nikita barked and whined as if in answer.

"Where's your daddy, huh, girl? Where did he disappear to?"

I stand and sniff the rose as I look inquisitively down the hallway. I hear the ding of the elevator, and he appears holding a bottle of what appears to be expensive champagne. What a sight he was at that moment standing there with in his long brown coat, black V-neck sweater, jeans, and gunslinger boots, looking right into my eyes with that smile of his. I ran and literally jumped into his arms wrapping my legs around his waist and my arms around his neck. My mouth pressed against his, urgently covering his lips with feverish kisses that were returned in kind.

In that moment, Grace, as he held me against the wall just outside my door, I had a vision of the dam within me, the one that had held for so long my passion at bay. I watched it fracture, splitting down its middle and disintegrating into a thousand indistinguishable pieces. I gasped with audible wonder as my longing for him flooded my senses. I could hear the roar of its release in my ears as my body was transported through sensations that left me weak-kneed and breathless.

Somehow he carried me into my loft with Nikita on his heels, but as he kicked the door closed, he slipped on the snowdrift of invitations. His amazing reflexes someway enabled him to cushion our fall. We looked at each other for a brief moment, with our hands over our mouths still in shock over the mishap. Then as if on cue, we burst out laughing.

"Well that was fun," I said, rising to my feet. "What do you do for an encore?"

"This," he said with a smile, pulling me back down on top of him.

His kisses were a supple combination of fierce and tender as he pulled me close slipping his hands over my body, his desire feeding mine with every stroke and caress.

"You know," I said some moments later, "there are more comfortable surfaces in this general locale."

"A place more comfortable than this bed of invitations, I cannot imagine," he said with a smile. "I missed you, Faith," he said as he caressed my cheek.

"Well if this is you missing me, then I think I might be able to get used to it."

"Thank you for what you wrote and for sending it the way that you did. Your sense of timing is remarkable."

"How so?"

"I had just reached my limit of 'distance makes the heart grow fonder' when I received your letter."

"Well, truth be told, I had reached my limit too."

We managed to get back to our feet, and Gabriel made hasty work of collecting the invitations, which he folded neatly and placed in the pocket of his coat. We made our way to the kitchen where we found Nikita next to the water bowl where I had laid out a bone for her.

Gabriel winked at Nikita, who rewarded him with a small whine of contentment.

"You've just made a friend for life you know."

"And her me," I said, giving Nikita a wink.

Gabriel opened the champagne as I pulled two flutes from the cupboard.

"So what's the plan?" he asked as he poured the bubbly.

"There is no plan," I replied. "That is why they call it a lark."

"Excellent point," he said, raising his glass with his boyish smile, "to the lark then, the lark in the city."

"And so it begins," I said, touching my glass to his.

Grace, as I dressed for the night's adventure, I had to ask myself what exactly is it about romantic hope that is so singularly exhilarating. Is it the energy that comes from finding someone who gets you, someone who believes in you, and holds the promise of granting you an acceptance so unwavering that even your deepest worries, doubts, and fears evaporate in its wake?

"Yes, that will do it for me," I said to myself out loud as I pulled the dark violet Armani cashmere over my head. I enjoyed the sensation of the sweater's caress on my skin

as it fell around me, bringing with it a silken warmth that held me in a snug embrace.

Or maybe, I thought as I pulled on my black jeans, this exuberance is more about the excitement of connecting with a refreshingly beautiful masculine presence, one that I believe in, with a belief that is growing by the minute. Maybe it is this believing in him that makes me ache to be close to him, and then again, I think with a smile, maybe it is because he looks so beautiful and the way he looks at me makes me feel so beautiful.

"Oh my god," I say, thinking out loud again, "maybe I'm losing my mind."

And then I could hear your voice in my mind speaking so clearly, Grace, it was almost as if you were in the room with me.

"The illusions of bliss mark the borderlands of intimacy. This bliss is the hope for an intimacy not yet realized, and while it is a nectar to be savored to its final drop, keep well in mind that it cannot bear the weight of your being."

"So keeping your words well in mind, Grace," I said as I pulled on my boots, "I'm off to do some savoring."

Grace, there is a St. Louis cabby named Joshua. He is a living example of unsung hero and is a bona fide soldier of hope and peace, a true guardian angel. I met him several years ago on a hot summer's night in the heart of the city. I had lost track of time that night, and I was walking down Washington Avenue a little later than I should have been. I had just left a club after catching the man I had been dating in the arms of another woman. I was zoned out and deep in thought as I often am when I walk. I suddenly hear the honk of a horn and a squeal of tires as a red and white American taxi pulls up alongside me. The driver gets out and in an urgent tone says, "You've got a tail, lady. If you don't want trouble, you best jump in."

So startled and frightened by the urgency in the cabby's voice, I immediately jumped into the cab. As the car door slammed and the cabby jumped in and pulled away from the curb, I was struck by a sudden fear that I had just been duped and had unwittingly facilitated my own kidnapping. Somehow seeming to read my mind, the cabby spoke to me in a strangely soothing voice, "I'm circling the block, ma'am, so you can take a look to see if its someone you know. Those windows are tinted, so they won't be able to see you."

Sure enough, Grace, we rolled past five men wearing what appeared to be thug wear complete with baggy pants, muscle tees, and tattooed biceps. They were talking loud and fast and seemed very upset about something. I could make out some of what was said and definitely heard the words "Where the hell is she?" and "How could she vanish like that when we had her boxed in?"

That was more than enough for me. "Could we please get out of here?" I said with a tremble in my voice.

"Consider it done," the driver said as he sped off toward the heart of the city.

"I'm Faith," I said, reaching over the seat to offer my hand.

The hand that briefly shook my own was rough and huge, swallowing my own in its surprisingly gentle grip. "The name's Joshua."

"How nice to put a name to the face of my guardian angel," I said with a sincerity that caused Joshua to look at me in his mirror.

"I'm no angel, Ms. Faith, just the right man placed in the right place at the right time."

"My only wish right now, Joshua, is that you accept my deep gratitude and allow me to thank you in some sincere way for saving my dignity and most probably my very life," I said as my voice broke and my tears began to fall.

He brought me to my doorstep, and I hugged him tight at my door thanking him again, but he would not accept payment for the ride. "I will not be paid for the privilege of being an instrument for honor." He'd said with air of finality that seemed beyond challenge.

So I told him, Grace, with that look of grim determination you would say I get when I go after something in that dog with a bone manner of mine, "I have no plans to pay you, Joshua, but I will be finding ways to thank you for the rest of my life."

To this, he gave me a gruff smile followed by a grunt and a "Good night to you, Ms. Faith."

And I can assure you, Grace, that those thank-yous did surely come to pass.

That day marked the birth of both a new friendship and a renewed caution surrounding my love for "night-larking." As for Joshua, he became both a preferred driver (also the recipient of a constant flow of gifts and hugs) as well as a beloved St. Louis guide and guardian. As a frequent rider in his cab, I discovered that he wrote poetry. I began to call him the St. Louis Warrior Poet, a title that he tolerated with a cryptic grunt that while hard to read seemed to indicate a grudging acceptance of my growing affection and appreciation for his presence in my life. My parting kisses on his cheek had brought more than his share of raised eyebrows and curious smiles from fellow cabbies who happened by, but his growl and fearsome stare kept the gossip at bay.

Having made prior arrangements to hire Joshua for the night, I felt it necessary to share the guardian angel story with Gabriel. He listened intently, occasionally gazing into my eyes with penetrating looks that ranged from disapproval at my foolishness, to respect for my efforts at showing gratitude without condescension. At story's end, he took my hand, kissed it, and told me that he, too, felt indebted to Joshua for his heroism, but if I ever did anything that foolish again, he would personally lock me in an ivory tower and throw away the key.

Grace, while he gave me a rueful smile with the ivory tower comment, his eyes held a ferocity in that moment that seemed to suggest that he possessed a conviction to go to great lengths to protect me. That ferocity made me feel both safe and frightened at the same time. There was something quite delicious about that feeling and the notion that such terrible strength and skill was devoted to me with such solemn resolve.

Some moments later, the intercom buzzed with Joshua's arrival, and armed with a small tote bag packed with "dressed to kill" wear and our appetites for adventure, we headed out the door. Josh greeted me with a smile as he stood beside his cab just outside the front entrance.

"Is this perfect lark weather or what," he said in his deep drawl, "clear and cold."

I introduced the two and watched fascinated as they studied each other with their eyes almost like soldiers before a duel, measuring both strength and weakness, searching for both flaws and hidden agendas. They must have both passed their initial screening, as the tension holding their mouths in tight lines seemed to leak from their faces with a *strange synchronicity. Something that might be called the hint of a grudging smile relaxed their faces, and they went into a warrior-like handshake that surprised me with its rhythmic series of masculine pounds, taps, and grips, like some secret code known to only to a chosen few.*

"OK, that's enough, you two, it's getting cold out here. How about helping a woman into this warm and cozy cab."

"Well, I don't know about the cozy part," Joshua said as he opened the door to his cab, "but it is warm."

"Thanks," Gabriel said with a look of respect that seemed to indicate he was saying thanks for much more than Joshua's social graces, "thanks for everything."

"Why don't you get into the car, son, before you freeze to death," Joshua said in an effort to slip away from Gabriel's offering of gratitude.

Gabriel slipped in beside me, smiling to himself, as Joshua shut the door and went around to the driver's side. He climbed in, put the car in gear, and pulled away from the curb. I snuggled close to Gabriel, who put his arm around me, and as I took in that familiar winter sound of snow and ice crunching under hard rubber, I had this feeling that I was the most protected woman on the planet.

"So where to first, Ms. Faith?"

"Just down the street, Joshua. The place you call the laughter factory."

Grace, our first stop was a place very close to home and one that has become very dear to my heart. Once a thriving hive of industry and commerce, the International Shoe building housed both a sprawling shoe factory and warehouse. The building stretches over a city block down Washington Avenue sitting well within the boundaries of

Lawrence Gabriel

what is known as the St. Louis Loft District. In 1983, innovative artist Bob Cassilly bought the nearly vacant building along with his wife, Gail. Cassilly's artistic vision for the space began to take shape with construction that started in January 1995. Two plus years later, on October 25, 1997, Cassilly unveiled his masterpiece with the grand opening of the now famous City Museum.

The museum primarily employs architectural and industrial objects in bold and innovative artistic designs. The result was an artistic wonderland truly located somewhere over the rainbow and through the looking glass. Descriptions of Cassilly's creation have been described as an extraordinary tapestry of funky funhouse, fantasy playground, and alien architecture, all woven together with a constant thread of artistic magic.

Each and every individual who enters the museum is instantly transformed into explorer/adventurer. Museum staff, trained to encourage visitors to touch and feel their way through the maze of art and architecture, help individuals rediscover and release the giddy, wonder-struck, Christmas morning child within.

It is no wonder that the sounds emanating from the museum walls create an infectious energy that pulls at the corners of the mouths on even the most determined of frowns that may pass by on the streets below.

The museum attracted up to three hundred thousand visitors in 1999 with exhibits that continue to make those numbers rise. The museum consists of four floors and a roof. First floor exhibits feature the "Bowhead Whale," which is a walk through whale-filled aquariums of all types and sizes. There is the "Giant Slinky," the "Tree House," the "Enchanted Caves," and the "Shoe Shaft."

There is a food court on the mezzanine, and going up to the second floor, you will find the "Vault Room," which contains two three-thousand-pound vault doors built in St. Louis in the mid-nineteenth century. The second floor also features the "Hamster Wheel," the "World Aquarium," which includes stingray petting, and the "Shoelace Factory," which houses a collection of vintage shoelace machines from the 1890s. Should you possess the patience, you may choose to design your own custom shoelaces.

The third floor features the "Everyday Circus," which consists of a circus school with instruction for individuals from age six to eighty. They also hold daily circus performances with several showtimes. Right next door is "Art City" where art techniques are offered to anyone who wants to give art a try. Other exhibits include "Toddler Town, Beatnik Bobs," where you can see the world's largest underwear, the "Architectural Hall," and my favorite, the entrance to a three-story slide that leads all the way down to the first floor. The third floor has also been the subject of some mystery with reported incidents of hauntings. These reports include the sighting of a piano playing with player in absentia and children sitting and pointing to the revolution of a grand scale ALCO train.

The fourth floor holds one of the largest vintage clothing shops in St. Louis. The name of the shop is the Bale Out, appropriately named for the sheer number of cotton bales represented by the store's collection of cotton designs and creations for sale. I have also heard a different version for the shop's title based in the romantic notion that each item purchased is fashioned cotton "bailed out" from a past life to be resurrected in the present. I found the notion to be both intriguing and endearing.

The roof exhibits feature an old-fashioned Ferris wheel, a pond with stepping stones, and a rope swing to name a few. There are several new exhibits under construction with plans to add even more, two of which include a school bus and an actual airplane.

Joshua pulled up to the museum entrance and walked around to open the door for us just like a real chauffeur. We climbed out of the cab, and after giving us specific orders to enjoy ourselves like there was no tomorrow, Joshua gave us that wink of his. He told us that he would pick us up here at the entrance when we found ourselves ready for our next destination. I watched him lean back against the cab with this look of satisfaction on his face as he watched us make our way toward the door.

"You two are going to be trouble I can already tell," he called after us, "but I will say you're a real nice-looking couple. You both look like you stepped off the cover of one of those fancy magazines."

To this I turned, and putting my hands together in a prayerful pose, I gave him a bow of gratitude and blew him a kiss.

Joshua gave me one of his rare smiles, and then returning to his gruff disposition, he waved me away and disappeared into his cab.

As I turned, I found Gabriel watching me. His face held an expression of fondness mixed with reverence. The fervor of that look struck such a deep chord in me, I had to look away. But he was having none of that. He took my face in both of his hands and, under the gaze of his blue eyes, kissed me hard and full on the mouth.

"I had to do that," he said, releasing his hold on my face, "both because I wanted to and to make sure that you are not a dream."

The Dreamwatcher Diaries

"Well," I said, still recovering from the spell that his lips seemed to cast on me, "shall I expect these reality tests frequently, or are these visions more or less sporadic?"

"It's difficult to say," he said with a wide smile. "I contracted the condition just a few weeks ago, and as yet the frequency seems quite unpredictable, but I shall make a point to keep you well informed, Herr Doktor."

"Please do," I said, taking his hand as he led me through the museum door, "and I shall look forward to our next session."

I gave him a wink, and we gave way to the laughter that pushed its way through the doorway of our smiles.

Once inside, I took the lead, smiling at the wonder-struck look on his face as we made our way across the palatial entrance—way toward the ticket counter. As I paid the entrance fee, I found myself licking my lips in my anticipation of all the delicious surprises that awaited him just on the other side of the turnstile.

Grace, there seems to be a subtle transformation that takes place within many of the adult souls that enter the "City Museum." The natural conditioning of the artistic design places urgent demands upon the individual soul to release the internal ties that might bind the child within. As a frequent patron of the museum, I have had the opportunity to observe this transformation firsthand.

Upon entering, I would sometimes secretly choose a couple as I casually strolled through the exhibits and would discreetly follow them through the museum. As I conducted this covert field study on the psychological impact of Cassilly's magic, I would always be surprised at the consistency of that inner child's release. For many couples, that child did not appear until they reached the seventh or eighth exhibit. For others it might be sooner, and as there are exceptions to most rules, there were times when no transformation took place at all. For Gabriel, such was not the case as his child within leaped out almost immediately, sporting both mischievous eyes and an infectious grin.

It was just in front of our first exhibit, which was the Mark Twain–inspired caves where he hugged me, kissed me, told me I was brilliant, then giving me a playful shove, said, "You're it," and disappeared into the caves.

I got that giddy ticklish feeling as I stepped cautiously through the narrow passages of water-carved stone. While I whispered his name, I felt like the little girl, playing hide and seek, walking through a dark room at home, feeling safe but at the same time anticipating a scare. The girl fights with her nerves, loving the silly fun of it, while at the same time wishing her friend would just jump out and get it over with.

"Gabriel, come out already," I coaxed. "This is making me crazy. I...oh," I shrieked as a hand grasped my arm and pulled me into a little crevice. "You scared the life out of me," I said as our laughter dialed down to low giggles.

"I think I can fix that," he said, giving me a kiss that made my head spin. The crevice was narrow, and I could feel the cool stone on my back pushing me against his warm masculine shape. My body began to memorize that shape melding each line and curve into the archives of my romantic memory. I lay my head on his chest and listened for a moment to his heartbeat.

"I wonder if this is how Becky Thatcher felt after being kissed by Tom Sawyer," I whispered, looking up at him.

"Maybe," he said, "but I am certain that she couldn't hold a candle to you."

The Dreamwatcher Diaries

"Thank you," I said, kissing his dimpled chin, "but I think we should move on before the lights go out, and we actually need Ms. Thatcher's candle."

"Yes, let's press on, shall we?" he said with that grin of his.

"Let's shall," I said, sliding with him out of the crevice and back onto the stone path.

So we laughed and played our way through those early hours of the lark. We let our inner children run the show as we went from one exhibit to the next with the exuberance of high school sweethearts at an amusement park.

Feeling a little thirsty from our exertions in the dodgeball pit, we purchased some bottled water. We sipped the water as we threaded our way through the museum's final offerings, pausing for a moment at the huge model train display. We watched the train make its way over what I have heard amounts to over one mile of track. Gabriel pulled me close as we watched the trains progress. The rhythmic sound of wheel on rail ushered in that mystical sense of comfort that comes with travel. It almost seems tangible, Grace, that spirit that comes with a soul's linear progress toward some person, place, or thing where hope and freedom converge, with journey and fate.

The train followed its course across a bridge and through a tunnel carved in the stone of a small mountain sculpted to scale. As the train made its way toward its scheduled stop, I laid my head on his shoulder and softly told him the ghost story about the specters of children standing across the way at the Lilliputian train station. The sightings described the children as angelic radiating an ethereal beauty. Strangely their faces did not portray the animation of children at play, I told him, my voice *taking on a breathy whisper. They appeared instead like travelers weary but patient in their wait for the transport that would carry them safely to their destination of hope and comfort. I like to imagine that the look of patience on their young and tender faces came from their simple faith in the wisdom of the divine. A patience that declared how genuinely they believed in that being that cradled them in some carefully crafted design. An unspoken declaration of confidence in their hope in a divine presence that even in these moments of grave uncertainty, though unseen, was sensed as it is when children somehow know that someone on the other side of their fragility hears their prayers.*

"OK," Gabriel said, "you are really headed for the storytelling hall of fame. Feel my arm 100 percent gooseflesh, and it wasn't just the story, it was the way that you told it."

I obliged him, touching the bumps on his biceps, but my brain registered heat of desire rather than flesh of goose.

"My that is gooseflesh alright. I will definitely have to ensure that such stories are not told around any female geese as I fear for their need to imprint on you," I said, pressing my mouth to his.

His lips devoured mine as his hand went up the back of my neck, cupping my head in his palm while his fingers slipped between strands of my hair. As we parted to catch our breath, his mouth went to my ear.

"Dare I say I believe in you, Faith, yes, I dare," he whispered, "how strong and sweet your words, Faith, yes, I dare."

I threw my arms around him and held him tight, squeezing from that place in the heart where hope and joy embrace.

It was an adult-size hunger that pulled us out the door of that place where children rule. Though I must confess, I was probably more guilty of this pulling as my mounting hunger coupled with my fondness for food had begun to nudge me toward our next destination.

We ran out to the cab and grabbing our "dress to kill" wear, we both did a hasty freshen up and change in the museum restrooms.

We almost ran into each other as we headed back out to the cab, stopping for just a moment to take in our stylish transformations. My heart skipped a beat as I took in his physique now draped in sleek Armani, the navy-blue suit a perfect complement to his eyes. Under the jacket, he wore the soft white of an Egyptian cotton, crisp collar opened at the throat, the kind of shirt that looked dressy and yet cozy all at the same time. The shirt had that kind of weave that makes you want to caress it, as if some spell had been cast on the cotton itself, not to mention the spell cast on me by its owner.

He took in the deep purple of my Chanel dress, which featured a low but classy V-neck, accessorized with vintage chain and heart-shaped locket given to me by my father (worn special just for the occasion). I secretly thrilled at how his eyes devoured me in a way that was even more than I had hoped for.

"Faith, you look... you look... well... I'm speechless."

"Well, Mr. Speechless, I'm Ms. Famished," I said, smiling wide as I linked arms with him. "As I am an avid talker, you sound like the perfect dinner companion. Would you like to dine with me?"

"Sounds brilliant," he said as he escorted me out the door and toward the cab, "and what will we be having for dinner?"

"Why, Italian, of course," I said as we jumped back into Joshua's cab.

"Where to, Ms. Faith?"

"Joshua, where can we score the best Italian food in St. Louis?"

"That would be the Hill, Ms. Faith."

"Next stop, the Hill," I said, giving him a peck on the cheek.

Grace, of all the neighborhoods in St. Louis, there is one that seems to touch that deep familial nerve at its very root. The "old country" magic of this place seems to travel through the soul rippling back through layers and layers of lives long since past resonating at last in that ancient hearthstone where the warmth of family was born.

Immigrants in the 1830s traveling primarily from Northern Italy and Sicily first discovered the area. It was the discovery of rich clay mines that in the years to come drew growing numbers of Italian families. The settlement dubbed Little Italy in the late nineteenth century was by then rich with Italian culture and influence. The spiritual forces of the region included a blend of Italian-bred family, food, and Catholicism that effectively transformed this square mile of midwestern soil into a genuine slice of what is fondly called the old country.

At the turn of the century, the Sicilians founded the Parish of Our Lady Help of the Christians, building the Roman Catholic Church in the downtown area of St. Louis.

The Dreamwatcher Diaries

Meanwhile in 1903, the Northern Italian immigrants built St. Ambrose church, modeling the structure after the St. Ambrogio church in Milan. The church was built in close proximity to the highest point of the landmass upon which St. Louis City rests. Originally called St. Louis Hill, and for some time coined Dago Hill (a term popularized by the blue's singer Luella Miller, who recorded "Dago Hill Blues" in 1926), the neighborhood settled for its current title some years later, becoming what is called to this day the Hill. It is a neighborhood where everyone knows everyone, and the church is the heart of the village from which all the destiny-borne tributaries flow.

This Italian community is comprised of twenty square blocks of kindred souls woven together by the ancient roots of family, work, church, boccie ball, and of course food. It is the Italian's ongoing love affair with food that makes the art and soul of the dishes you will find there both a delight to the senses and an inspiration to the spirit.

Speaking of inspiration, the Hill is also renowned for being the birthplace of baseball greats Yogi Berra and Joe Garigola, as well as the soccer heroes that comprised approximately half of the 1950 US soccer team that upset the top-ranked England club in the World Cup. In 1948, in the back kitchen of a Charlie Gitto's restaurant on the Hill, the famous chef discovered how to toast his delicious ravioli, thus giving birth to the internationally celebrated dish known as toasted ravioli. Count on me, Grace, to close the description of this wonderful St. Louis neighborhood with inspirational food.

Our ravenous appetites led us through the door of Charlie Gitto's restaurant, where we were greeted with warm handshakes and gracious hospitality. I felt a bit like

I was in one of those Italian movies where every customer in the restaurant seems to have their own table. We were ushered in and seated almost immediately in a cozy corner booth. The table was immaculate with thick white tablecloth, gleaming china, sterling silver service, and chilled water glasses. We sat next to each other in the booth, and finding each other's hand, we made a link. We took a moment to inhale the dark-lit, candle glow ambience of the room. Suddenly I felt his lips on mine, and I thanked the Gods that I had not yet drank the wine as his mouth did things that left me dizzy with a desire that spread a liquid heat throughout my body.

"Gabriel, why does it feel like I'm falling," I whispered in his ear.

"I think it's because you do me the honor of believing in me," he said in a husky whisper. "Does this help?" he asked slipping his arms around me.

"No," I whispered into his cheek, "it makes it worse, but it's a good worse. How about you, do you feel like you're falling?

He took my face into both of his hands and said, "Faith, I've already fallen." Then he kissed me with a deep and tender ferocity, and yes, Grace, the earth did at long last move.

I then laid my head on his shoulder and wrapped in his embrace, breathless. I waited for my desire to slow from a gallop to a trot. The waiter came with the wine, and we fell to that artful task of choosing the grape of the moment. Steady now our desire, we laughed at a joke the waiter made about the smelling of the cork and how he had stumbled through his first day at wine service, which had ended in near disaster.

The Dreamwatcher Diaries

And so we supped there, Grace, in the soul of the Hill, there in St. Louis, my sweet dream and me. There was laughter and talk and forkfuls of food passed from lover's hand to lover's mouth. There was comfortable silence, the kind that comes with that genuine gratitude that is beckoned from the presence of a sunset's glory. There were looks of desire and expressions of unspoken appreciation that seemed to pass from soul to soul.

At meal's end, we sighed and stretched in hopes of making room for those final forkfuls of the divine cuisine that our bellies had warned against. As we walked out of the restaurant, the crisp fall air greeted us. We walked for a spell, breathing in the colors of the fallen leaves as we made our way down the street. I guided him toward Milo's where we played boccie ball and sipped bourbon. We pulled Joshua in for a game, and I smiled wide as I watched the competitive natures of the two men on display as two out of three games became three out of five and then four out of seven. Joshua emerged the victor but being a graceful winner accepted Gabriel's challenge to a rematch in the very near future.

We piled back into the car, and I told Gabriel that our next stop would require a little trust. He allowed me to blindfold him, and we headed out for our final lark destination. Having arrived at the building, we said our thankyous and goodbyes to Joshua. I paused for a moment at the entrance when a beautiful brunette dressed in jeans and waist-length leather jacket with vanilla scarf stepped out the door and brushed by me. I turned to look at her, and she smiled and gave me a conspiratorial wink before disappearing around the corner. Giggling to myself, I took his arm, and after what must have seemed to him an enormous number of twists, turns, and rights and lefts through hallways and up stairways, I managed to lead him to that after place. He had me laughing all the way, telling jokes about how bruised up he would be by the time we got there and how he was getting so many good ideas about how he was planning to use this blindfold someday soon with me in the bedroom. Thank God he was blindfolded in those moments as my mind had been cruising down similar deliciously decadent avenues, and the bloom on my face was not just from my exertions on the stairway. Stepping through the final door, I was beside myself with sweet anticipation as I walked him to the perfect spot for the unveiling.

As I removed the blindfold, it was candlelight that first greeted his eyes, shimmering across that geography striking deep and pulling out the deepest chords of blue. I was immediately rewarded by his look of wonder and deeply gratified by the way he pulled me close as he marveled at my final surprise.

"Where in heaven's name are we, and please tell me we can stay here for more than just a while?"

"You are on the rooftop, just three floors above my loft at 707 Castleway, and yes, we can stay here for as long as we damn well please."

At this, he busted a gut laughing, embraced me, and swung me around as if we were on the dance floor.

"OK, so how did you do this?"

"You know better, a woman never tells," I said coyly as I pulled him toward the cozy rooftop table for two, covered in white cloth, set with two crystal flutes, and two orders of crème brûlée.

"I'll get the truth out of you," he said, pulling me back into his arms. "Are you sure you want to go through my interrogation, Ms. Adams?"

"Hmm, that depends," I said, my lips quivering in resistance to my urge to smile.

"Depends on what?" he asked, his eyes taking on that look of hunger for my lips.

"On whether or not you want desert, Mr. Aaron?"

"Faith, that seems so unfair. You know how I love desert," he said, releasing me just when I thought he had given in to that hunger.

"Gabriel, many things in this life are not fair," I said, pulling away from him. *"Things like this,"* I said with a teasing smile as I flashed him some leg, lots of leg. I then kicked my heels off and laughingly took off, running around that rooftop with my sweet dream in hot pursuit.

Dearest Grace, as I'm sure you have guessed by now, leather jacket girl was Layla ducking out with hardly a moment to spare, putting the finishing touches on the rooftop setup, which I had prepared days in advance minus a few essentials. To complete your vision of the rooftop finale, imagine an open-air candlelit café featuring a picturesque view of the St. Louis arch along with the riverboat traffic flowing along the mighty Mississippi herself. The crisp air is laced with the heady perfume of river scents mixing with the fragrance of rich cuisine offered at the restaurants and cafés along the cobblestoned streets of the landing. The rooftop decor features a Japanese garden complete with bonsai trees and hand-carved wooden walkways. Layla had set up a small sound system and nice mix of jazz and blues plays in the background.

We laughed and talked and danced and drank, nibbling at our crème brûlée and feeling in those moments of rare joy that occurs when you find yourself, as they say, "on top of the world."

As the air grew colder and our bodies began to signal to us the notion of weariness, we took a final stroll around the rooftop boardwalk. His jacket was around my shoulders, and he seemed amazingly unaffected by the frigid air. He told me this tolerance was a gift from the great state of Vermont and coupled with the effect that I had on his body temperature, that it was more than a match for the moderate chill of early winter in Missouri. I smiled to myself at this, so secretly pleased at the way he had reciprocated what I, too, was feeling. I linked my arm in his, and completing the boardwalk circuit, we quietly bade the St. Louis skyline a God bless and goodnight.

We engaged in a quick cleanup, which included dashes with items from rooftop back to the loft and back again. He kept trying to steal kisses from me when we passed each other, and this made me smile. He began to tease me about my smile. "What are you smiling about, could you please turn your smile down?" he says, looking way to suave and sexy in his blue Armani considering the night's mileage and the late hour. I got the giggles and could hardly stop. I ducked into the bathroom on one of my return trips to splash some water on my face and regain my composure.

"Will tonight be the night?" I asked that face in the mirror. "Does the time seem right?"

"The vote is not in yet," says the voice of that woman behind the door. "Certainly possible," she says.

"Certainly wanted," I replied.

"Oh yes, most certainly," she says. "The wanting is good. It is now only a question of whether our romance has reached the place where virtue could be honored."

"Of what virtue do you speak?"

The Dreamwatcher Diaries

"The virtue of the birth of authentic intimacy. If the act be determined by the urgency of bliss, your intimacy will forfeit its authenticity. True intimacy as you know will not be deceived. She knows too well the rhythm of the bond that has matured to the place where virtue is whole, and yes, Faith, I do believe you have found the man who also listens for that rhythm to share with you that reverence. In the meantime, why not enjoy the mystery of why the 'when' is sweeter unknown."

"How comforting is your wisdom," I say to that voice, and blowing her a kiss, I give her a wink and to my mystery I returned.

I walked out to find Gabriel in the kitchen sipping a cup of coffee and smiling down at Nikita who was fast asleep in the cozy basket bed I had made for her.

"So how is my weary larker," he says offering me a cup of coffee to which I added some cream and a pinch of sugar.

"Ready to stretch out and rest these tired feet," I said, kicking my shoes off, "and I'm not certain but I don't think larker is a word."

"I'm afraid you may be right, but I was hoping that considering the fact that I am under the influence of champagne and the fact that I am an expert in foot rubs, that I might be allowed to take some liberties with the English language."

"Given those facts, most especially the latter, you have my permission to butcher every word."

"You're on."

He was right; he was an expert at foot rubs at the end of which my body took on the consistency of Jell-O, and the second wind that I had discovered several hours earlier evaporated into the mists of the most delicious slumber. He stretched out with me on my bed, and in keeping with the romantic fragrance that we had created with the blooms of our growing affection, he pulled a blanket over us, wrapped me in his arms, kissed my cheek, and whispered those two words in my ear, "Sweet dreams."

We slept late, and except for a quick dash by Gabriel to tend to Nikita, we remained horizontal till almost noon. There was kissing and cuddling and the urgency to yield to the rising temperature of the fever within us. I felt a kinship to my prayer boat in those moments how it must have been when the mild current of the creek spilled into the white water of the river's undeniable force. How small I felt against the intensity of this passion. Yet at the same time, I sensed an inner strength, one that seemed to commune with a higher purpose, a purpose held in sacred trust with that woman behind the door. She whispered to me in those tender moments about the ancient wisdom of intimacy's rhythm and in that rhythm revealed to me a beauty so vast and majestic that desire became but a pebble in the great sea of possibilities. This experience of finding this sacred presence so capable in the face of flesh-borne appetite filled me with a resolve so serene that it seemed even sweeter than desire's destination.

It seemed as if we both sensed this wisdom as we discovered this moment of hesitation that gave us pause. We smiled shyly from this place of reserve, and slowly we kissed each other again. I could actually sense my body travel from passion to purpose and back again as I felt my being cross the border with him into the country of true intimacy. This deep and soulful communion summoned a resolve so absolute that it seemed to contain a presence that could even defy the laws of bliss. It was with this resolve that we *dared to swim there, our souls naked, our hunger revealed in the ocean of desire. I recall, Grace, the moment of mutual discovery of a strange and wonderful rhythm, one that held both light and intelligence. A wave of bliss might rise and begin to sweep me away, and suddenly I would feel his arms, the strongest swimmer of the moment, pull me back from the brink. Then only moments later I would do the same for him. How extraordinary to experience the sensation of potency and vulnerability in a single transpiration; in that moment, I felt as if we were paradoxes swimming side by side.*

Sometime later, we would find ourselves face to face, treading water in the interim, smiling and breathless. Buoyed by our bubbling passion, we embraced till that smile would again become a kiss. Our eyes would then gloss over as were swept away again by yet another wave rising from that blissful deep. In those brief moments during which I found myself able to engage in conscious thought, I found myself marveling. How extraordinary to finally discover a masculine presence who could read the motion of intimacy's rhythm flowing far beneath the surface of the waters of desire. He somehow sensed that subterranean intelligence, and listening for her voice, her design of ebb and flow, he seemed to know just where to kiss and then caress. He seemed to know just how hard and now how soft, just what to breathe softly in my ear, and just when to embrace and then to let me go. I felt as though the tide had placed us on an island that was truly all our own. I told him as much my head propped on my pillow during a soulful interlude, and I asked him what he would bring to such an island on such a place that we called home.

We talked about that island for some time, and then feeling the need to pull ourselves from our nest, we threw on our running togs and took a jog together down along the landing. Talking and laughing as we ran, we made our way along the Mississippi, feeling like sunshine in spite of the day being dressed in a cold gray. I hated it that he hardly seemed to break a sweat, and at times I would try to outrun him. Of course he would always catch up and say something like "Ma'am, please pull over, you just caused an accident back there, and I'm going to have to write you a citation." To which I would say "I will see you in court, and would you please stop following me!"

We cleaned up and had a truly late breakfast at Kitchen Kae's. We went back to the Loop and caught a movie at the Tivoli Theatre, then back to my building where I took him down the hall to my workshop and showed him some of my recent projects. He picked out a couple of sculptures.

Pulling me close, he asked, "If I make you some coffee, could you maybe tell me the story behind these two pieces?"

"Maybe," I said, kissing his mouth, "but only if you include a shot of brandy in that coffee."

"That could definitely be arranged," he said, kissing me back.

We went back to the loft, and over a hot beverage, I told him my sculpture stories. At my request, he read more from the violet-covered book we had started days earlier. After the reading, I told him that I had fallen in love with the character Caroline and even more so Hope and was keen to hear her next adventure. I made a deal with him that I would not read ahead if he promised to provide regular readings until the book was finished. He held out for a handshake deal that included extra helpings of quality nest time, an agreement that was sealed with a smile and a kiss.

The Dreamwatcher Diaries

Lazing about through the evening hours, it was after midnight when he left with promises that I would be hearing from him soon. He whispered to me during a lingering "see you soon" kiss that I would be in his heart and mind for the hours in between.

Hugs and kisses to you too, Grace, and more to come when I see you soon in the next entry.

~~~~~~~~~~~~~~~~~~~~~~~~~~~~~~~~~~~~~~

November 25, 2003
Prophecies and Revelations at the Library
Sweet Dream Time: 115 Hours of You and Me
Gabriel's Gift

~~~~~~~~~~~~~~~~~~~~~~~~~~~~~~~~~~~~~~

Dearest Grace, it seems I've reached a plateau here on cloud nine as they often call it. I am with little doubt currently residing somewhere in that upper atmosphere and have no plans from my present lookout point of ever coming down. I have lost for the moment anyway the notion that there could even be a higher altitude, and if one exists, it seems I've reached some semblance of my summit to that Mount Everest that resides there within the deep country of my romantic heart. The air of contentment here is far richer than I imagined. I just want to walk in this mountain pasture and breathe the fragrance of these heights. There is no urge within me to climb higher, and there is no need or wanting here as the tall grass rustles in the mountain wind, whispering, "This could be home, child, yes, this could be home."

I was returning home late Sunday afternoon after spending the day with Layla shopping, lunching, and updating her on all those recent and remarkable romantic details when I spied a FedEx package leaning against the door to my loft. I literally dropped the packages in my arms and, reaching the door, snatched the cardboard envelope and eagerly scanned the label. I caught the key words "From: Gabriel A. Aaron" and "To: Dearest Faith." I quickly retrieved my irreverently discarded packages, which had so suddenly lost their value. Had there been a passerby in that moment, I'm sure they would have remarked on radiance of the smile that had my dimples working a pleasantly unexpected overtime shift. I scurried inside, and flinging my parcels on the dining table, I carefully opened the envelope and emptied its contents on the table. A sealed envelope hit the table, and I scooped it up and flew to the couch where I sat studying the vanilla-crème-colored stationary. I admired how he had scripted my name across the envelope and then gently broke the seal and pulled out a neatly written letter. Taking a breath, I reined in my anticipation that threatened to gallop unseeing through the countryside painted in the word journey that lie before me. Regaining my composure, I sat back and read the most recent message from my sweet dream.

Dearest Faith (Beauty from Elysium),

So here we are, My Dearest, somewhere on the other side of Epiphany's whisper. These are the words, Faith, that I have discovered here in this Elysium, the place to which the grace of your being has delivered me. My hope is that this affirmation might honor the beauty of your presence in my life and all that you have come to mean to me.

The Dreamwatcher Diaries

"Us"

I feel the embryo of "us"
a living wonder.
The life of an ancient hope
rising inside me
growing now
with each breath
of you in my life.
I wake now to the hope
of being with you.
and when I sleep I dream
of that birthing day
when the fragile kiss
of our "us baby's" breath
first touched our cheeks.
When come the moment sweet
we are walking hand in hand
I can hear the music
of our surrender
to our rhythm
as we embrace
the way we are together.

With deep affection,
Gabriel

It took me a moment, Grace, to recover from those written words. How strange that words could work such potent magic on the heart, not to mention the body. How words could be phrased in such a way to cause a woman's soul to fly while her knees in turn grow weak. My cheeks were aflame with both longing and desire, and God save me, Grace, how I wanted him in that moment just right then and there. If in that moment he had been there, I felt no force on earth could have held back such fevered passion. I sighed, took a few deep breaths, stretched, and went to the kitchen where I opened a bottle of red wine, and after gulping down a half a glass, I poured another and went back to the couch and picked up the letter. Careful not to reread the poem just yet, I read on.

I wanted to say a special thank you for sharing your sculpture stories with me. I must say, Faith, the way that you tell a story is so very beautiful. There is something remarkable in your manner, the natural way that you pull the audience in, especially this audience of one. This brings me to the brainstorm that I had that night as I drove home from your loft. This storm involves the library where I volunteer at a literacy program, the children and staff I work with there, and you and your sculptures in a very limited speaking engagement.

My wish is that you might come to the library this Monday at noon (storytelling hours go from noon to 3:00 p.m.) as a special and spontaneous guest speaker to share those stories with this unique audience. Please do not concern yourself with any anxiety regarding the audience portion of this request. The majority of your listeners will be children who are guaranteed to adore you and have at some level already discovered you in the "new light" in my smile (actually that is a direct quote from one very inquisitive twelve-year-old girl in the group). While other patrons of the library are welcome to step up to the storytelling circle, I am certain they will be most entertained by your presentation. To completely take the pressure off you, I should

The Dreamwatcher Diaries

let you know that this is a special wish performance meaning that you are a hopeful plan A, and there is a well-sketched plan B waiting in the wings should you have other pressing matters or engagements that require your attention. I do send a deep apology for the dreadful imposition of this short notice and promise to keep you apprised of any brainstorms that might occur on future horizons. It's just the vision of you speaking at the library (not to mention my craving to see you) was more than I could resist.

Oh yes, I almost forgot, the details. Dress is casual, punctuality is nonsense, and parking is free. Directions are on the map at the end of this letter, and the contact person once in the door is Mildred Baker. Mildred, who prefers to be called Millie, is the greatly feared and devoutly adored head librarian. She does fancy herself to be quite the matchmaker, but you didn't hear that from me. She comes off rather like a psychic because frankly she is, and the children and I could tell you stories about how she truly does have eyes in the back of her head. The woman misses nothing. She is expecting you and will know you by the cream-colored cashmere scarf also enclosed in your package. Not that anyone could miss you, but just in case there are other strikingly exquisite blonde starlets in the neighborhood, this will help with the initial identification. I do hope the color works for you as it seemed a rather good match with your brown camel hair, "gunslinger coat" as I call it.

Grace, at this I bolted for the envelope, knocking over a chair in my headlong dash. I giggled as I reexamined the envelope and reaching inside my fingers sighed with pleasure at the plush caress of cashmere. I pulled out the scarf, eyes bugging at the Versace label, and wrapping the delicious fabric around my neck, I walked back to the couch with that school-girl smile plastered back on my face. I sat back and reassembling the letter's pages read on.

Speaking of gunslingers, if gunslinger skill levels were to be used as a metaphor for quick wit, then Millie would be considered the fastest gun in Missouri if not the entire Midwest. Just thought I should warn you. Good luck and don't forget to duck. I will keep an eye out for you, and although I am tucked away in a corner without a view of the entrance, I do have several little spies that will keep me well informed.

While I do hope you can make it, if you cannot I do have a backup plan to ensure that I will see you very soon. In the meantime, how delicious the anticipation.

Genuinely yours,
Gabriel

Sleep did not come easy that night, Grace, though I did all I could to escape the grip of that anticipation. While my head was in a spin, my heart was doing pirouettes and I fought to regain some semblance of balance. I took a quick run, but as I sorted out a plan for the telling of my stories, my heart kept coaxing me to sip again from the sacred cup of heart's affection and taste the bliss there from those words that he had poured into that poem.

So I used your poem, Mamaw, the one you said to use when the mind in my heart runs wild with love's fever.

The Dreamwatcher Diaries

"Patience over Passion"

*Not until the morrow,
did I then tell my heart,
let that wine a while mature.
That sip you may then savor,
when your mind is not a blur.*

This seemed to satisfy my heart for a time as the woman behind the door sighed, and reluctantly her dancing gave way to preening as she sat at her vanity while looking into the mirror with a knowing dreamy gaze. And with that dreamy gaze, Grace, sleep did then finally come.

Julia Davis Library sits on Natural Bridge along the northern outskirts of St. Louis City. The woman after whom the library is named is nothing less than a St. Louis treasure. Ms. Davis devoted her life to the very soul of education. Teaching the youngest of minds from 1913 to 1961, Ms. Davis spent forty-eight years of her life in elementary education. Even at the conservative number of fifty students per year, you've got somewhere in the neighborhood of twenty-five hundred souls ushered by her light, illuminating for each soul the way to that hallowed path of knowledge. Think of it, Grace, twenty-five hundred souls touching twenty-five hundred more souls, and so on. Such exponential force created by one woman who believed in the power of learning. Just with her students alone, she created a virtual sea of enlightenment that to this day continues to send ripples of knowledge and understanding across the land. Amazingly she did not stop there. She held a deep passion for her culture. It was as if Ms. Davis possessed a unique vantage point in her soul that enabled

Laurence Gabriel

her to see with such clarity the ways in which her African American culture had touched the soul of America. Driven by a deep pride in the beauty of her people and heritage, she embarked on a spiritual mission to help open the eyes of Americans to the grace and charm of the African American soul living within their midst. As a researcher on black history, Ms. Davis published many significant works including a calendar of African American achievements and a compilation of biographical notes on the twenty black Americans for whom St. Louis schools were named. On the day of her retirement, in November 20, 1961, she established the Julia Davis Fund at the St. Louis Public Library. The fund was designated to the specific collection of African American contributions to world culture, leading to the creation of the Julia Davis Research Collection on African American History and Culture. This collection, which expanded at a surprising rate, is now housed at the Julia Davis Library, which opened in February of 1993. Julia Davis lived for almost one hundred and two years and died on April 26, 1993. She was able to see the opening of the library, which proudly bears her name and upon her death added her personal collection to the library's enormous collection, which continues to pay homage to the grace of a culture that changed the face of a nation.

As I made my way to the library, I wondered about Gabriel and how it was that he came to be involved with of all things a literacy program. Don't get me wrong, Grace, it is not that I found this strange truth in any way a concern. It was just unexpected is all, surprising but not in a bad way.

"Say what you mean, Fay-Fay, and stop running around your point like some dizzy girl around a maypole." I can still hear your voice, Mamaw, pushing me toward *clarity in that no-nonsense way of yours. OK, OL, what's my point, well frankly, Grace, he just doesn't seem the library type. He just keeps surprising me so unexpectedly. As I thought about the words unexpected and surprising, I smiled to myself, realizing that no two words could have described Gabriel better nor would I want him any other way. The fact that he was gorgeous was just icing on the cake, and only you, Gracie, know of my affinity for icing.*

The literacy program itself now just two years old is called Rainbow Literacy. I googled the program and found myself fascinated by the organization's innovation and creativity. The name came from the program's visionary leader (who seems to prefer anonymity) who put together a team of teachers from every creed, color, race, and nationality that could be found in the St. Louis kingdom.

Now here, Grace, is where things get really interesting. The teachers themselves (called literacy guides of which there are three levels: junior, apprentice, elder) cover the entire spectrum of reading levels and individual ages. The youngest teacher on the team is six years old, and the oldest is ninety-three years old.

Let's say an adult comes in and tests out at a first grade reading level. This adult was matched with say a ten-year-old who was struggling at the third grade reading level. The ten-year-old teaches the adult until that adult is proficient at the same level as the ten-year-old. The research on the program indicated that the experience of teaching improved the struggling young reader's proficiency by 90 percent. Within a year of working at the Rainbow Program, the ten-year-old was reading three to four grades above his age.

If the teacher can stay two grades above their student, they may keep that student. If not, they may adopt a new student. The teachers and students are supervised by a literacy elder guide who matches teachers with students, measures teacher-student progress, and monitors teacher-student relationships. (Students who graduate from a senior high school reading level are then eligible to join volunteers already reading at that level and above to be literacy apprentice guides who are allowed to teach students at all levels.)

Each time a student progresses to the next reading grade, they are given a coin colored for that level. When they have acquired twelve coins for the twelve levels, there is a big celebration for that student who commemorates the day by performing a reading from a passage of their choosing. The student's accomplishment is then honored in a ceremony in which they trade in their twelve colored coins for a single rainbow coin inscribed with the student's name.

In its short life, the program has already inspired other cities to adopt this vision as Rainbow programs are beginning to pop up all across the Midwest.

I pulled into the library parking lot and was immediately greeted by two boys who appeared to be in their mid-teens. They were excitedly pointing and waving at me. My guess was that Gabriel had given them some sort of description of my car, which they now guided into a waiting space. I had barely put the car in park when one of the two boys, who appeared to be of Ethiopian descent, bowed politely and opened my door.

"My name is Khuma, and this is my friend Manny," he said, pointing to a lanky brown-skinned boy who was flashing me with a winning smile. Manny reminded me of the boys who had helped me set up my display at that art festival in Brazil.

The Dreamwatcher Diaries

"Faith Adams at your service," I said, stepping out of the car and offering my hand.

"Right now, I think it is our turn to serve you," the boys said almost in chorus, both of them bending this time in a quick formal bow.

"Is there anything we can carry for you?" Khuma asked.

"My pieces are in those baskets in the back," I said, clicking open the back hatch. "I can handle my bag," which I pulled from the front seat while they collected the baskets.

We made our way into the library, which immediately struck a chord deep within my olfactory memory. It was the comfort-borne scent of knowledge laid to paper bound in leather. There was the sound of brain matter consuming and digesting reams of information and stories. There was the feeling of electricity, the light bulb moment, the moment that excites neurons to discover hidden pathways to unseen destinations in the mind. It was into this little universe of enlightenment where not surprisingly, my sweet Grace, I, too, would soon be enlightened.

Millie was exactly as Gabriel had described, an intellectual force to be reckoned with. She sat there comfortably in the African American skin of a pleasingly plump woman who seemed clothed in a kindness that suffered no fools. As we walked up to her enormous desk, she studied me over the rim of her wine-colored reading glasses.

I took in her elegant attire as she stood to greet me, the deep purple of her cashmere cardigan over the silk of her maroon blouse complementing the classy navy-blue skirt complete with stylish black flats. Her deep brown eyes twinkled with both wit and wisdom, a truth that though *presupposed I gleaned to be authentic—a theory that was soon proved to be sound.*

"So you're the one that has my star elder guide stumbling over his own feet. Well I can see why, and it's about time Mr. Picky find someone to lose his head over. That boy thinks far too much as it is. Khuma, Manny, sweethearts, why don't you take those baskets to the reading circle and we'll be along shortly. So how about the dime tour," she said linking her arm to mine. "My, you are a beauty and so tall."

"You're too kind," I said, suddenly feeling a bit awkward. "I'm Faith, Faith Adams, and you must be Ms. Millie."

"Please, girl, you can leave the miss in the river that flows through our beautiful city. Millie is just fine here, and I know exactly who you are, Faith. I've even seen you work."

Grace, at first I thought oh, she has seen some of my pieces, but then I thought she is too smart to have said "you work" rather than "your work," and then it hit me.

"So you were there at the park when I finished that piece that I dedicated to the homeless."

"Yes, that's the one, the art festival is always such a marvelous event. I thoroughly enjoyed those seven days at the park. I was fascinated at how you could work with such focus under the gaze of so many onlookers. I was very touched by the story you told about your grandmother who had inspired that piece. What was the sculpture, about ten feet high?"

"Yes, almost exactly."

"The romance in that story seemed quite magical, and, Faith, at a time in my life when I thought all of that was behind me, I happened upon the most wonderful man *there. Someday when there is more time, I would love to exchange stories with you. It seems," she continued now in a cryptic whisper, "we may have both stumbled upon the last two knights in the city walking among us disguised as common noblemen."*

Millie's cryptic whisper disappeared behind an equally mysterious wink, and she shifted seamlessly from Millie, the woman who fell in love with a knight at an art festival while under the spell of a romantic sculpture, back into Millie, the librarian.

She showed me each and every wing of the sprawling facility, proudly explaining the function of area. I however, my sweet Grace, was in a state of semi-bewilderment, not so much because she seemed so all-knowing, most specifically about me, and not even because of her mystical reference to knights and nobleman, but much more so because she had used the word we. "What," as Grandpa used to say, Grace, "in tarnation was she talking about."

After making all the polite "oohs," "ahs," and "wows," and hopefully in the correct rhythm and sequence that acknowledged the honor she deserved, I found myself back at her desk where Khuma and Manny stood, practically at attention, waiting patiently for my return.

"Millie," Manny said, "Gabriel is ready for Ms. Faith. If she is ready, we can take her back to the reading circle."

"That sounds marvelous, Manny, and I want to tell you and Khuma that you gentlemen have both done yourselves proud today." Seeking a strategy to regain my composure, I discreetly asked Millie for directions to the ladies' room.

"It's just down the hall, sweetheart, just a left then a quickie right, and you're there. If it's last minute jitters,

a splash of cold water on the face works wonders. But you've really no worries on that score, Faith. I have every confidence that the children will adore you."

"Thanks for that," I said, giving her a smile. "Be right back," I said to Manny and Khuma, giving them a slight bow. I was rewarded with wide smiles as they returned the bow.

Moments later, I was taking Millie's advice marveling at how something as simple as cold water could calm the gathering wind of thoughts that now swirled through my mind. I took a deep breath and letting it out exhaled the whirlwind of musings that surrounded the mystery of Millie and romance in the park. I gave my face a final splash, and gently applying the face towel, I raised my eyes to the mirror—that's when I saw her, Grace, and time actually seemed to stop.

At first I thought that she was an apparition staring at me from behind the mirror. A woman-child certainly no more than twelve years old, she had long raven-black hair that hung full and straight as if she stood under a waterfall of liquid black silk flowing over her shoulders and cascading down her back. There was a glossy texture to her lush mane, creating a luster that whetted one's hunger to touch. Within this luxurious frame, it appeared as if someone had poured a deep cup of rich, pale cream over the most exquisite bone structure that I had ever seen. Her complexion was flawless, creating a natural beauty that would send even the most gifted of makeup artists scurrying out the door. There was simply nothing that could be improved upon. Red full lips parted, slightly revealing a hint of the even columns of pearl that lay beneath. Thick black lashes set off large almond-shaped eyes that framed the most luxurious green, a green like that of a garden that grew silently, hidden deep within the mysterious valleys of the woodlands. Those eyes mesmerized, casting an ethereal countenance that seemed to entrance the beholder. Her calm demeanor held such depth as to be unsettling, but it was the intensity in the forest green of her eyes that saw right through to my soul's inner sanctum. Suddenly there she was, Grace, standing there just a short walk from the place where stood that woman behind the door.

It was then, as her green gaze penetrated the brown pane of my eyes, that I sensed this girl was a seer.

I turned around and was strangely both relieved and disturbed to discover that the girl in the mirror was not a ghost. I gave her a barely perceptible nod as I took in the deep mountain hue of her lavender dress that reached well below her knees. She wore black flats laminated with a polished shine that reminded me of Dorothy's magic slippers. As my eyes again met hers, she spoke. "So you're her."

"I'm sorry... I am... her who?"

"The one who makes the light in Gabriel smile."

"Oh my," I said, placing my hand on my heart, "such kind words from a stranger."

"Truth is not always so kind."

"And what is your name?"

"Serenity, but most people call me Rennie."

"I rather like Serenity. It seems to suit you."

"Thank you. What is your name?"

"I'm Faith. It's very nice to meet you, Serenity."

"You saw her too, didn't you, Faith. You saw the girl with the red mouth?"

"I... I..." A sudden knock at the door pulled me from my speechlessness.

"Ms. Faith," Millie called, "are you ready? The natives grow restless."

Laurence Gabriel

"Coming, Ms. Mille," I called, rolling my eyes at Serenity earning what I believed to be the rare beginnings of a smile.

My mind was swimming again as I made my way toward the reading circle. Walking with what seemed something akin to a military escort, I tried to regain that glassy calm on that blue lake in my mind, but that surface resisted me, rippling with the waves of some dark disturbance rising from the deep. I stole a quick glance behind me, but Serenity seemed to have vanished just as mysteriously as she had appeared. I begin to wonder if my imagination had conjured her somehow, invoking her cryptic query about the girl with the red mouth.

Then quite suddenly I saw him, and my mind gave way to my heart. He stood at the head of the circle, and I don't believe I will ever forget this snapshot moment.

Gabriel had not yet registered my presence. He was sharing a story using his hands and well practically his whole body in the telling. His intensity was electric and his charisma so magnetic that not a single eye wavered from his presence.

Grace, I have to tell you that the essence of this snapshot was the children's faces. I'm not sure that I have witnessed that much soulful adoration in one room before. The boys were scope-locked definitely into the story, though on a different level, they were studying Gabriel's masculine presence. Hungry for a hero, the souls behind their eyes were busy absorbing information about how he thought, spoke, and moved. They seemed to be eating up each morsel of his character, savoring the suggestions, and memorizing taste and texture for later consideration.

I had to smile at the young girl's faces; they were so childhood-crush stricken. I could relate and a certain grade *school teacher came to mind. Though as I imagined how I might feel if I replaced that long-ago face with Gabriel's, I reflexively covered the blush that rose to my cheeks.*

That's when he saw me, and again as it had happened before, the world seemed to stop. Surprisingly for the children, so did he, and suddenly they were all looking at me. The boys eyed me with a guarded interest, sending me the message that I was an interloper who must earn the right to enter their circle. Many of the girls giggled, sharing secret whispers behind delicate hand cups. A few of the girls actually frowned at me with an all but transparent jealousy, and I forced myself to suppress the smile that threatened spread across my face. With quiet deliberation, I focused on my purpose here, and as I caught my sweet dream's eye, I heard his voice in my mind, Just tell a story, Faith, just tell your story.

So, Grace, that is what I did. Piece by piece, I told my story. So immersed in my anecdotes, I did not come up for air until I arrived at the final piece left in the basket. I was surprised to register the change that had taken place on the faces of the children. Something in their eyes seemed to say that they saw me now in a different light. There was also something in the room's atmosphere. It was that sort of magic that occurs sometimes between storyteller and audience. The kind of magic that transports the soul to that learning place, the place where truth is discovered and destination pathways are altered. I paused before beginning the last story, smiling at their thoughtful faces. My smile grew wider when, to my pleasant surprise, several smiled right back.

"I must tell you something very strange," I said, leaning toward them as my voice took on a conspiratorial whisper. "Mistakes can actually be quite beautiful."

Many of the children looked at me as if I had suddenly lost my mind. A few giggled, and one girl actually laughed out loud. I threw her a wink and went on.

"The beauty of a mistake is how it alters the shape of one's life. Which is to say that a life without mistakes has almost no shape at all, and what I must ask you is the fun in that? Let me tell you the story about my final sculpture, the piece that I have aptly named 'Mistakes Design.'"

So I told them about my relationship with stone and how the stone would give me a vision of the being that was trapped within the stone. My art, I told them, was found in my ability to free that shape from the stone walls that held it captive. The vision I had that day was the form of a perfect egg. Deep into my process of freeing that flawless oval figure, my chisel slipped mostly, I told them, because I had neglected to refresh the resin on my hands. Now I had a deep groove where I did not need one. The children laughed along with me as I described the temper tantrum that followed and how I had yelled at the stone for being so weak.

I left the stone in the dark, I told them, and did not return to my studio for two long days. When I did return, I felt foolish and more than a little sheepish as I sipped coffee while walking around the stone studying my mistake, which seemed to be glaring at me. I sat down at my desk and put my head in my hands and let out an ugh of frustration when suddenly I had a vision of how I might fix the flaw. I flew to the stone knocking my coffee cup over in my haste. I worked through the morning past noon and into the evening. My hammer chisel pace was feverish, and then guess what happened again?

"You forgot the resin!" a boy yelled. "And grooved another mistake!" shouted a little girl (who couldn't

have been more than eight years old). The entire audience along with the speaker did a good sixty-second belly laugh, and when finally the laughter in our tummies was spent, I conceded, "Yes, you are exactly right. I grooved another mistake."

But this time I told the kids I did not throw a tantrum. I just said, "I don't get it?" and left my studio not really sad or mad but more like resigned.

The next day, I did my coffee sipping circle around the stone, and then again sat down at my desk with my head in my hands and nothing, no vision, no light bulb moment, not even a single clue as to what this shape was trying to tell me.

Two weeks later, I had a dream. In my dream, I was in a field filled with perfect bird eggs, but when I picked them up to study more closely, I began to find that each one had a flaw. There was a dent on this one, a bump on that one, one too big, one too small, and one that seemed to have dents and bumps all over it. I picked this one up, and as I held it up to the sunlight, I saw something I had not seen before. I saw design. Yes, there was a design, an actual plan in the shape of every egg in that field. That's when it dawned on me these eggs were not flawed, they were just designed to hold different shapes. Each shape held within it a distinct plan, a unique destiny. Suddenly the egg in my hand moved, and there right in front of my eyes something broke through the top of the egg. First the beak, and then the head, and there I was looking into the eyes of a newborn baby dove whose eyes were staring right back at me. "Would you like to meet her?" I asked the children. "I named her Missy, short for Mistake." I pulled the veil off the sculpture. They all took a turn, coming up for a closer look, touching the sculpture with looks of wonder as I pointed out the areas where my chisel had slipped.

"I'm glad you forgot the resin, Ms. Faith," one boy whispered, "otherwise Missy would never have been born."

"Truer words were never spoken," I whispered, giving him a wink and a smile.

Once they were all seated again, I summed up the story for them. "So what I learned in the end was that what oftentimes seems like a mistake is really just part of a plan, a plan that was designed to take a unique shape to a special destiny, and what can you please tell me is the flaw in that?"

The group broke out into an unexpected round of applause. I gave them a bow, and as I raised my head to give them a heartfelt thank-you, my eyes locked with the emerald-green intensity of Serenity's gaze.

She stood on the outskirts of the circle, leaning against one of the tall bookshelves. The lavender in her dress stood in bold contrast to the dark cherrywood that currently supported her slender frame. Grace, I swear, she even leaned gracefully, making it look as though she could maintain that position even in the event that the bookshelf suddenly disappeared. The expression on her face was not just difficult to read; it was impossible. Her look was not happy, nor sad, not interested, nor bored, not blank, nor expressive. She definitely seemed to be studying me, but there was no hint to what she might be thinking or feeling about her subject. I gave her a smile, and she returned my acknowledgement by placing her hands together in a prayerful pose and bowing to me. The reverence that came wrapped in Serenity's gesture washed over me, and in that moment, I was filled with a deep and abiding sense of worth and contentment.

The Dreamwatcher Diaries

"Oh, I almost forgot. I have a surprise," I said, tearing my gaze from Serenity in an effort to regain my footing. "Manny, could you bring me that blue basket please."

With basket in hand, I told them about Thomas, the toy maker from Buffalo, New York, and how he used to work for a company called Fisher Price.

"Thomas saw Missy at a show that I had in that area, and he asked me if I would consider having him make a miniature Missy so that children everywhere might have a chance to meet her. Well I said yes immediately, and about one year later, he called me and showed me these."

I pulled the cloth cover off, revealing a basket full of multicolored porcelain eggs. The children gave a chorus of oohs and ahhs.

"Thomas loves variety, and he wanted children to have a choice, so he made a collection of twelve different eggs. In addition to being different colors, there is something unique about each egg that sets it apart from all the rest. All of the eggs do however do this. I pressed on a small knob hidden at the bottom of the egg, and the top of the egg slowly cracked open revealing a mini Missy. Each egg contains a different bird. This brown-spotted egg holds the white dove, the red egg with white spots contains the cardinal, and so on. There are cards that come with each egg along with a little stand on which you can mount your egg. Each of you will need to give your bird a name, which you write on the card. The card is then placed in the little slot at the bottom of the stand. Let's have you come up one at a time, but instead of having you choose the egg, I'm going to ask Gabriel to come up and hold the basket high enough so you cannot see which egg you choose. That way you see it is more like the egg is choosing you."

Once every child had been paired with an egg, Millie came up and formally thanked me for coming to speak. There was a final round of applause and then several offers of help from the children who, with the leadership of Manny and Khuma, set about the task of packing my car. Gabriel and I packed up the most fragile of my pieces, as the children scurried about and with the efficiency of Santa's elves carefully placed bundles and baskets onto book carts. Then under the watchful eyes of Khuma and Manny, they shuttled the packages out to the SUV where they were neatly packed in the rear compartment.

"So where do rock stars go after the show?" Gabriel asked with that delicious smile of his.

"Somewhere where they serve massive portions of food. I'm famished, I could eat two of those proverbial horses right now."

"I think I can do better than horse meat, darling, that was one inspirational performance you just pulled off. I mean it, Faith, I thoroughly enjoyed watching you and especially watching them watching you. You really connected with them."

"Thank you for saying so. I was a little nervous at first, but once I took your advice and just started telling the stories, it started to be fun. But look who's talking, what was that story you were telling them when I walked in? You had them hypnotized."

"How about I tell you over large plates of shark steak seared in butter with a couple of bowls of chicken wings covered in hot mustard sauce on the side."

"You're on, cowboy," I said, staring down at his boots, "and I am awfully sorry about my reference to horse meat."

The Dreamwatcher Diaries

Syberg's is a family restaurant exclusive to the St. Louis region. The original Syberg's started out as a mom-and-pop style tavern with home-style food so delectable and family atmosphere so inviting that patrons were soon spilling outside the door waiting in lines that wove around the block. That popular demand led to the birth of six additional locations each one like a child growing up with its own identity, fostering a fondness within its own exclusive neighborhood. The restaurant is famous for their shark steak and chicken wings, the latter being made unique by the trademark mustard sauce, a family recipe that has become a traditional taste of St. Louis.

Sitting in a cozy booth at the downtown Syberg's on Market Street, Gabriel and I chatted and laughed over steaming platters of shark and chicken washed down with ice-cold Budweiser.

"It amazes me that something with such ferocity and dietary indiscretion can taste so good dipped in butter sauce. I mean sharks will eat anything. Case in point, if you will notice the row of license plates hanging on the wall to your left." Gabriel pointed like a tourist guide, pontificating on some historic artifact while using an Australian accent.

"Please tell me that those were not extracted from the very sharks on which we now sup."

"Well maybe not those exact plates, but I did order the Louisiana plate–encrusted special, so don't be surprised if you detect some hot sauce in that metallic aftertaste."

"Stop," I giggled, "where do you come up with this stuff."

"What, it's just good investigative journalism."

"Please, I'm trying to enjoy my food here without choking," I said while giving him the time-out sign.

He zip-locked his lips and threw the key over his shoulder.

Some moments later, having eaten to the point where our tummies began to inquire about a less restrictive belt size, we both leaned back to stretch and as it happened let go a burp as if on cue. We laughed together and then reclined back in our seats, taking a moment to catch our breath.

"I know a great desert place," I said, breaking that comfortable silence that we had somehow discovered with each other. "Are you in the mood for something sweet?"

"That is a dangerous question," he said with a smile so sexy, it made me blush.

"It's a great place," I said, suddenly shy looking down at my plate. "It's at 777 Castleway. They have the greatest coffee and pastries there."

"Yes, I've actually been there a few times, but I'm not sure that it's a good idea to go there."

"Why not?"

"Well it's like I've got the wildest crush on the coffee stylist over there, and I think it might be a bit awkward."

"You are in so much trouble," I said, wadding a napkin and throwing it at him. "But because you remembered the coffee stylist thing, you're forgiven. There is a fee, however."

"How could I forget a word like stylist, and yes, I would love to go with you to 777 Castleway. What is this mysterious fee?"

"You must tell me your full name."

"Gabriel Artemis Aaron at your service, ma'am."

"What an extraordinary middle name."

"I should love someday soon to hear about what is so extraordinary about the name Artemis."

"And so you shall."

We drove back to the loft where we made quick work of returning all of my pieces to their proper spaces in my workshop. Back in my loft, I placed Gabriel on nest-making duty as I made us some coffee, which I laced with Frangelica, Bailey's, and a touch of brandy, topping it off with some homemade whipped crème. As I carried the steaming cups up to the living area, I smiled at the look of careful concentration on his face as he put the final touches on his arrangement of blankets and pillows that now covered the couch.

"I hope that my nest construction is up to fluff," he said in that suave English accent of his.

I giggled. "Just let me get my fluff meter and I will let you know," I said handing him his coffee.

We both took a tentative sip, taking a moment to savor the brew.

"OK, you are definitely going to have to give me your recipe on this concoction."

"Yes, it turned out better than I expected. I think it's that touch of brandy. Gives it a little kick," I said as I put down a couple of coasters and placed my cup on the coffee table. I looked up to find him smiling at me.

"What, too strong, a little too liberal with the brandy?"

"No," he said, his smile growing wider, "it's just that you seem to have developed a little moustache problem. Here," he set his cup down, "let me fix that for you."

He stepped up to me, took my face in his hands, and then he kissed me. God save me, Grace, I felt that kiss travel all the way down to my toes. My crème mustache evaporated along with my composure, and I felt as *if my body was no longer my own. Our lips parted and I pulled back. I traced my fingers down his cheek in a slow caress and swam for a moment in those pools of blue-eyed intensity.*

Something happened in that moment, Grace, something in that deep inner sanctum where that woman no longer behind the door silently stepped forward, allowing herself to be revealed, allowing Gabriel to feel her presence. There were no words to capture what I was feeling in that moment as she just stepped right into his arms melding there into the man who could finally see her, the woman that I am.

I could sense that it was not the hope of a dream that had invoked her appearance at this moment. It was rather the hallowed birth of a sacred affection not only anticipated but also familiar. It was as if she were registering the face of an ancient love long lost, now mysteriously beheld in the eyes of the man that stood before her. As the woman and I became one, my resolve that I held my sweet dream in my arms led to an embrace so deeply sincere that the natural fence lines that separate two souls dissolved, and in that moment, it was as if we were a single being.

How long we held each other in that rapturous embrace, I do not know. I just remember feeling as if I was floating somewhere just outside the earth's temporal sphere. Then like the arrival of a cool wind breezing in through the kitchen screen door on a hot summer's day, there came this knowing, and the woman whispered in my ear. She told me that this affection bloom is rare and true but also young and fragile. So she surrendered that embrace, retreating slowly to that room from whence she came, saying as she withdrew, Let this flower flourish, feed it faith and reverence, raise it carefully up to the sun of your regard, and discover its mysteries under the moonlight of your imagination. Do this and the day of its maturity will surely come.

My dearest Faith, I heard her whisper, just trust that the intelligence of this intimacy's natural rhythms will shepherd you to that moment when the rites of consummation will abide in both your heart and mind. You will sense your arrival at this wondrous milestone when you wake to find your affection's flower has opened to the point of fullest bloom. On this day, the morning light will greet you with the fragrant wisdom of the rose. She smiles at this knowing, blowing me a kiss as she slips silently back behind her door.

Whether Gabriel intuited this happenstance within my heart, I do not know, but how extraordinary that he let go that embrace almost exactly at the moment of her retreat. We stepped back as lovers often do to take in the face of the one with whom they hold so much hope. In that moment, he looked so deeply into my eyes, it seemed as though he, too, registered the woman as she retired to her deep and sacred inner sanctum.

"*So do you have like a sprinkler system installed, or should we just take separate cold showers?*"

I threw my arms around him pulling him close and surrounding him with waves of deep heartfelt gratitude. "*Thank you,*" *I said with a tear in my voice,* "*thank you for who you are, Gabriel Artemis Aaron.*"

"*You're welcome of course, but I have to tell you, Faith, I've done nothing,*" *he said as he pulled back to face me.* "*Waiting to love your body, to give in to those desires, is not about sacrifice. It's about not making something less than it so remarkably is.*"

"How is it that you always know exactly what to say?"

"I'm not sure. I guess I just try to speak from my heart."

"Well, Mr. Aaron," I said touching the cleft in his chin, "I think your heart is batting a thousand."

"That is very nice to know," he said, taking a strand of my hair and placing it behind my ear.

"So tell me, slugger," I said, pushing him playfully back into the nest on the couch, "what pray tell is your heart telling you now?"

"I'm afraid that information is classified," he said, laughing as he pulled me down on top of him. "But for a price, I might be able to accommodate you."

We settled into our nest searching for our signature snuggle situ, that place where lovers' hearts can whisper while their owners float in that bliss along that endearing stream. Our conversation ebbed and flowed with tender kiss intermissions and smiling sighs of hearts that sense the crossing into the borderlands of contentment. We fell into a tranquil hush, and sleep took us, pulling us down into that deep, otherworldly place of our dreams.

I woke up many hours later to that familiar sound of morning rush hour traffic in the distance. I had only recently begun to marvel at how those city sounds had traced a subliminal path to that comfort place within me. I marveled at how such noise had somehow become the endearing music of the place that I call home. I reached for Gabriel to tell him as much saying out loud, "Gabriel, isn't traffic wonderful," but I found only a pillow in his stead. Turning my head toward the coffee table, I saw a note propped up on a coffee cup. Squinting through the slowly dissipating fog of sleep, my eyes registered the now familiar script of my sweet dream. I *plucked the note from the table and burrowing back into my nest I began to read.*

Dearest Faith,

I had to go feed my darling Nikita who I fear may be feeling a bit neglected (I also fear looking at the shoes in my closet as she has a particular way of informing me of her displeasure with my dereliction of duty). I just could not bear to wake you mostly because you look so beautiful while you are sleeping. How can a man so smitten alter the sleeping beauty of the one he is so smitten with? Alas, I could not. But I shall return on Thanksgiving morn somewhere around the tenth hour. That's o-ten-hundred military time (to this I giggled). Thank you for the most extraordinary Monday of my life with the single exception of the Monday of my 13th birthday when I awoke to find that my sister had covered me in whip crème. Sorry, it's just that I love whip crème (to this, I belly laughed). Until the dawn of that day that began somewhere just west of Plymouth Rock... (It had to be west right, I mean, if it were east, they would have had to eat corn on the cob underwater and that actually sounds quite difficult. "Cut it out," I said out loud, giggling and wishing he were here.) Until that dawn, please read the letter in the envelope under that delicious though now albeit ten-hour-old coffee. See you soon, and from my heart, Faith, I will be missing you all the hours in between.

Affectionately yours,
Gabriel Artemis Aaron

I laid my head back and held the note to my heart, murmuring the words affectionately yours to myself and smiled to myself with what seemed to be my whole body. My next thought was the letter under the coffee cup, but before I could reach for it, I heard Serenity's voice in my mind, saying, You saw her too, didn't you, the girl with the red mouth.

Grace, I think that I might be more worried, even alarmed at this puzzling portent, were it not for your wisdom pearl on the nature of bewilderment, gifted to me not so long ago (to me, Grace, even now it seems like yesterday).

I was just ten years old, and we were sitting on the porch at Grandpa's store. I was fussing about my missing calico, Camiel. "Where could she have gone?" I asked. "The whole thing bewilders me," I said, trying out a new word.

"Break it down, Fay Fay," you said, "what does bewilder tell you when you break it down?"

"Be wilder? How will it help if I am more, wild?"

I still remember your chuckle at my furrowed brow as I asked the question. "More wild means taking out the walls and fence lines in your mind. Open yourself to the possibilities beyond your fence lines, Faith. Bewilder takes us out of our comfort zones and pushes us to explore and discover. The discomfort of bewilder, that feeling of not knowing, drives us to search for truth. Bewilder is a travel companion, the one who says with just one look, this is not over yet, sweet heart, the journey continues..."

It is with this fond memory that I leave you now, Grace. I shall see you again soon, hopefully laden with bundles of sweet dream moments and clues to that which bewilders, some days hence in the next entry.

Sneak Peek Into Book Two

The Dreamwatcher Diaries

Diary Mid-Day through Diary Dusk

Lawrence Gabriel

Part – One

Diary Mid-Day

Prologue

Lindsay Parker having just moved into her new loft in downtown St. Louis was sitting misty eyed in the window seat of her new home going through the throes of what she called the soul mate blues. Recently divorced she is struggling to navigate the stormy waves of disheartenment that threaten to pull her down into a chasm of desperation and despair. Give me a sign, she implores the universe, what more can I do?

Moments later a dove sitting just outside her window, embodying the mystical presence of serendipity guides her to a path filled with discovery and illumination While focusing on the bird Lindsay notices that the window seat is actually a window box. Opening the lid of the box she finds an old hat box. The gold lettering across the lid of the box spells out the words, The Dreamwatcher Diaries. Startled by the dove's sudden departure she drops the box and kneeling down discovers both a letter and a diary.

Placing the diary back into the box, Lindsay begins to read the letter. The letter written by a grandmother to her granddaughter resonates so mysteriously with her wounded heart that she is compelled to enlist the aid of her best friend Gabriella Menendez. Lindsay and Gaby spend that night pouring over the letter's content while try-

ing to discern the deeper meanings woven into the author's profound message to her granddaughter.

The heart of the message surrounds the notion of self-discovery along with alignment with divine design as a way to find one's beloved, what the author calls one's sweet dream. The grandmother whose name is Grace gives her granddaughter Faith the gift of the wisdom and rituals that encompass this journey towards one's sweet dream. Grace passes on this gift while noting for Faith that this gift as been passed down from grandmother to granddaughter for 4 – generations.

The primary ritual involves quoting the Dreamwatcher Prayer to a dove, then releasing that dove to find, watch over, and guide the sweet dream couple to the place where at last they first meet. After completing this ritual Faith must complete the self-growth milestones including self-discovery, self-reliance, and self-worth. As she does this journey work, she may consult with her inner spirit guide that Grace refers to as Faith's wisdom angel. Grace includes many lessons within the letter about the nature of illusion and authenticity. She instructs Faith that once she finds her sweet dream, she may start to write about him and their moments together in what Grace calls Faith's own Dreamwatcher Diary. She clarifies that she should date her sweet dream for 40 – days and 40 – nights (960-hours) before telling him about the diary and the journey work that brought them together.

Gaby is so inspired by the letter's passages that she gets up in the early morning hours and begins to read the diary to which the letter referred.

Completely immersed in the magic emanating from both the letter and the diary Lindsay and Gaby design a plan to share the letter with Gaby's mother Margarita who is an accomplished Shaman and Mystic. Seeking further clarification for the letter's segments on illusion and authenticity as well as those on the journey of self-discovery the two friends meet up at Gaby's home for eggs, enchiladas, and explanations. Margarita and Gaby's brother Eduardo sit down with the college chums and probe the lessons spun throughout the letter's pages.

Margarita introduces helpful passages from a rare book that she found in a small second-hand bookstore in Alton, Illinois. The book entitled Hope's Journey through the Forest of Illusions, was written by Hope Aaron and published by Word of Mouth Publishing. The tome is shrouded in some mystery as the publisher and the author seem to be both completely unknown and untraceable. The book however, gives uncommon clarity to the notions of authenticity and the self-growth journey. Among the passages that shed light on the complex meanings surrounding the quest for the authentic self is the story of Caroline and how her inner self helps her find the path to self-discovery by invoking the aid of the virtue angels including Hope, Destiny and Worth. This story includes the impact that a sexual violation event has on the soul's ability to find the self-growth pathway.

Having traveled deep into the soul's inner realms the two friends take a well-earned nap and after freshening up set out to continue their read-

ing of the diary at the very place where Faith's Dreamwatcher Diary began, the Venice Café.

Our story begins 5 – hours later as Lindsay and Gaby are finishing their reading of the 7th entry of the dairy.

CHAPTER ONE

Signs from Serendipity in the Midnight Zone

The light had long since drained from the rainy March day and lamplit warmth framed the Venice Café. Inside patrons were wrapping café favorites to be enjoyed in the wee hours of the morning or perhaps for lunch the next day. Diners in attendance during the late Sunday evening hours were generally sparse in the off season. However, during the summer months college students could be counted on to keep bartenders and waitresses on the run right up to the last call.

Mary walked up to the service station, "2-chicken, 1- chick-wing, 2-buds and 1- blood of my namesake."

"Coming right up for our resident songstress," Darnell boomed, deftly flipping a burger in the air while holding up a toasted bun that he had somehow pulled from the grill just in time to catch the burger and put it to bed on a plate full of onion rings.

"2-cheddar-b, 3-buff-chick-salads, 3-buds, 2-bud-lite," Rachel bade in that deep alto voice of hers.

"As a woman who proudly prefers women, I take offense to the term buff chick," Mary said flashing her impossibly white teeth at Rachel in a winning smile.

"It's, food-speak silly girl, or should I say chef-speak at least our chef that is," Rachel replied giving Mary a smile of her own.

Mary stood on tiptoe and reaching up pulled 3-service ware bundles from the tub. She placed them on her serving platter and leaned on the bar to watch Madeline the mixologist put her drinks together. Standing 5-feet 6- inches with the last 2-inches more gorgeous afro than skeletal frame, Mary made up in voice and attitude what she might lack in size and stature. She had performed at several open mike nights at the café and had quickly earned the name TT-Girl for her raw Tina Turner vocals.

"I saw you crushing on the pair in station-7. Did you get a number yet," Rachel asked, grabbing a beer bucket and filling it with ice?

"Not yet, but I already have a nice consolation prize."

"Oh really, do tell?"

"I actually got a visit from the Gee-Man."

"You did not. You've only been here for 6-months. I've been here for 2-years and that womanizing inventor has not even tried to flirt with me."

"That's because you are home-spun gorgeous, 6-feet tall, naturally nonchalant, and practically married. Not to mention that you look like a tomboy, walk like a tomboy, you even talk like a tomboy and yet at the same time all you have to do is put one curl in that straight brunette hair of yours, throw on a burlap dress and you look like you just walked off the cover of Vogue magazine. Haven't you figured that out yet girl, you're like, too beautiful?"

"Alright, alright you're forgiven, but wait how could you have had a visit from Franklin when they haven't even closed out yet."

"Ok, so check this out. They come in, right? They go straight to station–7. Before I can even take their order, the beautiful blonde stands up ushers me aside and takes my hand. She asks me for my name. She then places a folded bill in my palm and whispers to me "this is for rent Mary. We are going to be here for more than just awhile. We will be reading a very, in depth love story and as we are on a quest, we are going to need an unusual favor from you."

"Anything," I say to her.

"Anything? Yes, that sounds about right." Rachel says in that casual, offhand manner of hers and then gives me one of her rare giggles.

"Oh my God Rachel you really do have a sense of humor. You know I just said that to see if you would laugh, don't you?"

"Sure, okay, so what happened next, she said smothering a second giggle?"

"She says. "after you take our order, we need you to just give us the space, kind of like after the delivery guy drops off the pizza. The difference is that you are a woman and you can intuit things that guys don't seem to get. Like how and when to leave the universe alone." Say no more I said. So, Then I go straight to the serving window and check out the bill, right? I almost screamed. I think that they are finally ready to close out."

"What exactly is the total elapsed time here," Rachel asked?

"Five hours can you believe it," Mary replied incredulously?

"I have had longer but not by much," Rachel said as she began to pull her orders off the serving bar and load them onto her platter.

"Shooters for the house on the house," Madeline bellowed, placing a platter of tequila shots on the serving bar.

"To whom do we owe the pleasure," Mary asked scooping up a shot glass before the question could be answered?

"Darn, shooters in the spotlight, shoot it or lose it," Madeline yelled towards the kitchen.

"Definitely shoot it," Darnell said appearing suddenly while turning to flip his spatula circus style to his protégé and kitchen lieutenant Demetrius. Mentor mimed a high five to his protégé as he expertly caught the kitchen tool holstering it into his apron.

"To what do we underlings owe this dubious honor Herr General," Madeline asked with more than a hint of a smile forming on her generous mouth?

"A toast to being smitten with the splendor of September," Darnell said with an ardor so genuine that the women instinctively felt a tingle even before they drank.

The group threw back the prescribed measures of alcohol, slamming the dense glass on the bar in a ritual that was as common to most villagers across the globe, as was the ritual of prayer.

"Alright so let me get this straight. You have gone through 8 out of the 12 months of the year minus of course May because that is your mother's name, in a romantic quest to find your Beloved Moor."

"Well why don't you just tell everybody." Darnell said sarcastically.

"I think she just did," Rachel said with her very unusual, third giggle of the night.

"Yes, I suppose she did, but that is okay as I have no problem with people knowing that I have a plan surrounding my quest for my Beloved."

"So, you are saying that if a man or a woman uses the calendar as a guide to find the name of their dream-mate that they have a better chance of finding their soul mate," Madeline challenged with the glimmer of a smirk?

"Mary are you as astounded as I at the narrow minds in our midst here," Darnell asked with a genuine ire?

"So, I think that I will choose Switzerland surrounding this particular issue," Mary said impassively.

"Well done Mary, and I would have to say that you are ahead of the curve on that response," he said winking at Rachel while simultaneously nodding at Madeline.

"And she is ahead of the curve because," Madeline said trying valiantly to reign in her defensiveness?

"Maybe because she does not draw the conclusion that having a strategy is not worse than having no strategy at all. Like going to a bar to find the one or being a bartender as a way to encounter Mr. Right, while at the same time denying that in some secret place inside this is your specific way to cultivate that hope that maybe this could lead to that penultimate connection."

"Whoa, just a second here," Mary said making the time out sign with her hands. "Please do not ruin my awesome rapport with the best bartender I have ever known."

"No worries there Mary in fact your stock just went up a few points," Madeline said flashing a smile as she set her drinks on the bar.

"Oh my God thank goodness I made it up here just in time to catch the nightly Madness vs. Darn sparring session. Who is winning," Rose asked as she placed hot plates of food on her platter?

"Darn just threw a kidney punch but Madness is about to throw that famous left hook of hers." Rachel said as she ducked out of the serving area with her tray.

"Okay so you're saying that proactive is better than no-active?" Madeline said forcing herself to reign in her frustration.

"Simple as that Madness," Darnell said with a wink and a smile.

"So, what happens when you meet Miss Right while you are finding out that you are currently with Miss Wrong?"

"You keep your ears open for serendipity while at the same time keeping both eyes on your present choice. You let science work it's magic and magic work its science."

"You two keep this up and I'm going to call Oprah. I'm outa here," Mary said as she held up her tray and spun deftly into the server traffic.

"Darnell 911, fire ball on grill 2," Demitrius yelled.

"*D,* what did I tell you about using too much grease? Class dismissed ladies, Darnell said tipping his white hat and darting back into the kitchen.

Rose and Madeline looked at each other with pursed lips and raised eyebrows grudgingly impressed with Darnell's response.

"So, what do you think Rosie girl," Madeline asked grabbing 2 – mugs and dunking them in soapy water.

"I think you are in love with Darnell that's what I think," Rose replied pulling a fresh tray off the shelf.

"How could you possibly even think that. We argue just about every night that we work together, which is, well, just about every night," Madeline said as she dunked the mugs in clear water and placed them on the bar.

"Exactly, need I say more," Rose said grabbing a fresh towel from a shelf below the server window.

"Oh, I see so you want to play house shrink. So, doctor what is your sage advice?" She asked sarcastically pulling 2- more used mugs off the bar.

"Tell him how you feel, get laid immediately, or in the immortal words of Shakespeare, get thee to a nunnery." Rose giggled throwing the towel at her friend's surprised expression.

Finishing the last sentence of the 7th diary entry Lindsay paused for a moment. Emitting a deep sigh of longing she placed one of her business cards into the seam to mark their place and carefully closed the diary. Exhausted and spent on all fronts Lindsay and Gaby lay their heads back against the hard cherry of the straight back seats of their booth. They took a deep pull of oxygen and then as if on cue expelled their breath in chorus.

"Gaby, I think I used up all of that pluck that your mama mentioned earlier. I am truly not sure whether I can even stand let alone walk."

"I cannot even feel my butt, its completely gone. It's like I have been out of my body for the last 5 – hours and I am just now returning to find that my muscles closed shop early to go fishing."

"Wait did you just say 5- hours?"

"Five it is at least according to the clock on the wall behind you, unless of course it too is from the

80's. It is after all sitting just above a picture of the *Six Million Dollar Man."*

"What's this, when did our food get all wrapped and bagged," Lindsay asked pointing at the several bags that littered the table.

"That happened about an hour ago, while you were reading," Gaby said with a yawn.

"Oh my God our waitress must be so pissed!"

"On the contrary thanks to my small talk and your big tip we totally won her over. Plus, she is such a sweetheart, cute as a bug and maybe even a little smitten with one or both of us."

"Really, wow I totally missed that."

"Not surprising. You were more than just a little preoccupied at the time."

"Okay well let's settle up and hit the road. What do you think your place or mine," Lindsay asked stifling a yawn?

"Definitely yours, its closer and we won't have to disturb Mama with a late entrance. She definitely looked beat after that impromptu cerebral marathon."

"Works for me. Oh, thank God here comes Mary."

"Don't worry about the tip sweetheart it was worth every minute both for the journey and the service," Lindsay said in response to Mary's profuse gratitude, as she and Gaby made their way out of the booth.

"Wow this really must be some quest," Mary said.

"Yes, it is but don't you dare short sell the service," Gaby said smiling and placing her hand lightly on Mary's shoulder.

The smile that lit up Mary's face ran from pleased in the mouth to shy in the eyes.

"Thanks again," Lindsay said giving Mary a warm hug.

"Well I hope you find what you ae looking for," Mary said, her shyness now taking over her whole face.

"Right back to you," Gaby said as they stepped towards the exit.

The pair walked stiffly to Lindsay's car shivering as they sat back on the cold leather. Giving in to both weariness and the more unconscious sense of reverence surrounding the magic of the words that now moved within them, the friends maintained a communal silence during the drive home. Parking in the underground garage they went straight to the elevator which trundled them laboriously up to the seventh floor. Once in the loft they hung up their wraps and went straight to the bathroom for washing, brushing, putting on sleep gear and other sundry rituals that seemed so essential to the enjoyment of a well-deserved slumber. Working in tandem they pulled back the bedclothes of her California King.

"Wait, be right back," Lindsay said suddenly.

Gaby smiled to herself as she waited. Although she was well schooled on her best friend's turn on a dime system of thought she was curious as to what this dime would purchase.

"Okay so don't laugh and I know it is silly but I want to keep the diary close," Lindsay said placing Faith's Diary under the middle pillow.

"I'm too tired to laugh and I think it is an excellent idea," Gaby said as they fell into the bed an pulled the covers up to their chin.

"Oh my God these sheets feel so good, Lindsay. I love feeling this exhausted."

"Yes, they are my recently purchased satin purple sheets and purple polka dot pillow slips."

"Now you know what to get me for Christmas," Gaby giggled. "Good night girlfriend."

"Sweet dreams," Lindsay said as she laid on her side. Letting go a sigh that seemed to be a mix of both weary and wistful Lindsay slipped her hand under the pillow and placed it on the diary's cover. While waiting to hear those pages whisper, she fell, quick and silent feeling the gravity pull her down into that deep inner province where dreams hold dominion.

Sleep and her sister Slumber both clad in flowing white satin slips touch down on the illusion floor of the nights dream destination. Landing neatly with their precious cargo in tow they step lightly down a tree lined lane located in the southern most region of Lindsay's Midnight Zone. This southern province is filled with scenes and memories from Lindsay's past. These scenes are logged daily and organized chronologically according to second by second recordings of her life from the womb to the present day. This enormous collection of historic sound-bytes, some of which Lindsay herself would be hard pressed to recall, were catalogued while she was sleeping. The trio walk towards the staging site where the cast for this night's dream feature await their arrival.

Lindsay catches a secret smile passing from sister to sister along with a hint of hero worship in the shy looks they steal while she is focused on the path ahead. She intuits that something important is happening and it feels as if some urgent dispatch is in the wind. She wishes to say as much to her companions and turning to look at Sleep she opens her mouth to speak. Before the words can form on her lips Sleep nods towards her sister. Turning to look Lindsay is surprised to find that Slumber has vanished. Quickly turning her head back towards Sleep she finds that both sisters have vanished. Lindsay is now standing on the path alone shrouded in a sudden mist.

As the fog dissipates Lindsay is surprised to find herself on that familiar mountain path not far from her home. This is the path on which she had watched her parents walk while she had secretly observed their mutual affection. Then suddenly there they were side by side, arm in arm, strolling liesurely around the bend. She wanted to run up to greet them but she sensed the reign of some hidden order. She had the fleeting thought that the force that held her seemed much like the protocol of the royals. It was a procedure that sent the message; boundaries are sacred, and the rules surrounding these natural fence lines hold both meaning and grave importance. Holding her position there she watched her beloved soul mate vision walk bravely up the mountain path. Only seconds later she sees her first boyfriend Brett come around the bend followed by her 13-year old self. Brett is about 10-yeards ahead of her and she is asking him to wait up for her. Brian her high school sweetheart comes next with her following again at the same distance. Then Brad her steady in college and finally Bruce walking ahead of her more recent self. She cringes at the truth that her strident pleas for him to wait seem to be more, shrill and yes at times even desperate.

Then she sees her, the girl in the red checkered blouse. She flashes Lindsay a conspiratorial wink and places her index finger to her lips. Whipping her head back before Lindsay could capture the contours of her face, she heads down a hidden fork along that treasured path from Lindsay's past. The signature blonde ponytail like the pipe of the pied piper pulls Lindsay down this unfamiliar lane. Entranced she follows the flight of the red butterfly on the girl's barrette which seems to have come alive. Moving in sync with the bounce in the woman-child's step, Lindsay finds her voice. "Are you real Faith, tell me true. Please give me a sign that this Dreamwatcher journey is not just another grand illusion," Lindsay calls out hoping to connect with the intelligence that radiates from the child's purpose driven stride. Faith did a quick spin and holding up a prayer boat about face high she pointed to the sail. Lindsay is surprised to find that the sail is made from a cloth with purple polka dots. Coming around a corner they arrive at a creek and Lindsay watches Faith place the boat into the current of the white-water rivulet. Faith then wades to the shore on the other side. They run parallel along the water's edge as the creek flows rapidly towards the river. The brush along the river's edge runs so high that the woman and the woman-child cannot see each other. The duo turns a corner and the river abruptly doubles in width. Faith has become a red checked speck in the distance. Lindsay notes with some alarm that the prayer boat has been pushed ashore by a powerful wind. The purple polka dot sail has been torn from its mast and is wrapped around some obstruction that stands along the river's edge. Lindsay tugs at the sail unveiling an alabaster statue carved from stone.

CPSIA information can be obtained
at www.ICGtesting.com
Printed in the USA
LVHW010558270420
654496LV00003B/801